"Set in an age when marriage was strategy, love was temptation, and treachery was a tool of survival, Nicole Galland's *The Fool's Tale* creates a vivid twelfth-century world and three unforgettable characters whose lives entwine with war and politics and climax in an ending as haunting as it is powerful."

—William Dietrich, author of *Hadrian's Wall*

"The characters and descriptions in Galland's world certainly are worth stopping by to meet as the story gallops through a time of treachery, rife with infighting among the four kingdoms of Wales and border clashes with the English barons.... As we share life from the perspective of each of the three main characters, understanding takes its turn amid powerful emotional tides, awash in realities of today."

—*Albany Times Union*

Revenge
of the Rose

ALSO BY NICOLE GALLAND

THE FOOL'S TALE

Revenge of the Rose

Nicole Galland

HARPER

NEW YORK · LONDON · TORONTO · SYDNEY

FOR MY GRANDPARENTS,

WILLIAM AND RACHEL GALLAND

HARPER

A hardcover edition of this book was published in 2006 by William Morrow,
an imprint of HarperCollins Publishers.

FIRST HARPER PAPERBACK PUBLISHED 2007.

Designed by Nancy Singer Oleguera
Map by Steve Lewis, the famous fourth-grade teacher emeritus

The Library of Congress has catalogued the hardcover edition as follows:

Galland, Nicole.
    Revenge of the rose: a novel / Nicole Galland.—1st ed.
        p. cm.
    ISBN-13: 978-0-06-084177-5
    ISBN-10: 0-06-084177-X
    1. Holy Roman Empire. Emperor (1138–1152 : Konrad III)—
Fiction. 2. Holy Roman Empire—History—843–1273—Fiction. 3.
Knights and knighthood—Fiction. 4. Courts and courtiers—
Fiction. 5. Minstrels—Fiction. I. Title.
PS3607.A4154R48 2006
813'.54—dc22   2005054491

ISBN: 978-0-06-084179-9 (pbk.)
ISBN-10: 0-06-084179-6 (pbk.)

07 08 09 10 11 WBC/RRD 10 9 8 7 6 5 4

Contents

BOOK TWO

Holy

Roman

Empire

Kingdom

of

France

Duchy
of
Bourgogne

County

of

Burgundy

• Mainz

• Worms

Speyer

River Rhine

• Strasbourg

• Koenigsbourg

• Colmar

Oricourt •

• Montbéliard

• Besançon
Dole •

Rome

Revenge *of the* Rose

Prologue

[a passage introducing key elements of all that follows]

7 June, late in the twelfth century

in the ninth year of the reign of Konrad the Fair, Holy Roman Emperor
some seven or eight years after the Third Crusade
two decades into the era of courtly love, which proposed that
females just might have value above the waist

The women were completing their transformation into ladies. They did this in the largest pavilion of the unfinished alpine palace as most of the men broke the fast outside.

"And who are you playing at this time?" one woman asked another.

"I'm the chatelaine of Bern," a dark-haired girl said.

"By whose request?" asked a blonde.

"The Duke of Bavaria," she answered, and several of the others murmured enviously.

Under Marcus's direction, two dozen pair of hands rummaged through the piles of elegant robes and tunics. All of them—even those grumpy few who truly did this only for the coin—were smiling now, smiling at the outfits, the sumptuous brocade silks and fancy, exotic weavings, sleeves edged with gold, silk and leather girdles, fabrics that troubadours could drone on about for hours. The broad pavilion was bright; it had been rigged to let the cloth roof be drawn away so that the summer-morning sun could come pouring in through the tops of the firs and birches shading the pavilion.

This was a palace still in the making. The courtyard walls were unfinished (but already overdecorated), and the kitchen was conveniently in working order. There were rough wooden huts for the workmen and their tools, but such men had been removed from the site for this fortnight, and no other permanent structures yet stood. One end of the yard, where the women's pavilion was staked, was not even enclosed yet. Here the hill they were on rose so steeply above them, it was nearly a wooded cliff, and His Majesty liked the aesthetic of this: nature peeking timidly into what would soon be a magnificent, artificial world, the most sumptuous and glittering of his many glittering courts. In the meantime, with the necessary tents and pavilions, it provided the illusion of an idyll, and illusions were always useful to a monarch.

"I'm to be a shepherdess for a few days," announced the most buxom woman in the bunch, and then added, winking, "for the bishop of Friedberg." Everyone—except Marcus—laughed, and she turned to the tall one, with the heart-shaped face. "And you, Jeannette? Who are you to be?"

"The naked sister of the Count of Savoy," Jeannette said with mock solemnity.

"By whose request?" asked someone else.

"The Count of Savoy," she answered, grinning, and the tent roared with their laughter.

"From what I've heard of his sister, I'm surprised she didn't come herself," one of the women muttered to another, and they all laughed at this as well.

There was a lot of laughter in this pavilion, every year, whatever hillside it was pitched on. The prelates, knights, and noblemen outside heard only the bright cheer of such laughter, not the cynicism that inspired it, and the women knew that this was part of the appeal. Besides Marcus the imperial steward, only Konrad—their sovereign and host—had any inkling of what the women really found amusing.

Marcus was a black-haired man with a narrow, keen-featured face. Each year the women teased him, claiming he was so attractive, they should beg him to take their virtue if only they had not misplaced it. Usually he enjoyed their attentions, and he was popular with all of them for being undemanding. But this year he was agitated and distracted.

What Marcus had in dark good looks, Konrad—King of Germany, of Sicily, of Burgundy, and Emperor of the Holy Roman Empire—had in charm. He was a tall, solidly built man with perfect teeth, pale eyes, light red hair and beard, and a ring of a different gemstone on each finger. He loomed large now in the doorway in scarlet and gold, beaming with the hearty confidence of an empire builder. He had earned, by a balance of bloodshed and diplomacy, the right to peace, to prosperity, and to this unorthodox (but to the women, profitable) summer ritual: two weeks of the finest illusory debauchery in the Empire. This year the debauchery was taking place in the woody hills below the Black Forest, safe from the troublesome Italians farther south and the troublesome Burgundians to the west. The common women who worked near the royal courts competed for an invitation to this fortnight of easy abundance: two weeks of wearing gowns that were far finer than any they would ever own, of eating *doucetes* and other delicacies they never could afford at home, of being treated almost as politely as the landed ladies they were trussed up to resemble, and finally, bags of generous material reward from the emperor's own elegant palm before they left. Their only duty—beyond the usual ones of their vocation—was to loosen the lips of the excitable young lordlings, men whose fathers and uncles and older brothers and counselors were not always well inclined toward their emperor. Only Jouglet the minstrel unearthed better intelligence for Konrad than did these women in their playful masquerading.

"Your Majesty!" the women said nearly in one breath when they realized who had come in through the flap, accompanied by his bodyguards. They all curtsied, unselfconscious in their ratty shifts.

Konrad chuckled. "Welcome, ladies, to my final summer as a bachelor. Those shifts will never do. We've brought you better undergarments—yours to keep! Have your boy bring them round now," he said to silent Marcus behind him. He turned back to the women. "Venison of rose for dinner, my pearls, and goose in verjuice. Are there any complaints I should hear before we begin?"

"*My* only complaint is that Seneschal Marcus has not asked me to carve out time in my busy schedule for him," said the buxom shepherdess, and there was a round of giggles.

Marcus, uncharacteristically, blushed. "Too busy this year," he said, eyes slightly averted.

The women made teasing sounds of disappointment, and Konrad shook his head with comradely sorrow. "I know, my lovelies, I know, he's breaking all the rules. He won't tell me what he's up to. I suspect he's brought his own distraction." Under his breath he added warningly, "And I intend to find out who she is." Marcus involuntarily winced, and Konrad laughed, smacking him on the arm. "See you all outside," he announced, and gesturing for Marcus to hold open the canvas flap, he strode out into the clear, cool morning.

Jouglet the fiddler had not shown up this summer, to Konrad's great annoyance. For years the young tenor had dutifully abandoned other adventures to appear, fiddle and bow in hand, and lead commencement revelries. Konrad could not conceive that anything would be appealing enough to turn his favored court musician truant. But truant Jouglet was. Such an absence was particularly irritating this summer, when the cacophony of rumors regarding a royal wedding required constant damping. The French king's outrageous land ambitions had made it clear that the emperor needed to heighten his own presence in the west; since he was overdue for wedlock, he had decided to seek a wife from the western flank of his empire. More specifically, he wanted a bride from his infamously independent border county of Burgundy, which historically had deeper ties to the sovereign Duchy of Bourgogne, just across the Saone, than to the Empire itself. Burgundy happened to be ruled by Konrad's paternal uncle, Alphonse, whom Konrad could not abide. Alphonse, like every Count of Burgundy before him, sought opportunities to defy Imperial power; Konrad, like every emperor before him, therefore sought opportunities to more closely weld the heart of Burgundy to his own court. Alphonse's daughter Imogen was heiress to Burgundy, and Konrad's marrying her would have been a simple, deft solution to the conflict. But Rome forbade a marriage of first cousins, and so Imogen had been betrothed to Marcus instead, while other Burgundian brides were being sought for His Imperial Majesty. Unfortunately, the emperor and his Assembly of Lords had mutual veto power, which so far meant every suggestion had been nullified, for Konrad would only contemplate a match that might increase the power of his throne, while the Assembly, with the pope's encouragement, would only contemplate a match that did no such thing. As a result, every marriageable noblewoman in Burgundy was verbally paraded before Konrad's wearied attention, and he wanted Jouglet present to artfully deflect them all.

Once the women had refashioned themselves into great ladies, Marcus signaled the musicians. The little throng of courtesans made its way outside behind him. There was an instant and thunderous response from the collected lords.

Konrad had a mind to find the ersatz Duchess of Austria later
that afternoon, but he had given himself the morning to swagger
paternally about the dewy yard, assuring himself that everyone was
dutifully misbehaving, and that they were grateful to their sovereign
for the chance of it. His two bodyguards followed him at enough of
a distance that he could pretend they were not there.

Since it was impractical to provide private tents for everyone here
in the remote alpine site, there was a very casual ambiance to the copulation. Only Konrad and Marcus had quarters of their own. Both tents,
like the pavilion, were swathed in images of the imperial black eagle
and Konrad's family crest, a black lion rampant. Konrad had watched
the flap to his seneschal's tent from the corner of his eye all morning.
Nobody had gone in or out, and when Marcus himself retired to it, he
had done so alone. Signaling his guard to wait outside, the emperor
slipped into the little tent, grinning with smug anticipation.

Even in the secrecy of his own tent, Marcus was being secretive.
He had thrown a sheet entirely over himself and his companion,
whom he was clearly on top of, although they were both trying to be
quiet. Konrad paused a moment to see if they would notice him—he
was used to being noticed instantly, and especially by his steward.
But they were far too engaged in each other. So he reached down and
in a sudden sharp move plucked the sheet from off the couple, whipping it out of reach behind his back.

Like startled rabbits, Marcus and the young woman leapt apart
from each other. She buried her head against a bolster, but Konrad
snatched that up as well and tossed it to the ground. She cowered,
curled up defensively, trying to hide her nakedness and her identity.

But Konrad recognized her.

The emperor, seldom at a loss for words, simply gaped. Marcus
hung for a moment in horror, seeing his life at court crumbling to
dust before his eyes as he tried to read Konrad's expression.

The king burst suddenly into bellows of laughter.

"So my little cousin Imogen is marrying a swine!" he roared. "Can't you even wait until the wedding, man?" Then he saw that the still-traumatized steward was not properly prepared for fornication. "You're still in your drawers," he said, accusingly.

Marcus, dark-complexioned, became the color of a radish. "I would never presume to lie so freely with a lady of my Lady Imogen's virtue," he stammered, which only made the emperor laugh harder.

"Marcus, for the love of Peter, you're in bed with her at a bacchanalia, and she's naked as Eve before the fall!"

The girl, who was dark-haired but attractively pale and considerably younger than both men, had found Marcus's silk bed-robe and thrown it around her shoulders. Her expression was as troubled as Marcus's. She huddled behind him now, and he shifted protectively to shield her. "Sire, cousin, I beg you, please don't tell my father," she whispered, stricken, looking down.

"One of you tell me why the devil Marcus still has his drawers on and I'll consider it," Konrad said agreeably and perched on the silk sheets of the portable bed. "Honestly, the consummate seducer, forgive the pun, spending an entire orgy in bed with his intended bride, *not* naked and *not* ravishing her—it is so perverse it borders on suspicious."

Marcus lifted the corners of his lips in a feeble attempt to appear amused. Then he grimaced and fell into a confessional tone. "Sire, this will sound inane, but the truth is, we're in love—"

"So why are your *drawers* on?" Konrad demanded again.

"I . . ." Marcus was flustered, and Imogen herself spoke up, with grim matter-of-factness.

"Your loyal servant is too much the gentleman to claim me before we are properly wed. He is protecting my virtue should I ultimately be married to another. We are both aware this is a political engagement, which Your Majesty might sever at your expediency," she said from behind Marcus's right shoulder, gripping his arm nervously.

The amusement immediately drained from Konrad's face. "Yes," he agreed, irritated partly about the situation, but mostly about having to *think* about the situation, even at an orgy. The couple winced in anticipation of the famous royal temper. "In fact . . . in the name of *Christ,* this was *stupid* of you."

"I know, sire," murmured the steward, ashamed. Imogen slid her hand from his arm forward onto his chest protectively, and he blushed.

"Her father will demand your hide if he learns, and *then* where will I be? You know he hates my ministerials, Marcus—he'll use this as an excuse to demean your entire class! How could you be so *selfish,* dammit?"

Marcus, cheeks burning, was looking down. "Forgive me, milord," he whispered.

"This is so unlike you! You haven't a foolhardy bone in your body! This is on a par with those idiot knights in Jouglet's troubadour songs."

"I would hardly rank myself among the romantic heroes, sire."

Konrad gawked. "Did you just speak of *romantic heroes*?" he demanded. "Are you possessed? My friend Marcus does *not* say such things." Marcus said nothing in protest, just sat very straight and looked down at the ground. Konrad made a contemptuous, dismissive sound. "I'll see you are left alone," he said gruffly. "But she will not leave this tent, even in disguise, do you understand? Nobody— *nobody*—is to know she's here. Ever. They'd never believe her chaste if she was caught in your tent like this. That would reflect poorly on us both and render her *worthless* if I require her to marry somebody else."

"She won't be caught, sire," Marcus promised.

"And you will *never* put me in such a compromising position again," Konrad went on. "Or this will be a whip next time." He struck Marcus across the cheek once, hard. Imogen bit her lip; Marcus did not even flinch.

His outrage somewhat abated, Konrad took a deep breath and demanded, "Do you have a way to spirit her out of here?"

"Yes, sire—"

"If Jouglet assisted in this, which I assume he must have, he'll pay for it too. Where is he, anyhow?"

"Jouglet?" Marcus shook his head nervously. "Good God, sire, he's a dreadful gossip, he knows nothing about it. I've seen to all of it myself. But I promise you she will not be compromised."

"Good," said Konrad in a harsh tone. "Because I do not want problems from her father. He plagues me enough as it is. This would play right into his hands, you moon-drunk idiot." He groaned. "Never mind what *Cardinal Paul* would make of it!"

"Her father thinks she's visiting a nunnery," Marcus said hurriedly.

Konrad stood to leave. "If he learns of this, Marcus, I know nothing. If he informs me, I shall be shocked and outraged and I will punish you severely and in public. You know I mean it."

"As long as you don't punish her, Konrad," said Marcus, daring in private to plead upon decades of familiarity. Konrad only frowned at him.

"I'll punish whomever the wronged father demands I punish; the last thing I need is more problems with the Count of Burgundy while I'm trying to find a bride among his vassals. *Christ* in *Heaven*." He started to let himself out of the tent, then turned to deliver a final warning. "Keep your drawers on, Marcus."

Alone, the two lovers looked at each other with both relief and distress.

BOOK ONE

1

Idyll

[a poem or short prose in a bucolic setting]

16 June

Jouglet the minstrel and Lienor were flirting again as they waited for Willem on the steps in the small courtyard. Lienor's green linen tunic was laced tighter in the back than her mother would have liked, but Jouglet and Lienor each seemed quite pleased with the effect.

"I'm astonished Willem said yes to this," said Lienor, who was possibly the most beautiful woman in the county of Burgundy, and knew it, but was not much bothered by it. With a grateful smile, she added, "It's only for your sake, Jouglet. My brother never lets me do *anything*."

"He is concerned only for your safety, milady," the minstrel answered neutrally. "Think of all the scrawny itinerant musicians who would prick your honor, given the chance."

Lienor fidgeted with her wreath of rosebuds. "He's overcautious. I would have more freedom in the cellar of an abbey."

"Come now, milady," Jouglet cooed. "He is a man of great indulgence. I offer my own friendship with him as proof."

Lienor rolled her eyes and sighed dismissively. "It's different for you, you're a *man*." Her eyes ran over the lean young body and she added, giggling, "Well . . . very nearly."

Boyish Jouglet, although used to such jabs, looked affronted nonetheless. "What does milady mean, *very nearly*? Must I prove myself yet again? I beg the lady to assign me a task only a great hero could achieve, and I'll demonstrate that I am worthy of your feminine regard." But they smiled at each other; this was an old game between them.

"Very well, you lowly knight errant," Lienor recited, feigning disdain. She gestured grandly toward the manor gate. "Travel the earth for ten years and bring me back . . ." She glanced at her pale hands a moment. "Bring me back a magic ring that will make me queen of all I survey."

"Your happiness is my Holy Grail, milady," Jouglet announced, with an absurd level of gravity, and bowed deeply.

"Is it?" Lienor scolded. "I have been waiting three years already, you might at least have slain a dragon for me by now. But I am so gracious and undemanding, I shall be content with a magic ring."

"It is as good as done, milady. And when I return I hope I shall be granted the honor of resting upon your delicate pink bosom."

"*My* bosom is *white*," Lienor said, mock-petulant.

Jouglet grinned wickedly. "Not once I get through with it."

Lienor giggled; her mother, Maria, standing watchfully a few paces away, clicked her tongue disapprovingly but said nothing. Maria had come, over the course of three years of Jouglet's unannounced visits, to trust the fiddler with almost unimpeded access to the entire household; even if Jouglet could have claimed the brute masculine strengths that might endanger a young lady's purity—and Jouglet couldn't—Lienor would have been impervious.

Willem stepped out of the musty shade of the stable. He squinted in the bright light, a hooded falcon tethered on his wrist. Willem was a handsome man, his gentle demeanor belied by the crooked nose that was evidence of too many fights. He saw his sister and their guest at their usual banter and smiled despite himself. Their behavior was appalling, but he was too fond of each of them to chastise effectively. Although the musician made it this far west infrequently, there was no one outside his family to whom Willem felt so close. In a world where he had learned he could trust almost nobody, he trusted Jouglet, intuitively and entirely.

Willem was followed out of the stable by the groom, who led three saddled horses. Together they passed a wooden tub of soaking walnuts, the rabbit-tortured herb garden, and the little wooden chapel, before stopping in front of the hall steps.

At the top of the steps, Lienor clapped her hands in delight. "Oh, this will be such a treat! And such a change in our domestic philosophy," she added, pointedly. "Surely you've noticed, Willem prefers that I am not the hunter but the prey—of rich men in search of a mate."

Jouglet loomed over her and crooned suggestively, in a husky tenor voice, "Do you blame the rich men? If I were a rich man, I'd try to mate you."

Lienor looked delighted by the declaration; Willem said, "Behave yourself, fellow," but only because he knew he ought to.

"Yes, you'll *never* be able to marry me off if word gets around that I've been cozying up to some migrant musician," said Lienor, smiling. She and Jouglet descended the steps together, white hand resting on tanned one.

"I'm only trying to help, friend," Jouglet assured Willem. "I've been trained to cozy up at the highest courts in Europe. How do you expect her to learn feminine wiles if she never has a wooer to practice flirting with?"

"Wooers are one thing she needs fear no lack of," Willem said with a patient smile. "It's the *sort* of wooers we get that are the problem."

"Anyhow it surely doesn't count as flirting when the wooer's voice has hardly changed," Lienor teased.

Before Jouglet could protest, Willem said, "Careful, Lienor, I asked him the other week over chess whether he might be a eunuch and he nearly gave me a bloody nose."

"And then *you* gave *me* a black eye," Jouglet reminded him, sounding inexplicably delighted.

"And then *you* gave *me* a kneeing I should have hanged you for."

"Well, at least we know *you're* not a eunuch," Jouglet pointed out, slapping Willem on the shoulder.

The falcon made a mewling sound, sensing Jouglet's nearness; the musician drew away. With a sweetly coquettish attitude, Lienor took her horse's tasseled reins from the groom. "Jouglet, have you hunted before? You seem to be scared of falcons. How amusing."

"Lienor, don't be rude," said Willem.

"It is my lady's courtly way of showing affection, so the barbs are as caresses to me," Jouglet said smoothly, and was rewarded by Lienor's smile. The groom held out the reins to a second mount, a chubby chestnut, and Jouglet took them with a wary glance at the horse's enormous head.

"Wait until we have Lienor up and then my groom will help you," Willem offered kindly, trying not to sound condescending.

Jouglet looked so relieved that Willem, not for the first time, silently questioned the wisdom of taking his friend on this hawking trip. He was accustomed to being cajoled by his sister into dubious ventures—she had a history of getting into them herself, for all her demure posturing. And he had become used to it with

Jouglet, who'd been his sister's ally (and wooer) throughout their friendship. And so they were going hawking, although not three weeks before he'd vowed no more such outings. That vow had been made the day when, against all Willem's best instincts, they'd convinced him to let them both tag along to a training session for some of the knights and squires stationed at the fortress in Dole. Lienor had merely been sunburned, and eventually repulsed by the excessive violence that her presence inspired. Jouglet, however, had jumped impulsively into a boxing ring with some of the older boys and briefly made a good showing—but ended up with bruised ribs and two black eyes, and was immobile for three days from the pain.

When Lienor and her brother were both mounted, the groom turned to help Jouglet. The fat chestnut stamped a rear hoof, started a little, and lifted its head to listen to something far outside the gate. Then with its midriff inflating, it whinnied long and loud into the afternoon breeze. Jouglet leapt back. The other horses' ears pricked up, and Willem's horse, Atlas, let loose too, to be answered by a similar neighing out in the hills.

The siblings exchanged knowing glances and announced in one voice, with amused resignation, "Erec."

Then Lienor whispered, "Let's slip out the river gate and have mother tell him we are away for the day."

Willem frowned and shifted the hawk to his other arm a moment, stretching his shoulder. "That is rude and deceitful, Lienor."

"From what I've heard of Erec, I don't blame her," Jouglet said. "Your irrepressible cousin, correct? Your little squire?"

Willem was surprised. "Have you two never actually met? In three years? Yes, he's the infamous cousin. And squire." He grinned. "He's also your rival for the lady's hand."

Lienor craned her neck to see around Willem and smiled down at Jouglet. "No he's not," she assured the minstrel.

"If he's your squire, he has to do what you tell him, so just send him away," Jouglet suggested breezily.

Willem wondered how much he would have to explain; he did not like to talk about this, even to a close confidant. "He *was* training as my squire, but he has just unexpectedly become my lord—"

"Your lord?" Jouglet echoed. "Your lord is Alphonse, Count of Burgundy, you are not subservient to some lesser—"

Lienor pursed her lips; Willem flushed, but his expression did not change, and he ignored Jouglet's interjection. "Erec is younger than I am, younger even than Lienor, barely seventeen. But he's got an uncanny way with horses, and he's been an excellent squire, which pleased the family—knighthood is a good calling for a second son—"

"—but then his father and older brother both met their Maker in the same week, and suddenly he is lord of a sizable estate," Lienor concluded.

"But he's not *your* lord?" Jouglet pursued, looking confused. "You're your own man, aren't you? Besides homage to the king and count, of course."

The siblings exchanged unreadable glances; the small falcon, sensing her master's unease, mewled briefly, and Willem was glad of the excuse to coo calmingly at it rather than answer the question.

Jouglet gestured helpfully to the grand homestead around them. "What is this?"

"Uncle Raimond's charity—or now, his son Erec's," Lienor said, without a trace of self-pity. Wanting a return to levity, she cackled, rubbing her soft pale hands together around the leather reins. "The bait to lure fat little husbands into our diabolical web of poverty."

Willem shook his head at her with affectionate disapproval. "It's not *quite* so dire, Lienor." And to Jouglet: "Our father was killed a month before her birth, and he had made no provisions for her."

"And men want heiresses," Jouglet concluded, understanding.

Willem nodded. "Although we receive offers from those who would never consider such a poor girl if she were not so charming."

Lienor's smile was somehow both bashful and proud; it was just the sort of smile that might make one the most beautiful woman in Burgundy. "I never receive them when *you're* visiting, Jouglet, since you're much more satisfying company. But they do bring remarkable gifts. I have more jewelry and dress gowns than—"

"Yes, but most of them would just take you for a mistress," Willem said tersely. "And we've no *idea* what to do about poor Erec. He's a good lad, really, but he's still adjusting to his sudden acquisition of lordship. It makes him buffoonish sometimes, especially toward Lienor—"

At that moment the gate swung open, and they turned grudgingly to receive the visitor.

Erec was close enough in kin to resemble each of the siblings: like Lienor he was fair-haired; like Willem he had a soldier's build. But there similarities ceased.

Erec's face was aflame with the imbalances of late-adolescent humors, and he carried himself with a reckless intensity that Jouglet found alarming. He was dressed as if for a feast day—a bright silk tunic, long pointy poulaines on his feet—although it was an unremarkable Tuesday afternoon and they were, moreover, in the middle of nowhere. Behind him, three dusty, stumbling serfs, sweating profusely in the warm moist air, pulled an enormous dusty clay vat on a dusty wheeled platform.

"Good day, cousins!" he cried out as he came through the wooden gate and steered his mount—a well-bred charger in extravagant gear—toward them. He spoke in the family's native Burgundian. In a smooth arc of movement, clearly intended to visually thrill the lady, he dismounted and fell into a sweeping bow beside Willem's Atlas. "My lord," he intoned, then stood and spun around to face Lienor and dropped to his knees on the dry packed dirt. At his signal, his horse did likewise. "My lovely lady," he addressed her, or rather her breasts. Lienor, physically affected by the intensity of his ogling, held a protective hand against her chest.

"Please get up," said Willem calmly. "Your groveling is unattractive and inappropriate."

"But I'm your squire," Erec protested, twisting to look over his shoulder at Willem without actually rising from his knees.

"And now you are my lord," Willem said, tired and resentful of having to repeat this so frequently. Jouglet, realizing that Erec liked hearing Willem repeat it, decided at that moment to dislike Erec profoundly. "And we've discussed the awkwardness of this, milord," Willem continued. "It requires that you go elsewhere for the remainder of your training."

"But cousin," Erec pleaded, the grandness of his delivery deflating. He obediently got up from his knees. His horse followed suit, and he gave it an approving swat on the shoulder. "You're the best knight in the county, I *want* to be your squire. Your training is the best and your home is the fairest one to pass the time in." He smiled, apparently content that the matter was now resolved. "That reminds me, I've brought the mistress of the house a trifle." He gestured for the perspiring peasants to wheel their burden closer.

"How kind of you, I'm sure the mistress will be delighted," Lienor said graciously. She looked toward the house, where her mother hovered still at the doorway. "Look, Mother! Erec has trundled you a large vat of something that's attracting flies as an expression of his regard!"

Erec shook his head. "I meant you, milady. No insult intended, Aunt!" he called out with hollow heartiness to Maria. She remained silent.

"We thank you for the gift. May I ask what you have brought us?" Willem queried and protectively edged Atlas between Erec and his sister's horse.

Erec took a wide step sideways, to again address Lienor's breasts directly. "I have brought the beautiful lady a little honey," he announced, resuming his grandiose manner. All of them were startled by the enormity of the gift. "So that she might have some sweetness in her current earthly privations. But all the honey in the world is not as sweet as her fair visage," he concluded with what he seemed to consider great artfulness.

Jouglet snickered quietly, and Erec spun around, glaring. He was not tall for his breeding, and although Erec was burlier, the two were of a height.

"Who are you?" he demanded.

"Your cousins' boon companion," Jouglet said, with an exaggerated bow.

Erec looked disgusted. "How can a vagabond make such a claim on persons of gentle birth? Explain your rudeness, clod."

"That insult would be more effective in German, you know," Jouglet said, in German. "I assume milord speaks the emperor's language, and that these ersatz trappings are not just a bad disguise for provincial coarseness?"

Erec hesitated, frowning, then switched to German. "Do you know the value of a vat of honey that size?" he demanded, with an atrocious accent.

"A hell of a lot for someone newly risen to lordship, milord," Jouglet observed.

"All the more opulent the gesture, then. Are you so well-endowed with riches that you can offer something better?"

"I have been told I'm well-endowed, but why do you treat me as your competition when neither of us may ever have her?" asked Jouglet calmly. "You are manufacturing a conflict where none exists, milord."

"Then why do you seek to discredit me with your snide reaction?" Erec demanded. He flicked his teeth with his thumb in Jouglet's direction.

"Erec!" Willem and Lienor scolded in the same voice at the extraordinarily rude gesture.

Jouglet blinked and looked suspiciously sincere, bowing very low. "Milord, I would never dream of discrediting you, but I would be honored to correct your misunderstanding of the one thing in this world on which I am an expert."

"You're not old enough to be expert at anything," Erec scoffed uncomfortably. "You don't look like your balls have even dropped."

"I was known as a child prodigy," Jouglet said evenly. "I am now known, variously and sometimes inaccurately, as a jongleur, a minstrel, a minnesinger, and a troubadour. I make my living, in part, singing of romance and of courtly love. You abase both yourself and your beloved when you practice these so clumsily."

Erec blushed but was too curious and eager to deny it. "And what have I done wrong?" he demanded.

Jouglet's tone of voice was diffident. "To begin with, of course, you would do better to choose a woman of greater, not lesser, rank than yourself. And married, preferably, but whomever you set your sights upon, you must court her with utter discretion and secrecy, never letting another man even know her name. Trundling a honey vat the size of Flanders in front of her brother's nose hardly counts as discretion." The musical voice stayed diffident. "You should dress to please her fancy, not your pride. *This*"—a gesture taking in Jouglet's own simple fawn tunic—"is far more to her liking. You should never mock or insult anyone, as such behavior would be ugly to her. Further, I must point out the object of the game is not to impress upon her guardian, be it husband or brother, that you are much better off than he is . . . yet your gesture is clearly intended, first and foremost, to have that affect upon my gracious host and friend, Willem Silvan of Dole. That is not just bad wooing, it is bad manners."

Willem, who agreed with this assessment, stared fiercely into

Atlas's mane, grateful but chagrined that his friend had called Erec to task in a way he never would have.

"I don't—" Erec began.

"Excuse me, but interrupting the jongleur is in extremely poor taste as well," Jouglet said, pressing on, still diffident and polite. "Never done in the better households. I speak only for your edification. Finally, of course, the point of courtly wooing is not to sully the loved one by imposing your lust upon her, but rather to discipline yourself, and raise your own spiritual worth by worshiping her selflessly with no real expectation of physical satisfaction. The fair blond virgin before us is so entrancing, and you are clearly so extremely virile, that I cannot blame you for lusting after her, but you should not try to buy her compliance with a tub of insect vomit."

Willem could barely keep a straight face, and Lienor didn't even try to as Erec took a threatening step toward the minstrel and said hotly, "Do not speak to me that way!"

Jouglet looked profoundly apologetic. "Forgive me, milord, for accusing you of virility. I am sure I was mistaken."

"Who are you, you . . . *Hungarian*?" the young man demanded furiously, advancing again.

"I'm a poet and a singer," said Jouglet sweetly. "My only aim is to flatter and please. If I have failed, despite my best intentions, you may slug me without fear of political repercussions."

Erec grabbed the fawn-colored collar and shoved Jouglet up against the chestnut's flank as the groom shushed the horse. "I'll do more than slug you, I'll knock out all your teeth!" Erec shouted.

"You will do no such thing to a guest in our house," Willem said sharply. The squire, conditioned to responding instantly to Willem's commands, retreated. "Anyhow, Erec, he is far below you, save your wrath for those worthy of it."

Jouglet bowed quickly, and sincerely, to the knight. "I've never been so grateful to have my stature denigrated." And back to Erec.

"If you will excuse me, milord." Jouglet nodded to the groom, who shortened his grasp on the chestnut's reins. Jouglet clambered up gracelessly into the saddle. "Shall we go kill things, then?"

Erec, still irked, grabbed the reins from the groom and smacked them hard across the chestnut's left shoulder. "Erec!" Willem cried out angrily as the horse obediently responded to the trick he and Erec had taught it together: the animal snorted and then reared up abruptly, kicking its forelegs several feet off the ground. The move was a trained reflex, performed without energy, but Jouglet was not prepared for it and tumbled backward, landing hard in an uncomfortable and unflattering heap on the dirt. Lienor cried out in alarm.

"Ha," Erec said, satisfied, and took one long, proud stride to stand over his victim with a malevolent smile.

His victim, still collapsed, slowly reached out both hands, and then abruptly poked Erec hard behind each knee. Erec's legs buckled under him—and as he fell, Jouglet scrambled up and snatched the youth's knife from his belt. By the time Erec hit the ground, Jouglet was standing over him, his own blade at his throat. Willem did not intervene because, frankly, the fellow had it coming.

"What does milady wish me to do with the offender?" Jouglet asked, nodding toward Lienor on her dun.

Lienor grinned mischievously. "Let me ponder the possibilities."

"If you hurt me, you'll have to answer to my liege Alphonse, Count of Burgundy," Erec huffed nervously.

"Mm," Jouglet responded, unimpressed. "If you'd hurt me, you'd be answering to someone *far* scarier than that, so let's say I've done you a favor." Letting the knife fall point-down into the ground, a hand's span from Erec's head, the minstrel reached out to retrieve the chestnut's reins.

"Jouglet takes the honors for that round," Lienor announced playfully, to help dispel the tension. She pulled the rose garland from

off her head and offered it out to Jouglet, who led the chestnut closer
to accept it. Lienor turned to her cousin as he dusted off his fancy
tunic. "Thank you for giving him the opportunity to be so clever,
Erec."

Erec sighed. "Will you accept my gift, cousin?" he asked gruffly,
the pleasure of giving it extinguished.

"Certainly, I shall feed some of it to Jouglet at supper," she said
sweetly, and called out to the house steward to fetch the honey vat.

"Lienor," Willem said in a low growl.

"Yes, brother dear?"

He gave her a parental frown. "Erec has brought you a very fine
gift to express his familial regard for you. Please show him the
graciousness for which you are so widely—and I'd like to think
accurately—admired."

Lienor gave him a vexed look, but he was firm. She dismounted
gracefully but with a drawn-out sigh and offered her palfrey back to
the groom. "Cousin, forgive my rudeness," she said with dutiful resignation. "It is a remarkably generous gift and shall sweeten all the
days of the year. Please come inside with me and I shall have the
cook offer you refreshment. I would enjoy that so much more than
going hawking." Her brother nodded slightly, regretful but approving, as she led Erec up the steps and into the cool shadows of the
hall, followed by her ever-silent mother.

Willem and Jouglet watched them go. Willem handed down the
falcon to the groom. He wasn't sure if he should be relieved or sorry
that the trip had been delayed. "And *that*," he said conclusively, gesturing after Erec, "is why I dread the thought of giving her over to
someone just because he happens to have riches."

"I think you simply dread the thought of losing her company,"
Jouglet said flatly.

"Well, that too. Wouldn't anyone?" Willem said with a shrug.
He glanced over at his friend, who was fidgeting with Lienor's

rosebud garland, wilting now in the heat. He smiled. "I'm not blind, Jouglet, I know why you've been tarrying here with us so long this visit."

Jouglet gave him a strange and almost melancholic smile. "My friend, you do not know the half of it."

2

Eclogue

[a work set in the country but preoccupied with matters of the court]

19 June

Two weeks later outside Basel, in silver alpine mist that muffled even birdsong, Marcus efficiently directed the dismantling of the summer camp. A trumpet bleated a warning, slightly muted in the damp air, and horsemen approached through the as-yet-gateless gateway of the courtyard.

The emperor heard the hooves, the voices calling out with polite familiarity across the broad courtyard, but he paid them no attention. This was his last hour to be free of the burdens of state, and he did not want to be interrupted. So he slouched in his squeaking leather camp chair at the unwalled end of the yard, under a fir, and munched on a spring pear. He toyed with the gold thread embroidered into his beard and pretended for one final morning he had no need of bodyguards.

The women were back in their usual prostitutes' garb, which was fashioned less to display finery and more to display flesh. They were ignored once they had ceased to be creatures of fantasy, and now the men congregated at the far end of the clearing, doing the clever things young lords do to entertain themselves, some engrossed in a spitting contest, others arguing politics quietly and simplistically. All of them were noticeably more placid than they'd been two weeks earlier. In the permanent game of allegiances between pope and emperor, Konrad always gained a temporary upper hand after each summer's camp.

The noblemen paused to return a greeting from the small pack of fog-dampened riders. Still Konrad did not bother turning to look, listening instead to a lovely pipe tune coming with the breeze from the beeches outside the yard. Marcus had dismissed all the musicians earlier this morning, but somebody apparently had lingered behind, hoping for another handout.

His Majesty recognized Marcus's halting footfall and glanced into the yard—then cursed under his breath as he prepared (by deliberately slouching farther) to receive the well-dressed man Marcus was escorting to him. Imogen's father, Count Alphonse of Burgundy, was as tall as his nephew Konrad and as slender as his son-in-law-to-be Marcus, except for a protruding belly implying he stayed too long at table. Which was true. But then, by Konrad's measure, Uncle Alphonse stayed too long wherever he went, simply by arriving.

Marcus was limping, a battle wound from the last crusade that plagued him when he suffered agitation.

The count bowed deeper than he needed to as he approached his nephew. "Sire—" he began, but Konrad, alarmed and trying not to stare at Marcus, interrupted at once.

"Uncle! Come to drag us back to politics so soon? How characteristic. How have you been? How is your lovely daughter?"

"Imogen is very well, Your Majesty." He bowed again and tried,

"I have come here, sire, to speak not of politics but of matrimony—"

"Did you bring your daughter with you?" Konrad asked, a shade too heartily.

Marcus stiffened, and one side of Alphonse's upper lip twitched involuntarily. "This is hardly an appropriate setting for my daughter, sire. She is visiting the abbess of Mulhausen."

"Is she now?" Konrad said, his voice but not his eyes drifting toward Marcus. "I am very fond of the abbess and must inquire after their joint devotions."

"I have removed everything from the site that requires removal, sire," the steward said smoothly, and Konrad relaxed. "When would you like to ride out?"

"When the village bells ring terce," the emperor said, then looked again at Alphonse. "Pardon, you were saying?"

"Sire, I am here to tell you that we have found you a bride."

The music had stopped. Konrad was annoyed that the piper hadn't bothered to play so well until the festivities were over. He took his annoyance out on Alphonse. *"We?"*

Alphonse's ears reddened. "I meant, sire, those of us entrusted to safeguard your interests—that we are aware of an excellent choice."

Konrad looked at his uncle narrowly a moment. "I was not aware I had entrusted you with any such thing." His mouth opened with rueful amusement. "Ah. My darling brother has arrived from Rome and is thoughtfully casting his cardinal shadow for you to shiver in. Am I to guess that your suggestion comes with the church's seal of approval?"

Alphonse hesitated, which gave Konrad his answer. "Who is it, then?" He sighed.

"We recommend the daughter of the lord of Besançon. As Besançon is Burgundy's largest city—"

Konrad groaned. "Oh, Christ in heaven, man. She's full of even more braying opinions than her father is. And she's ugly. She must be the least engaging creature west of Jerusalem."

"You are not marrying her for conversation, sire," Alphonse pointed out carefully.

"I am not marrying her at *all*," Konrad corrected.

"Sire, Besançon is the best choice. It strengthens your position near the border—"

Konrad laughed sarcastically. "No, it strengthens *Rome's* position in my *court*. Besançon's loyalties lie with the pope, not with me. So do Alphonse's, if I am not mistaken, although I can't think why. What has this new young pope promised you? Eternal life? Entry to his personal collection of holy sisters? What?"

Alphonse's ears reddened again. "My loyalties lie with the Empire. It would naturally soothe and flatter my vassals to have your presence in any manner at all in Burgundy."

"They're my vassals, not your vassals," Konrad corrected. This was an arguable point, and he had spent too many years arguing it already. He began to look around for a distraction. "I do wish you would suggest somebody who might be worthy of the office. Please try to remember I will have to be intimate with her more than once. Why did that musician stop? Hey!" he called out into the damp, shifting greenery. "Piper! Where are you? I want more of that! And why the devil didn't you play so well over these past two weeks?"

"I did, sire, but you were too far away to hear it," said the husky tenor behind him. He twisted in his chair, to find himself gazing at the familiar young face, nearly the human equivalent of a greyhound. Slightly freckled skin and pronounced hazel eyes suggested northern breeding, but the accent had always been impossible for Konrad to place. "Does my music please you, sire?" Jouglet asked solemnly, with a very formal bow, holding up the ivory pipe.

"It would have if you'd *been* here." Konrad frowned. "I gave you one fortnight's liberty, Jouglet, not three."

The minstrel, who almost never looked sheepish, looked sheepish now and put down the hard leather case that cradled the fiddle.

"I must have misheard you say forty days—I was resisting temptation in the desert. I tarried in your interest, sire, I promise you."

Konrad wanted a better explanation, but he suspected Jouglet was being deliberately vague because they were in public. "Your desertion is never in my interest. The next time you disappear that way, do not bother coming back, you will not be let in. Do you understand?" Jouglet nodded, still sheepish, and Konrad's demeanor lightened. He reached out to wrap a brawny arm around the minstrel. Jouglet politely repressed a strangling sound and tried to disengage from the royal limb. "Ladies!" Konrad called out to the wagon of women, his humor instantly restored. "See who has finally presented himself!"

Jouglet waved broadly to the prostitutes across the damp yard. The group immediately sent up a raucous cheer, whistling and making come-hither gestures.

"The lovely light women!" the minstrel called and bowed elaborately. "Now a little less light, I presume? Weighed down with the king's food and gold and the collective male moisture of the camp, are we? Please forgive me for having missed your favors this time."

"As long as you spread the word of how captivating His Majesty found all of us," sweet-faced Jeannette cried out.

"I'll spread what I should spread as long as you do likewise," Jouglet shouted back cheerfully—then with instant sobriety turned to make a show of obeisance to Alphonse and Marcus.

"Where have you been?" Konrad demanded.

"On the road as usual, sire," Jouglet answered, handing the little pipe to one of Konrad's bodyguards. "I was just on my way to lovely Hagenau to remind you that you simply can't abide the world without me. How very considerate of you to meet me halfway there, sire—a generous gesture I shan't soon forget."

"You'd have missed us in lovely Hagenau, we're for lovely Koenigsbourg," Marcus said dryly.

Konrad made a face. "Ach, Koenigsbourg, I'd put that out of my mind." He returned his full attention to Jouglet. "You'll be docked your entire summer salary. You missed the whole event, dammit, and the musicians were a disappointment this year, weren't they?" he asked Alphonse, knowing Alphonse hadn't been there. At the abashed look on Alphonse's face, Konrad smirked. "Prude. Well, Uncle, I thank you for your most unwelcome news. Perhaps the August Assembly will make a better suggestion for a marriage. I shall veto yours." Alphonse's face did not quite hide his displeasure. "We are very much packed up here, but Marcus, tell the cook to find some refreshment for the count. I have some catching up to do with my little spy here."

Marcus bowed, respectfully, to his future father-in-law, of whom he was at this moment feeling terrified, although he knew Imogen was safely on her way home. Her scent still lingered on his neat beard; he worried, absurdly, that Alphonse would recognize it. "If you will follow me, sir, there is some Clermont cheese still out." The two men worked their way back across the yard, leaving Konrad alone with his minstrel and, at a discreet distance, his bodyguards.

"I hope you at least have worthy new gossip and songs to make up for your absence," Konrad said. "Take my mind off politics."

"But, sire," Jouglet said confidingly, crouching beside the leather chair, "the juiciest gossip around is of the impending imperial wedding. There's talk of it all the way to the Rhone! Wherever I travel, they're wagering entire estates on who the lucky lady will be."

Konrad made a face. "Not you as well, Jouglet. I am sick of it."

Feigning innocence, Jouglet asked, "Why is it suddenly so important?"

"Use your brain," chastised Konrad. "The Duke of Bourgogne has sworn fealty to that pope-kisser Philip of France. You *know* that—I first heard the rumor from your own mouth."

Jouglet shrugged. "The duke was never your subject. He was always independent."

"And now he's *not* independent," Konrad said impatiently. "Now he is France's. And he's directly between us and France, only now he is an extension of France, and France is an ambitious little whoreson who would love to unburden me of my western counts, several of whom, being shortsighted idiots, would happily conform. Which I'm sure the church would love as well. You *know* all this, Jouglet—have you been carousing so heavily all month that you have forgot your own stock-in-trade? And where have you *been,* dammit?"

"I regret to hear you so against matrimony, sire," Jouglet deflected. "It would keep me in verse for months, your wedding."

Konrad made a face. "It will come soon enough. I'll have to plant my staff in Burgundy"—("so to speak," said Jouglet)—"to insure security. All the minor aristocracy under Alphonse there are trying to turn that to their advantage—they all want to marry me off to their little nieces."

"Burgundy!" Jouglet said, as if the word had just registered. "I've just come from Burgundy!"

"You better've brought back a new song or story, then, I don't let you loose to go traipsing about just for your own health." Konrad closed his eyes and stretched out on the leather chair, and took a deep breath. "All right, let's hear it. Entertain me. Start with a riddle."

"Of course, sire." A pause. Riddles were not Jouglet's calling. "I discovered on my travels the bravest, boldest thing in the world. Do you know what it is?"

Konrad did not.

"It's a miller's tunic, for every day it grasps a thief by the neck."

Konrad made a face. "That is why you are not famous as a riddler."

"Nor as an acrobat, nor conjurer, nor juggler. My talents, alas, truly are quite limited."

Konrad gave Jouglet a knowing look. "No they're not, my friend.

You conjure and juggle more deftly than any of my enemies, thank God. Give me a song."

Jouglet grimaced apologetically. "I haven't a song, Your Majesty. I was planning to perform for you a medley of selected works of the Provençal troubadours, but—ah, *but*," the minstrel intoned, musically, arms outstretched. "Then just the other *day,* the day before I headed this way, I was reunited with the most marvelous pair. They are old friends of mine, and would be a brilliant addition to your court if they weren't so poor. But I have not put together a worthy song yet. Will you accept a prose description?"

Konrad nodded, eyes still closed, enjoying his slouch. "Very well. As long as you don't try to marry me off to their little niece."

"They have no niece of any size."

"Excellent! Then you may proceed."

"Well. They're of Burgundy. He is a knight straight out of a troubadour's romance, or a tale by Vogelweide. Quite the most astonishing young man I've ever met, sire—he grew up fatherless, and truly he seems to have taught himself how a man should be in the world from reading the Arthurian romances. He is a devout Christian without the taint of Rome. There is not a whit of politics in the fellow's blood, he worships you from afar, although he's never even glimpsed you, simply because you are his king and emperor."

Konrad looked up at the damp tree branches on the hillside above, pleasantly surprised. "A Burgundian who *likes* me? Have I heard of him?"

"*Reveres* you, sire. He goes by the name Willem of Dole, even though he isn't exactly from Dole. Well, he sort of is, but . . ." Jouglet deliberately let it trail off, to catch Konrad's interest.

"He sort of is, but what?" He closed his eyes again.

Jouglet coughed slightly, to suggest delicacy of subject matter. "I speak now as your gossip-monger, not your spy. What I am about to say is pieced together by conjecture and rumor only, and Willem himself will not quench my curiosity, although he considers me a confidant. From his father—it is whispered by former servants and local drunks—Willem was born to hold in fief, directly from the crown, both the town and the fortress of Dole."

Konrad opened his eyes abruptly. "But all of Dole has been in Alphonse's hands as long as I've been emperor."

Jouglet shrugged. "I was told by an old man who might know the truth, or might simply be senile, that Count Alphonse unburdened Willem of these estates before Willem could walk."

Konrad frowned and sat up a little. "When was this?"

Jouglet waved a dismissive hand. "You were not come to your throne yet. There was a lot of corruption below your father's ken. I would guess that you have never heard of Willem in part because the count has kept him in the dirt. But that is my guess only, sire; you know I do not claim anything as factual unless I can present some evidence, which I cannot do in this case."

Konrad began to sit up, as if he would call his uncle to account that very moment. "If it was held from the crown, then Alphonse had no right to take it! I'm sick of that scheming whoreson—"

"There's no proof of what I've just told you, sire. It is, I say again, merely gossip," Jouglet said soothingly, and waited until Konrad, with an annoyed grimace, relaxed back into the chair. "Anyhow, whatever the real story, Willem's uncle stepped in and gave him enough to support Lienor and his mother, and he has a rather tragic attachment to their poverty. Which is a pity, because he's the best fighter I've ever seen. He could probably win half a county with his skill in tourney, but he can't afford to keep enough men with him to fight often enough." That last part, at least, was something Jouglet knew for fact.

Konrad frowned. "Willem is a *Flemish* name. The Flemish are allied with the French."

"He's pure Burgundy stock back to the dawn of time," Jouglet assured him. "His father was a renowned tournament rider in his youth, and Willem was the name of his closest cohort, a Flemish knight with whom he went round the tourney circuit."

"I need good men in Burgundy," the emperor mused. "I have been thinking a few well-placed soldiers down there might be useful. In fact, I've been contemplating the creation of a new military order—knights who would answer only to me directly, not to Alphonse or any of the minor lords. A sort of secular Knights Templar. Knights Imperial, something like that. Is he so grand as to be worthy of it?"

Jouglet's eyes widened with a surprised pleasure that masqueraded, convincingly, as doubt. "I don't know if he'd have any interest in such a heady exaltation, sire. Count Alphonse has never acknowledged him as he generally does the local knights, so for lack of habit, he lacks ambition. Except to make himself as close to Galahad as anyone could hope to be." A grin and a lecherous little chuckle. "Now let me tell you about Lienor. Lienor of the golden tresses and adorable pert breasts."

Konrad smiled. "Very well. Tell me about Lienor. Of the pretty epithets."

"She's a pretty lady, sire." With both hands Jouglet outlined an exaggerated female silhouette in the air. "Imagine this: wide-set emerald eyes with long dark lashes, a perfect, *perfect* heart-shaped face, hair as blond as that of Lady Agnes, falling in soft ringlets past her elbows with flowers bedecking her hair—fresh flowers every day that smell so good when you sidle up beside her it takes all your chivalrous restraint not to throw yourself on top of her, and try to sip the nectar out of all her hidden little nooks."

Konrad laughed approvingly. "Jouglet, you're very naughty."

"Truly, sire, she is delicious. I would have seduced her were I not terrified of Willem's wringing my neck. But she remains as pure as the driven snow, as chaste, as virginal as—"

"Don't ruin it with obvious hyperbole," Konrad chastised,

interrupting. "How can she be married and yet virginal? Is she a child bride? Or frigid?—is that the twist to the tale?"

Jouglet looked taken aback. "But she's not married, sire." And seeing Konrad's confused expression, explained hurriedly, "Oh, no, I apologize. I said a pair—I meant a pair of siblings. Did I not say that? How careless of me. They are brother and sister and both un-married."

Konrad was suddenly very attentive. "The sister of this extremely loyal knight, from Burgundy, is a virgin?"

"Sadly, yes," Jouglet said. "She will not even speak to men when her brother is away from home. But when she does engage in com-pany, she has such a pretty wit, you can see the entire assembly fall in love with her. Not just the local bumpkins, either, sire—high aristoc-racy passing through the area court her all the time, I hear."

"Why hasn't she married, then?"

"She is no heiress, as I explained, so she is courted only to be mistress of their *hearts*, not of their *hearths*."

"Ah," Konrad said, with understanding; he had such mistresses himself.

"She and her brother have resisted stooping to such a thing." A pause. Jouglet shifted from the crouch to sit cross-legged at Konrad's feet and began to trace a circle in the humus of birch leaves and fir needles carpeting this part of the unfinished courtyard. "But I sup-pose her brother will have to hand her over to someone sooner or later. Men make such a fuss over her she's a bit of a liability—I my-self saw a lord so moved by jealousy of her favors that he came to blows against a rival no older than myself. A knife came into play by the end of it!"

"An impoverished orphaned virgin had that effect?"

"I suppose Willem will have to yield her up eventually," Jouglet said with affected offhandedness, still drawing circles. "I think there are rumors some of the higher churchmen have taken an illicit interest in her too. Has your brother the cardinal been in that area of late? He goes so rapidly between concubines, and I'm sure the church would be happy if he accidentally sowed a few ecclesiastical seeds in Burgundy. Bastards make excellent pawns. He likes them blond, doesn't he?"

Konrad tensed slightly. "She is not repulsive to look at? And has enough wit to entertain even you?"

Jouglet nodded and glanced up, looking smitten. "She is the most exquisite creature I've ever met. I would choose her over any lady of your court—no insult intended to you, of course, sire. It is such a rare condition, to meet somebody so purely chaste and yet so engaging. She sits, sire, all afternoon at the window—her profile is lovely in the sunshine—and she does the most elaborate needlework while singing in the sweetest little soprano voice. Sometimes we perform the songs of Kurenerg together for her brother, taking turns with the verses, or we might sing a canso together." The minstrel sighed happily, hand over heart, looking a little dopey. "And truly, sire, she does smell wonderful. And her skin looks like ivory with just a touch of rose dust upon it. None of that unbecoming porcine ruddiness of northern blondes."

The emperor was sitting up very straight. For a moment he looked smug about something. "Dole, eh? That's better even than Besançon, it's the capital of Burgundy, after all." He frowned and deflated slightly. "No, the Assembly would never agree." A small resigned smile. "But go on talking about her. I dare say you're in love with her yourself."

Jouglet blushed. "She is entirely above me. She deserves a higher perch than Fate has given her. She and her brother, Willem, both. If only he had the means to ride in the tourneys more, especially the big ones like the one you're sponsoring next month." That was a little too obvious, and Jouglet, concerned, risked a studying glance at Konrad.

But the emperor had taken the bait. "If her brother could win more tourneys he might, indeed, rise in the world." Konrad was musing. Distractedly he brushed away a water droplet that had fallen from a tree above. "He could become the first Imperial Knight. And if he rose in status, she would as well. And if she rose enough, perhaps the Assembly would not veto my marrying her."

"Your *marrying* her?" Jouglet looked astonished. "Sire, that's preposterous, if you will pardon me. Like that French romance about the baron falling in love with the milkmaid."

"The baron marries the milkmaid although she has no dowry," Konrad pointed out. "Because she has worth in other ways."

"But . . . but . . . Lienor's never been outside Burgundy, and I doubt she's stepped beyond Dole since she was ten. She's hardly material for the royal chambers."

"You said she engaged you," Konrad argued. "That she had a quick wit. Were you lying?"

"No, sire, she is excellently educated for her station," Jouglet assured him hastily. "And has a mind as nimble as fire. But she knows nothing of court, or indeed of the world beyond her home. Surely you need somebody with strong opinions and a command of politics—"

"I need no such thing," Konrad said dismissively. "I have Marcus to run the court and my own wit to run the empire, I need her for nothing but begetting sons and provoking envious stares when we're in public. I have an entire Assembly of Lords insisting that I marry at once, from Burgundy, but they do not want to see my own dominions too advanced by that. You're telling me there is a nearly landless virgin of gentle birth in Burgundy, whose brother has a blind devotion to my throne and is an excellent knight." He smiled serenely. "That makes her an attractive choice. And much more attractive simply for not being a suggestion of the lords."

"But . . . she's lowly."

"When her brother's status soars, hers will as well."

"But how could her brother's status soar?" Jouglet asked in an incredulous tone, afraid to breathe too hard for fear of hexing it. After seven years of preparation, of waiting for just the right moment to begin, this had been ridiculously easy. Perhaps the heavy mist had softened His Majesty's royal brain.

Looking pleased with himself, Konrad explained patiently, "I shall invite him to the court, and if he makes the same splendid impression on me that he has on you, I shall have him compete in the royal tournament outside Sudaustat next month. If he's as good as you say, and he takes the day—in front of all the lords who matter— he'll be a hero, and his sister by extension might as well be a princess. Nobody would deny me her hand, especially if her pedigree can be proved. But even if they do, assuming you speak the truth, I've still added an excellent and devoted knight from Burgundy to my inner fold."

Jouglet applauded. "So you have a winning stratagem no matter how the fates unfold it! Very clever of you, sire."

3

Epistle

[a work in the form of a letter]

22 June

The rafters of Willem's modest hall echoed with rowdy masculine voices, with a boisterous joy seldom heard here. The master of the house sported as many bruises as his guests did, but he was the day's undisputed champion in the art of simulated bloodlust, and had earned abundant gratitude by announcing he would host an impromptu feast for all the knights who had participated in the local tournament.

It was not really impromptu, of course. His cook had anticipated this event for days and was prepared to feed them all with jellies and summer meats; everyone for miles around had known that Willem of Dole would lead his team to victory, and that when he did he would feed and water them. He always did. But he was a humble man, and the pretense of improvisation added to the spirit of the evening.

Willem sat at the high table in his family colors of red and blue, a slash of sunburn marking what had been exposed between his helmet and his beard. Erec—dressed more demurely now, in Willem's livery—was serving him a leg from a suckling pig. The knight radiated a relaxed cheerfulness that was as rare on his face as such excitement was in his house. He had won a lot of gold in ransoms today; he'd also added an excellent grey mare to his stable and a staghound hunting bitch; three days' service from Sauvin of Poligny's serfs was due him as well.

But late in the day he had surrendered his iron helmet, and the knight to whom he'd lost it—Renard of Vesoul—had no interest in exchanging it for any ransom. "This bonnet is worth ten times its weight in gold," Renard had laughed, hoisting it atop a lance and waving it for everyone to notice. "I'm the second-best knight in Burgundy, but without this you won't be fighting any tournaments, so I become the first best!" Willem, to maintain a gentleman's demeanor, had laughed self-deprecatingly at this but immediately told Erec to try to buy the helmet back. Despite Erec's best efforts, Renard was not selling.

Willem wasn't thinking about that now. He was allowing himself to indulge in the deceptive pleasure of feeling rich enough to host a feast—a quick mental calculation would have told him that the feast almost wiped out the amount he'd earned in coin today—and the even greater pleasure of being appreciated by his fellow knights and all their men. He was only sorry Jouglet had left earlier that week; the local entertainers were dull in comparison.

There were some two dozen knights crowded with their squires in the small half-timbered hall, most of them exceedingly drunk. The extra servants hired from the town were all young women and suspiciously pretty; Willem had been taken aback by it at first. But they knew their business. They flirted raucously but stayed entirely clothed, were admirably prompt at service, and if they were doing anything on the side to make a little extra, they were doing it quickly, quietly, and most important they were doing it behind the stables. So the impression of wholesome, if inebriated, jollity was preserved within the hall.

Willem sat back against his carved oak chair and smiled with paternal satisfaction at the hubbub. The hubbub was consuming an amazing amount of larded chicken in pepper sauce, so luxuriously gushing with fat it could almost slide unchewed down one's throat.

"Excuse me, sir." The boy who had been minding the door was at his elbow. "But there's a rider come with a message for you, says he's ridden three days to get here with it."

Willem could not think of anyone who lived three days' ride away who wasn't already at the feast. "Bring him in then," he said.

As the boy departed, Willem felt a tap on his shoulder, and looked back to see his mother, almost invisible within the shadows in her dark grey widow's wimple. She gave him a look that he interpreted at once. "No, milady," he said gently, with an apologetic smile. "Lienor knows she must not come down here while the hall is full of drunken bachelors. I promise to share the news with her if it is of interest."

She nodded and slipped back into the darkness by the kitchen screens.

Willem and everyone who had heard the porter's announcement assumed that a messenger three days on the road would be dirty, hungry, and exhausted. But the young man who entered the hall through the sunset-shadowed door was so elegantly dressed, so debonair, calm, and collected that the murmuring that had begun returned at once to silence. There was respectful ogling as he crossed the room, his face clean, his black hair and beard neat, and—most peculiar for a man who had been three days on the road—a cape of expensive ermine without a mote of dust on it covering his livery. For the cape alone, this courier was dressed as well as any knight in the room, and held himself with greater dignity than most of them.

"Excellent knight," he said in German-accented Burgundian, and bowed before Willem's table with a practiced efficiency. He held a scroll in his finely tooled leather glove but little could be seen of it. "May I presume you to be Willem of Dole, the master of this house?"

". . . Yes," Willem said cautiously. "Who are you and what is your mission?" And then because he could not help himself: "You are in an excellent state for three days on the road."

"I have taken a room at the inn at Dole, sir. I arrived well before the bells tolled vespers, and bathed and changed my clothes before coming to see you." Seeing the uncomprehending stare Willem and others gave him, he explained pleasantly, "My master pays my travel expenses and is very generous for my comfort, sir."

This only further astonished the assembled provincials—a messenger so pampered was not even in the realm of their imagining. The young man took this in, hiding his amused condescension, and bowed very deeply again to Willem.

"I forget myself, allow me to deliver my message. I am Nicholas of Swabia, and I bring greetings from my master"—with a gratuitous flourish he flung back the cape, revealing a yellow tunic with a black eagle on it—"His Majesty the king and emperor."

This was Nicholas's favorite part of his job, and Willem gratified him by gaping as the room burst into astonished drunken speculation. Nicholas presented the scroll, which was sealed with gold leaf; Willem reached across the table and accepted it. He examined the seal—it was actually gold foil, adhered to the fine paper (the fine *linen* paper) with wax. The small imprint on it matched the eagle on Nicholas's chest. Willem was almost afraid to break it.

"His Majesty requests your presence at his court," Nicholas explained, seeing Willem's hesitation.

Willem was so startled by this announcement that he handed off the scroll to Erec, who in turn ogled the gold seal until another knight reached for it.

"What?" Willem said, trying not to sound moronic. "Would you please repeat that message?"

Nicholas bowed again. "His Majesty the Emperor has called you to his summer court at Koenigsbourg. He is awaiting your presence as soon as you can set out." Seeing Willem's confusion he added, reassuringly, "It is not a criminal summons, milord. He has heard good things about your mettle as a knight and he wishes to consider making you a member of his entourage."

Willem made a gasping sound, and the hall grew still. He breathed out a restrained, incredulous little laugh. "I am stunned. And of course His Majesty's obedient servant," he added quickly. He had absolutely no idea what was appropriate in such circumstances. "Should I depart at once?" He stood up, and seeing him, a few of his less-inebriated guests stood as well. A small group of them had gathered around the gold foil seal, staring at it openmouthed.

Nicholas smiled and held up his hand. "His Majesty enjoys a good feast and would surely wish that you enjoy the rest of yours. Let us begin preparations in the morning."

"Join us," Willem said earnestly, embarrassed it had taken him so long to think of this. "Please—" He gestured for his steward to find a stool. Finally thinking clearly, he switched to German to add, "They are about to bring out a currant-bread pudding that has made my cook famous locally. And then by all means stay as my honored guest tonight."

"For the feast, thank you, I will stay," Nicholas answered, smiling. "But not overnight—I have a very comfortable room at the inn awaiting me." Lowering his voice he added, "And a very comfortable young companion as well."

"Aha," Willem said with a polite smile. "Well. Perhaps you will break fast with us in the morning? You are welcome to observe mass here—it is a modest chapel that we have, but our chaplain speaks well."

"I would be very pleased to do that," Nicholas said and settled elegantly upon the leather stool the steward had brought.

The next morning, by the time mass had been performed by the family cleric, Willem's handful of devoted serfs, understanding the importance of their visitor, had diligently cleaned up what had turned out to be a very messy evening. The evidential detritus of every indulgence, from overeating to carnality, covered the hall, the courtyard, and the stableyard at dawn; by the time the chapel bell tolled prime, these areas had been restored to their usual monastic sheen.

Nicholas, refreshed from the various comforts procured at the inn, arrived for a breakfast of yesterday's bread crusts sopped in sauce, and ate beside Willem, describing what the journey would be like and whom Willem should bring with him for the circumstances. The young knight's eyes grew rounder as he listened. He was being asked to select an entourage of his own: all his squires and enough servants and page boys to attend them for an extended time (he murmured, falteringly, that he might bring one servant, and perhaps two pages, and he had no squire but Erec). He was to bring his armor and at least one ceremonial outfit (he had only one ceremonial outfit, which made the selection simple).

According to Nicholas, the journey would be easy, assuming they did not succumb to heatstroke, ague, highwaymen, or wild boars. They would be almost entirely on the edge of river valleys without having actually to ford any body of water; they would begin by following the River Doubs east and slightly north, into the gentle southernmost foothills of the Vosges. Willem knew this terrain from running the tournament circuit; as in Dole, the climate was mild and the soil superb, the land's lush virgin forests being reclaimed with growing rapacity by serfs and lords alike, and tamed to crops, vineyards, and livestock forage. Beyond lay the Rhine Valley, a flat, swampish expanse that ran north to south but was extremely broad from east to west as well. They would travel north along its western edge for several days, Nicholas explained, on ancient, refurbished trade roads raised several yards above the marshy valley floor, roads that traveled true north even as the Rhine itself meandered with silt-inducing vagueness toward the North Sea. Conveniently, Koenigsbourg Castle was to the west of the river valley, perched atop a mountain crag; the town of Sudaustat lay at its foot a half-mile distant, snug against the hills that connected the Rhine plain to the northern Vosges. A room at Sudaustat's best inn had been reserved, although Nicholas was vague as to who was paying for it.

When breakfast was finished Willem set his steward about the task of organizing the adventure. Erec was sent for. The few servants they had, except Lienor's maid, were corralled into preparations; the task enlisted even those who would have been otherwise harvesting the hay. Nicholas had quite offhandedly remarked that they need not bring much, they would be in a castle town where nearly everything required could be purchased. Willem saw no point in mentioning that he had very little with which to make such purchases.

Once the servants were dispatched on their errands, Willem gestured Nicholas to follow him across the small sun-drenched courtyard toward the back of the manor. "Allow me to present the only treasures of my home," he said, with an obvious eagerness to please His Majesty's servant. One thing he knew surely was that introducing his sister to any man would please the man enormously. Lienor's

relentless flirtations had disturbed him until he came to see—Jouglet
had pointed this out to him—that for Lienor, the whole point of flirtation was *never* yielding to *any* wooer.

They climbed the outside wooden stairs above the stable, to a
small platform and carved wooden door. Willem stepped aside and
held open the door for his visitor, wishing that the place were over-
run with page boys for such menial services. They went inside.

The women's chamber was a long, narrow room running the
southern length of the household. It had several windows to the south
that let in brilliant light, a view of hayfields, and a warm breeze that
was softened by the River Doubs. For such a modest house, Nicholas
noted, this room was sumptuously decorated and relentlessly feminine: there were flowery tapestries on the walls, flowery curtains by
the windows, and flowery draperies around both beds; there was one
chair and one stool, each embellished with flowery designs; there
were flower-painted chests with attractive but unuseful knickknacks
atop them, jewelry draped almost casually over every free surface,
and several gilt, but empty, birdcages. The clothes-pole held more
kirtles, robes, and tunics than a poor knight's sister would ever need
to own.

Sitting in profile, at the large middle window that had a linen
drape protecting it from direct sunlight, were two women. The older
one was wearing dark grey, and generally plain; the younger, blond,
was one of the prettiest females Nicholas had ever seen. They had
been bent over sewing frames, embroidering, but both looked up as
the door opened. With twinned expressions and similar bright green
eyes, they smiled on seeing Willem then looked startled, almost
alarmed, when they registered Nicholas's presence. They set the sewing frames aside hurriedly, and hurriedly stood up.

"Nicholas, these are the ladies of my house," Willem said with a
hint of pride. "Maria my lady-mother, and my sister and ward,

Lienor. Ladies, this is Nicholas of Swabia, messenger of our great emperor." He had sent them the extraordinary news before retiring last night, along with the gold seal from the scroll; by now even Lienor had managed to control her excitement. Nicholas bowed to the mother, then the daughter. They curtsied, eyes averted. "I am honored," Nicholas said in a silky voice, "to be granted access to the private regions of the manor."

Lienor smiled and spoke in the perfect aristocratic German that Jouglet always insisted on. "We are honored to receive you," she replied. "We have seldom in the course of my life received a visitor to our chambers like this. My brother is famous for being extremely protective."

"That speaks excellently well of him as well as of you, and only further deepens the honor I feel at having been invited here," Nicholas said, with another bow.

"Whatever I am master of is at the emperor's disposal," Willem said with quiet earnestness.

"I am sure that is more than your emperor requires of you," Nicholas replied pleasantly. "But he would be pleased by the sentiment, especially in this corner of the Empire."

"Will you sit with us?" Lienor asked, and held a dainty hand out to him. She was wearing one of her favorite tunics, made of brilliant green Ghent cloth—a gift from some Flemish knight whose name she did not even remember now. The sleeves were fluted to the wrist, and draped extravagantly, almost ridiculously, to the floor. This made any activity—even embroidery—extremely cumbersome, but for today's meeting she did not care, because it made her green eyes startlingly greener. Nicholas smiled, with a bow of his head, and kissed her hand without quite taking it in his, or touching it with his lips. "Please have my seat," she gestured; he sat on the cushioned window seat knee-to-knee with the mother. "Would you like some refreshment?" Lienor asked. "We are blessed with excellent wines. Lisel," she said to the servant girl without looking at her. "Bring a flagon and a fresh cup for our guest."

The girl withdrew silently.

"How was your journey?" Lienor asked. She sank onto a brocade cushion at Nicholas's feet, in a demure posture that nonetheless deliberately offered him an unimpeded view down the front of her tunic. Nicholas, although immune to far less subtle behavior from the ladies of Konrad's court, found the girl's flirtation endearing.

"It was uneventful, which means it was very good, thank you, milady." He glanced around the room. "This is a beautifully furnished chamber, milady."

She smiled. "Thank you. Nearly all these things are gifts from our friends. The cages of course came with birds, but I let them all go free. My heart weeps to see things caged." She gave her brother a brief, meaningful look, then returned her attention to Nicholas and gestured to one of the two beds, with a confidential smile. "That is from the Lord of Auxonne, who courted me, although he was married. My brother would not accept the gift, and when His Lordship deposited it anyhow, Willem insisted he reclaim it, but he was killed in a tournament the next day. We have given it to mother, as it seemed improper for me to lie within it."

"An excellent course of action, milady." Nicholas smiled. He pointed to a corner of the room, where there was a worn, oval-shaped fiddle on an enameled table set almost as if upon an altar. A faded image of the imperial eagle was visible beneath the strings, between the flat bridge and the fingerboard. "Are you a musician, milady?"

"I play the psaltery, of course," Lienor said offhandedly, then noticed where his gaze had gone. She smiled. "Oh, yes, the fiddle. That was left here by a fiddler who tried to teach me to play it, after he had been given a much finer one by his patron. I do not have the knack for it, I fear."

"But my sister sings quite beautifully," Willem put in. "Lienor, would you please entertain our guest?"

She made a self-deprecating gesture. "Consider his life, Willem. He hears the entertainers of the emperor's own table, it would be an embarrassment to both of us to subject him to my unsteady warble." Then she smiled languidly at Nicholas, an expression he interpreted to mean: *I know my voice will enthrall you, but first I want you to appreciate how modest I am.*

"I would be honored to hear the lady sing," he said.

She smiled again, pleased. "Of course I cannot deny the emperor's ambassador."

When the wine arrived, she served it to him, then offered him a pillow for his feet, and settled again on her cushion with her carved psaltery, to sing: *"A delicate breeze of longing blows through my lover's window . . ."*

Nicholas listened, enjoying with dispassionate pleasure the combination of Lienor's truly childlike smile and not nearly so childlike physical comportment. He glanced at Maria, the mother, sitting in the window seat across from him. She had returned contentedly to her sewing, humming slightly to Lienor's song. She had not spoken once.

"You have handsome children, milady," Nicholas said, bowing his head to her. She smiled and bowed her own head to acknowledge the compliment.

"I never dreamed my lover would betray me," Lienor was singing. Her voice was very pleasant, if not brilliant. *"For I always yielded to him with a smile."* And with an expression as sweet as honey, she concluded daintily, *"Oh, God of love, I just want to rip off his accursed head, and I don't mean the one on his neck."*

Willem grimaced and shot her a chastising look, but Nicholas laughed. "That is how our jongleur Jouglet sings the final verse," the messenger commented, smiling archly. He'd recognized that weathered fiddle on the table.

Lienor's entire face widened with her smile. "Jouglet!" she said, delighted. Nicholas nodded. "Brother, did you hear that? I knew this was somehow Jouglet's doing!" Willem, without speaking, registered flustered, pleased interest. Lienor turned back to Nicholas. "Jouglet has written several songs about me. I wonder if he's ever sung them for His Majesty?"

Nicholas's eyes widened. "Is it you? Jouglet is known for his romantic lays, almost as much as his romantic exploits—"

"Romantic exploits? *Jouglet*?" Willem laughed despite himself. Lienor frowned.

"Oh, yes." Nicholas smiled knowingly. "For a fellow still working his way toward burliness, there is something there already that makes the females swoon, and he has a reputation that pricks his rivals' jealousy. He will be notorious when he's older. More notorious than he already is, I should say." Seeing the squelched outrage on Lienor's face, he added diplomatically, "But there is only one lady to whom he devotes his poetry, whom he is too discreet to name—he's let it slip that she is a blonde from Burgundy, so I assume it must be you."

Lienor was somewhat appeased. "The only one?" she said, with fetchingly wounded dignity.

"The only one. And now that I've seen you I am convinced his heart is entirely devoted."

She smiled. "As long as I have his heart, I don't much care what he does with the rest of himself. His Majesty's court must be an excellent assemblage of personalities, judging by the two whom we have now had the honor to know."

Nicholas smiled at the flattery, so obvious yet so benign. Jouglet had good, if predictable, taste—Konrad would like this one. She would make pleasant company and never bother anyone with willfulness, Nicholas thought.

Until the time came for them to leave.

Maria, her chaplain, and the family's aging steward had come into the hall for a final interview with an anxious Willem. He assured them Erec had assigned men to guard the property. He advised the steward to remember to air and turn the stored grains and feed his falcon and close the house securely before retiring each night; he advised his mother to air the furs and linens when it was dry outside; he advised the chaplain to deliver alms each morning to the village after mass. He advised them each to do exactly what they had been doing anyhow since before he had been born, and they promised him, smiling, that they would try to remember his instructions.

While waiting for the official leave-taking, Lienor went out the back gate, to the flat and fertile river plain mown low by livestock, to breathe in the green smells of the field and throw sticks for the dogs. She had the rare sort of translucent skin that looked as if it would burn at once under such summer sun, or at least mottle with freckles. Her mother, concerned about that, went to the back gate to call her inside.

"Give her a few moments more," Willem called out from near the river, where he and his servants were greeting Erec. "It may be awhile before she has the liberty again."

Lienor froze, stick in hand. A young pup danced about her feet impatiently waiting for her to throw it. After a moment, stunned, she simply gave the stick to the dog, who accepted it with disappointment.

"Brother dear," she said, using a tone that hinted there was trouble coming. "One might *almost* think you meant for me to be sequestered in the house the entire time that you are gone."

Without speaking, Willem handed Atlas's reins to Erec and took a few steps toward her, holding his arms out in a conciliatory way. She backed away, a horrified expression on her face.

"No," she said, quiet but ferocious. "You cannot mean that, Willem. You absolutely cannot think to keep me penned in the house for what could easily be months. I spend enough time in there, with you out at your accursed tourneys all spring."

"Those tourneys are our only hope of advancement, sister." Willem continued approaching her slowly; she continued backing up toward the gate. "Lienor, there is no other way for me to know that I am looking out for your safety."

"You could trust me!" she cried. "You could trust me to sequester myself when a man comes here. How many male visitors are we likely to have while you're away? How much of my life would you have slip away inside the house?"

"You make it sound like prison," Willem said and stopped following her, because he was afraid she would trip on the ludicrous long sleeves of her gown walking backward. Out of the corner of his eye, he saw to his dismay that Nicholas had come out to the back gate and was watching curiously. "You have the run of nearly the entire house, and the whole courtyard as well."

"The *whole courtyard*," she mimicked with bitter sarcasm, then suddenly lurched sideways so that she could, moving forward, get past him. "The yard is not thirty paces across and all summer it reeks of manure! I will not do it. Send me to a nunnery while you're gone, I'd have more freedom there."

"Lienor," he said unhappily, reaching out an arm to stop her, but she sailed past him and broke into a run, arms raised to keep from tripping on her sleeves, a hand held up to her crown of flowers so it would not fall off. She ran as if she would try to take wing up into the brilliant blue, or else—more effectively—hurl herself into the shallow Doubs. "Somebody stop her!" Willem called out to the cluster by the river, and Erec obligingly leapt from his horse and darted toward her across the field. She tried to stop and spin off to the side, but he was quick and agile and extremely pleased to have an excuse to close his arms tight around her.

"Let go of me," Lienor hissed at him when he had wrestled her to a standstill. "Your breath smells of spoiled mustard."

"You are being disrespectful to my vassal, your lord and brother," Erec said. He spoke quietly, mostly because it gave him an excuse to keep his head near hers. Lowering his voice still further—which required bringing his pimply face even closer to her porcelain one—he added, "Do not forget it is the emperor's messenger you misbehave in front of, cousin."

"Damn the emperor," she snarled, but too quietly for Nicholas to hear.

"Cousin!" Erec snapped.

Lienor hurled her headdress furiously to the stubbled ground. Hearing her brother approach them from behind, she said it again deliberately for his benefit. "Damn the emperor. And damn his fussy little messenger. And most of all, Willem, damn your precious Jouglet. Tell him I'll spit in his face the next time I see him. Tell him I'll lock *him* away because of some scheme that *I* dream up for my own entertainment—"

"What about Jouglet?" Erec asked, confused. He knew he should offer to hand her over to her brother's physical custody, but he decided not to make the offer because she smelled too good.

Willem made a dismissive gesture. "We don't know why Konrad sent for me, so Lienor has decided Jouglet must be behind it for some reason."

"You tell that stupid little fiddler I'll bury his face in *mire* the next time I see him. It's all well and good for you, you're going out to have an adventure. It's bad enough I cannot share in it, but I will not be *miserable* so that you may enjoy it."

With the patience of a grandfather, Willem said quietly, "Lienor, shall you and I have this discussion inside in private? It is inconceivable to me that you would subject the emperor's messenger to such ungentle behavior."

She made an awful face at him, then sighed heavily with resignation. "You and I alone," she agreed and nodded toward the gate. "In there."

"Yes," he said, and gestured for Erec to release her, which Erec did quite unwillingly.

They sat facing each other across the table still set up from dinner, each clearly displeased with the other. Their mother anxiously hovered nearby, watching but not speaking. "I'm not a child anymore," Lienor began in a low voice.

"Then stop behaving like one," Willem said reasonably. "Anyhow, it's *because* you are a woman that it is not safe for you to be unguarded."

"Hypocrite!" she snapped. "You like it well enough that the Widow Sunia is unguarded, don't you?"

For a moment Willem was too startled to speak. "It is precisely because I know what women may do when left to their own—"

"But I'm nothing like her, *I* am not a *whore*," Lienor announced defiantly.

"You will not refer to Lady Sunia in such a manner," her brother informed her curtly, wondering how she had heard about that.

"You help to guard her farms, and she repays you by giving you access to her bodily orifices," Lienor said impatiently, unimpressed.

Willem blushed, not for the fact of it, but for unexpectedly hearing it from his delicate little sister's delicate little lips. "The private life of the Lady Sunia is irrelevant to this discussion, Lienor."

She made a frustrated sound but decided not to pursue it; it would gain her nothing. She tried a new tactic. "We all know why you're doing this," she said with exasperation. "You think I'll seek out mischief if you are not hovering over me. But that was *ten years ago*, Willem. I was a *child*."

He grimaced. "Lienor, please don't dredge up—"

"When will you stop punishing me for a childhood mistake?" she demanded. "May I ask how long you intend to keep me on probation for one single, juvenile misadventure?"

"Misadventure?" Willem snapped. "We were almost *killed*. And for the love of God, that poor—" He stopped abruptly, grimacing, and crossed himself.

"I'm not planning to *confront* anyone this time," she argued. "I'm not going to walk to Oricourt again—why do you think I would do that? I simply want the freedom to step outside my own front gate, or down to the river."

Willem slouched back in his chair, wishing he were already on the road. "Lienor . . ." He sighed, and stopped, not knowing what else to say.

"How do you think Jouglet would react if you told him I was locked up here alone?"

Willem laughed softly. "He would probably come back and offer to be locked up with you."

"I'm serious. He would want to know that I was left behind in a state of relative contentment. If this is his scheme, and I think you must admit it probably is, he would be stricken to learn that he had contributed to my misery. Do not make that the truth of it. Leave me here content." She smiled, pleased to have finally found the persuasive argument: "Do it for Jouglet's sake."

Willem, unconsciously tapping his foot on the rushes, sighed as if the fate of the world hung on his decision. "Very well," he said at last. "Only if Erec's guards escort you. On your honor." She clapped her hands once with satisfaction and threw herself on him to kiss his cheek. "But if I have any reason to suspect you have abused the arrangement," he went on, smiling despite himself at her instantly renewed affection, "that is the end of it. There will be no second chance. I will keep you under my thumb until we manage to marry you off."

She placed one hand over her heart. "I shall remain as chaste as if my wedding day were already set," she promised with a smile.

4

Exemplum

[a narrative that instructs]

27 June

Checkmate, sire." Marcus sounded dutifully apologetic. Jouglet chuckled—respectfully—from the window seat of this, the handsome royal dayroom of Koenigsbourg Castle.

Konrad, swathed in a gold-encrusted chamber robe, stared down at the board as if he could not imagine how Marcus had done it. "How is it that you are the only one who ever beats me at chess?"

"Perhaps because I'm not skilled enough to strategize a losing game, Your Majesty," Marcus said demurely.

Konrad laughed. "So all the others *can* best me but devise games that make them seem to lose? You're saying that I am, in fact, the worst chess player at court and you are the second worse."

"I would simply make the observation, sire, that I lose to everybody else, and you always lose to me. In fact, Alphonse of Burgundy, whom you always checkmate within twenty moves, is one of the best players I know."

"How do we account for this bad chess player being so strong in strategy in the court and on the battlefield?" Konrad demanded with cheerful smugness. He signaled a page to slice him a bit of cheese, and reached down to pat his favorite bloodhound, who lay dozing happily in the rushes by his leather slippers.

"Oh, that's easy, sire," Jouglet said from a relaxed slouch at the window seat, laying down the fiddle. "Many great warriors cannot think in the abstract, they must be in situ to grasp what lies ahead of them. Willem of Dole, for example, cannot even win a chess game against his own mother, yet he—"

"I find it odd that this Willem fellow has such an illustrious record and yet we've never heard of him," Marcus interrupted.

"You're just jealous because your best days are behind you," Konrad said.

"He also sounds suspiciously magnanimous," observed Marcus.

"I refuse to consider that a failing," said Konrad, laughing. "It's a relief, frankly, to know there is somebody in the Empire other than the emperor himself who makes a habit of generosity."

The word *generosity* made Marcus think of the trusting look on Imogen's face the first time he had entirely undressed her. With an embarrassed blink he shook the thought away. "Sire, with all due respect, it is reasonable and believable that *you* would host a feast after a tournament, but for a knight who can barely keep one squire—"

"Oh, hush, Marcus," Konrad said cheerfully, enjoying the cheese. "Jouglet, Marcus is getting petulant, and we both know why, so go and summon my uncle, would you? Wine," he added, to another page boy.

"I saw milord Count on my way up here, Your Majesty. I think he was going in search of carnal debauchery," the minstrel answered, not wanting to get up from the sun-drenched cushions quite yet.

Koenigsbourg Castle deserved its reputation for cold and damp, but in summertime the window seats of these southern chambers were sublime, with a warm breeze and a commanding view of the foothills tapering toward the Rhine Valley.

Konrad made a self-righteous face. "Yet he turns up his nose at my summer bacchanalia as if it were the devil's own invention."

"I believe your Lord Uncle prefers his carnalities in a blunter form," Jouglet said dryly and added with quiet disgust, "he simply rapes the kitchen girls."

"Oh," Konrad said, disinterested. "Well, then, look for him in the kitchen, I suppose." Beside him, his expressionless page boy decanted a skin of Moselle into a thick glass cup. The boy handed him the cup, and he drained it in one swallow as he gestured impatiently with his free hand at his musician. Jouglet reluctantly rose from the striped cushions, slipped past the two men, bowed, and left the room.

"I always beat Jouglet at chess," Konrad said after a thoughtful pause.

"No, you don't, actually," Marcus informed him.

Konrad grinned ruefully. "I knew that."

A pause. Marcus fidgeted with a black bishop from the chessboard, whose tapered head felt to his fingers like one of Imogen's nipples. In his distraction he almost brought it to his mouth. "If you are calling Alphonse for the reason I think you are, I thank you, Konrad."

The king shook his head and yawned, rubbing his broad face with one broad hand. "Don't thank me yet, I'm not going to demand he set the wedding date." Seeing Marcus's dismay, he added with irritation, "Oh, Christ, you haven't got her with child, have you?"

Marcus looked insulted. "Of course not, sire."

"If you're playing me for a fool, Marcus, I'll banish you."

"I told you she is still a virgin, sire."

"Good, because I may yet need to marry her to someone else, and she's too important for me not to punish whoever sullies her before she's wed."

"I would never . . . sully her, sire," Marcus said quietly.

"Then what's the rush?"

"I want to be with her," Marcus said softly, knowing it would be impossible to make him understand that.

Konrad made a dismissive gesture and tossed the wine cup back to the serving boy with a gesture for more. "Oh, I thought it was something serious. Alphonse has got us by the balls right now. I hoped a betrothal would satisfy him—he can't marry her to *me,* so I gave him my very right arm, the man who is practically my own heart—"

"I am honored, sire," Marcus said quietly.

"Don't be." Konrad accepted the fresh wine cup. "It is his religion to loathe your entire class, Marcus, regardless of your particular worth. As long as it's only a betrothal, not a marriage, he has leverage to drum up another match. He'd marry her to the pope if he thought he could. I know he's got his eye toward Bourgogne, which I find annoying—the last thing I want is to marry my only legitimate kin to France's lackey."

Marcus felt a seizure of fear. "If you would insist upon *my* marriage to Imogen finally taking place, that danger is removed."

Konrad downed the wine and belched a little. "I cannot force Alphonse. The delicate dance of pretending we respect each other could not survive it. But there are ways to encourage his cooperation." Seeing the look on Marcus's face, Konrad added disapprovingly, "Oh, for Christ's sake, you really are lovesick, aren't you? Must you *complicate* things?" Before Marcus could defend himself, Konrad held up a hand for quiet: all the doors were open to welcome the afternoon warmth, and the footsteps mounting the steps outside were growing louder. The two friends said nothing as the guard outside briefly patted down the ascending count. Jouglet bowed Alphonse into the far room of the suite, and then Konrad called out, "Jouglet, don't you think love is an illness?"

"Absolutely," the troubadour said heartily, entering. "But I make a good fat living off it, so I'm glad we live in an age of epidemic outbreaks."

Alphonse of Burgundy bowed to His Majesty, an action consisting of bending his tall, otherwise gaunt frame over the bulk of his stomach. "Your Majesty," he said solemnly. "I was on my way to you already. His Eminence your brother has humbly begged me to humbly beg you to reconsider Besançon's girl as a bride."

Konrad grimaced. "His Eminence my brother can go bugger himself. Innocent should be castrated for sending him as papal chaperone. I can't believe you gave him a southern room, Marcus, it should have been saved for something more worthy, perhaps an indoor privy. Uncle, play chess with me. I shall be white."

Marcus immediately stood and offered his stool to the older man, who took it, looking at his sovereign a little suspiciously. Jouglet knelt by the board and returned all the pieces to their starting positions with impressive dexterity.

"Your Majesty has summoned me to play chess?"

"Of course not, you're an awful player, I always beat you," Konrad said. "But now that you're here you might as well practice. I called you because I need you for some clarifying."

"Clarifying? What does Your Majesty need me to clarify?"

"A small matter, Uncle, but I didn't specify which of us would be the clarifier." Konrad carelessly moved a pawn two spaces forward. "Your turn. Am I correct that my father gave you the border fort near Dole?"

". . . Yes, sire, I received that honor," Alphonse said warily.

"Oh good," said Konrad. "I'm so glad to know that it is firmly in family hands." As if it were an unrelated thought, he said,

"I've heard a rumor that your neighbor just across the river there, France's new lackey, is looking for a new bride for his son and heir. The last one just died in childbirth or something inconvenient like that."

This was a lie—a setup—but the count looked so hungry at the news that Marcus almost felt sorry for him.

"I did . . . I did not know of this, Your Majesty." Trying not to look too eager he ventured, "We might offer my daughter Imogen."

"Well you see, that's the thing," Konrad said with barely masked triumph. "If she inherits all the land right up to the border, then marries the man who inherits the other side of the border—suddenly the border becomes meaningless, in a way that is not, I think, in my best interest. Of course you see the folly of my approving such a match, don't you, Uncle? Unless of course I were to divest Imogen of her inheritance, which is within my power to do, especially if you don't marry her appropriately. It's your move."

The Count of Burgundy drew a careful breath. "I do see the problem, Your Majesty." He moved one of his pawns forward a single space.

Konrad immediately pushed his pawn up, bringing it unprotected to the diagonal of Alphonse's.

Instead of taking Konrad's pawn, Alphonse pushed another pawn forward two spaces, distractedly.

Konrad smiled. "You have neglected to take my pawn, Uncle. I shall now neglect to take yours." Instead he moved one of his knights out onto the board.

"Speaking of pawns, Your Majesty," Jouglet said airily, "how is your little cloistered bastard?"

"Quite well, I hear, and of an age to marry this very week," Konrad said with exaggerated nonchalance, and took from his page's hand an ebony toothpick. Marcus realized with a silent burst of gratitude that this moment had been rehearsed; this was the actual purpose of the summons.

"That means she has come into her maternal inheritance, I suppose?" Jouglet obediently recited, neither knowing nor caring what this inheritance actually was. "Which amounts to much more than, say, a mere border county such as, oh, Burgundy, is that not right?"

"Much more," Konrad said, as if it had just occurred to him. "And close enough to Rome to be politically . . . interesting."

"Then I suppose you'll want to marry her to someone you can trust with your very life."

"I suppose," Konrad agreed, picking his teeth with the ebony toothpick. "A pity Marcus is already spoken for," he said around the toothpick. "He really would be the perfect choice. Your turn, Uncle."

"Well, if his current betrothal should fall out—" Jouglet posited offhandedly.

The count bristled. "It's not going to fall out," he announced and looked up at Marcus accusingly. "Is it?"

Marcus managed, somehow, to remain expressionless. "Not by my doing, sir. Unless of course His Majesty required that I wed his daughter . . . before I was actually wed to his cousin."

Alphonse eyed the three of them, imagining the laughter and rude gestures that would erupt once he left the room. "You will be wed to his cousin very soon," he said sullenly, then deliberately turned his shoulder to Marcus, as if he were suddenly not in the same room with him. He slipped into a confiding tone but did not lower his voice. "But, sire, I must tell you once again that it grieves me to see my only child and heir debased from royalty to serfdom. You know that is the only reason I have delayed the match so long."

Marcus ground his teeth together and let his master answer for him. "He's not a serf, Alphonse," Konrad said evenly, chewing on the toothpick.

"Technically he is, Your Majesty, and therefore my daughter would become one too."

"He is a knight and he is my man. In this Empire there is no higher honor."

"As a Burgundian, sire, I must explain to you that I value my freedom and my pedigree above all—"

"You're only a Burgundian because your brother the emperor gave you the office of count there," Konrad corrected sharply. "Until then you always insisted you were German to the marrow." He sat up much straighter on his cushioned oak chair and glowered at the tall man across from him. "You will never use the word *serf* in reference to Marcus or any of the Empire's other appointed ministerials, do you understand me? Do you forget what I am, Alphonse? I've given Marcus land—I've given him the very land where Charlemagne, and myself, and my blessed father who was your infinite superior, were all crowned emperor."

"Actually, sire, that particular site belongs to the church," Marcus corrected dutifully.

"*Near* the land where we were crowned," Konrad said with off-hand impatience. "I can give him more than that, little count, and I probably will, to suit my needs. Plus he holds one of the most prestigious offices in Christendom. Do you think I would marry my own child to a serf?"

"A bastard you've never met, sire, not your cherished heir," Alphonse said quietly, eyes averted.

"My seed is always cherished," Konrad snapped. "Yes, Marcus has the lineage of a peasant, a bondsman, but he is *my* bondsman and I have exalted him as my father exalted his father. I can give him a dukedom. I can *invent* a dukedom to give to him. God knows he deserves such elevation more than others around here who have only their blessed *pedigree* to back them up. It's still your turn." This was not how he had intended to reveal his intentions to Marcus, but the steward's astonished face was still a very satisfying sight.

So was Alphonse's. "Sire," he said in a low voice, trying to contain himself. "Are you serious? Are you telling us that you shall make Marcus—*Marcus*—a *duke*?"

"I did not say I *shall*, I merely noted that it is my prerogative," Konrad said, pretending to be absorbed in the chess game. "And that it would not be undeserved."

Marcus was staring at him with his jaw hanging open.

For a moment, Alphonse seemed to be contemplating the private mysteries of his own digestion. Then he stood abruptly and bowed. "With your permission, sire, may I be excused to dictate a letter to my daughter regarding her imminent nuptials?"

"Certainly, you obviously can't keep your mind on chess. Here's a present for being such a good sport." He pulled off one of his many rings without bothering to notice which one it was, and tossed it. Alphonse looked insulted but caught it anyhow. Konrad dismissed him with a wave, and he went out.

The emperor and the minstrel turned in unison toward Marcus. He shook his head, stunned.

"You owe your gratitude to Jouglet, it was his idea." Konrad smiled.

"Actually, sire, that's not quite accurate, as I have always *genuinely* advocated Your Majesty's child as Marcus's perfect match," Jouglet pointed out. "Especially since it would make him a duke. A duke, Marcus! A count is a pullet next to the rooster of a duke! And you'd get even more from her than from Burgundy's Imogen—"

"Thank you, Jouglet, I don't require your further assistance in statecraft," Konrad said, yawning. "From the way you have been carrying on, I'm half inclined to offer this Willem fellow my daughter."

"Sire," Marcus stammered. "I want—I don't—I should not believe, should I, th—"

"I meant everything I said," Konrad said. "But there will be no more discussion of it until it becomes timely." There was a noise outside the window, which looked down from a great height onto the only entrance to the fortress. "That must be our papal spy's return from his official tour of the town," said Konrad, sighing. "My brother always did like people to make a fuss about him, jealous little whoreson." He gestured toward the window.

Jouglet peered down, then looked back into the room, beaming. "It's not the cardinal, sire. It's Nicholas the messenger, returned from Dole."

Once he was satisfied that Willem and his minuscule entourage had settled comfortably into their lodgings, Nicholas rode through the town and the sunny fields, up to the castle. There was a cool breeze on the slope, but this was always a difficult climb for the horses; even with the switchback road, it was a steep ascent up what was virtually a cliff. He was grateful Konrad never came here in winter.

Just inside the main gate of the lower courtyard, a groom took the heavy-breathing mount from him. Nicholas sighed with satisfaction at being within the sheltering arms of a castle, any castle—he had gone to Dole straight from the damp and dewy summer camp and had not slept near a royal hearth in at least a month. He turned to face the final ascent up to the palace proper—narrow steps cut crookedly into the living red sandstone—when he became aware that he was being, literally, shadowed: somebody walked directly behind him, step for step, only a hand's breadth from his back. He stopped and spun around, automatically raising a hand in self-defense. The minstrel ducked and leapt back, almost colliding with two laundresses at the well.

"What do *you* want?" Nicholas asked, lowering his fist.

At a jut of Jouglet's pointed chin they began to climb, slowly. With the high sheltering curtain wall to the left and the enormous keep towering above them to the right, the long narrow steps nearly felt enclosed. "What will you tell Konrad?" asked Jouglet as they went.

"Willem is a goodly man—charming, decent, modest. Very easy on the eye, the ladies will like that."

"Not just the ladies, I suspect," Jouglet said wryly.

"I prefer them smaller, actually. But he's also an excellent rider and hunter, I learned along the way; he killed a boar that was about to rush my hackney. A little innocent, perhaps—you should have seen his reaction when he first saw the castle as we approached town. He . . . reveals his humble origins. But he's an impressive specimen."

"Yes, obviously. And she?"

Nicholas smiled a little. "A beautiful girl, that, and very winsome. But I must say she is shockingly headstrong—"

Jouglet had anticipated this and was already untying a quadruple-knotted belt pouch. "No, she isn't." Stopping at an arrow loop that looked out over the green slopes, the minstrel pulled from the pouch a silver coin with something that passed as Konrad's likeness stamped upon it. Nicholas stopped beside the fiddler and raised an eyebrow with interest.

"This is a bribe? You wish me to lie to His Majesty?"

"No, simply forget to tell the truth. I've got another one of these if you require it."

Nicholas looked at Jouglet, puzzled. "You are not the sort to stoop to this," he said. "I know you for a schemer, Jouglet, but usually your work is seamless."

They stepped out of the way of a knight who was descending from the armory. "If that is a compliment, I decline it. But I propose a wager, Nicholas. Give me one chance to guess precisely why she was, as you say, shockingly headstrong. If I'm right, you will not mention her lapse from graciousness to Konrad. If she's imperfect in any other way than how I guess it, tell him the whole truth."

Nicholas smiled a little despite himself. "I will tell him what I deem important, but I have not entirely decided what that is. Very well, then." He nodded. "What's your guess?"

"Lienor did not want to be sequestered while her brother was away. She hates being shut up in the house. Willem is . . ." Jouglet considered it. "Willem is more solicitous to her chastity than to her happiness. Although it genuinely pains him to be so."

Nicholas arched one brow. "Well. I'm impressed."

"And?" Jouglet prompted, holding up the coin.

"And I shall certainly tell His Majesty about her unadulterated graciousness."

Jouglet held out the coin, but Nicholas declined to accept it. The minstrel frowned. "It was a wager, Nicholas."

"Of course it was," the messenger said, with a superior smile. "But I'm not for sale." He took the mark from Jouglet's hand and chucked it spinning out of the arrow loop. "I'll abide by my word out of honor, not bribery. His Majesty need only know that Lienor is . . . spirited."

Jouglet retied the belt-pouch, four times over, watching the coin disappear into the weeds dozens of yards below. "That was a waste, but I thank you." Then in a brighter voice, "So Willem is arrived, I take it? Where is he staying?"

They had retired to prepare for bathing when there was a ruckus from the small yard below. *"Dole!"* a voice sang out.

This inn, just past the merchants' square near the southeastern gate, was mercifully removed from much of the noisy, noisome urban stimulation. There was a small garden behind them and a horse market to one side, which gave way to the green market. It was late afternoon, and the markets were closing up; healthy horse-flesh and sun-wilted cabbage were the heaviest aromas, despite the horror stories both youths had heard about the smells of life in town.

Erec and Willem hunched over while being undressed in their low-ceilinged room. Their pages slowly peeled the exhausted men out of their armor—chain mail from the knight, waxed leather from the squire—but all of them paused and looked toward the open door. Willem, still in his hauberk, went to the door, smiling, as Jouglet's voice rose up again: "Willem of Dole, knight of the realm! Where is Konrad's new delight?" Footsteps were heard lightly running up the wooden stairs, and then Jouglet's lanky frame appeared in the door-way dressed in a neat tan tunic and burdened with the ubiquitous fiddle case. "Well upon my life, everyone, look who's arrived, the most talked-of man in the Empire! Willem of Dole himself!" The minstrel bowed very elaborately and deeply, setting the case by the door.

Willem beamed. "Jouglet! You *were* the rascal behind all this. Lienor guessed—I should have too."

Jouglet straightened and embraced Willem gruffly around the neck. "Welcome, welcome, welcome! I'm delighted you've arrived safely. What a switch this is, eh? *You* traveling to *my* world at last!"

Willem returned the embrace briefly, then pulled away a little so he could see his friend's face as he spoke. "Jouglet, I am speechless with gratitude—"

Jouglet clucked happily. "Never mind that, you're here, that's what matters. Good God, you're actually here!" This was delivered more to the heavens than to the knight, but Willem, beaming, wrapped his arms around Jouglet with such a strong hug the minstrel was almost squashed against Willem's chain-mailed chest. They clutched each other for a moment, both grinning.

"Have you been rolling around in a rosebush?" Jouglet asked ironically. "You almost smell as good as your sister. And I see you have brought your little nephew along with you."

"Cousin," Erec corrected coldly.

Jouglet released Willem and for a moment studied Erec, who like a peasant laborer was now in nothing but his drawers. "This look suits you better than the gilded-lord costume you had on when we first met," Jouglet decided.

Willem held out a warning hand to Erec. "Your first meeting was not the brightest, but I hope you will both rise to the occasion. Jouglet, my cousin will be with me for the duration of the visit, as my squire. Erec, Jouglet is the very reason we are here. I beg you both, make peace."

Jouglet immediately slid to Erec's side, bowed deeply, and spoke in a swift, quiet, pandering sort of voice. "I apologize for my arch disposition, milord. I fear it sometimes fails to avoid cutting too close to the marrow of the offending victim."

Erec wasn't sure what this meant but liked the self-recriminating tone in which it was delivered. "You are forgiven," he said with grudging magnanimity, and even bowed a very little.

Willem, amused, chose not to explain to Erec what he'd just forgiven and continued undressing for his bath. Jouglet leaned back on a cushioned chest beneath the one sizable window in the room. "I was sent here by an already enamored monarch to summon you to sup with His Majesty and the royal vermin at the castle court."

Willem and Erec exchanged delighted looks. "Truly?" Erec demanded, stepping out of his drawers so that he stood naked in the middle of the room. Jouglet barely resisted the temptation to accuse him of strutting.

"Truly. So bathe if you will, but let's be quick, we don't want to keep His Imperial Majesty waiting. He's called for a feast tonight especially for your arrival."

Again the cousins exchanged amazed and happy looks. Then Willem turned back to Jouglet. "All right now," he said as his servant put aside his chain mail hauberk to help him off with his tunic. "How on earth did you cause the ruler of the Holy Roman Empire to desire the company of an impoverished knight from a disaffected corner of his realm?"

Jouglet shrugged. "I mentioned you in passing, and he was instantly entranced at the idea of your existence. Truly, I deserve no credit; it was a fluke that your name even came to be mentioned."

"How astonishing!" Erec cried. Willem gave him a droll look as he pulled off his shirt and handed it to his servant.

"Erec, he's *lying*," Willem said patiently.

"Oh," said Erec, sobering.

Willem turned his attention back to Jouglet, clearly expecting a better reply. Jouglet shrugged comfortably. "The answer lies in the question, my friend. *Because* Burgundy is disaffected, and run by an untrustworthy ninny, Konrad needs well-armed and loyal Burgundians in his court, especially impoverished ones whose lots he may best improve. Luckily for him, you happen to be impoverished."

Willem smiled gratefully. "The stars were well aligned when you came through my gate three years ago," he said quietly. "You are better than a brother to me and have been from the day we met."

"In this court, that's not saying much," Jouglet laughed.

Erec, exuberant again, announced, "We saw the castle on the hill as we were approaching—and the Emperor's flag flying from the keep!"

"The castle is *magnificent*," Willem said with sudden excitement, his face lighting up.

"It's cold and wet," Jouglet sniffed, then sat up to exclaim, "Willem! *You* are what's magnificent!"

The knight looked down at his own well-muscled physique and shrugged indifferently. He untied his drawers and let them fall to the floor. Somehow his nudity did not resemble strutting the way Erec's did. "I'm still bruised from my last tournament, and I lost my helmet," he said, almost as if apologizing.

"The innkeeper has a pretty daughter, perhaps we should call her up here to heal the wounds," Jouglet hummed suggestively, chuckling when Willem blushed. "For God's sake, my friend, how can one man be so comfortable in the raw and yet so uncomfortable at the thought of a woman?"

"My cousin is uninitiated in the ways of women," Erec taunted.

"I am not," Willem rebutted unconvincingly, looking out the smaller window.

"Well, excepting the Widow Sunia," Erec said. Willem swung around to stare at him.

"How do you know about that?"

"Everyone in the *county* knows about that."

Jouglet, looking startled but delighted, clapped and made obscene hooting noises. "This is marvelous fodder for some new tale, a fabliau I think. I must admit I'm relieved to hear the fellow has an appetite, he feigns saintliness in my company."

Willem ignored this. "Erec, tell me how you know that."

Erec's pimpled face grinned wickedly. "You're hardly the only one she gives her favors to, you know, cousin." Willem blinked at him, frowning. "Except with you she knows you would never take advantage of a lady, so she invents frivolous tasks for you to complete so that you feel you've earned it. Although I must tell you, she was relieved when she talked you out of that nonsense about trying to woo her according to the rules of courtly love. The poetry you insist upon reciting for her? She'd rather you not bother. Why you'd waste your time begging for anything but fornication, when fornication is really all you're after, is beyond her. She asked me to mention it."

Willem stared at him as if he were speaking Russian. This tickled both of his companions even more. "I must memorize this!" the minstrel whispered very loudly to Erec. "I'll earn a year's wages in a week for singing this one." And then to the dumbstruck knight: "Oh, really, Willem, don't be such an innocent. Take a bath and clothe your most magnificent body in your most magnificent clothes. I'm here to take you to the start of your new life tonight. Don't stand there flabbergasted because some old lady is kind enough to indulge your peculiar form of chivalry."

"She's . . . not an old lady," Willem said in a tone of embarrassed yet paternal defensiveness.

"Is she rich? Why don't you marry her?"

Willem hurriedly shook his head, a blush starting on his cheeks. "I am not worthy of that."

Jouglet examined him, then grinned at Erec. "I thought only women developed a fond attachment to their first partner in carnality."

Erec grinned back. "My cousin is an unusual gentleman in almost all regards."

"Where is the *bath*?" Willem demanded, bright pink. He threw a linen robe around himself and went out on the balcony to call for it.

"He's not actually attached to her," Erec continued in a low conspiratorial voice to Jouglet. "He simply feels that he *ought* to be, because he believes that would be *proper*. It amuses her no end. But she really could do without the serenading."

"Our dear Willem," Jouglet said with affection, glancing after him down the steps. "He'll be·in for a shock at court."

"She won't even accept trifles from him anymore, she knows how poor he is," Erec went on, with a certain satisfaction. "That mortifies him, and he tries to stay away, but then he burns and eventually on some very feeble pretext ends up at her gates—"

"And she lets him come straight in," Jouglet concluded in a low, lecherous tone, with illustrative gestures.

Erec howled. "Always. His sister's got a perfectly pretty serving girl, which would be much more convenient, but she's a bit of a prude, and he believes the knightly code should extend even to peasants."

"Actually, it does," Jouglet corrected, sobering, then sat back and affected nonchalance as Willem reentered.

"Actually, it does *in theory*," Erec corrected, doing the same.

"The bath is ready, in the courtyard," Willem told his cousin, and the two of them, disrobed, went out. Jouglet followed.

They settled into the tubs by the stairs. The page boys scrubbed their backs and the innkeeper's daughter made eyes at them across the small cobblestoned yard as she helped her mother pound moth eggs from the linens. Jouglet perched at the edge of Willem's tub and quietly coached him in preparation for the evening.

"Don't bring up your lineage," the minstrel began. "And if you're asked about it say as little as possible. Don't mention Lienor, and if you're asked about her don't say much either—the way these fellows' minds work they'll assume your affection is incestuous." Willem looked disgusted, and Jouglet laughed. "Do not ever suggest you are not rich. In fact, make offerings, give gifts, empty your purse to appear heedlessly magnanimous—"

"Jouglet," Willem protested uncomfortably.

"Trust me, all this is for your betterment. If it helps, consider it your Christian duty—you're proving you're not avaricious. One cannot be sinful by way of greed when he gives all he has so merrily away." Jouglet looked at him comfortingly; the familiar hazel eyes winked. Willem, staring into them, felt himself relax a little and smiled gratefully. Then Jouglet grinned and called out to the innkeeper's daughter: "Musette, my darling!"

"Is there anyone you don't know?" Willem demanded as Musette began to cross toward the tubs.

"Hello, Jouglet." The young woman smiled adoringly.

"Hello, pretty lady. My knight Willem here wants to give you a little gift. Upstairs in his chamber, lying beside his hauberk, is a hairpin with beads in it that happen to exactly match your eyes. He meant to bring it down, but he's so overwhelmed by all this excitement—did you hear he's going to sup at the castle tonight?"

"Yes, I heard that!" Musette said, smiling at Willem with almost the same smile she had bestowed upon the minstrel. Willem and Erec, in perfect unison, eyed her curving form from head to toe with appreciation. But Jouglet was the one she winked at, after blessing Willem with thanks for the gift and leaping up the stairs to retrieve it.

"But Jouglet, I did not bring a hairpin—"

"Yes, you did," Jouglet said. "And lots more. I've seen to it."

They stared at each other for a moment in silence. "This is an elaborate project you've set for yourself," Willem observed, not sure if he should be amused or alarmed. "You're tossing me off a boat into deep water."

"Which will teach you how to swim," Jouglet concluded, and with an avuncular chuckle, slapped the surface of the bathwater so that it splashed into Willem's face.

Willem grabbed the musician's wrist and almost pulled Jouglet into the tub with him.

"You two are enjoying yourselves far too much," Erec said in a lazy voice of contentment as the boy massaged his scalp. "Stick to business. What else does he need to know? Surely you realize how ignorant the fellow is, you'd better spell it out for him."

Jouglet squatted on some musty straw between the tubs. "He's not the only neophyte in this courtyard, milord; you should put some attention to your provincial accent or you'll stand out like a country clod. And try to refrain from teeth-flicking if someone irritates you, it makes you boorish." Knowing he deserved the jab, Erec grimaced. Jouglet softened, gave him a friendlier look. "I know your heart is sound, m'lord, and if you will be ruled by me a little, I think you'll find we're natural allies." Jouglet turned back to Willem. "Most of all you should know that the brother recently arrived from Rome, Paul, is an unwelcome visitor."

"Why unwelcome?"

Jouglet smiled knowingly. "There is an occasionally entertaining history of familial jealousy. More to the point, though—Konrad and the old pope had some troubles with each other. His Holiness very publicly excommunicated His Imperial Majesty, so His Imperial Majesty very publicly rounded up an army to attack His Holiness."

Willem nodded. "I wanted to enlist, but my uncle would not let me."

"Yes, I was looking forward to it myself, great fodder for song-writing, but alas, Konrad was talked out of shedding holy blood. In their settlement the pope demanded that one of his close officers perpetually maintain a presence at the royal court. When Innocent became pope earlier this year, he appointed Konrad's own brother Paul for the honor. Paul had expected to be elected pope himself, and in the hopes that he might yet earn the office, he endears himself to the Mother Church with various little schemes to gratuitously un-dermine Konrad's authority."

"So I had best not discuss religion," Willem said. Jouglet nodded. "What may I discuss, then?"

Jouglet buffeted the knight's wet shoulder. "Your prowess, of course! Tell them how you came to be knighted before your majority."

Erec laughed. "Willem was knighted by the archbishop of Basel because he saved His Eminence from a band of angry knights during a tournament His Eminence was preaching against."

Jouglet grimaced. "Ah. Then perhaps don't tell them how you came to be knighted. But you may talk about tournaments in general. Or tell them all how eager you are to follow that Fulk of Neuilly lunatic on his holy war against the infidels."

"I can't even consider such an honor until Lienor has been safely mar—"

"Don't tell them that!" Jouglet insisted. "Your only concern should be proving your manliness. The only females you should bother yourself about are the Blessed Virgin and whatever lady is lucky enough to eventually become your patroness. You gain nothing at all by showing solicitude for an orphaned baby sister. And most of all, Willem, you must not be so wide-eyed. Don't gush about how magnificent the castle is. The spoons are solid silver—don't heft them with wonder, or gawk at anything else you see. Don't express amazement at the number of courses served, or the quality of the tapestries, or the extravagant cut of Konrad's tunic. And don't trust a soul there. Even Konrad. He's disarmingly friendly most of the time, but he can snap, and when he does—and I am not speaking figuratively—heads roll. Do not make any alliances or enemies until you understand what is really in your interest. Smile politely and keep your guard up. You'll be under intense scrutiny. Be careful how you speak. Every sentence must suggest you are beyond any kind of reproach. Don't say, 'I can't ride in the upcoming tournament because I have no helmet.' Say instead, 'Ah! A tournament! I'm the man to win it! All I need is a helmet!' "

Willem rolled his eyes, but Jouglet was serious. "Say it."

The knight took a breath and repeated, dubiously, "Ah, a tournament, I'm the man to win it, all I need is a helmet."

"That was convincing," Erec said with mild sarcasm.

Jouglet clapped Willem's wet shoulder approvingly. "Good man. And when in doubt, just keep your mouth shut. That always impresses Konrad because nobody ever does it. He'll think you are profound."

Willem felt dizzy contemplating how entirely his fortune was hanging on the minstrel's plans. It was thrilling and yet terrifying—and for a moment, extremely claustrophobic. "Will I know anyone there but you?"

Jouglet hesitated. "Perhaps you'll recognize some garrison knights from tournaments. And . . . from here to the western border, things are prickly, so Konrad likes to keep an eye on the counts and margraves, especially with France recently become so aggressive. So there are a number of nobles here from your backwater part of the world."

Willem tensed slightly, then made himself recline against the back of the wooden tub. He voiced a sigh so tense it could be heard across the yard. "And would that include His Majesty's uncle, fat old Alphonse, Count of Burgundy?"

Jouglet shrugged. "Probably. So what? He won't hurt you."

Willem glanced toward Erec, whose attention was distracted by watching Musette saunter back down the stairs. Willem whispered, tensely, "I have a vendetta with Alphonse. He sinned against me and tried to cover that sin with another far more heinous." Automatically, as he always did at the thought of this, he crossed himself. "He'll try to undermine me—"

"Don't worry about anything, my friend!" Jouglet insisted. "I'll be there as your guardian angel, and the whole point of the evening is that you will meet the emperor and some potential patronesses who already think you are sensational."

A tentative smile of disbelief washed over Willem's face. "This is all extraordinary, Jouglet," he breathed, and for reassurance again sought the minstrel's calming gaze.

Jouglet smiled back and whispered, with sincere affection, "I am delighted that you chose to play along."

5

Occasional Poem

[verses commemorating a particular event, such as a feast]

27 June

*M*arcus, in his duties as court steward, never liked introducing unmarried gentlemen to Imogen's father; he could almost hear the balance shift against his own favor as Alphonse sized up every bachelor as a potential son-in-law. At least this fellow, however rugged and hearty, had no land to speak of and no proper title; also his tunic, although a nice bright scarlet, was simple and hardly suggested wealth. He had the bedazzled look of a country boy entering the gargantuan sandstone fortress for the first time—coupled with the unease of a knight who'd had to surrender his weapons at the gate.

They stood at the extreme lower end of the hall by the primary entrance. "Willem, son of the late Henri Silvan of Dole, and one of your vassals," Marcus said, politely but as offhandedly as he could.

"Willem, you may recognize your liege lord, Alphonse, Count of Burgundy."

The count's pale eyes began to widen in the appraising manner Marcus was so used to, but then the widening increased until he was indecorously close to bug-eyed. And yet he smiled.

Willem was neither bug-eyed nor smiling, but his lips were pressed taut together. The distracting enormity and opulence of his surroundings vanished from his mind; he was staring hard at the count.

For all his height, Alphonse of Burgundy had to look up slightly at Willem. "God in heaven, son, you've grown up to a strapping fine young man," he said heartily. Perhaps a little too heartily.

"Thank you, milord," said Willem, expressionless.

"I'm glad you've turned out well. I shall remember to summon you to the Oricourt garrison. I tend to forget about the little knights on the borders, please forgive me." His eyes flickered beyond Willem, and his face lit up with genuine relief. "And is this not Erec of Tavaux, my newest-risen vassal!" Alphonse brushed past Willem and warmly embraced Erec; Erec, even more dazed than Willem by their remarkable surroundings, hardly registered who was speaking to him. "But why are you costumed like a squire?" the count chitchatted nervously, ushering Erec away.

Once the two were out of earshot, there was an awkward pause. Marcus smoothed the trim on his blackberry-colored tunic.

"You know each other," he commented, gratuitously.

"As you say, I am his vassal," said Willem in a neutral tone. His slight accent was identical to Imogen's—Burgundian—and it hurt Marcus's heart to hear it in another voice. A shadow passed across Willem's face briefly and he asked, "I know the count is His Majesty's uncle, but is he in fact an intimate?"

"That depends on who is speaking," Marcus answered. "He would say he is."

"What would you say?"

"I would say he is my future father-in-law and politely decline to comment on the issue." He felt an adolescent thrill, stating it to an outsider; he wondered if Willem was aware of his lowly lineage and would challenge him for making such a claim.

But Willem just looked thoughtful for a moment. "I do not know his daughter but I trust she is . . . a lady of her own merits," he said respectfully.

"As different as Gabriel from Lucifer. Her mother the countess is a goodly soul, that must account for it." And in a lower voice, "I assume your dealings with him did not leave a pleasant taste in your mouth?"

Willem released a blow of breath that was a disparaging laugh, but then stopped himself. Jouglet had insisted he not make alliances too early. He glanced after the count, who had already released Erec and was making his way toward the high table before the fire.

"It was a long time ago," Willem said to Marcus. "It makes little difference now." Thinking of Jouglet he glanced around the room and noticed for the first time how bright it was, much brighter than his little wooden hall at home—there were more windows, more chandeliers, and the walls were limed and painted with bright colors, preponderantly gold. He'd never seen gold paint before.

Before he could locate his friend, Marcus took his arm. "So," the steward announced. "To the master." The trestles were set up running on either side of the hall, but no cloths as yet covered the boards as Marcus led Willem toward the most ornate chair in the room, canopied with gold and scarlet, in the middle of a dais.

Seated there, at the high table, was a man who only vaguely resembled the images stamped in coins or sealed in wax, but there could be no doubt who this was. A large man of middle years with pale eyes and reddish blond hair, hefting a sleek hooded falcon on his leather-wrapped wrist, he was dressed in brilliant scarlet silks and velvets—dressed more magnificently than anyone Willem had ever seen, with a gold circlet literally glittering with gemstones—

"That's the emperor!" Willem said in a voice checked with excited awe. Marcus looked at his astonished face and smiled despite himself. So the much-heralded Willem of Dole was a pup. Marcus found his artlessness endearing.

"Yes, His Majesty, and on his wrist is Charity. The cardinal beside him is his brother Paul who has recently joined us from Rome as papal nuncio."

The two men were not speaking to each other. More precisely, Konrad was not speaking to his brother. He seemed to be speaking to his falcon, whose hood sparkled almost as brightly as the king's own headpiece. Paul was earnestly, but unsuccessfully, trying to rally the few other men at the high table to converse with him. Willem felt a little sorry for him.

"Look at that," he said with continued artlessness. "They are alike in feature, but there is something to the king that the priest lacks."

"Good fortune in birth order," Marcus observed.

Konrad recognized Willem from Jouglet's many loquacious descriptions—brown hair, brown eyes, handsome build, handsome rectangular face and a fighter's handsomely broken nose, an air of confidence mixed with modesty. He returned Charity to her perch behind him and rose to greet the young man. He was pleased to see how strong he looked—he must be a good fighter, at least; the slavish dedication to the throne, so exalted by Jouglet, would prove useful. If nothing else, he could perhaps be made a reliable constable somewhere back in his home county.

"Ah! The fabled Willem of Dole!" Konrad said, which brought all eyes to the young knight. The hum of the hall quieted a little. Willem was startled that the great man called him by name and bowed deeply; the emperor further astounded him by taking his elbow as casually as Marcus had, and drawing him back toward the table. He couldn't wrest his eyes from the emperor's jeweled hand on his arm. On the emperor's little finger, simpler but larger than the other adornments, was his gold signet ring, the very ring that had sealed the invitation Nicholas had brought to Dole. Willem resisted a childish urge to touch it. "We have all been very much looking forward to your arrival," Konrad said, booming. People were still gossiping in huddles, but it was noticeably more quiet as everyone tried to study the emperor's new find. "Jouglet has sung your praises for weeks now, and Nicholas has added to the chorus since this afternoon."

He had Willem on the royal dais before the younger man had collected himself. "Allow me to introduce my little brother," Konrad said with an insulting casualness, not addressing the priest directly. "This is Cardinal Paul, our official papal spy. Brother Paul, this is Willem of Dole, a celebrated knight of Burgundy whose arrival we've been anticipating for days." Paul was on his feet before Konrad had finished the introduction. Everyone looked wary of the newcomer, but Paul looked almost frightened.

Willem bowed. "And what great exploits have brought you to my brother's attentions?" demanded the cardinal with an anxious smile, as if he were jealous that yet another person in the room might outshine him. Despite sharing the emperor's fair features, he appeared an oversize adolescent, soft in all the places Konrad was firm. And while Konrad's expansive geniality heralded how entirely confident he was of being the center of the known world, the equivalent attempts in Paul betrayed the creeping realization that he was not, and might never be.

"The court musician assures me he is worthy of attention," Konrad said with suspicious offhandednesss. Paul was appalled.

"You may as well believe the commendations of a prostitute," he said in a loud whisper to his brother.

"That's not a bad idea," Konrad mused. "But he's no ordinary musician, Paul, haven't you sniffed that out yet with that little blood-hound nose of yours? Come, Willem, sit with me—shove down, Alphonse," he ordered his uncle, who had taken the seat closest to the king's right. The count rose, with a look that Willem found shockingly disrespectful. Konrad ignored it. "Uncle, this fellow is from your county. Have you been hiding him from me and all the ladies?"

The count almost choked. "Of course not, sire, but I have a thou-sand knights under me, and only a few of them ever make it to your halls. I need the rest along the Saône," he stammered.

His nephew had already lost interest in him. "Sit beside me while we wait for supper, Willem." The count and knight exchanged un-comfortable, startled looks.

"Oh, sire," Willem said carefully, finally finding his voice, and bowing again. "You honor me, but it would be unseemly to take such a privileged seat. I am a stranger here, surely there are men more deserving of the distinction—"

"They will sit next to me another time," Konrad said placidly. There was constant competition among the knights and courtiers for the coveted spot to the king's right, and he wanted to see how they would all respond to an unexpected usurper.

But Willem did not provide an opportunity to find out. "Truly, Your Majesty, I would feel an imposter," he said, fighting the urge to fidget under the continued intensity of so many judging eyes. "Espe-cially as your own esteemed brother and uncle already flank you. Simply being in your court is honor enough for me. I've brought my squire Erec with me—please allow me to sit with him until he is more confident with his German?" He glanced about briefly and fi-nally saw Jouglet at the lower end of the hall, near the door, beside Erec and the lower minions of the castle. Jouglet had probably had an eye on him since he'd walked in.

Without expression, Jouglet nodded once, approving Willem's comportment.

Konrad was staring at the knight, astounded. Men *groveled* to earn a place at his right side—groveled, pandered, stole, blasphemed, murdered; some occasionally even tried to get there by merit. He had never met anyone who would turn down an opportunity to sit beside him. He wondered, not for the first time, what Jouglet's real motive was in initiating Willem's introduction to the court. Perhaps the knight's much-touted dedication to the throne was a front, and this was his opening gambit to make it clear that he would need currying. Suspicious but intrigued, Konrad invited his guest to sit at the end of the high table, three seats down from him. He made it clear to the men between them—a dyspeptic-looking Alphonse and the Count of Luz—that they were to push their bench back to let the king speak directly to his new visitor. "So," Konrad began, allowing one of his Italian greyhounds to hop up onto his lap and nestle in against his surcoat. He had turned his back directly to his brother, who peered over Konrad's shoulder, attempting to be part of the conversation. Again, Willem felt a flash of sympathy for Paul, although he did not like the way the man was looking at him. "I hear you're superlative in tourneys. Do you know there is soon to be a huge tournament at the foot of this mountain?"

"A tournament!" Willem said immediately, loudly. Twenty-five paces away, seated on a wooden bench beside Jouglet, Erec sat bolt upright to listen. "Excellent! I'm ready to ride in it, sire, and happily I made the trip with all my armor, so all I need is a helmet." This time he managed to say it with something approaching enthusiasm.

On the far side of the hall, Jouglet grinned with satisfaction and whispered to Erec, "I think he's about to get a helmet."

Almost simultaneously with this, Konrad announced grandly, "Come to think of it, I have a helmet I would be honored to give you.

Boidon!" he called out to his chamberlain. "The Senlis helmet—bring it from my armory."

Alphonse of Burgundy looked horrified. Boidon the chamberlain and Marcus the steward exchanged brief, incredulous looks across the room. "Yes, sire," Boidon said tonelessly and took the exit nearer to the high table.

"Now remind me," Konrad said to Willem, "exactly where your estates are again. Are you directly on the border? On the Saône, I mean?"

Risking a fleeting glance at Jouglet and avoiding Alphonse of Burgundy altogether, Willem answered as quietly as he could, "I have a small holding outside Dole, sire, not quite at the border—on the River Doubs. I live there with my family. It keeps us fed and well enough maintained."

"Excellent. And what else?"

"That is all, sire," Willem said softly.

Konrad frowned. "I did not know your father well, but I do recognize the name," he said. This was true; Jouglet had mentioned it to the emperor repeatedly as he was being dressed for supper. "Silvan is one of the oldest families in Burgundy. Surely your ancestors distinguished themselves enough for great estates."

"Most assuredly," Willem answered. "Yes, they did." He felt himself turn slightly pink. Between them, Alphonse tried to disappear into the wall.

"Then how came you to lose it?" Konrad demanded, testing how Willem would respond to an impossibly awkward situation.

"Brother," Paul said with warmth from behind Konrad's shoulder. "You do not understand the pain of deprivation; do not ask your guest to be reminded of it publicly." He smiled comfortingly, understandingly, at Willem, who gave him a grateful look.

"Lack of advancement only stings when one is prideful," Konrad rebutted airily to his brother, who had narrowly missed being elected pope the year before. "As a *good* Christian, my guest is surely not burdened with the sin of pride."

Paul grimaced and pulled away again, a chastised child, as Konrad returned his full attention to Willem.

Willem looked down into his lap, afraid of accidentally meeting the count's gaze. Many pairs of eyes were staring at him, hanging on the answer: he realized he was new blood, and whatever the explanation, this would be good gossip. "It is a complicated story, sire, hardly an engaging anecdote for a supper feast. Anyhow, I may have lost my land, but there are more important things. I have my own reputation to enrich me, and the joy of my sister and mother's company."

Across the hall, Jouglet cringed and sprang to action, afraid Willem had gone too far expressing a noble heart in a setting where no such thing actually existed. Konrad simply disregarded the comment, intent on testing Willem's diplomacy. "And who has the land now?" he queried disingenuously. "How did they get it?"

Willem shifted uncomfortably. "I have lost track," he said vaguely. "I have no legal recourse to it, so it is no concern of mine."

"Uncle," Konrad said, and Alphonse nearly jumped. "Uncle, does this sound familiar to you? You're his liege lord, you should be trying to prevent these things."

"My good knight Willem, isn't that the latest style from France?" Jouglet interrupted loudly, abruptly, and too cheerfully, from the foot of the dais. "You stylish fellow! The undecorated look is all the rage now, among the Gallic aristocracy. Did you know that, sire?"

Konrad glanced down at the musician and chose not to play along. "Do not presume upon my patronage too far," he warned. "I'm holding an interview. You will not interrupt my queries, or I shall interrupt your throat."

It was the first time Willem had ever seen his dapper young friend look abashed.

But then Boidon returned, burdened with a box; the emperor

decided to prod the Burgundians some other time. He turned his attention to his chamberlain, so that was the end of it. The count and the musician, for their very disparate reasons, both looked relieved. The chamberlain set the box on the table by Konrad; Konrad himself carefully extracted an iron helmet.

The entire bubbling hall went silent. Willem had never seen any headgear like this. Where most helmets had a top that tapered to only a noseguard, this one, masklike, covered the wearer's face almost down to the jaw, with oval holes for eyes. It had decorative gold strips on it that were covered with chased designs; it looked more like a ceremonial piece than something intended to be used in battle, but Konrad, holding it out to Willem, promised, "This is one of the strongest helmets ever forged."

"It's beautiful," Willem said in an awed voice, and reached out to accept it, handling it as if it were an infant. At an encouraging gesture from Konrad, he lifted it higher and then settled it down over his head. It fit remarkably well, although it felt a little as if he'd stuck his head into a slatted box. "I feel invincible!" he said excitedly, and there was a murmur of amused approval around the room. Willem took it off again and handed it to Boidon to be put back into the box. "Thank you, sire, I shall wear it well and bring it safely back to you."

"Oh, no," Konrad said with grand offhandedness, petting his dog. "It's a gift. It's yours to keep."

There was a smattering of envious applause around the hall. Konrad was known for his ostentatious generosity—but it was usually reserved for court-level aristocrats. Who was this landless borderman to receive such an honor on first sight?

The landless borderman, flummoxed, glanced down the steps and saw Jouglet nod once firmly. Willem blinked in disbelief then looked back at Konrad and said in a warm voice, "May God reward you, sire."

"If you are half the knight you're rumored to be, he already has," Konrad replied. "Jouglet," he added, forgiving, "well done in bringing us this fellow."

Jouglet was looking up at Willem from the foot of the dais with great satisfaction: now Willem had a helmet, and Konrad, thinking Willem required purchasing, believed he had the bill of sale.

Paul the Cardinal, who had offered Willem such sympathy, glanced down at the minstrel with a scrutinizing glare.

Jouglet ignored Paul.

Willem decided the nuances of court enmities were more than he could decipher, so he gave up trying.

Marcus received a signal from a servant at the kitchen screens and motioned to Konrad that the meal would be served soon. The emperor pushed away the whippet and rose to his feet, and the entire room scrambled to follow suit. Everyone stepped to one side of the hall, where a row of boys held silver handbasins full of rose water, and a row of girls beside them offered scented linen towels.

Willem was stunned at the size and volume of everything—there were more children helping with the hand washing than he had servants, total. The hall was actually modest for the exterior vastness of the fortress, but still bigger by far than any he'd seen before, and brightly decorated. On the vaulted, plastered ceiling was painted the imperial coat of arms, and colorful murals illuminated all four walls. There were rows of windows on both long sides, unsealed and unshuttered to let in the summer light, although the view to the east, into the surprisingly claustrophobic courtyard, was only of the red sandstone walls of the other wings. There were more than a hundred men in here, all of them ornately dressed in greens and reds and yellows, furs and gemstones, and all of them familiar—or affecting familiarity—with eating at the emperor's board. Most of them had coloring closer to Lienor's or Erec's than his own. A few of them looked to be ministers or visiting dignitaries; some of them were local lords; many of them were seasoned knights fulfilling their feudal obligations in the king's bodyguard. A very few of them had ladies attached, sitting in the lower end of the hall nearer to the servants. There would clearly be no courtly pursuits that way tonight, and Willem was glad of it.

Despite Konrad's own welcoming congeniality, the general mood struck Willem as colder and sterner than any feast he'd attended within Burgundy. Everybody in the room was viewing him appraisingly, jealously, even resentfully. He felt self-conscious and yet oddly exhilarated by it. Without vanity he saw that he was better-looking than most of them, and younger than many. He was wearing the most expensive garments that he owned, but they were lackluster compared to the gilt of the evening. He would have to ask Jouglet where he could order better fabrics on credit in the town tomorrow.

As Alphonse was returning to the high table from the washbasins, Konrad gave him a meaningful look and gestured to the place at the end of the table, where Willem had sat. The count grimaced but bowed in acquiescence, and took that seat. When Willem returned to the dais—trying not to gawk at the beautifully woven table coverings and extravagant settings that had been placed during the hand washing—there was only one seat left. And so he found himself sitting at Konrad's right side, after all—which everybody noticed.

At the far end of the hall, Jouglet looked delighted. And Erec shot him an encouraging wink too, nearly giggling into Jouglet's shoulder. Willem felt a pang of jealousy at how lightning fast those two had suddenly taken to each other in the course of the afternoon. Possibly this was a calculated move on Jouglet's part to cultivate Erec's goodwill—but still, they certainly looked to be enjoying themselves more than he was at the moment.

A trumpet sounded to announce the first course, and the room grew quiet as Paul gave a lengthy, sonorously nasal blessing. Marcus stood between the royal brothers to taste whatever food was set

before them. A man seldom given to fancy, he imagined it was Imogen's health he was safeguarding.

Over the first few courses—first cherries, then peppery cheese
soup, puréed cabbage, lamprey, roast heron in garlic sauce—Willem
attended only to his table manners, deferring to the Count of Luz,
with whom he shared his trencher, holding the goblet by the base to
avoid greasing the enameled sides, washing his hands after each
course as the page boys came around with the basins of rose water.
He spoke little, except to thank the pretty woman who served the
drinks, but he listened to those around him. It nearly put him off his
food: all of the lords and knights, and even Konrad, were earnestly
discussing the upcoming tournament, but they spoke of it as though
it were a cockfight, or a gambling match. There were many swagger-
ing wagers being placed over the venison stew on who could unhorse
whom, and by what time of day. The rest of the discussion was men
making fun of absent knights, mostly Flemish and French. The
mockery was not of their horsemanship or breeding, but simple and
base insults—the shape of this one's nose, that one's pockmarked
face, the Englishman William the Marshal who was getting long in
the tooth, another one who stuttered, and many warriors' rumored
lack of—or excess—virility, a topic that inspired shocking commen-
tary about a number of well-born ladies.

The only person who shared Willem's distaste of the general
attitude was Cardinal Paul, and for that reason Willem began to
warm to him, directing many of his comments over Konrad's shoulder to the slightly pudgy younger brother. But his enthusiasm faded
when he realized that Paul, speaking as the shrill voice of the church,
was *entirely* against the tournament, no matter how it was approached.
In Willem's own household, discussions of tourneys were nearly on a
par with discussions of faith. They were always very much focused
on discipline and technique, a verbal preparation for the actual deed.
It was detailed and technical enough that Lienor, on those rare

occurrences when she succeeded in winning her way to the table to join them, had learned many of the basic terms and strategies.

Suddenly he missed his sister terribly and wondered what she was doing right now, what she would have to say of these well-dressed overfed louts hammering the air with hollow braggadocio. He fell into a reverie of home, of his maddeningly contrary sibling and all that was familiar to him, smiling slightly without realizing it.

"What are you musing on?" Konrad asked as Marcus served them each a wing of roast capon.

Willem answered promptly, "I was thinking I would best all of these men at the tournament, in your name, in honor of your stupendous gift." Jouglet, he thought, would have been proud of that.

Konrad doubted this was the true answer, but he approved of the impulse that had sponsored it. He wiped his hands on the embroidered tablecloth and clapped Willem on the shoulder. "Earlier I said this because it was proper, and polite, but now I say it from my heart, Willem," he said in a low voice. "You are most welcome to my court." He sat back.

Willem felt both Paul's and Alphonse of Burgundy's eyes upon him again. Alphonse's displeasure he could understand—it must be uncomfortable to be outranked by the grown man one had betrayed and terrorized when he was a powerless child—but Paul was a mystery to him.

Then Willem caught Jouglet's gaze from across the room. Jouglet, like the cardinal and count, had seen the quiet exchange between Konrad and Willem, and gave Willem a reassuring nod that helped put him at ease. He wished the minstrel would be summoned to join them, stay right at his elbow for the evening. He was still so nervous he could hardly appreciate the whimsy and finesse of this, the most exotic and sumptuous meal he'd ever sat down to in his life. Mostly all he noticed was that the food was saltier and saucier than what his own cook made in Dole.

Bellies were digesting figs and gingerbread, some seventeen exotic courses later, when the trestles were cleared away for evening
entertainment. Several people stretched out on the rushes of the lower
hall playing backgammon or a Spanish dice game; others, including
most of the sparse female population, clustered nearer the hearth close
to His Majesty. The Count of Burgundy and his nephew Paul, the
papal spy, disappeared together. "My family," Konrad said with a
droll sigh, smiling at Willem. "The phlegmatic and the bilious. I
would my father and I had been each an only son."

Jouglet, asked to lead off the entertainment, announced a song
from Provence, translated to the German. The bow ran droning
smoothly over all the strings as Jouglet fingered an introduction on
the top one. "It's a love song, and I dedicate it, as I do all my songs, to
my secret beloved," the musician explained in a throaty voice, hazel
eyes slowly taking in each woman in the room. Willem watched, astounded, as each of them in turn blushed, giggled, or grew moony-
eyed. With a start, he remembered Nicholas's declaration that
Jouglet's secret lady was probably Lienor. It had never occurred to
him to take Jouglet's flirtation with her so seriously.

*"Ah, white shining rose, I will desire you eternally.
I can never be allowed to have you as a mistress . . ."*

Each woman in the room—wives, maids, and aging crones—
looked as if she would have thrown herself at the singer's feet, and
Jouglet basked in the attention. Willem had never seen his friend in
action before this kind of crowd. Even while chanting dolefully, the
jongleur had a quiet cockiness, the charismatic confidence of a young
gallant; Willem felt a surprising wave of pride that he himself had
been singled out for the young gallant's confidences.

The love dirge was followed by a more upbeat tune typical of the
Danube, by the young Dietmar of Aist, about a typical little bird on
a typical little linden tree. Then Jouglet sat beside Willem for a

while, presenting him in glowing terms to the moony-eyed ladies (who all clearly liked the look of him but found Jouglet more entertaining, at least tonight). Dancing girls were brought out, ruddy and unhappy-looking yet smiling bravely—Slavic conquests of war, Jouglet whispered discreetly, from Konrad's campaigns in the east. They were followed by acrobats and jugglers who had been carted up to Koenigsbourg for the occasion, and finally Jouglet was asked to close the evening.

The minstrel chose to enthrall the male audience this time, with a translated passage from *The Song of Roland,* but paused at a most dramatic moment: the dying Count Roland is surprised by a Saracen who, after feigning death, steals Roland's sword . . . but Roland gets a second wind and begins to beat the Saracen to death, when . . .

Jouglet lowered the bow and grinned at the assembled company. "If you'd like me to finish, this spot at my feet is an excellent place for those hard little round things you carry in your wallets."

There were groans and protests around the circle of listeners at this familiar and imperially sanctioned extortion. But that was followed by a rustling of silk and linen, a creaking of leather, as men reached for their belt-pouches, and a moment later there was a considerable pile of coins at Jouglet's feet. The performer nodded approvingly. "You all know perfectly well what happens next, but here is my divine craftsmanship to conclude it." It took another seven verses before Roland was finally tragically, romantically, handsomely, graphically, heroically deceased.

His Majesty, the hooded falcon back on his wrist, bade an avuncular good night to all the knights and squires but amazed Willem by telling him to stay. Konrad led him, the page boys, the guards, and Jouglet through the lower entrance of the hall and up one flight of a spiral staircase of stone—a bit of architecture nothing more than functional, but Willem still had a hard time not gushing over it.

They stepped onto the second floor, and all but the guard, who stayed by the door, entered Konrad's personal suite. This was a string of three rooms opening onto one another, running the length of the south wing: bedroom, dayroom with its enormous window alcove of which Jouglet was so fond, and a small receiving chamber at the end, with a door out to an external spiral stair. All three rooms had hearths, an extraordinary luxury.

Willem was given a brief glance of it all before they settled in the bedroom. It was the most opulent room he had ever sat in, so opulent that by the next morning he would hardly remember a single distinct thing of worth or beauty—except the breathtaking view of the woods-and-hedgerow-decorated landscape in the midsummer twilight, and the scent of the beeswax candles all around the room in their enameled holders.

The emperor handed off his falcon to a boy who took her into the dayroom with the dogs. At His Majesty's invitation, Willem settled onto velvet cushions while Konrad himself reclined on the tilted bed, and they spoke in reasonable voices rather than shouting over masses of men. Jouglet put the fiddle away in its leather case, picked up a small gut-strung harp, and began playing something soft, almost dronelike, as they ate cherries and sipped wine. There was a small pack of omnipresent page boys in one corner of the room, who entered and exited from either door with the quiet efficiency of worker bees; when Konrad had no need of them, they and their monarch seemed oblivious of each other's presence. They all huddled together now, taking turns losing pennies and glass beads to one another over dominoes and dice.

In private discourse with His Majesty, Willem was comforted to see that Konrad was in fact a learned and cultured (if not pious) man, that he was capable of conversation nearly as engaging as Jouglet's or Lienor's, and that he was, however calculating, generous of spirit.

For example—Konrad explained—the landless freemen in certain of his burgeoning castle towns, the growing class of merchants and artisans, were not taxed the way most towns were by royal tolls or levies; Konrad on a seasonal basis simply invited them to make a gift to the royal coffers.

"And they do?" Willem asked, surprised, trying to imagine how his serfs might respond if he made their week-work on his fields voluntary.

Konrad smiled and spat out a cherry pit. "I get more now than I did when they were taxed in the conventional manner," he said confidingly. "They are made so grateful by the *principle* of not being taxed, and so aware that other towns will pay according to their own ability, it becomes a competition to prove which community is most prosperous. Filling the royal coffers becomes almost festival in feeling. His Holiness in Rome is sick with envy."

"What if they grow wise to it, and cease . . . gifting?" asked Willem.

"Then I'll start taxing them again," Konrad said offhandedly. "And anyhow I always tax the Jews." He smiled. "I love my Jews. Germany could not be the power that she is without them. I so prefer them to those blasted Lombards for enhancing trade. They know enough to revere *this*." He held up his right pinkie and wagged the signet ring.

"Oh, yes, that! My sister set the seal in a brooch, so she would have a king in the house," Willem said with boyish enthusiasm.

Konrad grinned at Jouglet. "This fellow is almost too good to be true." He turned back to Willem. "Would you like to see it?" He held his hand out and rested the signet ring in front of Willem's nose. Willem automatically reached up toward it, but Konrad pulled his hand slightly away. "For obvious reasons I cannot let you examine it."

"I don't think he knows the story, sire," Jouglet prompted, when Willem looked confused.

"Ah," Konrad said in concession, and relaxed back against the bed. "Of course, you were a child when my father died, so you don't remember the scandal."

Willem bit his lower lip. "I remember His Majesty's death because he died in Alphonse's castle. It was the most dramatic thing to happen in Burgundy for years. I don't remember hearing of a scandal around it though."

"Yes, well, Father's signet ring was stolen from his finger on his deathbed. Paul and I were taking turns standing vigil, and to this day we bicker about whose negligence it was, but of course it was his. He was probably in the garderobe, trying on father's crown. Lord knows Alphonse did that often enough. What a headache—for years after my father's death, every petty document that was presented to me with his seal on it had to be inspected for authenticity. Not the big ones—the town charters, the establishing of baronies—those were all affixed with the great seal. This was the pettiness of court etiquette— personal gifts, dispensations, penalties, minor proclamations and transfers of land, and on and on. Thank God I had Marcus to oversee it all. So I am even more diligent of securing my signet than Jouglet is of securing those little magic tricks in his drawstring bag."

"What magic tricks?" Jouglet asked innocently, attention on the harp. "I'm merely keeping careful guard over the generous salary Your Majesty provides."

Konrad tapped Willem's shoulder conspiratorially. "Most people think it's herbal powders to keep his voice boyish and his face pretty." He winked. "I'm guessing it tends toward more lascivious concoctions."

Willem looked narrowly at his friend; the minstrel smiled with secret amusement and said comfortably, "Merely lucre, I assure you, sire. I already have Venus entirely in my thrall. Would you like to hear some Sevelingen?"

As Jouglet serenaded them, they played a game of chess. Throughout the match, Konrad grilled the young knight on his knowledge of battle strategy, which Willem frankly admitted he had only ever had a chance to practice in tournament, and never on a real field. He reminded His Majesty that strategy was considered unworthy of a knight, and seen as a form of deviousness. But for each scenario that Konrad threw out, often based on his actual experiences against the infidels, or with rebellious princes (or entire rebellious Italian towns), Willem matter-of-factly answered with tactics that matched or bettered Konrad's own. The emperor was delighted.

And yet Willem lost the chess match.

("And he really did lose," Jouglet quietly assured Konrad, spitting out a cherry pit. "Unlike me, my lord.")

"Now that we are away from the vultures of court gossips," Konrad said, "speak candidly to me, Willem. Tell me about your land being taken. I want to remedy that."

"Oh, sire," Willem said with a quick breath and began to fidget with one of his rooks, running the edge of his thumb around and around the base. "I don't think there is a remedy. We have questioned the justness of it, but it was lawful. And consider that whoever has that land now, his children are growing up considering themselves the rightful heirs to it. And so they are. It would be folly to rob them of their patrimony—they would seek vengeance."

Konrad smiled condescendingly. "That is naïve."

"Sire, I speak from my own life," Willem said awkwardly, continuing to fidget. "My sister and I were infants when our land . . . became another's. And young children still when we were made aware of the injustice—"

"And you clearly did not seek retribution."

"*I* did not—" Willem began, nearly breaking the base off the rook. He would have said more, but he was interrupted by a loud knock from the direction of the gallery. The door swung open.

Marcus the steward stood there in his elegant dark tunic. "Pardon me for interrupting your leisure, sire," he began. "But I am concerned

with a matter of . . ." He glanced meaningfully at Willem—who, misunderstanding the look, abruptly put down the chess piece as if he'd
been caught stealing it. He began to sort nervously through the bowl
of cherries with great concentration. Marcus lowered his eyes and
bowed. "The cardinal, sire, is presenting a challenge to my duties."

The emperor sighed. "Who does he want excommunicated this
time?" Seeing Marcus hesitate, he said brusquely, "Speak freely, we're
among friends."

Marcus grimaced. "He demands the removal of a considerable
portion of the household, sire. Already we've had to replace two
chamberboys, his groom, and a young woman who served drinks to
the high table, and now—"

"Why?" Konrad knew the answer to his own question; he asked
it entirely for Willem's edification. Willem looked up from the cherries, curious.

"He accused them of deviancy, sire, or in the woman's case, simple lechery. Tonight he demanded the dismissal of a particularly
pretty hall boy who holds a washbasin, and he wants another groom
gone. If I hesitate he says he'll report to the pope that you keep a
court of sodomites and whores."

Konrad grunted. "And His Holiness doesn't?"

"Sire," Marcus pressed softly, looking at his sovereign's slippers.
He coughed demurely. "I cannot empty the court of servants merely
because your brother knows he lacks the willpower to keep his hands
off the winsome ones."

Willem blinked in shock, but Konrad and Jouglet threw their
heads back and hooted laughter. "I wasn't aware he had started re-
straining himself," Konrad said, and signaled a boy for more wine.
"Pity him his burden!"

"It is not a laughing matter, sire," Marcus said, without looking
up. "He has begun to insinuate similar things about certain members
of the court. Including Jouglet."

Willem blinked again, and Konrad stopped laughing. But Jouglet, with a characteristic shrug, said in a lisping, girlish tone, "Oh, heavens, I'm flattered His Grace noticed me at all."

Konrad shook his head. "Marcus, you should not have let him get away with that."

"I am hardly in a position to naysay the emperor's brother—"

"Balls to that," Konrad snapped impatiently. "That's exactly what you're in a position to do—you're my deputy, if you can't stand up to the pope's deputy, then what's the point of having you? I don't need you to demonstrate your servile family pedigree, Marcus, don't prove Alphonse right about that or you'll suffer the consequences." He grabbed the wine his boy offered and drank it all at once. His irritation was acute; Willem felt uncomfortable being present for the rebuke. "We cannot let Paul think for a *moment* he can affect the fabric of my court. Reinstate the servants he's had sent off and make sure he understands that he has no more say over who is expelled from court than over who is included in it. And send us up more fruit. Willem seems displeased about the state of the cherries."

Marcus, looking grim, withdrew. Konrad relaxed a little and turned his attention back to Jouglet. "Nicholas will be jealous," he said wryly. "Usually he's the one singled out for fancy. He's handsomer than you are, and a better dresser."

"But I have milkier skin," Jouglet crooned, pulling up a sleeve to bare a skinny arm, much paler than the sun-toughened calloused hand it was attached to. "That's worth more in the dark."

Willem looked mortified until the other two broke out into adolescent laughter.

Vespers was tolling that night, when Willem accepted an invitation to return to the castle for breakfast in the morning. He was exhausted from long travel and his first evening at court, and it was not a short trip down the mountain to the town; he really wanted only to sleep. But Jouglet followed him down the uneven sandstone stairway to the lower court and waited with him to retrieve his sword and horse, as if presuming an invitation back to the inn for further carousing. More out of affection and gratitude than enthusiasm, Willem invited his friend to ride behind him. Nicholas the messenger followed on his own mount to bring the celebrated helmet in its wooden box, and to guide the way: the path was well marked, and the five small watch-towers of the town twinkled, but it was still a steep and treacherous road after dark.

When they finally approached the northern gate to the town, some half-mile distant of the castle mount, Nicholas offered up a wax imprint of Konrad's ring, and they were allowed through, al-though curfew was long past. The street threaded through the dark-ened, quiet artisans' quarter, past the Street of the Bakers, behind the church—the biggest church Willem had ever seen—along the pavil-ion of jewelers, and through the green market.

As they approached the inn, which was still well lit and full of sounds, the knight gestured for Nicholas to enter the courtyard be-fore him. Then Willem stopped Atlas outside the gates on the cob-bled street and sat for a moment looking up into the clear night sky, where the waning moon was creeping over the town walls. The town air, even here, was thicker than the open fields, but the difficult bou-quet of smells woke him up a little, and he decided he was glad after all that Jouglet had returned with him.

"Jouglet," he said quietly. He felt the jongleur press up against his back to catch his words. "I would never have survived this evening without you. I cannot pretend to understand what inspires your gen-erosity toward me but I am deeply, deeply grateful. I hope I did not disappoint you with my behavior any time tonight."

"Are you serious? You were a perfect success!" Jouglet chucked

him affectionately on the shoulder, then slipped to the uneven cobblestones and leapt away from the charger's haunches. The curve of
Willem's back where the minstrel's body had pressed felt suddenly
cooler in the night breeze; the space behind the saddle felt conspicu-
ously empty.

Usually the castle was asleep by now, but not tonight, in the after-
math of such a lavish supper. Marcus was at the table in his antechamber hearing the droning daily reports from his household
officers, when Alphonse of Burgundy paused at the outer doorway,
on the spiral steps that led up to his guest quarters. In the torchlight,
his hair for a moment looked like Imogen's, dark and wavy; Marcus
suddenly felt hers between his fingers. He made himself look away
and put her out of his thoughts.

Alphonse had paused for no apparent reason other than to eye
the steward appraisingly. Marcus, knowing why he was being appraised, tried to appear ducal while discussing the fermentation of
horse manure with the marshal but doubted very much he was convincing.

His Majesty came down into the room from the other direction,
with only the gold-encrusted bed-robe thrown over his shoulders
and shadowed by his night guard. Yawning into his rings, he said to
Marcus, "When you're done with that I want a cure for my insomnia,
preferably blond. I send the page boys, but they never quite understand what it is I'm after."

Suddenly there was a cry of boyish laughter from the inner courtyard below, followed by irritated hushing noises from the kitchen,
beneath Marcus's own suite. The laughter darted about the small
enclosed area, then headed for the stairway and bubbled up so that
the count had to leap away to avoid the source of it: Jouglet and
Nicholas, who came bursting past him through the narrow door and

into the room together, in high humor—and well dressed in tunics much too large for them.

"Sire!" Nicholas gushed, referring to tunics Jouglet had absconded with at the inn, against Willem's protests. "See what Willem of Dole gave us!"

"And you should have seen the rings he gave the ladies!" Jouglet added.

Alphonse, his face set in a neutral mask, took a step up the tight circular stairs—but then paused, to study Konrad's reaction. Marcus watched Alphonse watching Konrad. There was a calculating expression on the count's face that worried Marcus.

Konrad looked astonished. "What a peculiar fellow," he said. The pair approached, offering him and the cluster of domestic officers pieces of their appropriated clothing to feel. "He's going to give away everything he has."

"Everyone at the inn *adores* him, sire," Nicholas said, as if this somehow justified it.

"And not just for the gifts," Jouglet added to all of them, heartily. "The gifts are just an expression of his generous and loyal heart."

Konrad considered them a moment, then looked around the room for Boidon. "Boidon, send a hundred pounds of new coins to Willem at his inn first thing tomorrow."

Everybody gaped at him.

"Sire?" Marcus said in a shaky voice.

"I want to see what he does with it," Konrad explained, looking straight at Jouglet, who suddenly had an itch in a most inconvenient place and had to turn away to scratch at it.

Marcus glanced quickly at Alphonse and then away again; Alphonse glanced quickly at Marcus and then away again. Hardly able to contain his abrupt anxiety, Marcus tried to return his attention to his evening sums. The count nodded a little to himself and finally continued up the stairway to his appointed room.

His work finished, Marcus threw on a sable-lined cloak and slipped downstairs and outside into the cool, moist evening air of the stone-courtyard, trying to stay calm. He sat on the lower steps of the broad staircase that led from Konrad's suite straight down to the courtyard. He smiled wanly at a passing female form in the torchlight, but he was so distracted and disturbed he did not even register whether it was lady or servant. She wasn't Imogen, so she didn't interest him.

Marcus's greatest strength as steward, as seneschal of Konrad's itinerant court, was his ability to anticipate and therefore avert every conceivable thing that could go wrong. As with any extreme of mind, this trait was a danger as well as a strength: he was far too quick to see the worst calamity that might materialize from any situation. And Willem's appearance, although an apparent delight to everybody else, reignited his one great, lurking fear.

He's just a knight, Marcus told himself. *He's just some minor knight from nowhere. The count and Konrad will not even remember his appearance by next week. And the count himself just said today my wedding will be soon.* Already that chess game felt like it had happened weeks ago. He wondered what Jouglet was up to in championing the young Burgundian.

"Marcus?"

It was Konrad's voice, above him. He rose quickly and turned to look up, bowing. "Sire!"

Konrad made a dismissive gesture and continued down the stairs, the night guard dutifully shadowing him. "She was lovely, that blonde, but she did not cure my insomnia."

"My apologies, sire."

Konrad sank onto the bottom steps and gestured Marcus to join him, then smiled conspiratorially, speaking too softly for the guard to hear. "It will be intriguing to learn the purpose of Jouglet's game."

"With the knight? I was musing on that this very moment, sire," Marcus said.

"It is no doubt in my interest; his games always are. I'm curious to see how he tells Willem to spend the money, though. Speaking of curious—I've a passing query for you."

There was no such thing as a passing query from His Majesty. "I'm entirely at your disposal, sire."

"Your astonishingly idiotic adventure, bringing my little cousin to camp. Were you telling me the truth when you said you didn't—"

"Absolutely," Marcus said briskly, flushing. "I swear it. Both as your subject and as your oldest friend."

"She is still a virgin?"

Oh, God, Marcus thought, horrified. *He has to know if he can give her to someone else without a scandal.* "Of course she is, I would never dishonor her that way."

"I'm not asking if *you've* dishonored her, I'm asking if she's still a virgin," Konrad said. "As I recall, you were the one concerned about protecting her maidenhead; she seemed blithely indifferent to it. I don't trust women like that. Make sure she's a virgin."

"You're taking her away from me, aren't you?" Marcus said abruptly, in a choked voice.

The emperor frowned at him. "No," he said with almost parental firmness, "but do not forget yourself, Marcus, it's a political betrothal. It is only a perverse fluke that you've fallen for the girl, that is irrelevant and frankly rather tasteless of you. It was *extremely* impolitic of me to turn my back on what I saw at camp. I did so as your friend. But you must promise me, as a friend, that I, as your emperor, will not look a fool for pretending nothing happened. I will not suffer looking foolish at the hands of my own steward."

"I promise," Marcus said. "You don't even need to ask. It's her own honor I'm concerned with."

"So my cousin is a virgin, and I have no reason to suspect otherwise."

"She is a virgin who is betrothed and deeply in love with—"

"Oh, stop that!" Konrad said impatiently. "I didn't say I was taking her away from you."

"No, sire," Marcus replied softly. "You did not *say* that."

6

Bildungsroman

[German, "formation-tale," a coming-of-age story]

28 June

Later that night, after making sure the sentries on duty were all sober, or at least awake, and claiming he had been called away to his ailing uncle's bedside in Aachen, Marcus rode out—not to the north and Aachen, but south. He rode hard until morning, swapping out his horses at relay stations as he spent them, and after sleeping briefly he was up again, riding south some more along the raised trade roads of the Rhine valley. The roads were lined with shade trees to keep animals from dropping dead of sunstroke, but they offered no protection from the vicious mass of biting bugs that shattered the summer heat. That evening, as the sun was slanting sharply from the west, he followed it away from the river to a small grove of willows, elms, swamp oaks, and bush-roses around the ruins of a nunnery. Here there was a woods-woman, one who harvested medicinal herbs and berries. She lived in the ruins, and she was the great-aunt of one of Imogen's handmaids.

And she was discreet. Over the past year he and Imogen had three times rendezvoused here, twice for a single overnight, once for several days together. The woods-woman fed them and made up a bed on the floor of the old chapel for them, asked nothing in return, and indifferently stored up the coins and jewels Marcus insisted on giving her. She had nothing to spend them on.

Imogen had arrived before him and now ran out of the oak-overrun cloister with her yellow tunic unbelted, smiling with anticipation. At the sight of that pale skin against that deep brown hair, his heart skipped and sank at once. "I've only been here a few moments!" she called to him in delight in her soft, murmuring voice. "Such perfect timing, all our while here can be together!" And grabbing his sleeve she pulled him toward the old chapel, laughing.

In the mottled shade of what had been a place of prayer, their hands were all over each other's clothes and their lips all over each other's faces. In an impressively short time they were lying facing each other, between layers of soft sheeting that Imogen had brought with her, on a bed of elm leaves and dried marsh grass. It was a bright sunny day, but inside here everything was warmly, lazily dappled. As always when they did this, Marcus was still in his drawers.

"I've missed you," one of them said to the other, and they immediately forgot which of them had spoken. She rolled a little and tried to pull him on top of her, grinned as always to feel him grow hard against her.

"Now how shall we take care of that?" she purred, but her smile faded when she saw the expression on his face. "What's wrong, love?"

He gave her a look that worried her, as if he would never see her again and wanted to memorize every fleck of color in her eyes. "We mustn't," he whispered, mostly to himself.

"Actually . . . ," she said, smiling up at him. "I had something very special planned for today."

He sat up, looking tormented, almost frightened. "I shouldn't have come, Imogen, I don't have the strength right now to—"

"Good," she said, placing one shushing finger over his lips. Her fingers smelled of apples. "Because I'm the queen of your heart and you must do my bidding." Her voice, without her trying, was inherently seductive in its shy velvet softness. "My bidding is that you know me as a husband would."

"Oh, no," he groaned, pulling away from her. She sat up and climbed after him across the shaded sheets. "Imogen, you can't keep doing this, you don't know what you're talking about."

"I'm talking about consummation," she said, innocently delighted with her own naughtiness. "And of course I don't know what I'm talking about . . . yet."

Every time they met it had become more frustrating for him to honor what seemed like a maddening technicality. Today there was both more and less reason than ever to respect it.

"We have other ways of pleasing each other, Imogen, please, you must save that for your wedding night." And unable to stop himself he added, heavily, "What if your wedding night is not with me?"

Imogen understood him, and their situation, well enough to have anticipated this objection. "If it's such a precious gift to give, I'd rather give it to my lover than to some stranger who happens to become my husband."

"It's not as simple as that," Marcus said. "It'll hurt the first time, love, and then all you'll have to show for it is pain that you associate with me, and a husband who will throw you out for harlotry."

"You're as bad as my father!" she suddenly snapped. "He locks me in, you lock me out! Don't treat me like a child, Marcus!" She calmed herself, and the easy sweetness of her voice again softened him. "I doubt one woman in a thousand has the grace to feel for someone the way I do for you, and maybe one in ten thousand will have it reciprocated. *That* is the gift. We throw it back in God's face not to act on it."

Marcus was so startled by this reasoning he laughed. "I don't think the church would much agree with that."

"Scripture speaks only against coveting thy neighbor's wife. I am not thy neighbor's wife. And nowhere does it say the bride must be a virgin on her wedding night. Our Savior never said that. Our Savior didn't care. One of his dearest followers was a woman but neither wife nor virgin." She managed to smile at him, an incongruously coquettish look that always made him bend to her. "I'll force myself on you," she warned.

For an eternity of perhaps one heartbeat, Marcus stared at her, believing he would control himself. Then he pushed her down beneath him, his mouth pressed against hers almost violently. She reached for the forbidden drawstring of his linen drawers to untie it; he stared at her while she undressed him. He had seen, touched, tasted this pretty young body before but always with the knowledge that he had to hold himself in check. Without that knowledge it was even prettier.

It did hurt, a little; not as much as she had feared. Marcus was so overwhelmed by the moment that he sobbed into her hair, drowning her with kisses, stroking her face. "Oh, Imogen, you impossible beauty." He kissed her once more, gently on the cheek, hoping desperately that he had not just ruined both their lives.

*W*illem awoke late, the morning after meeting Konrad, to find Jouglet's angular face grinning into his, looking sleep deprived but no less jocund for it. The minstrel held a heavy leather bag that clinked promisingly with each movement. "Good morning! You've already slept through breakfast, but I made excuses for you to His Majesty. He sent me with this little gift for you."

Willem yawned and sat up. He always slept well, but his dreams had betrayed how nervous he still was about making the right impression; Jouglet's unexpected company was a reassuring way to start the morning.

The servant and pages were not in the room; Erec, already dressed, was slouched comfortably on the chest by the larger window quietly drilling himself on German grammar. The young man grinned as his nude cousin threw off the covers and reached for his bed-robe. "You will never believe what the emperor has sent you," Erec announced.

Jouglet hefted the bag again. "Money!"

Willem blinked in confusion. "Why?"

"You don't ask *why,* you ask *how much,*" Jouglet corrected him glibly, and lowered the bag, then began to untie the leather stays around it. "One hundred pounds. Each one with our dear emperor's handsome profile upon it."

Willem's face registered astonishment, then relief. "Thank God, I can pay off my creditors," he said. "I need to order lances and new shields from Montbéliard, and I already owe my supplier far too much. We had a harvest that went moldy last year—"

"You're not paying off your debts *now*," Jouglet said, as if this should have been obvious. "*Now*, you're buying people gifts. You're buying yourself better clothes. You're making a huge donation to the brotherhood of St. Hippolyte. All the money will stay within the town walls so you can be seen using it, but *never* on *necessities*."

Willem made a face and tied his robe closed. "That's an absurd way to live. If this is what life is like at court, I am not sure I want to be a party to it."

The minstrel sat beside Willem on the bed and with fatherly gravitas smiled at him. "Not in court, just in town. Families are so scattered here that pedigree means little, and townspeople by definition don't live on great estates, so while you're staying here, how much you spend is how much you're worth. But it need be like this only until the tournament. I swear on your sister's curving rump."

"You're not getting anywhere near that rump," Erec scolded cheerfully.

Jouglet stayed focused on Willem. "I will write the man in Montbéliard in your name and convince him to send you what you need on credit."

"If he's as blindly trusting as I am, he'll fall for it," Willem said with a nervous laugh. He suddenly felt not reassured but overwhelmed by his friend's omnipresence. He stood up to get away from Jouglet and turned to the open door, where a boy sat attendant. "Is there a scribe available to the inn?" Willem asked him. "Find him for me, lad." He headed for a chest. "I need to write some letters of my own."

"You'd best do it quickly or we'll be late for dinner as well as breakfast," Jouglet said.

"We?" Willem echoed, a little more sharply than needed. "You're free to go to court whenever you care to. You are not bound to me as if you were my hound."

There was a brief silence as Willem busied himself retrieving his discolored blue riding tunic from a chest.

"You should have taken Konrad's offer of a woman, milord, you need relief from all your tension," Jouglet scolded softly from the bed. "I am not the hound, *you* are—and a pup yet, hardly ready to perform well without your trainer. Your trainer whom you must not bite or you will be abandoned on the side of the road like an ill-tempered little mutt."

"I apologize," said Willem gruffly, shaking out the riding tunic. He tossed it down and grimaced at it. "I need to dress well for dinner, don't I?" he said wearily. "*Usable* clothing has little worth at castle tables ever, I imagine."

"Showing up in riding gear might make a good impression, actually," Jouglet suggested. "The earnest knight preparing for the tourney, all of that. The ladies will like it. Were you taken with any of them last night?"

Willem, honest to a fault, admitted that no, he had not been.

When the scribe arrived, leather box of parchment under his arm, Willem sat him by the larger window and dictated as he dressed. He wrote first to Renard, the knight who had his former helmet, telling him about the tournament and encouraging him to summon the knights of Burgundy to come and ride with him.

"If you can gather enough of them," Erec hummed to Willem, "you might lead a whole battalion."

"I think he'll be doing that anyhow," Jouglet said with satisfaction, still seated on the bed and picking loose threads from the coverlet. "And they'll all be the emperor's own men, I wager."

Willem huffed a little as he laced his boots. "Jouglet, now you are out of your element. If Konrad raised me above his own retinue, one of them would probably kill me in my sleep. Second letter," he said briskly, straightening and turning back to the scribe. This one was to his mother and sister, telling them also of the upcoming tournament, and with mild exaggeration describing what a magnificent character the emperor had. Then, with some understatement, he described how he'd been received at court.

"Add this," Jouglet instructed the scribe. "Jouglet says Willem is not giving himself enough credit, but that is customary, isn't it?"

"Don't write that," Willem told the scribe. He was getting irked, although he did not know why, by Jouglet's relentless championing. "Just sign it, with great regard, your loving son and brother, Willem." He pulled on his second glove. "Erec, call for the horses."

Erec departed at once with the scribe, and Willem turned to the only other person left in the room, still casually lolling on the bed. "Jouglet, it will take a while to saddle up, perhaps you should walk yourself to the castle so we do not make you late. Thank you greatly for bringing me the king's gift." He added with unusual archness, "I imagine I'm expected to buy something for you with it as well?"

"No you are not," the minstrel retorted with cool, contained annoyance, and sat up sharply. "In fact, look what I have brought you, sweetheart." Jouglet went to the leather fiddle case lying by the door, pulled out from under it the two appropriated tunics from the night before, and tossed them with force onto a chest. "I was bringing these back to you. I only took them to make a show of them to Konrad. I am not trying to profit by you, Willem."

Willem reddened. "I apologize," he said, not meeting Jouglet's eyes. Then, meeting Jouglet's eyes after all: "I would like to know what you *are* doing. I feel beholden to you—and I know I am, but I'd rest more comfortable understanding *why*."

"Beholden?" Jouglet echoed. "Last night it was grateful, and now—*beholden*?" The hazel eyes appraised Willem, hurt. "You insult me, Willem. You insult the very idea of friendship."

"Stop being such a woman," Willem said defensively.

Jouglet's face flashed with indignation. "And now I'm a *woman*? Calling me *eunuch* back in Dole was not enough of an insult? What must I do to prove myself, molest your sister?" And with a snicker, unable to resist it: "More than I have already, I mean?"

Willem laughed irritably. "I'm sorry I said 'beholden,' does that help? I'm grateful, I'm very grateful." A pause. "But I would still prefer you walk to the castle." Another pause. "It will be good to see you there, in company."

Jouglet shrugged dismissively, grabbed the fiddle case, and left the room without bowing or glancing back.

The minstrel never showed up for dinner at the castle.

This made facing dinner at the castle terrifying for Willem, and he was reminded ruefully how much he had depended on Jouglet's silent presence to ballast him the night before. The absence was unremarkable to all but Willem; young Jouglet, he learned, was known for disappearing for days or even weeks, returning with secretive smiles and other symptoms of having spent far too much time carousing—but also laden with useful gossip for Konrad's private hearing.

Dinner was served in the hall, kept cool and comfortable by buffeting mountain gusts even under a relentless midday sun. It was a substantial meal with less hubbub than the supper feast, the highlight being a stew of salmon transported live to the castle from the North Sea in great barrels of ocean water. Alphonse, Count of Burgundy, was absent, as was Marcus, and this time Willem did not protest sitting beside the king. Cardinal Paul sat to Konrad's left again, his morbid fascination with Willem's presence as unfathomable and unnerving as it had been the night before.

Over the course of the dinner—during which he drank more than usual, in a bootless effort to relax—Willem and his monarch made unexpected and singular impressions on each other. He expressed surprise that His Majesty, even in his youth, had never had a lady to worship by the rules of courtly love: the chaste, secret, and usually doomed adoration of a great lady one could never have, an adoration that compelled a man to relentless self-improvement in her honor, that compelled him to deeds of martial ferocity, spiritual generosity, and cultured sensitivity, that even compelled him, when given the choice between carnal satisfaction or poetry, to choose the poetry every time. Willem was openly disappointed that, in fact, nobody at court had such a lady.

"So at tournaments there are no knights carrying their lady's favors?" he asked. He felt foolish for his curiosity about a subject that clearly meant little to the court.

"Oh, of course there are—kerchiefs and torn sleeves and all that rot," Konrad said. "Usually the lady is the knight's dowager great-aunt who is about to make her will, or the mother of the girl whose dowry he's after." Willem's face fell, and the king chuckled suggestively. "You want a lady's favor wrapped around your lance, is that it?"

Willem shrugged, not registering the double entendre. "Of course I'd like to earn that honor, but . . . I don't know any ladies here."

Konrad chuckled harder. "You can have Jouglet's castoffs. Or we could simply have the seamstress make a pretty glove for you and you can invent yourself a lady. Then you don't have to write bad poetry for anyone."

Willem grimaced and tried to hide his disappointment. "Then there is truth to the rumor that chivalry is not valued in Germany as it is in France and Burgundy."

"Of course it's valued," Konrad reassured him. "Any doctrine that tells armed men they are bettered by unflinching service and devotion to a superior is always valued in my court."

Over the next ten dishes Willem was disabused—gently

disabused, once Konrad saw how innocent he was—of most of his understandings about the courtly life. He learned how peculiar he was for refraining from bearing arms on Sundays. He learned how indulgent it was of him to consider the chivalric code of decent behavior as applying to the use of peasant women's bodies—had not Andreas Capellanus himself advocated taking them by flattery and force? He learned he was naïve for fearing that traditional values such as honor and loyalty were lost by the increasing popularity of money in lieu of the stable interdependency of manor life. Konrad roared with laughter over that, trying to imagine what would happen to his empire if, for a single afternoon, he ruled as though loyalty were a stronger force than greed.

But however strange the emperor found Willem's disposition on such matters, Konrad genuinely liked him for it. Though there were not two decades separating them, he felt almost paternal toward the young man; he was touched by Willem's simplicity, and pleased to have found someone so artless who was yet skilled in the art of combat. Konrad had never thought much of Burgundians—("They make pretty things, they pray well, but they're dull for dinner conversation")—and Willem was an unexpected delight. And so Konrad switched matters to more neutral ground—falconry, hunting, horsemanship. They discussed their mutual acquaintance the minstrel, and how uncannily each had felt, from the moment he'd met Jouglet (three years ago in Willem's case, at least seven in Konrad's), that they'd been friends a lifetime.

Paul, attempting as ever to insinuate himself into some conversation where he felt even marginally welcome, sarcastically suggested that such large, accomplished men as Konrad and Willem might square off to test each other's mettle by trying, for example, to bash each other's heads in. Willem took the cardinal seriously and begged off the idea, which tickled Konrad enough to want to try it out. He informed Willem that they would test their lances against each other's next day outside the town walls. Willem was flustered and would have given up his helmet all over again to have had Jouglet in sight then. Afraid to contradict his sovereign, he agreed to it; he doubted he could win such a match, but then again, he was baffled as to whether he should even *try* to win it.

In late afternoon, he retrieved Atlas and his weapons from the stable in the lower courtyard and began the steep descent down the mountain, into the hilly vineyards, through the town gates, along the narrow, haphazard streets, and finally to the inn. He dismissed his servant from the room, sinking immediately onto the hard bed and letting out a sigh—more a groan—of psychic exhaustion.

"It's easier once you are used to it," promised Jouglet from the far corner.

Willem jumped, though he realized that he had somehow expected the minstrel to be there. "Come over here," he ordered, and Jouglet did. Willem looked up at his friend wearily from the pillows. He seemed about to speak two or three times, then changed his mind and finally said, with a sigh, "I'm very glad to see you. Sup with me."

4 July

*I*n the slate-and-amber-dappled dawn, Imogen was smiling languidly in her sleep. She shifted closer to Marcus's leanly muscled frame, to snuggle against him, and he thought, for the thousandth time in those four days, that his heart might shatter with happiness. That this girl—and she was barely more than a girl—would sprout such unquestioning and passionate affection for him, a man almost old enough to be her father, was to him miraculous proof of God's work among mankind.

Or perhaps the devil's. This was so stupidly dangerous, what they had done, what they were doing. He was not a stupid man, and he had always been by nature too cautious to truck with danger. And when he was thinking straight—which he obviously had not been doing—he was far too protective of Imogen's well-being to forget himself.

Alphonse, Count of Burgundy, was a man whom nobody at court had ever liked, a second son without sons of his own, desperate to secure his immortality by marrying his daughter well. Suggesting Marcus had been a ploy of Konrad's—Marcus had the greatest authority within the royal court after Konrad himself, but no pedigree and no independent power. He was Konrad's creature, a childhood companion who through merit and favor had earned an extraordinary position of authority. He had agreed to the match because he did not have the right to refuse it, and anyhow, he always did whatever Konrad wanted. Imogen's mother, Monique, who had known Marcus for a lifetime, saw no impropriety in his meeting with Imogen when first they were betrothed; in fact Monique had requested it, to put her daughter's mind at ease that her intended was a gentleman.

He had seen her a few times in passing as a young girl, but when she walked into Konrad's chamber in Hagenau the day of their actual introduction, her face lit by the setting sun, he did not recognize even a trace of the child, she had bloomed and grown so beautiful. She looked at him and put a hand to her throat, gasping slightly. "Oh, it's you," she said, in a soft voice bursting with relief. "I wasn't sure which one Father was referring to. I'm so glad it's you." That was all it took. It was what Jouglet, in those ridiculous French romances, would have called a *coup de foudre*. There was no explaining it. They did not take their gazes from each other for the entire conversation, and later neither of them could remember what they spoke about. He could not wrest her voice and eyes from his mind, and with no evidence he knew, with absolute certainty, that she was just as distracted by thoughts of him. He initiated an exchange of letters, and within six months they had arranged—it was her idea—to find a way to be alone together now and then.

Why, he wondered now, *why* had they kept something that innocent a secret? There had been an adolescent gleefulness in the secrecy; Marcus, who had never felt gleeful in his own adolescence, was seduced by it. The first time, when they had each ridden for days to this sequestered spot, he had not lain a finger on her despite his relentlessly throbbing erection; they talked for two days, then he'd kissed her hand and they had separated. She'd written to him as soon as she returned home, explaining how she had felt in his presence, artlessly detailing what he recognized as feminine arousal, and from their second visit on they never kept their hands and mouths off each other.

Soon they would have to separate again. The tournament was coming up, and Konrad needed him for that. Four days was an eternity, and now that they were entirely lovers, it was an eternity of greater contentment than he had known the world could offer. But today was the last day. Until they were married. They would be married soon. Jouglet and Konrad had bullied Alphonse, and Alphonse, duly bullied, had said they would be married soon.

When Imogen stirred against him again, he stroked her cheek, beaming at her, and bent over to kiss her temple. Her hands, under the sheets, moved automatically toward his waist to pull herself closer to his warmth. There was a musky smell between them from three days of gentle but almost unrelenting fornication; it wafted up from the sheets when she moved and made him want to take her again.

But she looked so innocent and content as she slept; he only sighed instead and rested his cheek on her tousled dark hair. He supposed many men must claim to feel this way about their lovers, but he could not believe anybody felt as deeply as he did.

Half asleep, she rolled over and pushed the cool skin of her buttocks against his thighs, which made him almost instantaneously erect. And then in her soft, murmuring voice she whispered, half-yawning, "I like it when you take me this way. I like to feel you pushing against me on the inside and pushing against me on the outside at the same time." She wiggled a little, pressing back against him; he groaned and laughed.

"I've created the perfect lover," he whispered into the back of her neck, teasing.

"No," she corrected him, smiling with her eyes closed as his whiskers tickled her. "A shameless whore."

He sobered instantly and hovered over her, so that by turning her head toward him he could look straight down at her. "You are *not* a whore," he said in a very serious voice. "You are a lady. I will never let you be known as anything else."

7 July

Go into the attack," Willem called out patiently as Erec stepped back from his opponent. Like the squires he was training, Willem had stripped down to his breeches; the rolling field outside the fief of Orschwiller was full of sweaty, bare-chested youths in the hot afternoon sun. "*Meet* him."

Jouglet, lazing supine on the reddish dirt at the edge of the training area, suggested helpfully, "Pretend it's a woman."

"Ah!" Erec said with exaggerated heartiness, as if this made it all clear. "Sweetheart!" He threw down his sword theatrically into the dusty soil and leapt forward, pelvis foremost, with arms wide open toward his fellow squire, a smaller boy in service to the Duke of Franconia. The younger boy stared at Erec, not certain how to respond. He hefted his blade straight up, as if entertaining thoughts of swinging it.

"Dammit, Erec!" Willem shouted angrily. He turned to the boy. "Put up, Georges! He's unarmed. Never strike an unarmed opponent, even if he deserves it, which this stupid child does. And don't encourage him with laughter, Jouglet," he ordered, turning on the minstrel, who instantly went stone-faced.

Unrepentant, Erec picked up his sword and muttered, loudly, "We've been at this since sext bells, and it's after nones, certainly we've earned a break by now." He wiped his pimpled forehead with the whole length of his sunburnt arm.

Willem took a step toward him and raised his voice. "You don't earn breaks in battle, Erec! And Saracens are used to fighting in much harsher climates than ours. What will you say when you find yourself exhausted in the desert someday facing a scimitar? 'Excuse me, Milord Saracen, but I'm fatigued, shall we pause for *refreshment*?' " The other squires exchanged looks and chuckled, nervously, glad the sarcasm was not directed at them. "For the love of God, I'd die of shame to have one of my men behave that way. No wonder Lienor doesn't fancy you."

Erec, red-faced, started to thumb his teeth at his cousin but saw Jouglet watching him, and thought better of it. He resumed the stance he'd had before, ready to engage with Georges again. The smaller boy glanced over Erec's shoulder toward the slope and his face lit up. "His Majesty is coming to watch!"

Willem glanced up to see Konrad, mounted, riding over the gentle crest of the foothill in a broad path between rows of grapevines.

His vanguard, two mounted knights in livery, held high a banner with the imperial coat of arms to make sure he would not be unrecognized. He was followed by a group of some dozen nobles and knights, also mounted, and their servants, who were all on foot and walking faster than seemed comfortable, to keep up with the horses. Willem—extremely self-conscious around Konrad since unhorsing His Majesty at the joust the week before—immediately went down on both knees on the dirt and bowed his head; Jouglet and the dozen squires followed suit at once. From the top of the hill, a few hundred paces away, Konrad gestured for them to rise.

"Carry on," he called out. "We will make ourselves comfortable at our leisure on the pavilion."

Jouglet, rising first, saw who was riding to either side of the emperor. "It's a family reunion," the minstrel said in a loud whisper to the knight. "Tell these pretty boys to put their shirts back on or Brother Paul will throw them all out for deviancy." Willem made a dismissive gesture.

Erec looked far too excited about the king's arrival. Willem gestured him closer, and he approached, certain he was about to be given an opportunity to show off. But instead Willem shouted in his face, so abruptly that the younger cousin jumped back in shock: *"Erec!"* This got the attention of even the most distracted squires. "Your penalty for breaking concentration is to put down your sword for the rest of the afternoon and tend to Atlas." Willem's horse had been off his feed since they had arrived at court. "Examine his manure and see if there is anything peculiar about it. Smell it. Taste it if you have to."

The other squires exchanged glances, at once scared and trying not to laugh. Erec's face puckered. "You can't order me to eat horseshit, Willem, I'm your *lord*."

"You're my *squire*, that's why you're here at all," Willem corrected brusquely. "Here at *your own insistence*." He turned his back on Erec, and immediately the other youths pretended to be busy practising. He clapped twice to get their attention; they were all too preoccupied with showing him how hard they were working to notice this, and most of them did not regard him.

"Attention!" Jouglet shrieked in an almost ear-splitting falsetto, leaping up.

They all froze. Jouglet made a pained face, signaled the page boy attending Willem for wine, and sat down again.

The knight chuckled. "Thank you, Jouglet."

Between gulps of wine, Jouglet declared, loudly enough to be heard by the spectators, "Always an honor to serve such a great knight."

Willem ignored this and pressed on. "All right now, let's show His Majesty what you're all made of. We will walk through the drill you learned this morning—*slowly*—and then up to speed."

He had been standing to the south with the sun at his back. But now that his emperor was settling directly across from him, he felt himself too much on display and worked his way around the edge of the hollow until he was standing just below Konrad and the others. Jouglet followed him.

At a gesture from Konrad, Jouglet moved up the swell to the covered, open-sided audience pavilion, where the heralds had raised the banner. "How has this been going?" Konrad asked. Down the slope, Willem was squinting into the sunlight and calling out numbers to the fighters, who moved almost dancerlike through the drill.

Jouglet nodded. "He's very patient with them, but very strict. He's coaxed terrific work out of them. He could teach your knights a thing or two, sire."

Paul, seated to his brother's right and entirely ignored, stared narrowly at Jouglet. Jouglet smiled comfortably, knowingly, smoothly in response. "As His Eminence appears to question my . . . investment in the knight's ascension, might I ask whether His Eminence has his own investment in preventing it?"

Paul jerked upright, nostrils flaring like an indignant stallion. "I was actually going to comment that you are spending an inordinate amount of time gaping at these half-naked youths." He tried to make it sound like sarcastic humor, in the hopes that perhaps a few people nearby would laugh.

"You're right, Eminence. It's envy, plain and simple," Jouglet responded at once, unruffled. "I know that envy is a deadly sin, and I shall confess it when next I go to shrift." The vaguest hint of a smile. "I am overdue to be shriven. Perhaps Your Eminence would do the honor, if he knows of any dark and private place nearby we might—ouf!" This was in response to Konrad, barely squelching his laughter, smacking the minstrel hard on the side of the head.

"Have they worked the horses yet?" asked a knight's mistress, near the throne, eyes on the squires at work. She grinned confidingly at Nicholas, standing beside her. "I like watching them lance the ring." Paul, hearing this, sighed with benevolent exasperation, letting everyone know this was precisely the sort of suggestive comment he would expect in a court like this.

"I'd let Willem lance my ring," Nicholas chuckled in response, and several of the ladies tittered. Konrad gave his messenger an infuriated look of warning, which sobered him. The cardinal rolled his eyes theatrically and pursed his lips.

"Seven," Willem called out, then noticing one of the boys overreach, commanded, "stay on balance." He walked among the five teams; Georges, without a partner, went through the movements as though he had an invisible opponent. At Willem's call they came to a finish at the same moment, froze, then brought their swords to a neutral position, held upright from the waist and slightly crossing their chests. Willem nodded with satisfaction and clapped once, then began to call out numbers but much faster this time. In this tempo, they looked like an abbreviated army in choreographed battle.

"That is a beautiful sight," Konrad said expansively. It was the closest he had come yet to delivering a line directly to Paul. "Strong, healthy, capable bodies, and all of them laboring for me."

"You underestimate them, Konrad," Paul retorted. "Their ultimate goal is to go on crusade, where they will labor for our eternal Lord, not a mere temporal statesman like yourself."

The emperor stared at him a moment. Then he flashed a smile and slapped his brother hard across the shoulder. "Do you know what, Paul, I almost enjoy your company when you display a hint of wit. Try to do it more often." He turned his attention back to the exercises.

"No wonder the ancient athletes trained in the nude," a lady said with relish. "Man is a beautiful creature."

"I think the court ladies should all spin and weave in the nude," Konrad suggested.

"I'd rather see the ladies bounce around a little," Jouglet contributed, winking in the direction of the cluster of women in such a way that each was sure she was the intended recipient of the wink.

The drill finished, the squires were applauded by the onlookers, but they were too scared of Willem to break concentration and acknowledge it. At his signal they lined up front to back, facing him. Then he held out his hand, and the page gave him a sword—a blunted blade like the boys were using—and gestured the first squire forward. He sprang at the boy with considerable force, his shoulder and upper back muscles rippling briefly in the sun, which made the ladies titter. The boy parried the blow neatly, fended off three more lunges, saluted with his wooden sword, and went to the back of the line as the second squire stepped up to practise his own defense.

"That's one of mine!" Konrad said, delighted. "That's Tomas! I had no idea he could do that."

"I'm not sure he could before this morning," Jouglet said.

"Look at Willem of Dole *move*," Konrad said approvingly, ignoring the ladies' hilarity behind him. "I looked like that ten years ago. That is genuine beauty."

"If you like that sort of thing," Jouglet said placidly. "I prefer a little *bounce*." Another wink at all the ladies earned another round of brief, private smiles of anticipation.

"Jouglet," Konrad said, suddenly lowering his voice. "Look over my shoulder. Do any of my men look jealous or put out?"

Jouglet stood and pretended to stretch, turning in a slow arc, as if trying to catch a cooling gust of breeze. Paul, sitting next to Konrad, looked directly over his shoulder and then answered before the minstrel could. "A couple of them."

Konrad gave Paul a look that let him know how graceless he was being, but then he smiled to himself. "Excellent," he said. "That is what we'll do when the training session is finished."

"What is?" Paul and Jouglet asked in unison.

Konrad whispered with anticipation, "We'll see what your young man is really made of."

As a final precaution, on his way back to the town, Marcus rode well out of his way so that he could return as if from Aachen. It was, he hoped, the last time that he would have to resort to such subterfuge. The next time he saw Imogen they would meet before a church door. He'd spent almost every moment of the homeward journey revisiting the sensations of his body within hers, but now was almost nauseated with anxiety at the thought of what could happen should Alphonse slither out of his commitment. It was almost enough to make him confess Imogen's deflowering to Konrad . . . no, he could not do that, not after telling Konrad he'd never do such a thing. Konrad's trust in him was nearly his sole asset. Anyway—nothing would go wrong. They would be married soon, and then it would no longer matter when they'd first been together.

As Marcus approached the swell that opened down into the training field, he saw there was a training session just ending, with the emperor in attendance. Richard of Mainz, one of Konrad's most accomplished knights, was wearily walking off the field; Marcus supposed he'd overseen the squires' training session today, although usually he would not condescend to do so. Marcus recognized a number of the dusty, exhausted boys who had been honing their skills. Towering among them, to his surprise, was Willem of Dole, dressed in an undistinguished-looking linen tunic—but still damnably young and handsome. He looked by far the most exhausted of the lot. Marcus dismounted and led his mare around to where the trainees watered their mounts at the southern end of the hollow. He signaled to a blond youth with bad skin, whom he thought he recognized as Willem's squire, as he was rubbing down the largest of the horses.

"Good day, lad. Can you explain to me why your master is training with the neophytes? I thought he had a little experience under his belt."

Erec smiled smugly. "He has more than a little, sir. The emperor challenged him to a one-on-one joust last week, and he unseated His Majesty three times, so His Majesty asked him to train the royal squires."

"Oh," Marcus said, disappointed. "I thought Richard was training the squires."

Erec beamed confidingly. "No, sir. After the training session, His Majesty set up three rounds—all of them were Willem against one of His Majesty's knights, and Willem disarmed them all. He just now defeated Richard of Mainz."

"Oh," Marcus said again. Something the size of an olive pit felt like it was digging at his inner organs. "That's impressive."

"Yes! Today was the first time His Majesty came to view the training, but I think he'll make a routine of it now. Even the ladies have come." He giggled. "Willem needs a patroness, and all the ladies fancy him, but he has no idea how to handle them, poor stupid ass."

Marcus had followed his gesture toward the pavilion but turned back now to sternly admonish Erec. "That is no way to speak about your master."

Erec made a dismissive, confident gesture. "He's my cousin and boon companion. His sister and I were suckled by the same nurse."

Marcus did not have time to work out why this was bad news, but instinctively he knew it was. "He has a sister?"

Erec whistled under his breath. "Damn all laws against consanguinity, yes, he has a sister. Prettier than any lady up on that pavilion now too. In fact"—he lowered his voice, feeling important to be sharing this with the only person at Koenigsbourg who didn't know it yet—"it's a bit of an open secret now. If Willem makes a good showing in the tourney, Konrad is going to make him a member of the court, and send for Lienor with matrimonial intentions." Marcus started violently, but Erec didn't notice. "Can you imagine that, sir? Going from poor obscure border-knight to the king's legal brother in the course of a month? That will certainly win him an heiress or two!" He shook his head. "I envy him, but I could not wish it of a better fellow. Except myself of course. Excuse me, sir." He turned back to finish dealing with Atlas.

Desperately, Marcus scanned the people milling about on the dais. He saw Konrad—and much worse than that, he saw Alphonse of Burgundy. Did Alphonse know of the handsome young bachelor's probable ascension? Panicked, Marcus found a groom and handed off his horse, then ran as quickly as his knee would allow him toward the viewing stand.

It was still hot and bright. Willem was exhausted, sore, red-faced from exertion and dripping sweat, but he was very pleased with how the day had gone. There was hardly a better way for him to polish his own skills than to lead these earnest young men through their daily drills and exercises—but the duels with Konrad's three best knights, well, he had not been expecting those, and he certainly had not expected to win the lot. He'd assumed that in the great court, his abilities would count as little; happily, he was wrong. It was an immensely pleasant surprise. And it was a huge relief to be in his own element, away from the peculiar politics that plagued the castle, even away from Jouglet's hearty but relentless presence. He could lose himself all afternoon in the minstrel's songs or stories—the fellow had a beautiful voice, certainly—but being with the squires and knights *accomplished* something; it was brisk, invigorating, useful. And here, at least, he was master. There were few opportunities for him to be in Jouglet's presence without feeling dependent, and he relished the chance to excel on his own.

As he headed up the hill toward the covered dais to greet Konrad, he saw the minstrel rushing down toward him. "Wonderful work! I think I'm beginning to understand how it all works. You clobbered Gerhard of Metz, my friend—that popinjay thought he would disarm you in a moment! You showed him what's what!" With an exaggerated lack of coordination, Jouglet tried to repeat the gesture that had knocked Gerhard down.

Willem smiled self-deprecatingly and patted Jouglet's arm. "Thank you. You could have watched from the bench, you know, gotten a closer look."

"Brother Paul was insinuating that I was *too* interested in getting a closer look, and anyhow I wanted to hear what the nobles were saying about you," Jouglet said confidingly, slipping an arm across

Willem's sweaty shoulder. "I made sure they were saying all the right things."

The knight's humor dropped a little and he pushed Jouglet's arm away. "It is not necessary that you spend all your energy inventing my success. I am capable of achieving some of it on my own."

To his surprise, Jouglet, rather than retorting, made a gesture of retreat. "You're absolutely right. I get carried away by my enthusiasm; it's an occupational hazard. You don't need me. I'll leave you."

Willem glanced up at the viewing platform and saw with a wave of alarm that four or five young females were assembled there waiting for him, almost visibly salivating. "No," he said, reaching out to grab his friend's elbow. "No, please help me deal with those . . . people."

Jouglet squinted, scanning the female ensemble with a seasoned eye. "An excellent smattering, perhaps you can find yourself a lady in that group. I think all of them are married. That's the ideal scenario, you know. It only counts as courtly love when there's an obstacle of some sort or another." A dramatic sigh. "As between myself and your fair sister. I'll get them in the mood for you." The minstrel chuckled and darted ahead of him up the hill, to resume flirting, harmless and impudent, with all the silk-draped married ladies. Willem followed more slowly, tired. He stretched his neck to release a knot in his right shoulder.

When he reached the edge of the dais, before he had to deal with the ladies, he was approached at once by the Count of Burgundy, who grabbed his hand with such enthusiasm he almost cried aloud with alarm. The count literally pulled him onto the platform to stand beside him. "My boy, that was brilliant. You've done our Burgundy proud," he gushed loudly, in a familiar tone as if they were old friends. This was the second day of such sudden, extreme, and forced behavior; Willem detested it. When he said nothing in response, the count lowered his voice slightly and added, sycophantically, "There's a rumor you'll be commanding the royal troops in the tournament."

Willem looked uncomfortable. "Some of His Majesty's men have flattered me by asking to ride on my team, but it would be hubris to say I am leading the royal troops when I'm not royal myself."

"But you might be soon, I hear," Alphonse said with that same grating chumminess. "Or at least brother to it—practically the same thing."

Willem was taken aback. "That is also just rumor," he said, reddening. "I would not stake my sister's future on my own luck in war sports—and I doubt His Majesty would stake his Empire's future on it either."

"Then the rumor is not well founded?" said a voice behind him. Willem turned to see Konrad's steward, the tall, good-looking fellow named Marcus, who had disappeared after Willem's first night at the castle. His black tunic was dusty, and his hair windswept; his narrow face was sunburned and expressionless.

"There is good reason to believe the rumor," Alphonse said, not looking at Marcus but beaming at Willem. "You are a fine fighter, and I wish you the best of luck at tourney, and great happiness for both you and your sister." He bowed—obsequiously low—and strode off.

Marcus and Willem stared after him. "I don't trust that man," Willem confided quietly. Marcus nodded in miserable agreement, and Willem amended, "And I do not understand him."

Marcus sighed, pained. "I do," he said and walked away.

7

Fabliau

[a comic tale in verse, tending toward the bawdy or obscene]

8, 9, 10 July

The hundred pounds from Konrad had been spent with extravagant frivolity, under Jouglet's expert tutelage, with at least a few
pennies going to every trade—and almost every individual trades-
man—in the town.

And then, the day after Marcus's return, in the undertow of a
gentle wave of summer rain, when Willem was broke again (but the
owner of many dozens of tunics, pins, boots, wooden chests, leather
satchels, spoons, capes, rosaries and sacred relics, spices, astrological
charts, cooking pots, fabrics, musical instruments he could not play,
jewelry, and even a few pieces of real paper) the merchant from
Montbéliard arrived with an entire caravan of jousting gear for
Willem to take on credit. This merchant had been his supplier
since Willem was belted and already had pennants in the knight's

red-and-blue. There were lances, shields, trappings for the horses, overtunics, and pennants and flags of all sorts. Standing in the warm drizzle, Willem tried not to think about the debt he was running up as he outfitted not only himself but also Erec and both his page boys entirely. The other knights—the twenty who had shown up from Burgundy and the thirty of Konrad's own who had asked to fight under him—would content themselves with pennants of his colors to crown their own particular garb. He thanked the merchant heartily and offered to put him up at the inn, where Jouglet brokered a betrothal between the visiting merchant and Musette, the innkeeper's daughter.

"You are in everybody's business, boy," Willem laughed helplessly, listening to the congratulatory hoopla down in the hall. Cooling gusts danced from one window across the room to the other. The sky was the color of grey glass.

"And everybody benefits," said Jouglet agreeably. "Come, put on your expensive new dress tunic with the Ypres wool. Konrad wants you supping at the castle again tonight."

The lance merchant had arrived in an abrupt and endless current of traffic that presaged the tournament. Despite the intermittent drizzle, huge crowds of knights rode into Sudaustat with all their squires and servants, first filling the inns and every other room that could be let out, then setting up camps outside the town walls; common women from around the area had flocked here seeking temporary occupation, and found themselves duly occupied. Farmers and peddlers crowded the streets in a potpourri of languages and dialects, and from prime until nones, sold everything from false souvenirs ("a tooth knocked out of a knight's head by Michel of Harnes at the tournament in Flanders!") to equally false miracles ("the holy elixir Willem of Dole drank to crush his enemies on Crusade!"). Konrad had a clever tax for all of them: in exchange for a required donation in their own local currency, each and every visitor was given a handsome badge with the imperial insignia. They were free to take it home with them to show their neighbors. And anyone who had come from Rome was given two badges for the price of one, should they choose to be generous and give one to His Holiness.

Two mornings before the tournament, Konrad gave the whole court leisure to peruse the phantasmagoria. Willem, heading back to the inn from mass at St. Foy's, noticed Jouglet in a crowd near the silversmith's, buying something small from a scurrilous-looking peddler apothecary. He was about to cross the square to ask the minstrel what it was when he was surprised by a familiar voice at his side, muttering with fond amusement, "So *that's* where he gets it." Willem turned to see the messenger, Nicholas, gazing likewise toward Jouglet's surreptitious purchase.

"Gets what?" Willem demanded.

Nicholas started but recovered at once and bowed smoothly. "Good morning, sir." He shrugged one shoulder in Jouglet's direction. "I was referring to the concoction Jouglet guards so jealously in his wallet."

"What is it, then?" Willem asked. Other than Konrad's one teasing comment, Willem had never heard anyone refer to it, but he had always noticed that the minstrel was protective of that little leather belt-pouch.

"It's to keep his singing voice light," Nicholas explained with a knowing smile. "Or so they say."

The messenger slipped away toward the Street of the Bakers, and Willem was about to ask Jouglet directly, but when he turned back toward the apothecary's cart, the musician had already disappeared. Almost at once, Willem heard the familiar husky tenor singing out the praises of Willem of Dole from the direction of the ironworks, and he hurried away through the green market.

Besides the dubious-looking peddlers, there were musicians, seers, players, acrobats, and jugglers of all abilities literally lining the streets from gate to gate, and well out the northern gate up toward the castle too. And of course there were abbots and crazed religious mendicants pushing through all the crowded areas, warning everyone at the top of their voices that perdition was upon them. Stews and bathhouses in the poorer part of town overflowed from a surfeit of bodies. The sewers grew fouler. The price of victuals tripled each day, even at the inn where Willem was staying; he was grateful that Konrad had taken to inviting him to dine at the castle so regularly. It was worth the climb.

Jouglet was trumpeting the name and deeds of the knight from Dole around the crowded town and out into the camps, as well as endlessly arranging opportunities for Willem to meet attractive young ladies attached to the households of visiting knights and lords. Within a single afternoon, Willem proved himself thrice over a phenomenal failure at flirtation, despite his best attempts; this in no way dampened Jouglet's attempts to find him someone rich and pretty ("Not to marry, you understand," Jouglet assured him confidingly. "Merely to worship, so that when I and all the others immortalize you in song, you appear a proper figure of chivalry"). The minstrel also dictated the knight's schedule, insisting that in these final two days of preparation, his every move somehow be public knowledge. An only-half-jesting rivalry had by now developed between the two: wherever they went, they overheard spontaneous commendations about the knight from Dole, which proved to Willem that Jouglet's trumpeting efforts were unnecessary, while proving to Jouglet that those same efforts were working very well.

The morning before the tournament, however, a complication of such unrestrained trumpeting revealed itself.

Fog mated grudgingly with sun to produce a morning of punishing humidity. Konrad had come to watch the squires at training. The royal retinue was enormous now, filled with many of Konrad's cronies who were in town for the tournament, all of them sporting the imperial imagery wherever they went. Nicholas the messenger had slipped off the crowded viewing platform and closer to the training area to sit on the ground beside his friend in banter, Jouglet. The two of them whispered archly obscene witticisms about nearly every adolescent on the field, and laughed so hard together that they were shushed several times by Willem and then by Konrad himself. After the royal rebuke, they grinned at each other in superior silence until Jouglet turned to look back onto the training field.

After a considered moment, Nicholas reached over to touch Jouglet's arm lightly, a subtle, experimental gesture of a sort to which the attractive young minstrel was unhappily accustomed. But never before from Nicholas.

Startled, Jouglet glanced sharply at the messenger. "Nicholas . . ."

Nicholas withdrew his hand and rested it innocuously on the dry reddish soil. "My mistake," he said smoothly and returned his attention immediately to the training session.

Jouglet, too taken aback to let it rest, said firmly, with a hint of alarm, "Surely you know that I am not—"

"I know that you *were* not," Nicholas corrected. "I thought I'd sensed a change of tune. Of late."

Jouglet eyed him uncertainly. "My interest in the ladies is unchanged."

"It's your interest in the gentlemen that seems to have changed."

"*What*? What would make you think . . . ?"

"*That*, perhaps," Nicholas answered, gesturing with a nod toward Willem on the training field, shirtless and sweating handsomely in the heat.

Jouglet gaped a moment before blurting out, almost angrily, "That's ridiculous!"

Nicholas shrugged, eyes still on the field. "If you insist. But I've never seen you champion any project with such *breathless* enthusiasm as you champion this one. I think you may be falling for your own hyperbole."

Jouglet laughed the signature Jouglet laugh, head thrown back, making a hooting sound. "It's not hyperbole, and I'm not falling for it." Then, sobering a little, conspiratorially: "I have a weakness for Lienor, I confess."

Nicholas nodded, smiling. "Yes, I saw your old fiddle in her chamber when I was there. I wondered if there was a story."

"No story. I am only saying that if I ever act oddly toward *him*, it is probably because at that moment he is somehow reminding me of *her*."

"Oh, that must be it," Nicholas said with a sardonic smile. He sat up and elegantly dusted the dirt off his hands. "His brawny sun-burned back must remind you of *her* brawny sunburned back. Obviously."

"Don't be an ass." Jouglet frowned. "Life is full of young men I openly admire, but with whom I have entirely innocent friendships." An almost taunting pause. "You, for example."

"Me?" With ironic detachment, Nicholas repeated the suggestive gesture that had spawned the conversation. "Not me, Jouglet."

"I was referring to *my* regard for the young men," Jouglet answered defensively, almost flustered, rubbing one foot back and forth across the dry ground in a fidget.

"Ah," said Nicholas smartly. "But as I have just demonstrated, one must take into account *their* regard for *you* as well."

After a confused beat, Jouglet laughed uncomfortably. "What, *Willem*? Are you crazy? We scheme daily about getting him a lady!"

With a smug, triumphant little smile, Nicholas whispered, "Yet he spends more time scheming with you than he does acting on the scheming with any ladies. If that keeps up much longer, do you think nobody else will notice?" He turned his head casually in the direction of the papal nuncio.

Jouglet looked flabbergasted, then alarmed. "Point taken," the musician said quietly. "Thank you."

Marcus had taken to attending the training sessions by his master's side whenever he could spare the time. He would usually end up watching the Count of Burgundy watch Willem of Dole, which always threatened to bring on a mania of fear: he'd tormented himself with pornographically detailed images of Willem laying Imogen down upon a wedding bed, and then discovering he was not the first to touch her.

But now it was Paul who caught his attention: the clerical gaze had been trained on Jouglet and Nicholas whispering conspiratorially together down the slope. Marcus glanced automatically at Konrad for guidance. The papal nuncio was eternally looking for cracks in the moral armor of the court. Both Marcus and Konrad knew Nicholas was vulnerable; after a recent severe warning, he'd learned to be more discreet, but sometimes—as now—he forgot himself.

Konrad grimaced. "Could you for just one afternoon *enjoy* yourself?" he huffed to his brother without looking at him, and fingered his gold-embroidered beard with his jewel-encrusted fingers.

"I always enjoy myself, brother," Paul said pleasantly.

"Then be original at least," Konrad said in a tired voice. "Try incest or bestiality or witchcraft for a change. Anyhow it's one-sided and has been for years. You've discovered nothing more dastardly than unrequited Bulgarian love amidst my minions. Very dull stuff, Paul."

Paul looked happily, smugly unconvinced. Konrad glanced quickly at his steward, and Marcus headed down the slope at once with a chastisement and some invented business that would take

Nicholas back up to the castle, or at least away from Jouglet's laughter and Paul's scrutiny.

That night, the eve of the tournament, Erec went to Vespers, a mock-tourney for squires and younger knights to try their skills in the field. Willem had intended a private vigil, as he always did before a tournament, but when Konrad invited him to dine in his rooms, he did not dare refuse. He left his horse and weapons down at the gate and was escorted to join His Majesty in the dayroom, surrounded by Konrad's menagerie of hawk and hounds. Jouglet, perched as always on the window seat, played the fiddle for them. They spoke briefly of the tournament, and Konrad finally made official the rumor that Willem had been deflecting for days.

"If you do as well tomorrow as I have every reason to suspect you will, I shall make you one of my own knights," the emperor began.

Willem looked pleased and tucked his chin like a shy boy. "Your Majesty honors me beyond my wildest dreams," he said.

"But more than that," Konrad went on, smiling, "I would make you my own *brother*. This remarkable sister of yours I hear about—for whom are you saving her?"

Willem swallowed. He admired Konrad's character generally, but he heartily wished he had even once seen His Majesty treat any woman in his court with anything approaching actual respect. "For someone who would treasure her as she deserves to be treasured," he said carefully.

Konrad smiled with a self-deprecating smugness and stroked his bloodhound's head. "I have never met a woman who deserved my treasuring, but if her spirit is anything like yours, she would be counted among my dearest. I would endeavor to learn to treasure her. Will that suffice, my friend? Given, of course, that my Assembly of Lords will agree?"

The knight glanced at Jouglet on the window seat, fiddle on lap. Over the last few days, as Jouglet had seen to it that the "open secret" about Lienor became more open and less secret, Willem had come to understand that this was the pinnacle of the entire scheme: Jouglet wanted Lienor at the royal court, to flirt with her at least, possibly to seduce her, and Willem's prowess was the only way to get her here. For a brief moment he was enraged, then admitted to himself that he had benefited enormously from being played as pawn. But he felt a passing resentment that Lienor, not himself, was Jouglet's true pre-occupation.

Nearly imperceptibly, Jouglet nodded from the window seat, face expressionless but eyes bright.

"Yes, sire," Willem said quietly. He was hardly in a position to refuse his emperor. "I would be honored, humbled and . . ."—a long pause as he sought the proper word—". . . and speechless to give you my sister's hand, should you ever choose to ask for it." Konrad looked satisfied. Willem hesitated, then asked, "But are you . . . are you not risking the church's censure in this choice, milord? Your brother the cardinal seems very invested in brokering a marriage between yourself and the heiress of Besançon. Surely the pope's blessing of your marriage is—"

"The pope! I don't need the accursed pope!" Konrad growled, almost hitting the bloodhound as he stroked it. "The empire is already intrinsically accounted holy, its very *title* proves it. The blessing of the pope would be . . . redundant."

He released his company early, aware of how important sleep would be that night for each of them. It had become routine by now, even when Willem did not issue an invitation, for Jouglet to ride behind him on Atlas back down to the inn. This evening there was dancing in the courtyard to celebrate Musette's engagement to the merchant from Montbéliard. Jouglet insisted that they dance a few rounds with all the carousers, and heartily made all the expected and unoriginal quips about the satisfaction Musette could expect to have with her man of great lances. A garish red and green cloak Konrad had given Jouglet, in honor of tomorrow's tournament, earned many compliments, and Jouglet flung it away to somebody in the crowd, crying, "I'm sure Willem of Dole will give me something even more wonderful before I leave tonight."

Willem managed to retire to his room shortly before the high-summer dusk, both flattered and exasperated that Jouglet would not leave his side. "Before I trudge back up the mountainside, show me what you're wearing tomorrow, won't you?" demanded the minstrel cheerfully. "Let's see how quickly I can compose a song about it, maybe I'll even sing it down there for them tonight and earn an extra penny or two."

"You'll see me in full gear tomorrow," Willem said with a yawn. "I'm exhausted. If you don't mind I'll just ready for bed and perhaps we'll have a quick flagon before you go. No more singing tonight."

"Very well," Jouglet said with a characteristic shrug. "I need to save my voice anyhow. I'll be busy tomorrow making up ditties praising your victories in front of all the ladies."

"What am I to reward you for that?" Willem asked and pulled off his tunic. His shirt clung to it and came off too, leaving him bare-chested in the lamplight.

"Nothing, of course," Jouglet said. "It's my duty as your friend. Anyhow, it's a pleasure. And in all seriousness, Willem—by this time tomorrow I think we'll have secured the perfect patroness for you."

For a man who knew what his strengths were, Willem had a smile that was disarmingly self-deprecating. "I'm just a landless nobody, Jouglet. And I doubt there was a single lady of the dozen-odd you introduced me to who found my shyness the least bit . . . chivalrous."

"Ach, don't talk like that," Jouglet said, with a dismissive gesture.

"You're better with deeds than words, and what lady doesn't like great deeds? If they want you to be a poet as well, I'll teach you all my arts. But you'll be a great success as you are." As Willem stood in the middle of his room, looking vaguely about for his bed-robe, the minstrel stepped up to him and chummily grabbed his muscled bicep. "After all, it's—"

Jouglet paused, and Willem saw a look on his friend's face that he recognized, found innately complimentary, but still was shocked to see there: the pleased and hungry flash of smile that the Widow Sunia made when first she'd touched his body. If Jouglet had made the face and then exaggerated it, the moment could have been lightly dismissed. But Jouglet, having involuntarily smiled, turned scarlet and released his arm abruptly, as if physically shocked. The two of them exchanged accidental, unnerved glances, and Willem stepped away.

"As I meant to say—" Jouglet tried again after a moment, unsteadily and too loudly, then with exaggerated machismo reached again for Willem's arm. Willem pulled it out of reach. But he really only wanted Jouglet to make a clever joke of it.

Jouglet did not make a clever joke of it. In fact, Jouglet—still scarlet—looked as surprised as Willem felt, and stared at the knight's bulky arm as if it were some mythical beast.

"Why don't you go now," Willem said. "It's late. I'll see you tomorrow morning." He disentangled his shirt from his tunic and pulled it back on, then with sudden busyness began to look around the chamber for his robe. He threw open a chest and rummaged roughly through its contents.

Jouglet coughed uncomfortably. "Why are you throwing me out?"

Willem continued to rummage without answering, and with exasperation slammed shut the chest. "Where is my robe?"

"It's here on your bed," Jouglet said and took a step toward it.

"Stay away from my bed," Willem warned.

"You're being absurd," Jouglet said, sounding more nervous than Jouglet had ever sounded before. "I am not leaving until you calm down."

Willem turned, glaring to hide his discomfort, and ordered, "Calm me down, then. Give me reason to be calm." He felt his teeth gritting as he added, "Tell me what Brother Paul would say if he were here." Again all he wanted was to hear Jouglet make light of it; again, Jouglet looked too spooked to think of levity.

As if the heavens were looking out for their friendship, they were at that moment interrupted by a clamor outside. Young Erec threw open the door and, his face flushed with wine and the exertions of the Vesper practice, cried out joyfully, "I've just learned where the common women are! Want to come along?"

"Yes," they both said, very quickly and too loud.

It was a quarter-mile's walk to the town's west gate, through streets increasingly greased with dank muck, untended sewers full of rotting offal, and the stench of tanners' vats. It was not really dark enough yet for lamps, but Willem was holding one because that gave him something to do. He was silent, letting Erec's drunken chatter and Jouglet's occasional darting quip fill the air. After several streets, the putrid odors of the vats finally softened to the buttery smell of tanned leather in the heart of the leatherworkers' quarter. Erec regaled them with a detailed history of his whoring but admitted with enthusiasm that he'd never been to an actual lair of sin like this; the common women he knew were itinerant and solitary. Jouglet assured him that was the general case, that they were lucky to be in Sudaustat, which provided more progressive attitudes and creature comforts for the lecherous—especially when a tournament was in town.

They neared the western wall. This portal got little direct traffic from the main trade route running up and down the Rhine valley, and was therefore considered the undesirable side of town. Clustered between open garden plots, garbage pits, and a one-room lepers' hostel were the communities that good Christian society could not survive without but did not want to have to acknowledge: the Jews, the midwives and herbalists, and, of course, the prostitutes. It was strangely lively for so late in the day, and figures of various races and ages were squatting in their open doorways, gossiping about tomorrow's tournament, listening to the doves' and cuckoos' insistent evening lullaby as the loud unmusical swallows finally began to quiet. Without exception the people in the streets and doorways greeted Jouglet with familiar warmth.

"You truly go to the common women?" Erec asked in slight disbelief.

"Why wouldn't I?" Jouglet answered with an unwonted hint of defensiveness, stepping over a pothole filled with rusty-looking water. "I'm young and I've got a healthy appetite, but I can't *really* lay a hand on the ladies of the court." And adding with a slight swagger: "I've built a bit of a reputation for myself with these women."

Erec snickered playfully. "Have you now? I hope I don't usurp your throne."

"You would be hard-pressed to," Jouglet replied, puffing up. "Watch."

They had reached the place, a small half-timbered building directly next to the western gatehouse. Like many properties, its narrow end opened to the street, and most of it was only on the ground floor. Like most buildings in this part of town, it was drab and rickety-looking—except for a bright scarlet swath of felt covering the door.

"Excellent dye job," Erec said with studied insight. "They must have customers from Flanders."

Willem threw open the door, and the three of them entered.

They found themselves in a small room filled with smoke from a damp central firepit and reeking from the smell of too many unwashed male bodies. There were a lot of young men, some older men, two priests—and a few women of different ages and shapes wearing a variety of worn-looking tunics and kirtles, each sporting a torn strip of scarlet cloth as an armband. A harried-looking silver-haired woman was in charge; she was bustling about the smoky room, selling bread and ale to the waiting men at exorbitant prices. The house was clearly not set up to accommodate this level of business; they had the tournament to thank for that.

"We're here for the women," Erec announced brashly and unnecessarily.

The old woman rushed by them without looking. She began to retort, "Well, you'll just have to wait your—" But then she noticed Jouglet, and paused at once to smile at the trio. "It's His Majesty's fiddler," she said with friendly warmth, and finally looked at Erec—and then, with rather more attention, at Willem, who was one of the largest, most self-conscious men in the crowd. "We'll see to you gentlemen right away, then." Jouglet, feeling Erec's surprise, grinned at him.

They were shepherded through clusters of men who growled resentfully for their having received instant service. They crossed down through the narrow room to a door in the far wall and out into a narrow yard, delineated by the length of the neighboring building on one side, the high town wall to the other, and a hedgelike structure at the far end, on the other side of which—to judge by sounds and smells—lived swine and poultry. A dozen makeshift canvas structures in two long lines took up most of the space, each no bigger than a soldier's sleeping tent and each being used, but not for sleeping; at the end near the hedge, farthest from the house wall, was a small willow lean-to with a hole in the roof that anemically hiccuped smoke into the evening air. They were still adjusting their eyes, and

Erec was trying not to giggle about the sound effects from the tents, when three cheerful voices called out from the darkness, "Jouglet! Hello duck! Jouglet, over here!"

In response to Erec's startled expression, the minstrel made a gesture of exaggerated modesty and ushered the two young Burgundians toward the voices. Clustered halfway down the right line of tents, three tired women in colorless loose tunics, red armbands, and loosed hair immediately rose to their bare feet.

"My favorite meretrices! Ladies," the jongleur announced. "Be good to my friends this evening. This is Erec, he's young and fresh, he'll probably take some energy. This is Willem, and he's such a good man I don't know what to say about him, but I'm sure he'll be a handful. Probably two handfuls, no doubt with fingers spread. He's supposed to be holding vigil for the tourney tomorrow, but he's practically bursting out of his breeches." A dramatic pause. "And then there's me, of course, my ducklings."

"I'm for you, Jouglet," said the tallest of the three immediately, elbowing her companions back. She had a trace of a French accent. Her tunic needed mending, and her pretty heart-shaped face could have done with a wash, but she had a lovely smile despite her obvious exhaustion, and she smiled at the cousins long enough to wring a look of acute appreciation from them. Then she brushed past them to put a teasing hand on Jouglet's arm. "It's my turn for the hut," she said in a low voice. "Come with me, my little stallion."

"The fair Jeannette. Marthe and Constance are also delectable," Jouglet assured Erec, gently triumphant. "These are the three resident whores of Sudaustat, I'll have you know; all the rest are just vagabonds here for the tournament. We are getting genuine local craftmanship." The paired couple stepped around the second row of tents toward the stick lean-to, arm in arm. Jouglet's attention was entirely on Jeannette as they walked, smoothing her tousled hair with familiar affection, then stealing a kiss on her neck; she gave a sleepy-sounding, comfortable chuckle of pleasure. "Tell me, duckling," the cousins heard Jouglet begin, "what have you been about since His Majesty's summer retreat?"

Erec and Willem exchanged astonished looks.

"Don't tell Lienor," muttered Willem.

"Great gifts come in small parcels," said Marthe, the dark-haired one, knowingly. Then, with a wink at Willem, she added at once, "But myself, I like big parcels even more." She ran a finger along the cragged length of his nose, which sent a violent shiver down his spine. She gestured to the tiny, damp tent before them. "Join me in here."

When Jouglet and Jeannette were inside, and the canvas flap pulled down, she gave the minstrel a friendly kiss on the cheek and flopped down onto the hard rush mat. "Thank God you're here," she said. "It's been a hell of a week, all these crazed fellows in town for the tournament. My fruit can't stand much more plucking."

Jouglet squatted on the earth by the small fire pit, reaching toward the weak flames to soak up the warmth. "This smells like new wood."

Jeannette nodded and poked at the lean-to wall, yawning. "It is. The cardinal made his rounds as the crowds were coming in, and tore us down again. Those canvas things in the yard? They can fold up in less time than it takes to walk through the hall. Clever, that."

"I'll get Konrad to trim Paul's claws. What shall it be, now to dawn?"

"The whole night!" Jeannette's face lit up. "Can you afford that, duck?"

A jeweled bracelet magically appeared in Jouglet's hand and quickly passed over the fire pit. Jeannette cooed with appreciation.

"The rest of the night," Jeannette said, as if it were treasure. "I can actually sleep! Will I have been ravished ferociously or made tender, expert love to?"

"I think we must go for the ravishment this time," Jouglet said, poking at the smoking embers with a stick that lay nearby. "I stuck my foot in it tonight."

Jeannette, sprawled comfortably on the mat, and already half-asleep, asked, "What did you do?"

There was a long pause.

"Jouglet, tell me what you did or I will never fall asleep."

"The bigger of the two fellows I brought in with me," Jouglet finally began, still staring into the wan fire and sounding aggravated.

"Oh, he's a looker!" Jeannette grinned. "And he looks like an actual gentleman. When I'm not so exhausted I hope he comes back."

"I don't think whoring is a common hobby for him."

"A pity. What about him?"

Another pause. "There was a confused moment between us that . . . made him wary." The tenor voice was peevish.

Jeannette burst into laughter. "Oh, a *confused moment*! How did you survive?" But then she turned serious, and said with sympathy, "Jouglet, you idiot. How did you cover?"

"I brought him here!" Jouglet retorted, with a broad gesture toward the canvas door flap.

"Oh, duck, that's no solution," Jeannette said from the mat. "That only distracts him for the nonce—"

"I know that!" Jouglet snapped, scowling at the smoking flames.

"And you've got Paul at court now. He must be breathing down your neck." Jeannette's attitude was less compassionate than perversely entertained. "What are you going to do?"

An exasperated sigh. "I don't *know*."

"Well let me know when you do," Jeannette said. "I can't afford to lose my favorite customer to other . . . inclinations."

"Take a nap and leave me alone," Jouglet said in a surly tone.

"I will. Have fun ravishing me." Jeannette smiled. "If you had let me know you were coming I could have tried to round up someone more to your taste."

Jouglet scowled at her, looking almost alarmed. "You are *no* help to me with that kind of humor, woman. I'm on very thin ice these days—Nicholas actually propositioned me—"

"Nicholas is very attractive!" Jeannette giggled, punchy from exhaustion and amusement. "You've said so yourself."

"That's not the point! Paul and Konrad saw us—and that is not funny, Jeannette, don't laugh! Don't you know Nicholas was a fledgling courtier until Konrad made him a messenger to keep him away, to hide his lack of discretion? If that's what he did to a prince's son, what do you think he'd do to a vagabond minstrel?"

"Poor Jouglet, condemned to be purer than a monk." Jeannette laughed, not without sympathy, and half a breath later was asleep.

8

Panegyric

[a poem in praise of great deeds]

11 July

The next morning, Willem and Erec woke before dawn and went down to the taper-lit mass, surrounded by hordes of fellow knights and squires. This church, recently completed, had two grand towers and a magnificently high groin-arched ceiling. It smelled, reassuringly, of religion—even the omnipresent odor of the weekly fish market, which took place directly outside the high double-arched doors four days a week, could not cut through the sharp warmth of the frankincense.

Most unexpectedly, Paul officiated. He was there to preach hotly against the tournament, threatening all of the participants, down to the squires and heralds, with excommunication and worse. Willem was almost ill over this—until Erec returned from gossiping with other squires, and brought the assurance that Paul did this whenever he found himself within twenty miles of a tournament. No knight had actually ever been punished for it. "The consensus is that one of the best things about being in the tourney is a whole day spent away from the cardinal," Erec concluded, almost shouting it into his cousin's ear to be heard over the echoing drone of the church's organistrum.

Willem took time after the service for private reflection, at the back of the church, and begged blessings from the quartet of military saints he liked to imagine watching over him: George, Theodore, Mercurius, and Martin.

Once back in the straw-banked courtyard of the inn, Erec and the page boys reverently strapped Willem into his padding and chain mail. When he was finally mounted, Willem led the way out the gate, his squires on foot to either side of Atlas. Erec had the honor of carrying Willem's lance and shield. The streets were already so crowded that Konrad's castle guards came down into town and—to the townspeople's annoyance—closed the gates to all but the tourney parties. Not to be deprived of the thrill of a parade, all the merchants and artisans with houses giving onto the wider streets and market squares threw open their doors to anyone who wanted a view, and all the windows and roofs were crowded with cheering spectators, hurling flowers and streamers of tied-together colored rags, and banging makeshift percussive inventions that would have made less-seasoned mounts throw their riders.

Even with only tournament traffic the narrow streets were jammed. Willem and Erec moved slowly north to the green market, drawn by the relentless noise of pipe and tabor emanating from the square. They were surprised to find the emperor's enormous riding party waiting directly opposite them in the marketplace. This was utterly gratuitous of Konrad, who could have more easily and more safely reached the tourney field without going through town at all. He was surrounded by anxious bodyguards, who eyed the gawking, adoring townsfolk as if they might be insurrectionists. The royal heralds held aloft only pennants of the family crest, gold with a black lion rampant; Willem wondered where the imperial pennant was.

Konrad hailed Willem. Surprised, Willem raised his hand to return the greeting from a distance, but Konrad shook his head and beckoned broadly, demonstratively, for him to join them. Little *oooo*'s of intrigue and respect went up from all the surrounding windows and rooftops. Willem had never felt so absurdly on display.

"Come to me," Konrad said, with an outstretched arm draped in vermillion and gold. As other riders and their footservants scrambled to get out of the way, the two men rode toward each other and met near the central well, where two dozen village urchins had perched precariously to watch the terrifying knights parading past. Willem, bowing his neck, brought Atlas directly up alongside Konrad's horse, head to tail; Konrad dropped his reins and threw both arms around the knight, embracing him. A number of horses around the square, responding to their highborn riders' tensing with envy, whinnied, fidgeted, even bit one another. But the commoners were all delighted and applauded, anticipating some great honor. Willem looked flushed. "You will use this today," Konrad said, and gestured to Boidon. Boidon handed something made of thick fabric up to Konrad, who unfolded it and held it up for all the gawkers to see.

It was a golden banner emblazoned with a black eagle.

Willem gasped in astonishment and realized he could not possibly decline the honor of bearing the imperial standard, however staggering it was, in front of so many of His Majesty's subjects.

"Sire," he said hoarsely, receiving it, "I shall strive to be worthy of it."

Konrad turned his horse about and they all rode together out of the northern gate, Willem's small party subsumed into the emperor's large one. Jouglet was riding behind Marcus, wearing a new extravagant mantle from Konrad (this one nearly rainbow-colored), and deftly avoided greeting Willem. Willem had not spoken a word to either of his companions when they returned from the whores last night, and he had not invited Jouglet back to the inn; the minstrel was keeping a respectful distance but did exchange hearty good mornings with Erec. Otherwise, Jouglet seemed content to jabber on to Nicholas.

Marcus tried to hide his dismay at Alphonse's behavior: the count did not take his eyes off Willem once. He nearly rode into a linden branch as they left the town walls for the tourney field. It was as if he were trying to ensnare the young knight with his eyes.

Over the past week, Willem had examined the tourney field in detail, though *field* was hardly the word for this broad swath of land between the town, the foot of the castle-mount, and the fief of Orschwiller. Most of it lay wide open, long fallow; parts were wooded, especially up on the slope. At an elevated spot in the center rose the open-sided royal pavilion, built to hold several dozen spectators. Three or four smaller platforms lined the edges of the fighting area, and one far boundary was the town wall itself, atop and below which hundreds of townspeople, villagers, and serfs had gathered to watch.

The day continued overcast and cool. Summer saw few tournaments because of the heat, but Konrad insisted annually on sponsoring royal games. He liked anything that threatened the power of his higher aristocracy, and promoting the lower aristocracy—the knights— did that stylishly, and much to the delight of the rabble.

Most of Konrad's knights would fight under Willem. A leader in a tourney had to be able not only to fight one-on-one, but also to plan attacks for many riders altogether, making the most of opportunities to take down opponents. This was a contest for gain, for ransom and booty—despite his general idealism about the honor of knighthood, Willem had always been clear that the purpose of a tourney was to get a lot of money or its equivalent.

The tourney was a huge one—Marcus estimated there would be five hundred knights here. It took a very long time, but by late morning the logistical sorting out had been taken care of, knights had hailed and greeted one another, shown off their newest lances and shields and battle scars and lovers' kerchiefs, expressed amazement at how friends' squires had shot up. Those not yet in arms finished preparation. The countryside resembled a military encampment, save for the incongruously cheerful atmosphere. The breezy morning wore on cool and fresh, the sun just hidden behind a gauze of clouds.

The steward, as Konrad's representative, had established teams. To begin with, he adhered to tradition and honored preexisting loyalties, so Willem had his men from his own county and many from Konrad's court, for a total of fifty riders. He was partnered with a dozen other knights leading groups from Swabia, Hainaut, and Lorraine. His was one of three teams, grouped by geography: the Empire (which Willem found himself heading), Flanders to the northwest of the Empire, and France. Marcus directed them to stations around the field, and there ensued a protracted period of hurrying about to place everybody's squires and servants in the correct safe areas. During this shuffle, the town gate reopened, and commoners of all shapes and sizes, serfs to wealthy burghers, hurried to climb trees and outbuildings, crowding into the few spaces left open to them. A mass of people two paces deep surrounded Konrad's viewing pavilion, shrewdly assuming the fighting would come near, but not too near, the emperor.

Konrad's senior herald blew a trumpet and another flashed a flag at His Majesty's wave. For a fraction of a breath nothing happened, then the three groups, hooves thudding in a canter, advanced on the center of the broad, green space. All of them slowed. The lord of Mauléon cried out a challenge to Richard of Mainz; the two seasoned champions ran at each other, ashwood lances couched against their shields, and five hundred voices screamed with bloodthirsty exuberance at once. The tournament had begun.

A contingent of knights from Artois and Valecourt challenged Willem's immediate party, and Willem headed toward them over the field grass. Their leader was a man he didn't recognize—a large fellow with an ominous surcoat of black and red. Willem tucked his lance tighter under his right arm and with his left hand reined his horse toward the armored stranger. He felt Atlas pick up speed under him, anticipating the joust.

"Look at Willem, sire!" Jouglet said at the emperor's elbow. "He's taking down his first man!"

"Technically, he's merely *fighting* his first man," Marcus said from the other side of the throne. A pause. Marcus grimaced, tried to make it seem like a grin. "Ah. Now he has taken down his first man." This, he was certain, was the beginning of the end for him.

Unhorsing was easy, dismounting was not, but Willem insisted the felled soldier was his to take alone, and over the din of warfare, he signaled his fellow knights not to assist. He landed on his feet heavily in sixty pounds of chain mail and, grunting, drew his sword and grasped it two-handed, breathing hard. His unhorsed opponent was struggling like an upended insect, trying to get to his feet; Willem was on him in a moment and rested the tip of his sword in the one place the armor left the man most vulnerable—directly at his crotch.

Jouglet watched as Willem helped the vanquished man to rise. Then Willem beckoned Erec and one of his pages out onto the field. Erec took custody of the knight; the younger boy took the horse, a Castilian, and led him after Erec. Jouglet slipped off the dais and skirted skirmishes to reach the retreating boy. "Where are you going with the booty?" the minstrel asked.

Erec gestured to his bruised and limping captive. "Willem wants this fellow to pay ransom directly to the innkeeper, since we're staying there on credit."

Jouglet chuckled approvingly. "And the horse is for his supplier from Montbéliard, isn't it?"

Erec nodded, smiling, and continued toward the edge of the field.

Marcus wanted to freeze time, he wanted to stop everything that was happening, because he felt so foolishly impotent to prevent it. Between sext and nones, Willem fought eight jousts and won seven of them (one for each deadly sin, Marcus thought wretchedly); the eighth was a draw. He had captured men from Perche, Champagne, Amiens, Blois, and Poitou. Marcus realized what the knight was doing: he had challenged or accepted challenges only when he was on the outskirt of the field near the audience pavilion, where the joust could easily be seen by Konrad, without becoming part of the general melee. Jouglet had no doubt coached him to that, Marcus thought bitterly. Willem was bruised, bloodied, clearly exhausted, and his shield was literally falling apart, but he had sent seven horses to the inn for safekeeping—a small Welsh-Arab mix, four Danish stallions, a Hungarian, and the Castilian—and even made a wedding gift of one to the lance merchant, which Jouglet made sure the emperor and everyone within a half-league of the pavilion heard about.

The episode that sealed Marcus's fate—as Marcus would see it, later, with rueful clarity—began with Erec's running onto the field with a new ashwood lance and another shield for his master. Michel of Harnes, the leader of the French team and possibly the greatest living tournament rider after the aging William Marshall of England, challenged Willem. Willem recognized the man's colors; he had fallen to Harnes several times during his first year riding in tourneys. For the first time all day Willem felt serious doubt. He was exhausted and aware that Harnes had not himself been working very hard; his shield was hardly knicked. Waiting until late in the day and then taking down the reigning champion was a strategy for which Harnes was infamous. That accounted for every previous defeat Willem had suffered at his hands.

Willem grabbed the new shield and lance from Erec and spurred Atlas on, fixing the shield in front of him and couching the lance for attack. Harnes had a longer lance, and it struck Willem a fraction of a heartbeat earlier than Willem was expecting. The upper half of his shield took the force and it tilted back harshly toward his body, winding him and almost smashing into the lower part of his helmet—but Harnes's lance snapped in half just as Willem's own lance struck Harnes's shield, struck with such force and so squarely that the famous knight was jolted hard—and then to a cry of amazement from the crowd, he slid backward over his horse's rump, stuck in his highback saddle, looking as if he were yanked from behind. Hundreds of wagging hands pointed excitedly: the jolt had been so hard that both of the saddle's girth-straps had snapped. Harnes smashed to the earth behind his mount, saddle still clenched between his knees, and lay awkwardly prone, too stunned to do anything. Willem, his body moving faster than his mind could account for, wheeled Atlas around and chased after Harnes's horse, which had slowed to remain near its master.

From the pavilion there was hysterical cheering. It had been many years since anyone had taken down the great Michel of Harnes, and Willem's attack had been magnificent, and his catching the horse immediately was a flourish not even Jouglet could have dreamed up. The jongleur was thrilled, leaping about and making sure everybody knew exactly what had happened. The sun itself, Jouglet was later to

report, had peeked out from behind its cooling veil of clouds, to witness the victory. Willem's springing fully formed from Jouglet's head
could not have given the minstrel a more proprietary air of satisfaction.

Willem, on horseback, led the French knight away from the center of the field. Harnes walked heavily, panting under the burden of
his mail, and kept his helmet on so that nobody could see his face in
defeat. On Willem's other flank walked Harnes's horse, a gorgeous
grey Hungarian charger. Everybody knew it was named Vairon; half
a dozen ballads about Harnes had been making the rounds for the
past three or four years, and a famous knight's horse was almost as
famous as the knight himself. Vairon was less winded than Atlas,
and the thousands of eyes upon Willem collectively assumed that he
would take his prizes to a safety section on the edge of the field and
switch mounts.

But Erec realized his cousin was heading instead toward the
royal viewing platform, and rushed to meet him there. He grabbed
the high cantle of Atlas's saddle and pulled himself up onto the
horse's rump, then unlaced the Senlis helmet from Willem's metal
coif so that the knight could speak directly to his emperor. Although
the day was cool, the coif was almost hot to the touch.

Willem was a mess—his face was bruised and scraped all over,
despite the protection of the face guard, and his brown hair was plastered to his forehead and around his face from prodigious sweating
under the leather cap and chain mail coif. The few ladies present
murmured nervously, thrilled and slightly repulsed at the same time.
Willem ignored them. "Sire," he said hoarsely, exhausted, still trying
to catch his breath, and bowed to the throne. He blinked to keep the
sweat from his eyes. Konrad nodded in acknowledgment, smiling
but bemused that he was being drawn into the action. "Sire, I would
be honored if you would accept this splendid charger from me as a
gift to you."

The pavilion exploded with applause, and Konrad sat back, smiling. Marcus, seeing the appraising expression on the Count of Burgundy's face in response to this calculated gallantry, wanted to hit something.

When the noise had died down, the emperor announced, "I accept," and the noise started up again ebulliently, as one of his guards left the platform to retrieve the horse. Konrad held up his hand. "But what about the knight himself? I want to know what ransom you'll extract from this most important hostage."

"Well, sire," Willem said soberly, "I would not know how to put a price on such a knight, and so I think it would be best to simply let him go without ransom."

Jouglet almost fainted with pride. Konrad and the helmeted prisoner both did double takes, and Konrad himself started to applaud, at which point everybody on the platform followed suit, especially Alphonse—and Marcus, for whom it was an onerous effort.

Willem set Michel of Harnes free and finally took a moment to rest in a safety area. Konrad chose that moment to have Marcus summon a clerk to the viewing dais, with parchment and ink.

You are writing my death certificate, Marcus thought, but bowed and sent a page boy into town. "May I ask what Your Majesty feels the need to compose, in the middle of a tourney?" he asked, hoping he was wrong.

"Willem of Dole is champion, and the day is not half over," Konrad answered with satisfaction—as if that in itself were an answer. Then he added, slyly, "I think his sister should be informed of his successes, and the effect they might have upon her circumstances."

There was a pause, and then Marcus blurted out, "If she becomes your empress, sire, then Alphonse will—"

Konrad made an angry, dismissive gesture. "Marcus, it is a *tournament*. Allow me one afternoon's freedom from politics, for the love of Christ. You of all people should know how much I need that."

"Sire, please, as a favor to me—"

Konrad gave him an incredulous glare. "Marcus," he said pointedly. "*Fetch the scribe.* If you won't obey it as a command, then do it as a favor to me, and once you have done so, *then*, not before, I shall entertain the possibility of doing you a favor in return." He looked at Marcus expectantly; the steward stared back, frozen. "Marcus," the emperor repeated sharply. "You are delaying the one moment of genuine unfettered glee I've had in months."

"Sire, please, this is too important—"

"More important than your emperor choosing his bride?" Konrad demanded in a steely voice, more perplexed than angry. "Are you being insolent? Is that how you reward me for my trust in you? By aping my uncle and Paul? I asked for the scribe. Summon the scribe. You should be sharing in my delight, Marcus, not interfering with it."

Once the scribe arrived, Marcus stood expressionless as Konrad—his attention still half on the tournament—dictated a hearty if graceless message to Willem's sister Lienor, telling her that once he had coaxed permission from his Assembly of Lords, he would marry her.

But far worse than Konrad's message was Alphonse's gesturing to the scribe that he wanted to employ him when he was free. Marcus knew what that missive would be too.

Nicholas, to thank Willem for his hospitality in Dole, had brought wine and pastries to the safety area and was feeding the tired knight by hand. He turned this task over to Erec when he was summoned by Konrad—who gave him a scroll to courier to Lienor of Dole in County Burgundy. A smile passed between king and messenger; Nicholas understood what it was he was delivering.

And so, obviously, did Alphonse Count of Burgundy. Marcus

was on the far side of the platform from him, and there were many dozen gaping noble onlookers between them, but he tried desperately to move between the gaggles to get to the count. The count was furtively whispering to the scribe, an old fat man who squinted a lot. As Marcus approached, he saw Alphonse use his signet ring to seal the document—he was only ten feet away when—

"Marcus my friend!" Jouglet crowed gleefully, materializing inconveniently right in front of him. "Please let me honor you by making you the first audience ever for the ballad I've just composed about the gallantry of Willem of Dole! Come over here—" The minstrel took his arm and pulled him to the left, toward a corner where there was little fighting and therefore not as many spectators. "This will be on a par with *Ywein* or the northern sagas, I'm telling you—you know I'm not arrogant about my works, but really this one is incredibly inspired. Did you *see* that? Wasn't it *magnificent*?"

"Not now, Jouglet," Marcus said harshly. "I'm on an errand."

"What errand could be more important on the day of a tournament than celebrating the tournament's great hero?" Jouglet insisted.

"*Jouglet,*" Marcus snapped and shoved the minstrel aside. Jouglet, undeterred, and knowing Marcus had been delayed enough now, instantly turned to an aging duke with the same hearty invitation, and this time was accepted.

The timing was so horrible that Marcus thought the heavens must be mocking him. He finally neared Alphonse just as the scribe was waddling off in the other direction with the letter—the letter which he knew full well was to inform Alphonse's daughter, Imogen, that she would not marry Marcus, Marcus who was a nobody, merely the emperor's steward, from a family that had been serfs three generations earlier and even now was entirely dependent on His Majesty's beneficence for riches and honor. What was the worth of such a match when the emperor was about to have a marriageable brother-in-law who would be a legend by sundown?

He would have to find the scribe and waylay him before the message was even on its way. Then he would fly south to the castle of Oricourt and marry Imogen at once, before the confusion could be sorted out, before anybody knew the marriage was not to have happened. He would take her to bed and possess her so ardently that she would be carrying his child before her father could call for an annulment.

It was a dreadful way to do things, but any other way was even worse.

The direction in which the scribe had wandered off corresponded exactly with the direction in which the entire crowd now rushed to see Willem attack another famous knight, Odo of Ronquerolles. The two of them met on a mild slope that was turning loose and sloppy from the endless charge of half-crazed chargers, and in unison unhorsed each other violently in a joust. Staggering to their feet, they yanked frantically at the hilts of their swords, drew them, and immediately started dueling. This was a rare instance of actual swordplay, and it was impossible for Marcus to move through or even around the delighted mob.

By the time he found the scribe, on the edge of a safety area, the fat old man had already handed off the missive to a courier. "Where was that message being sent?" Marcus demanded, praying that somehow he was wrong.

The old man shrugged. "To Oricourt, his home in Burgundy, milord, to his daughter Imogen."

"Dammit!" Marcus swore aloud.

"Curses are foul things, milord," the cleric said.

"My life is fouler," Marcus said angrily and walked off away from the excitement, into the middle of a part of the trampled field every-one had their backs to.

It wasn't a disaster yet. If he had a horse—and there were some of them, riderless, wandering about the field—he could intercept the messenger and then the plan would still work. That's what he would have to do. There were two easily within reach, both grazing in their bridles, their saddles intact—but as he chose the bay and started walking toward it, he saw Konrad waving to him from the dais, ges-turing him back. He stopped. He groaned.

And then he walked back toward his emperor, because he could not do otherwise.

Konrad had summoned Marcus back to the dais because he wanted tripe and pork pastries brought to him as he continued to watch. He marveled that Willem and the other knights seemed able to con-tinue without so much as a break for defecation. "Remember when we were doing that, Marcus?" he said nostalgically, as if it were a long time ago; it had only been a few years. "Look at that, Willem and Odo are still at it. They should just call a draw and go smash up other people." Marcus looked over. Most of Willem's red and blue surcoat had long been torn off; his chain armor was ripped through in places; his latest shield was splintered into pieces, he wasn't even using it . . . and everyone was adoring him. How had the shy, bum-bling country boy from two short weeks earlier turned into *that*? How could he, Marcus, have let it happen?

"I will see that a late dinner is summoned for you from the stores at Orschwiller, sire. May I be excused to the castle after that?"

"Don't you want to watch the rest of the tournament?" Konrad asked.

"I wish I could, sire, but I have already seen Willem's abilities." Marcus hesitated—he had never actually lied to Konrad before. "And there is bookkeeping to be done." It could still be accomplished—he would grab a loose horse as soon as he was out of Konrad's sight.

Konrad shrugged. "As you please. I'll see you this evening, then. Oh, Marcus," he added as an afterthought. He signaled a pretty dark-haired woman, her elaborate dress revealing she was of royal favor if uncertain pedigree. "Escort Cecilia back up, if you are going anyhow."

So he would have to delay his escape until he had, in fact, gone to the castle.

But back at the castle, Marcus still could not escape. Before he had even dismounted, every conceivable headache presented itself at his elbow; there were emergencies that only a cruel God would have sent in confluence against him right now. Brother Paul, already upset by the very fact of the tournament, had sent guards out to round up the town's visiting male prostitutes, and Marcus had to stand as deputy for their arraignment. Domestic officers from all over the Empire were using any pretext of imperial business they could come up with as an excuse to spend most of the day at the tournament. They would take a brief, vigorous detour up the side of the mountain to plague Marcus with absurdities that should have been handled by the seneschals or castellans of the households they had come from: the hayward from Konrad's Bavarian estate, for example, was there to wail that the harvest was so full this summer he did not have the manpower, with all the reapers and boon-tenants available, to clean and gather the corn, and so sought permission to demand longer work hours of the serfs; the Bavarian bailiff had come as well, in a fit of pique, and wanted to go over the whole years' records with Marcus to counter that the serfs were already far overused for this time of year, and if it continued they would be dead from overwork before they could help to bring in the harvest—and *that* would make the harvest *much* more difficult. The provost of Hagenau appeared to report a shortage of wood and wanted advice on what to do about it. The chief waggoner of the Saxony royal stables wanted to complain that his overseer had miscalculated what he should be expected to do in a week, and he could not possibly bring up the amount of supplies he had been ordered to. He, as the others, tried to ease Marcus's judgment with a silver mark wrapped in a handkerchief; Marcus rebuffed it angrily. Once when a new face appeared in the door he caught himself praying it was news that the Count of Burgundy's courier had been found dead on the road somewhere. He wanted to shout at everyone who entered that his room was not a corridor; he could never remember so many people traipsing through here, most of them bringing problems that should not have been his to start with.

He imagined the sun sliding slowly across the sky and knew his possible salvation was slipping away. He wondered with pained tenderness what Imogen was doing at this moment, wondered with worry how many days and hours she had left before she would learn her world was shattered.

At the tourney field, Jouglet had improvised a competent but very earnest song describing Willem's gallantry, and was singing it loudly, bowing the fiddle, for everyone who had not been near the moment of Michel of Harnes's defeat. Willem's conduct was so extraordinary that the story spread fast around the field until every knight, squire, nobleman, servant, townsman, and villager knew about it. Willem, oblivious, continued to fight, and in the course of the afternoon, although slowing down from weariness, and aware that his team overall was weaker than the French, he collected six more horses and four more prisoners, who were sent back to be held for ransom at the inn.

When the final knight he took hostage—a fellow from Ghent

he'd never seen before—told him, quite flustered, that he was honored to be prisoner to the great Willem of Dole, he finally thought of
Jouglet and realized, with a mixture of appreciation and resentment,
the minstrel probably had as much to do with his instant fame as his
own prowess.

He thanked the man warmly. A month ago he would have insisted he did not deserve that kind of credit. Now he accepted it, and
even let himself enjoy it. That too, he realized, was a result of Jouglet's influence.

The sun was far from setting, but shadows were starting to grow
long; the air was cooling to the golden moment of a summer evening.
It had been a perfect day for the riders. The trumpets were sounded
to announce the end of the tournament, silver cups were awarded to
Willem and other knights who'd been outstanding, and victors took
their prisoners home, to inns, to camps outside the fighting arena, in
some cases to the castle. Konrad summoned Willem to the platform
and invited him up to Koenigsbourg for a supper feast in his honor,
once he had gone back to the inn to clean up and recuperate.

Willem saw Jouglet briefly through the crowd. Jouglet beamed at
him, with a strange combination of pride and awe, then disappeared
again behind a bustle of expensive tunics.

The knight knew he had been remiss toward his friend. With
silver cup in hand, he urged Atlas to move around the crowd to the
far side of the platform.

As the bells tolled vespers, a large, weary man on foot, with no armor, carrying nothing but the king's muddy pennant, arrived at the
gate of the inn. Five hostages were waiting for him; the others had
already paid their ransom and been released.

So bleary with exhaustion he could hardly keep his eyes open, Willem explained under duress to the innkeeper and his family, to the merchant from Montbéliard, to Erec and his hostages and servant, that he had given his armor away—except the helmet—to the heralds who were always in danger on the field and never in a position to gain anything themselves. He'd also given one of them his silver cup.

"So where's Atlas?" Erec demanded, alarmed by his cousin's excessive philanthropy.

"I gave him to Jouglet," Willem said, with a tired, evasive look.

"You *what*?" Erec shrieked. "He was a gift from my father! I helped you train him! I taught him to change leads! How could you *do* that?"

"I'm sure he'll give him back, but the gesture seemed correct," Willem insisted, and collapsed onto one of the staircases in the courtyard. He seemed drunk or drugged from his exertions. "And he made such a delighted fuss over it, right in front of Konrad, it was touching—the fellow acts like an eight-year-old sometimes." He sighed. "Come now, we must settle scores and wash up, Konrad wants us at the castle for supper tonight." He groaned. "I am bruised all over."

"Marcus, where are you going?" Konrad demanded from the middle of the narrow stone courtyard. He loomed larger than ever in the claustrophobic space as the steward came rushing down the spiral stairs, pulling on a wool traveling cloak.

Marcus came up short, almost cringing. He had nearly gotten away. He wondered what would actually happen if he turned his back on Konrad and ran off.

He tried to, but he couldn't.

"I . . . if you please, sire, I've received news of my uncle in Aachen, he's unwell and I—"

"Again?" Konrad said with no little impatience. "I should think he'd have died by now. Well you'll have to start out tomorrow morning, I need you tonight. Boidon is collecting money from my wardrobe—see to it that it's distributed around the camps for ransom."

"Sire?" Marcus frowned.

"I want to pay off all the ransoms for the poorer knights, the ones who would be hard-pressed to pay themselves."

"Sire?" Marcus was incredulous.

Konrad laughed. "Willem inspired me. Actually, I was planning to do it anyhow—the last tourney I sponsored, outside Marburg, there was a huge to-do afterward, don't you remember? The knights who couldn't pay ransom sent their squires around to rob all the local merchants and silversmiths, it was a nightmare and it ended up costing me a fortune as well. This is much simpler. And the Frenchmen will go home to their accursed Philip and sing my praises—ha! Pay for all of Willem's hostages, even the ones who could pay themselves, because he'll probably just let them go anyhow. Can you do that by suppertime?"

"N . . . not if you want me to oversee the feast as well," Marcus said with barely hidden sourness, pulling off the travel cloak. "There is only one of me."

Konrad frowned at him. "Are you being snappish with me? Are you for one moment even thinking that your malingering uncle deserves a fraction of the solicitude I do?"

"No, sire," Marcus said quickly.

"Because your tone implied that," Konrad continued, sharply. "And it is not the first time in the last few weeks. Not even the first time today. If your distraction is about Imogen, I'll call the marriage off—I will not accept this as an ongoing feature of your service to me."

"It's not about Imogen," Marcus said, something inside him dying a little as his conscience chastised: *two. That's two lies you've told him now today.*

"Good," said Konrad, a hint of warning still in his voice, but the sternness abating. "I'm exhausted from all the excitement, I'm going to my rooms to take a nap before supper."

Everything that had smelled and looked like fresh grass that morning now smelled and looked like dust or mud or dirt. In the late afternoon light, Jouglet was leading Atlas around the edges of the tourney ground to make sure everybody knew how the horse had come from the knight to the minstrel.

"Hey! Jouglet!" cried a cheery female voice off to the side. "We heard there's a song! We want you to sing it!" And then two women's voices rose in laughter.

The minstrel looked over, and smiled at once. With their scarlet armbands over otherwise drab gowns, Jeannette and Marthe were rushing up.

"My ducklings! I've a gift for you!" Jouglet announced, quickly untying the ugly rainbow-hued mantle from Konrad. "In honor of the champion's generosity. Who wants it?" Marthe accepted it, but only to be gracious after Jeannette made an awful face.

"He was quite magnificent, wasn't he?" Jeannette said in a voice intended to torment her friend. She brushed her long, loose hair off her cheeks. "Those magnificent muscles flexing, those magnificent thighs gripping his magnificent mount—oh, my goodness, speak of the devil! It's the very horse. Do you envy him for being ridden so hard all day by your hero?" And she broke into laughter, Marthe echoing her. "He was a regular little god! And to think he had such vigor left after spending half the night with a whore!"

As the two women laughed, Jouglet made a pained face and said, as if under duress, "Very well, then, since you obviously wish me to inquire, just how much of his vigor did he spend in Marthe's lap?"

Marthe held up a silver coin. "I gained this much for my discretion," she said sweetly. And then winked.

With a growl, Jouglet undid the quadruple-knotted drawstring purse, drew out a small coin, and held it toward her, just out of reach. "You'll gain this much more for your indiscretion."

Marthe took it, put both coins into the purse at her own belt, and said, smirking, "For that amount I can't even tell you the size of his cock."

Jouglet's face flashed impatience and annoyance in the cooling shadows. "What will it take then? You wretched women, you'll beggar me one of these days."

The wretched women exchanged glances and giggled, and Marthe waved her hand dismissively. "No more money," she said. "I can't tell you the size of his cock for any amount, because I didn't see it!"

Jeannette nudged her. "Of course there are many we've not *seen*, exactly, but could still measure well enough." She and Marthe almost fell against each other laughing.

Jouglet was blinking very quickly, trying not to blink at all. "What *exactly* do you mean?" It came out a whisper, an alarmed whisper.

"Well, he said it was on account of needing to save his *vigor* for the tournament today," Marthe said conspiratorially. "Whatever the excuse was, he did not touch me but he paid me *very* well to say he had."

Jouglet looked flabbergasted. "But he . . . there's a widow in Burgundy I know he . . . did he seem like he would have, might have had any idea what to do with you, if it weren't . . ."

"Darling, I am not trained to be a seer," Marthe teased. "I have only what I am given to know. And I know he did not touch me. But he wanted me to put it about that he had."

Jouglet gestured dismissively. "The last part makes sense under the circumstances; we both went to show the other one what normal appetites we had. I want to know more about the first part."

"She said she can't help you, duck." Jeannette smiled. "I think you'll have to investigate the matter further for yourself." She affected sympathy but was clearly about to burst with the hilarity of it.

Jouglet made a sour face and turned Atlas toward the castle.

9

Paralipsis

[Greek, "false omission," wherein a narrative provides less information than circumstances call for]

11 July

*W*illem regretted making a gift of his best horse. Not for the loss of the horse, because he knew Jouglet would return the creature, which was too expensive for a minstrel to maintain. He regretted the gesture itself because the moment of exchange had been peculiar. Jouglet blushed and blinked back tears when Willem held the reins out, and then gave him a look of such sheepish affection and appreciation, it made Willem self-conscious. For a moment he thought Jouglet was putting on an act, but there was no sly grin or wink to say the play was over, and uncertain how to respond, Willem simply walked away without a word.

Mostly he was upset because he'd been about to embrace Jouglet, but stopped himself when he realized how pleased he was by Jouglet's being pleased.

Up at the castle in the great hall, he was too busy being cheered and congratulated and compared to Alexander the Great to have to deal with the minstrel much at all, and the minstrel was keeping away from him as well. Though it relieved Willem not to have to deal publicly with Jouglet, it still irked him to be shunned, and so—irritatingly—he found himself more and more aware of the minstrel the more and more they ignored each other. He sat beside Konrad, served by the oddly fidgety Marcus, and drank a lot, forgetting he had not eaten since Nicholas fed him savories on the field much earlier. He got a second wind around the same time he got drunk. When Konrad announced that Willem had earned the right to enter the castle without disarming at the gate, and that, further, Konrad had written to Lienor about his intention to marry her, tears of pride wet the young man's handsome face, which all the ladies suddenly clustered around the royal dais found adorable.

Jouglet had received yet another ostentatious robe from His Majesty. The minstrel slipped down into the lower courtyard to pass the largess on again, this time to a servant—and, returning up the torchlit stairway, nearly walked smack into Willem. The knight was taking a brief respite from the attention inside; he had intuitively headed down the long stairs to the lower courtyard, which—made of simple, half-timbered buildings—felt more familiar to him than the red sandstone behemoth above.

Knight and minstrel responded to each other on the protected stairway with such synchronization that Jouglet almost suggested they perform a routine of double takes and pratfalls for the revelers: the instinctive response to seeing each other was a mutual cheer and pleasure; this was followed by mutual awkwardness from remembering their last encounter; and this in turn by a slightly-too-hearty buffeting of each other's shoulders to demonstrate—awkwardly—that the awkwardness was entirely forgotten.

"The hero of the day!" Jouglet said, heartily buffeting Willem's shoulder.

"My secret weapon!" Willem said, heartily buffeting Jouglet's shoulder. "My greatest ally!" He held a full cup of ale; it sloshed over his hand and the hem of his sleeve, but he didn't notice.

"What a day it was, eh?" Jouglet crowed, hating their mutually ridiculous behavior.

"Yes, what a day!" the knight gushed. "This was by far the most exhilarating day of my life, and I owe the chance of it entirely to you, my dearest friend." He threw his arms around Jouglet in a fierce embrace. His breath smelled sour from the ale; he was too drunk to even feel how battered up he was.

The minstrel, with a suddenly racing pulse, managed at once to slip out of Willem's arms, but not without getting splashed with the ale, though Willem seemed oblivious.

"I'm bruised," Willem said distractedly as he reached over to rub his own shoulder, and almost upended the ale entirely.

"Let's have a toast, there," Jouglet suggested, to draw his attention to the cup. "We'll drink each other's health." And added, feeling pathetic: "And the health of the pretty women who so inspired us last night."

"We will! Indeed we will!" Willem spoke eagerly, announcing it, defiantly, to the entire deserted swath of stairs. He held the mug high and cried out, "To Jouglet and his clever way with words, and wit, and women!" then drank a long draught as Jouglet clapped and hooted approvingly. "Here," Willem said, handing the cup over.

Jouglet took it and glanced in; the enameled pewter vessel was only about a quarter full now, and what was left was frothy from

being sloshed about so energetically. "To Willem! Whose lance un-
does men by day and women by night!" Willem grinned, looking
very pleased with this description, and Jouglet pressed on. "Willem!
Who has a heart so noble it makes the emperor want to kiss his brow
and the ladies want to kiss him everywhere else!" And Jouglet
downed what was left in the cup with a single swallow, coughing half
of it out again.

Willem looked at his friend's face and chuckled—almost giggled.
"You've finally grown some decent whiskers!" he boomed. "You have
yourself a full mustache of liquid barley!" Jouglet made a brief swipe
at the ale-foam, but Willem grinned and shook his head. Their eyes
met casually. Jouglet, breath shortening, suddenly could not look away
from the handsome bruised face, as Willem roared with laughter.
"Here, you clumsy oaf!" He reached out to wipe off Jouglet's upper
lip, grinning affectionately, and with a thrill of terror Jouglet knew
this, finally, had to be the moment.

So as Willem's hand came closer, Jouglet grabbed it in its tra-
jectory and kissed the knuckles very gently, eyes locked on the
knight's.

Willem was startled.

Jouglet pulled him closer by the arm, rose on tiptoe, and kissed
Willem full on the lips.

Willem, who was very drunk, almost kissed back reflexively, enjoying the warmth of soft, wet lips—until he realized, with awful
clarity, to whose mouth they belonged. His eyes widened as he pulled
his face away and coughed a little, uncomfortably. "Jouglet, please,"
he said gruffly. "If you are the kind of youth to seek pleasure that
way—" He thought, and suggested with an uncomfortable attempt
at humor, "Go to your friend Nicholas. Or find some other hen-
groper."

The hazel eyes bore into Willem's. "I've had ample opportunity
to offer myself to . . . hen-gropers. I never do."

Willem shook his head. "Then explain your . . . gesture. You must be drunk."

"Yes," sighed Jouglet, who was absolutely sober. At the bottom of the stairs, in the growing dusk, an old serving woman grunted and slowly began to ascend the uneven flight up to the inner court-yard. "I'm finally drunk enough to reveal the unnatural depth of my attachment to you. I did not plan it or expect it, please believe me; your sister's image is the one I've ferried in the depths of my heart between Dole and here. But what I'm feeling is no mere friendship." In a whisper, aware of the serving woman approaching: "And I believe, Willem, that it is mutual. But I know a man of your place may never admit as much. So please, milord, spare me from pain and humiliation, and do not suffer me to be alone with you again. Brother Paul already suspects too much of me, and I would not have you sullied or endangered for my weakness. There, it is said." The recitation over, Jouglet grimaced and studied its ef-fects.

Willem gaped in silent perplexity a moment, then snatched the enameled cup from Jouglet's hands and turned on his heel to walk back up the stairway. At the top of the stairs was a small drawbridge to the inner yard, barely three paces long. As he crossed it, he hurled the cup angrily into the ditch below without pausing or looking at it. Jouglet watched him go, saddened and relieved.

But then Willem stopped. And—to Jouglet's rising alarm—turned around. And walked back across the bridge. And down the stairs. Toward Jouglet. When he was standing directly beside his friend again in the torchlight, he peered into Jouglet's face. "I don't understand this," he said simply, frustrated. "I don't like not under-standing it. But I would rather stand here next to you and feel awk-ward as hell than go back in there and have a bunch of drunken strangers call me champion."

Jouglet, flummoxed by this turn, squirmed and stammered, "Are you commanding me to be in your presence even knowing it would distress me? Are you condemning me to misery?"

Willem shook his head, and Jouglet nearly shrank away, spooked by the gentleness of his gaze. Willem reached out and grabbed the minstrel's arm. "You have never steered me wrong or asked of me a single thing that I regretted. Perhaps I should not regret this either."

Jouglet took in a loud, pained breath and pulled desperately away from Willem's grasp. "You don't mean that."

Willem nodded almost shyly. "Yes I do, Jouglet. I would not give you false hope."

"You're drunk. You're saying it because you're drunk." Jouglet took several steps up the stairway, like a cornered stag looking for a chance to spring. The old servant was getting very close to them.

"I'm not so drunk I don't know myself," Willem said. "This is already a most peculiar moment, do not make it more difficult."

"I . . . you . . . *no*," Jouglet stammered, eyes wide. "*Think*, man. I know you, Willem—you do not mean this, even if you think you do. You'll wake up sober tomorrow and forswear it all. You're mocking me without realizing it. I won't fault you for it, but you don't mean this."

Willem frowned and took a step to grab at Jouglet's sleeve again, this time holding the minstrel tightly. "I would never mock anyone, you know me better than that."

Jouglet, stymied and in need of a distraction, managed to be sick on Willem's leather boots.

The knight abruptly pushed the fiddler away from him and tried to leap back from the vomit, his own gorge rising at it. "Hey there!" he called out to the servant as she reached them. "My boots!" The gnarled old woman immediately bent over his feet with a rag already damp from spilled ale, and Willem turned his attention back to Jouglet, who was leaning against the curtain wall by an arrow loop, arms crossed, face as red as the sandstone in the torchlight. Willem grimaced and felt foolish now, a feeling that transmuted very rapidly to anger. "You're playing me for something. You're playing me just like you've played all of them. What are you up to, Jouglet? I see through you like lattice. This is somehow the price I have to pay for your assistance."

"Yes, of course, I want to extort unnatural favors from you so that I can refuse them when you consent. Even I am not so perverse, Willem," Jouglet said, miserably. "But I cannot abide the absurdity of this. The emperor trusts only three souls in this court, and if two of them are revealed as deceiving him together it will devastate him. This cannot happen."

"Then why did you kiss . . ." Willem hesitated, glancing up at the old woman as she disappeared across the drawbridge.

"To scare you off, of course!" said Jouglet. "To bring it into the open so it would die of exposure."

Willem was briefly taken aback, then defiant. "You failed," he announced.

"The ale, the excitement of the day, it's all gone to your head," insisted Jouglet. "Go back up there, please, and see if the company of decent, civil men can cure you of this delirium. I'm sure there is some lady in there who would be thrilled to quench your thirst."

Willem stared incredulously a moment and sounded furious. "I have disregarded every tenet of my breeding to speak to you as freely as I did. And you repay me with remonstrations for doing it! After you yourself initiated such behavior!"

"I told you, I only meant to scare you off. I am considering the needs of His Majesty and of your—"

"You are a dishonest and misleading rascal," Willem interrupted in hurt, confused disgust and turned away to face the top of the stairs. He looked sharply over his shoulder. "I never said a thing to you in earnest just now. You will not accompany me up there or stand near me once you're in the hall, do you hear?"

He mounted the stone steps again, his tread heavy.

Alone, the minstrel muttered angrily, "You certainly rolled that die badly, Jouglet, you imbecile."

Upstairs, Willem so avoided Jouglet for the rest of the evening that even when the musician was called upon to make up new toasts to honor the knight, the knight did not acknowledge them. Nobody noticed this new tension, because nobody was sober—except Marcus, who was too distracted by his own problems to notice anything at all.

This will never do, Jouglet thought miserably, and on some feeble pretext slipped out of the hall again and into the narrow courtyard. There was only one way to resolve this, however, and it was the one thing the minstrel would have given almost anything in the world to avoid.

When the feast had been cleared, Marcus again tried to get away but was stopped by the cook, the baker, the butler, and the marshal, all of whom wanted to show that they had kept good accounts of this most happy and celebratory day, and none of whom had the decency to bring him news that the count's courier had been struck by lightning. Then Konrad informed him Willem of Dole, the great hero, would be sleeping as a guest of honor in the smallest of the three rooms in Konrad's suite, and would Marcus immediately see to it that young, handsome, perfect Willem have a bed brought in large enough to sleep him and his squire, as well as poultices and various other things so that Erec could attend to his wounds and bruises. Marcus wanted to hand this particular task over to a deputy but then realized all the deputies were out paying ransoms in Konrad's scheme to show up the king of France. He thought of the message heading south that would keep Imogen out of his arms forever. Out of mood and out of character, he shouted his page boys awake, to help him comfort the man whose arms she would end up in instead.

Moments after Willem was settled into Konrad's receiving room, his good friend Jouglet appeared at the top of the large staircase that opened onto the room, and asked for a quick word alone with the knight. Willem's page, used to Jouglet's unannounced appearance, withdrew down to the kitchen, happy for an excuse to scrounge for sausage ends.

Jouglet paused before knocking. "Come in," said a muffled voice from inside. Jouglet opened the door and stood at the threshold, knowing better than to enter.

"Do not come in here!" Willem snapped but reined himself in at once. "Why have you come? I don't want to speak to you."

Jouglet experimentally took a step into the room, and when Willem did not object, closed and bolted the door, came all the way in and tentatively sat across the small hearth from him. The knight was sitting awkwardly on one corner of the camp bed that had been set up for him, leaning back against the wall on musty woolen blankets, soaking his feet in a bath of mineral salts. He smelled like a crone's hut from the collection of salves and balms that Erec had dutifully administered.

"Konrad loves us both quite well," Jouglet began in a quiet voice, "and he wants us both at his court, but if I have to spend another evening like this one I shall die of putrefaction from a sour stomach."

"My boots fared worse than your accursed stomach," Willem muttered. He leaned his head back so that he was staring at the painted ceiling, and replaced a sopping poultice over one eye. He wished he was still drunk.

"You and I are going to come to an understanding before the sun rises or one of us will have to leave this court."

"Is that a threat?" Willem snapped from his awkward position. "Are you threatening me? I've been given my own room by the emperor, who makes you sleep on the floor with his dogs after seven years of service to him. I just won a tournament wearing his helmet!"

"I put that helmet on your head and I can take it off again," Jouglet warned. "With your handsome head still in it, if need be. Don't rest on your fresh-plucked laurels, Willem. I have a history with Konrad that outweighs yours, and I know how to play the games of policy that you are too naïve to understand. You were given this room *at my suggestion.* Make your peace with me tonight or you will find yourself on the road back to Dole before the week is out. I want good things for you but never at my own expense, is that clear?"

Willem shifted the poultice uncomfortably, still looking up at the ceiling, and nodded with a surly expression.

Jouglet calmed. "I did not expect anything about tonight to occur the way it did. But . . ." A heavy sigh. "Very well. I suppose we'll just have to soldier through this. Willem, we were at cross purposes on the stairs tonight—"

"You mean you didn't *plan* all that?" Willem said, glad he had an excuse not to make eye contact.

"Of course not. But I want to explain my behavior."

There was a long pause. Willem experimentally removed the poultice, then replaced it, needing an excuse not to sit up straight and look at Jouglet. "Very well, say what you have to say," he commanded in a clipped voice.

Jouglet took a long while considering the right words and finally, unsatisfied, began. "Imagine the circumstances were just a little different. Imagine, for example, if you had experienced such behavior from, let us say, a fellow knight, or say a woman—"

"A knight would absolutely never do that, and such behavior from a woman means the woman is a whore," Willem interrupted.

Jouglet's jaw tightened. "Imagine such behavior from a woman whom you regarded as you regard me."

"Jouglet, that's a ridiculous proposition!" Willem said impatiently to the ceiling. "You could not be a woman. The world would never let a female grow to be what you are."

"That's true," said the minstrel, and then added in a fierce whisper, "that's a very good reason for me not to be a female, isn't it?"

Willem's one free eye blinked. "What?"

Jouglet took a deep breath and added with difficulty, "Even if I were to have been born one."

For a moment the knight remained slouched against the wall, then he very abruptly pulled the poultice away and sat upright on the bed, staring. Jouglet was looking at him beseechingly, obviously as rattled as Willem himself felt. "What are you saying?" Willem demanded, a peculiar feeling in the pit of his stomach.

But when the moment came to say it outright, Jouglet couldn't. "I cannot . . . I do not want . . . balls, I thought I could do this intelligently," the fiddler muttered in annoyance. Then in a quieter but harsher voice, "I did not want to do this, Willem, you are pushing me into something against my will and I resent you for it—but still that's preferable to your utterly rejecting me and making life at court impossible for both of us."

"What are you saying?" Willem repeated, a little more firmly, kneading the poultice and then dropping it in disgust when it began to leak on him.

"I have said nothing," Jouglet said nervously, backing away and glancing nervously between the two doors of the room. "You cannot claim that I've said anything."

"I do not want to *claim* anything. Just tell me clearly what it is you haven't said!" Willem said with sudden vehemence. He struggled to his feet and took an unsteady step toward Jouglet, then pulled a knife from his belt, shoving it at the minstrel, who nimbly leapt up away from it. "Undress yourself," he ordered hoarsely.

Jouglet eyed the knife with genuine alarm. "If I undress for you at knifepoint and I'm a woman, this may be accounted rape."

Willem waved the knife impatiently. "If you undress for me at knifepoint and you're a man, it's not much better. Don't force me to force you to do anything!" A pause, and then, almost voicelessly and almost frightened, "Would it be accounted rape?"

Jouglet did not answer, and they stared at each other in silence. Willem put the knife away with a grunt.

"I never take a misstep," the minstrel murmured, in a tone that was both apology and self-recrimination. "There is no excuse for this coming to pass."

Willem closed his eyes. "Take off your tunic and shirt." He put a hand over his eyes. "Or don't," he added, gently, from that position. And then added, just as gently, "But if you are not willing to be honest with me now, go away and do not come back to me, ever."

There was a long pause in which neither of them spoke, or moved, or looked at the other.

The minstrel saw to it that both the doors were bolted from inside, then with trembling hands, pulled off belt, tunic, and shirt, and said, barely above a whisper, "Look, then."

After a beat Willem opened his eyes and brought a hand to his mouth to stifle a gasp. Clad only in an absurdly baggy pair of men's drawers stood a willowy woman, her small breasts completely exposed. She looked at him from his friend's face, smiling with a shyness Jouglet had never once displayed. The features that had never seemed quite masculine enough suddenly, on a woman's face, did not seem quite feminine enough either.

"I have just put my life in your hands," Jouglet announced quietly, then made a nervous expression that was half smile and half frown. "Willem, your mouth is hanging open."

He shut it abruptly, stood up gaping, circled the room ogling this inexplicable creature from every angle, absolutely unable to speak.

"What are you?" he said very hoarsely when he recovered his voice.

"I thought we had established that," Jouglet said with a failed attempt at laughter. "Or do you need me to take off the drawers as well?"

"A noblewoman? A peasant?"

"A minstrel," Jouglet said.

"You're standing naked by my bed," he said, as if he could not imagine how this had happened.

"No I'm not," Jouglet said. Fingers trembling, she untied the drawers, let them fall to the floor and stepped carefully out of them as Willem's gaping increased. "*Now* I'm standing naked by your bed."

"Are you a prostitute?" he asked at once.

Her face flushed with anger. Then she laughed. "No, I am your friend Jouglet the minstrel. Do not leap to simplistic assumptions."

He collected himself a little. "After such deception you have no right to tell me not to leap *anywhere*!"

"Keep your voice down! Anyhow you deceived yourself," Jouglet shot back. "Did I ever once claim to be a man? I have never uttered a single lie about my sex. I thought this revelation would be a relief for you. I thought you might . . ." A hesitation. "I thought you might embrace me."

"I can't embrace you," Willem said, slightly shocked. "You're a . . . you're a woman standing naked by my bed."

"Would you prefer me to get dressed?"

"No," he said, so automatically that despite her fear she threw back her head and laughed. It was a gesture so characteristically Jouglet that it almost made Willem dizzy with confusion to see it performed by a person with breasts.

"Well then, would you like me to sit down?"

He looked hurriedly around the room, as if the bachelor state of disarray from Erec's ministrations were a sudden embarrassment. "I . . . let me find you someplace comfortable," he began self-consciously and bent down to pick up a musty blanket that had fallen from the camp bed.

"Oh, for the love of the saints," Jouglet muttered and reached down for the tunic. "I'm putting this much back on until you can stop acting like a fool." She slid the tunic over her head, letting it hang loose without the belt.

Willem froze, gaping now at the blanket, at his own solicitousness in picking it up. He threw it down and looked hard at her. "Does Lienor know about this?" he demanded. "Have both of you been playing me for a fool behind my back?"

Jouglet waved a hand dismissively, reassuringly. "I've never told Lienor a thing. And I have never played you for a fool, Willem. I was perhaps a fool myself, and you were the victim of my foolishness. That's not the same thing at all."

For another long moment he kept staring at her, skeptically. She stood with resignation, arms at her sides, head high so he could scrutinize the suddenly alien face.

"Why?" he finally demanded.

"Why live as a man?" she replied with the usual Jouglet shrug. "Have you not noticed what my options are otherwise?"

"I meant why *me*? Why did you bring me here?"

"So I could have my dearest friend near me in a place where we might both prosper," Jouglet said. "Whatever else you have ever believed or might ever believe about me, Willem, please trust the truth of that."

Willem looked uncertain. "What else?" he demanded.

She made a defenseless gesture. "Only what is obvious! I hoped that you and I might advance your sister, whom I do cherish, even if my courting her is just an artifice. And I hoped to benefit my emperor, because he *would* benefit from both you and Lienor in his court. And I thought we—you and I—would have a grand time with all of it. Which we have. I did not mean *this* to happen, though, I swear I didn't." A pause. Jouglet took a careful step toward him. "But it has, and I think—I hope—I will not regret it. If you don't." Another step in his direction, with a tentative smile.

Looking alarmed at her approach, he took a large step backward and bumped into the camp bed, then crossed away from that too. "I have no interest in possessing you," he said awkwardly, almost defensively.

"Really? You considered it when you thought I was a youth."

Willem hesitated. "You are an attractive young man. You are, forgive me, not such an attractive young woman."

Jouglet laughed. "It's the same face!" And added pointedly, "It is your friend's face." Again she took a step toward him.

Again he pulled away. "You're not a virgin, are you?" he said in the same defensive, almost desperate tone.

"Willem!" said Jouglet in exasperation.

"If you're not a prostitute, or married, or—"

"*You're* not a prostitute or married, or a virgin," Jouglet pointed out.

"I'm a *man*," he said.

"There are a dozen witty responses to that insightful observation, but I'll refrain. No, Willem, I'm not a virgin. But," Jouglet added, in a softer tone, "I've always been on the road, without intimates. You're the only man to whom I have entirely revealed myself, and the first with whom—" He looked so alarmed she was afraid to say anything too direct. "The first with whom any embrace would not be a casual encounter." She risked another step toward him.

"Ah. So you're a harlot, then," he said, sounding unconvinced.

"You deserve another bloody nose," she snapped, and in a huff went to fetch her drawers. She pulled them on as she spoke, her hands shaking with anger so that it was hard to tie them. "I am not a harlot, Willem, I am someone with desires that you were not dis-pleased about earlier, and occasionally—*occasionally*—I find a way to fulfill them. It would be unhealthy not to. Do not ask me to be pas-sive and pure as the morning dew until the moment that I'm in your arms, and suddenly I'm vital. I'm *always* vital, Willem, that's part of what you've always liked about me." The drawers finally tied, she looked around for her belt and the purse she kept tied closed hanging from it.

Willem saw it before she did and grabbed it from the rushes where she had dropped it. "You've just given me the biggest shock of my life, I am entitled to be beside myself for a little while," he chas-tised.

Immediately she held up her hands in a yielding gesture. "I grant you that," she said, and with a small confessional laugh, added, "you gave me quite a shock yourself, when you came back to me on the stairs. I thought I'd managed to scare you off. I would never take you for a sodomite."

"I would never take me for one either! You underestimated your own charms," Willem said gruffly.

"I underestimated *you*," said Jouglet.

There was a moment of unsettled silence between them, with Jouglet's eyes looking almost plaintively at the belt and purse, forgot-ten in Willem's large palm. "My belt, please," she said as offhandedly as possible.

Willem glanced down at what he held. "What is it, then?" he asked, patting the small purse. "Obviously not herbs to keep your boyish treble."

"If you must know," Jouglet said in a grudging tone, "among other things, it's a concoction of nettle seeds and staghorn to keep my monthly flux as brief and light as possible, and also white pepper ampules from Jeannette, to assure there will be no little Jouglets running around—"

"Oh," Willem said hurriedly and handed it to her. She tied it on, and this time when she took a step toward him, he didn't back away. She reached out tentatively to touch his face. He took a hard, quick breath when he felt those familiar fingers touch his skin.

The gesture whipped something to life in him—he grabbed Jouglet's wrist and twisted it harshly to the side, so that the minstrel had to leap around beside him to keep it from snapping. "Willem!"

"You are a deceitful wretch," he hissed.

"My wrist—for God's sake, Willem!" Jouglet gasped.

"Apologize for deceiving me," the knight demanded, glaring.

"I didn't do it to deceive you, I'd—ah!" she cried as he twisted it more. "Stop, *stop*, Willem, you're a knight and you're hurting a woman—"

"I'm hurting a liar," he corrected angrily but let her go. She snatched her hurt wrist against her body and cradled it with her other arm, scampering several paces back from him and the fire, feeling trapped in the far corner of the small room. He turned away from her and looked into the flames. "Get out of here," he said in disgust and sat down again with a sigh born of too many bruises.

"You don't mean that," Jouglet said.

"Of course I mean it!" Willem thundered, turning again to glare into the darkness. "*I* am sincere—*I* never say or do anything untrue."

"Neither do I," she said quietly.

"You are the very *embodiment* of deception! I have no stomach for it, you've robbed me of my dearest friend."

"I *am* your dearest friend," Jouglet protested.

Willem shook his head adamantly. "No. My friend is not some lying woman."

"That's right, she's not—I have never actually uttered a lie to you about my—"

"My friend is not a woman *at all*!" Willem clarified furiously, barely remembering to keep from yelling.

"Yes he is," the minstrel said with quiet anger. "Your choices are now to maintain the friendship or forswear it."

"I'll make that choice once you admit that you were deliberately disingenuous," Willem snapped impatiently. "A lie by omission is still a lie, Jouglet. It offends me you would hide something like that from me. It is a crime against friendship."

"And when should I have told you?" Jouglet asked in a reasonable tone, and took a step out of the corner.

Willem looked confused. "The first moment you had impure thoughts about me," he said awkwardly.

The minstrel laughed. "That was precisely the moment that I needed most to *hide* it from you," she pointed out. "I am a woman of prodigious appetites, Willem, I—"

"Don't tell me that!" he said desperately, shaking his head as if he could toss the words out of his memory. He stood up and crossed to the outer door. "I want you to leave now. You are not welcome in my presence."

Sudden fear made her blanch. "I've endangered myself revealing this to you. If Konrad or any other—"

"Your wretched secret is safe with me," he said brusquely, looking at the floor near her feet. "What do you take me for? But leave now, for God's sake, until I've recovered from this shock."

"Are we friends?"

"Ask me tomorrow," Willem said impatiently, still staring at the floor near her feet. He couldn't bring his eyes to look any closer at her, even now that she was dressed again; he did not want to look at Jouglet and see a woman's face. *"Go."*

———

A little while later he was still pacing frantically through the rest of Konrad's suite, as the dogs eyed him suspiciously and Charity, the hooded falcon, squawked in concern from her pedestal. Willem heard the minstrel's musical warble waft up from the courtyard, in defiance of the croonings from the great hall. Of course it was a woman's voice, he could hear it now—a low, husky alto, not a delicate soprano like Lienor's, but lacking any real bass. Erec's drunken slur joined in, a little flat, and some other voices that Willem did not recognize. There was laughter, and then eventually the only sound was mournful overwrought harp music coming from the hall windows.

He went back into his assigned room, feeling as if he might go mad. Finally, mastering his impulse to scale down the curtain wall and flee, he exited the same door from which he had ejected Jouglet and stepped onto the grand stairs that led down to the courtyard. The moon was just past half full, and the courtyard, still torchlit, smelled of spilled ale and wine, cold stone, and perhaps a little vomit.

Erec sat with a woman on his lap near the bottom of the stairway. He looked over his shoulder and smiled up at Willem. "Cousin!" he called up in a loud whisper, pleasantly and drunk. "Come down and have a drink with me! His Majesty summoned this little lady for the tournament hero to play with, but you've been sequestered, so I had a round with her myself. She's got plenty of staying power if you're up to it—there's a convenient little place behind the kitchen cistern there." The female figure giggled, a low giggle that was almost a purr.

"Oh," said Willem quietly in disgust. "No, but I will join you for a drink. I'm amazed they're still serving us, it must be after midnight."

"For the champion? They never sleep!" Erec announced grandly and gestured toward the kitchen, where indeed a light still burned.

Willem descended the stairs and settled beside Erec and his purring burden—and then he recognized the burden. "You're Jouglet's friend," he said in an accusatory voice.

Jeannette smiled suggestively. "I am everybody's friend."

"She's certainly been *my* friend," Erec slurred happily, with a sudden, huge yawn. "Done wonders for my French vocabulary."

"Where's Jouglet?" Willem demanded.

"Did you quarrel?" Erec asked, sounding as if he were falling asleep as he spoke. "He was pissy when he came from speaking with you."

"Where is Jouglet?" Willem repeated, directing the question at Jeannette.

She shrugged. "I imagine he took himself back up to the hall."

Willem was irrationally furious and had to take a breath before he could trust himself to speak. He glanced around the courtyard to make sure he would not be overheard, and then whispered irritably, "Oh, *he* took *himself,* did he?"

Erec was entirely uninterested in this discussion, but Jeannette sat up a little straighter on his lap, her eyes widening. "Oh," she said softly. "Perhaps I know what you quarreled about."

"We did not *quarrel.* We had a . . . *gentlemen's disagreement,*" Willem said angrily.

Jeannette considered him, looking disappointed. She seemed about to speak to him but turned her attention very deliberately to Erec instead. "Milord," she chirped, running fingers over his little point of wispy beard to get his wandering, sleepy attention back to her. "If a female in distress places her trust in a knight, and he casts her away from him for any reason, is that not accounted unchivalrous?"

Erec began to ponder the question, and her nearer breast, with grave concentration in the torchlight. Willem said in a quiet, wooden voice, "What if she is not in distress, what if she is simply lying?"

Her face still turned toward Erec, Jeannette answered in a low voice, "What if she is lying *because* she's in distress?"

"She's not in distress," Willem snapped. "She has frightening control over her destiny—over *many* people's destinies."

"And that has damaged you, has it?" Jeannette asked, looking toward him, suddenly harsh. "Her machinations have ruined you, is that right? When you chastise her for duplicity, don't forget to chastise her for bringing you here and making certain you became a hero overnight."

It shocked Willem to be spoken to this way by an inferior, and for a moment he just stared at her. Erec, drunk to obliviousness, had rested his cheek on her breast and was dozing off.

"If I were like other men I would make you pay for speaking to me in that tone," Willem informed her with quiet anger.

"If you were like other men you would be terrified of a woman's strength," Jeannette answered evenly. "You would cast out the most deserving one because she dared to defy your expectations of her. How admirable that you are not like other men." She gently removed Erec's head from her chest and gingerly got off his lap. She tried to help his inert form to a supine position on the steps. He snorted a little and made sounds that his groggy mind probably thought were intelligible words, and then he was still again.

She began to step away from the staircase, but Willem's huge hand reached out and grabbed her wrist. She started and looked down at his hand, then back up at him.

"Why is she distressed?" he asked.

Jeannette tossed her head with contempt. "If you don't know that, you don't deserve to know," she said, and broke free from his grasp. "Especially since it is right in front of your face."

She excused herself and left. The harp had stopped. Konrad was in his room at last; the castle would soon be asleep. Willem stared up beyond the towering walls of Koenigsbourg, into the slate-grey sky, pondering Jeannette's words and listening to the sound of his own heartbeat pounding in his throat.

*U*nder the swollen moon, finally heading south too late to stop disaster, Marcus urged his horse into a gallop, too desperate to care that he was risking both their necks.

BOOK TWO

10

Romance

[a narrative about courtly life and forbidden, secret love]

11 July, late night

*M*arcus rode hard into a late-night summer thunderstorm, almost killing his horse under him, but he knew the messenger was still ahead. He did not even know why he rode—he could not keep the messenger from giving Imogen her father's edict; his presence would not make it disappear. He had a panicked impulse to *do something*, and to be near her—it was irrational, and no rational thought justified it. *We could elope,* he thought, shuddering at the thought of the spectacularly public upheaval that would cause.

He should have stayed at court. He should have tried to poison Willem. Good God, no, not that, he was not capable of that . . . although he could almost entertain thoughts of poisoning the Count of Burgundy. But even that would not undo the message being sent. Perhaps find a way to have Willem castrated? Marcus laughed at himself in shock as he galloped, then found the laughter was actually sobbing. Willem was untouchable now—and anyhow, Marcus had no stomach for such things. His bad leg pained him terribly, until it finally went numb from the knee down. He had hardly stopped to sleep; sometimes he felt he slept as he rode, his balance perfect in the high-backed saddle—the former nonpareil of horsemanship from his days of active knighthood. Sometimes he dreamt that the wind-driven raindrops on his chest and face were Imogen's sweet little hands teasing him with caresses. The only moments of relief he felt were when, in a twilight of consciousness, he half-convinced himself that possibly he had misjudged the count, that the message heading southward was benign.

12 July

Although Erec was hungover, he had an easier time facing the morning than his cousin. They both slept through mass, and Konrad told the pages to let Willem sleep through breakfast too. When the knight surfaced groggily to consciousness, he was alone in a warm, shuttered room. His mind felt as battered as his body was; he lay there a long while, thinking about the day, and the evening, before.

Toward midday, Erec entered, cheerfully shaking off raindrops, and helped his bruised cousin pull his clothes back on. They crossed through Konrad's suite and down the spiral stairs, past the guards and into the great hall. Konrad stood to greet Willem with open arms, the smirking but ignored Paul to his left.

The hall looked subdued, with all the shutters closed against the rain, but something else was different too, some subtle alteration of the mood. It took Willem a moment to realize what it was: the entire upper half of the room was filled with mostly older men, who had beside them at the trestle tables blandly attractive younger women. As each man rose to acknowledge Willem's entrance, he took his companion's hand with an intimate formality.

Konrad had filled his hall with married ladies and their wealthy, aging husbands.

The collected couples, recognizing Willem as soon as he walked through the door, began to applaud and huzzah him. Willem stared in confusion.

He crossed the length of the hall, horribly self-conscious, and once before the throne, he bowed. "Your Majesty," he said, uncomfortably aware of many ladies' appraising eyes on his back-side. "As ever I am grateful that you have invited me to join you at board."

Konrad beamed. "I am the one who is grateful, Willem, to have a man of such character in my court. If your loyalty is half as strong as your arm, I could not ask for a better retainer. We are initiating the office of Imperial Knight, and you will be anointed the first, within the month, if you pledge yourself willingly."

The room fell silent, and Willem's voice caught in his throat. "I am your man, milord," he said huskily, bowing again. "You offer me the greatest honor of my life."

"Excellent," Konrad said easily and slapped his hands together. "Let us say after the Assembly that convenes August first. The hon-orable cardinal my brother shall bless the ceremony." He said this as if Paul were in another room. "And now dinner!"

In the confusion during the hand washing, Willem saw Jouglet eyeing him carefully from the darkness between the hearth and the exit down to the kitchen—literally hiding in the shadows. He sighed uncomfortably, then gestured once with a jerk of his head.

The minstrel delayed a moment before slipping through the overdressed and perfumed congregation. By wordless agreement they stood in line for hand washing, just behind a lady whom poets might have described as homely were she not the daughter of a duke. Willem was behind Jouglet, both looking straight ahead toward the shuttered window where a boy held a washbasin.

"I owe you an apology," Willem said under his breath. "I deserve a better explanation from you, but my behavior last night was not gracious."

"I took you by surprise," Jouglet said in a clipped voice over her shoulder. "I had no right to expect any other response. Is that all? May I go?"

Willem leaned over to whisper against the dense mop of the minstrel's hair. "Much of what is good in my life I owe to you. Not to your sex, just to you. I'm ashamed at myself for forgetting that for even half an instant." Fumbling, he reached out very subtly between them and clasped one of Jouglet's long-fingered hands in one of his own. "You are the truest friend I have."

He felt Jouglet in front of him give a shudder of relief. "Even though I deceived you?" It was asked with a hint of sarcasm.

"You were not deceiving *me*," Willem murmured. He released the hand, aware that half the hall was craning for a look at the great champion. "You were deceiving *everyone*, but that is between you and God, it is nothing particular between the two of us." He could not see Jouglet's face directly, but by studying a spot near her left ear, thought she might be smirking. "I must say," he went on quietly, "that although I never would have married my sister to a jongleur, it saddens me that your flirtation was nothing but an affectation. It would hurt her pride to hear it told."

"Then don't tell it," Jouglet whispered back, tensing again. "Not to her, nor to *anyone*."

"I won't."

"Will you swear to that?" Jouglet demanded, still looking forward.

Willem frowned. "Is it so dreadful if you're discovered?"

Jouglet made an impatient, agitated sound and began to pull out of the hand-washing line. "So you will not swear it."

"I swear on my sister's chastity," Willem whispered quickly, which stopped her. "And I swear on my own life that our friendship will be unaffected by what I know."

"That's impossible, but I appreciate your intention," Jouglet said, almost too quietly for him to hear. The bony-buttocked young lady before them finished with the basin and stepped away. Jouglet moved to one side so that Willem could wash his hands beside her. Finally she looked at him, grinning a smooth Jouglet grin, instantly transformed into the cheery court entertainer who was, if not especially masculine, still wholly male in demeanor. "Let's get you to your seat so the grand game can begin."

"What game?"

The minstrel winked. "Come now, you haven't figured it out? He knows you want a lady, so he's given you a herd to choose from. To carry in your heart, to be made pure and ennobled by chaste love of. To lose your appetite over and be tormented by jealousy about. Like the poor idiot knights I sing about. Pick a rich one."

Willem looked appalled. "This is not a seemly way to find one's lady."

Jouglet, tickled, reached for the rosemary-scented linen towel a girl held out. "Come now, Willem, it's your fantasy he's indulging here, don't be ungracious about piddling details."

"*My* fantasy?" Willem countered as he took the towel. "You've been on about it more than I have; I would simply like a wife."

Jouglet made an amused gesture of dismissal. "Yes, yes, of course, in time—but first every knight needs an unattainable *lady*. So that when his friend the *musician* writes *songs* about him, to *immortalize*

him, he seems properly *poignant* and *romantic*. Here is your chance to
find the lady." Ignoring the appalled expression on Willem's face, she
slipped away to the lower end of the room, chuckling with anticipation.

That meal, and that day, were among the most peculiar of Willem's
life. He saw two people when he looked across the hall at Jouglet.
Sometimes he could not believe there was a woman there, but just as
often he could not believe others did not see through the disguise,
especially when the fiddler took to flirting with the ladies or acting
cocky with the men.

And the mealtime was ridiculous: on various feeble pretexts,
each wife was given her turn to rise from her place and travel around
the edge of the tables to bow before the king and by extension, to
Willem—before returning to her wordlessly masticating spouse. They
were literally on display for him, and the husbands seemed to have
no argument with it. The conceit of courtly love was usually adulter-
ous and doomed never to be consummated, but all the same—*arranging*
it by collusion this way embarrassed him. Fate, or God, was supposed
to cast one's lady into one's life.

As the trestles were being cleared, after a final course of figs and
dates, Konrad winked at Willem. "What do you think of the ladies
of the court?"

Willem smiled politely. "I think there is a sudden influx of
them."

"Oh, you noticed that, did you?" Konrad grinned. "So did our
little friend there—" He pointed to Jouglet, who had sidled up to the
Duchess of Swabia and was crooning things to her in a low voice that
made her blush.

Konrad turned suddenly to Paul with friendly offhandedness, as if he had not just spent all of dinner with his back to him. "Jouglet certainly likes the ladies, eh?"

Paul looked, characteristically, like he was seeking an excuse to sneer. "The minstrel is entirely too forward in his attentions."

Willem sat up a little straighter to see around Konrad. "He has never been improper to any female in my ken," he assured the cardinal.

Konrad laughed expansively, and pushed Willem by the breastbone back into his seat. "Of course he has!" he countered. "Jouglet is a demon with his appetites—there's never any doubt of his predatory tendencies, despite his being a scrawny youth."

Willem realized Konrad's ulterior motive and wisely refrained from further comment.

"Predatory like Nicholas?" Paul asked blandly, a comment his brother pointedly ignored.

"Willem is quite the demon too," Konrad went on. "The chivalrous demeanor is an act to fool the husbands. Isn't it, Willem? You know what they say about men with noses like that! How many of these ladies send you aflame?"

Willem looked out over the pleasant-looking collection of women in the hall. Nobody stood out. "They all have . . . promise," he said obediently in the most lecherous voice he could muster, which wasn't very lecherous.

"Yes they do." Konrad smiled. "Let us watch them fulfill that promise."

He clapped his hands and the chamberlain entered from the upper corridor, playing a falsetto march on a small, but very loud, pipe of horn. He led a trail of squires, walking in twos with carved and gilded chests between them. The chests were placed squarely in the center of the hall below the largest iron chandelier. "In honor of the great Willem of Dole's generosity to me yesterday on the tourney field," Konrad announced to the room, "I have been inspired to mete out indulgences to the honorable ladies of the court. Boys, remove the lids to those chests." In unison, the squires did so. The honorable ladies of the court squealed.

The chests were full of sensational robes and kirtles: sumptuous brocade silks and fancy, exotic weavings; sleeves edged with gold; silk and leather girdles; fabrics that troubadours could drone on about for hours. Some of the younger husbands looked startled to recognize the contents—they were the chests of "costumes" the common women had worn at Konrad's summer bacchanal. Since the clothes were donned so momentarily in the summer camp, they were not the least worn and passed as new.

"Today I am King Arthur in my generosity," Konrad bellowed out over the oohing and ahhing as the ladies flocked around to grab at dresses. "Take as much as pleases you. Gentlemen, you may assist them."

Willem, watching from the emperor's side, saw Jouglet wander over to the chests and run a critical eye over all that was inside. The fiddler's hand darted into the farthest chest and out again, extracting a tunic of red silk. The sleeves and collar were heavily embroidered with gold and silver, and the whole trimmed with ermine. With a very feminine gesture, the minstrel held it up. It was extremely large, and hardly the most decorated or daintiest thing in the chests, but it sufficed to make a woman of its wearer. "I'll be the best-dressed lady here today!" the minstrel called out playfully over the hubbub, and most eyes flickered briefly toward the voice. Willem almost leapt up in alarm.

Jouglet batted pale lashes and blew kisses to all the men nearby. The Duke of Lorraine, kneeling by a chest helping his pregnant wife to untangle a green robe, received an actual kiss on the brow. "Do I not make a *lovely* lady?" Jouglet demanded. "Shall I put this on?" In response to a mild round of laughter, she pulled it over her head, over her clothing, and looked extremely lumpy. She grabbed the tunic with her fingertips approximately where nipples would be found, and called to the usher, "Milord, a pair of apples would be well placed here! Who wants to be my wooer?" And as Willem nearly yelped in disbelief, the minstrel ordered, "Willem of Dole, good sir, come try to woo me to your bower." She struck a highly unoriginal pose of one who is coy yet lovesick: one hand supine at her forehead, the other stretched behind her. Willem felt spellbound; her convincing pantomime of a young man doing an unconvincing pantomime of a young woman bordered on the diabolical.

Everyone called out, "Willem! Willem of Dole! To the lady!" He looked at Jouglet, flummoxed. Jouglet winked at him audaciously for the benefit of their audience, but the expression on the minstrel's face was not playful. It was a challenge.

So he rose from his place by the king, and the applause grew louder, bolstered by whistles of encouragement. People cleared a path for him as he walked unsurely toward the minstrel in the middle of the room. His tentativeness evaporated the longer people looked at him, however; he was emboldened by his newfound celebrity, and by the time he reached Jouglet he was feeling, uncharacteristically, almost cocky.

He went down gingerly on one bruised knee and bowed his head. "My Lady," he said dutifully. "You are the shining star of my existence, and I would give anything to come to rest against your bosom." Giggles and catcalls percolated from the onlookers.

" 'Tis a goodly request," Jouglet said sweetly, blatantly imitating Lienor's diction, and dropped down onto one knee to be beside him. The minstrel laid a hand daintily on the far side of his head—then roughly shoved his cheek down onto her chest.

There was a swelling softness there, a small but distinct pillow of femininity, that Willem's ear and jaw could feel through the bulk of layered clothes. He had seen her breasts last night, in the firelight, had stared at them and the rest of her as if at a succubus, but already he had erased the details from his mind. This was something he could not erase; the immediacy of it seared itself like a brand to his skin.

Without pulling his head away, his eyes glanced up at her face, and—with his head so clearly couched against a woman—he read something feminine into the features too. She was a handsome woman. Not pretty, not delicate as ladies were supposed to be, she was not daintily perfect like his sister or seductively round like the widow, but it was a face to like enormously—and it was coupled with a spirit he had admired for years. He was staggered by his stupidity at turning her away last night. Feeling his eyes peering up, Jouglet glanced down and met his gaze a moment, grinned privately for a flicker of an instant. The grin made Willem's stomach flop over, especially as he became aware of the royal brothers' eyes upon him.

Beside him, Konrad sensed his brother's agitation without actually looking at him. He turned to ask Paul what was troubling him, hoping it was something he could exacerbate.

But there was a look on Paul's face that Konrad, running through a mental index of their adolescent run-ins, recognized: the sly, gleeful, sleazy triumph that usually presaged an enormous falling-out between them. He did not follow Paul's gaze to see the cause. He didn't need to. He knew Paul was looking at Jouglet and Willem.

Jouglet fluttered pale lashes at Willem very publicly. "Oh, sir, you are such a handsome man, so valiant and loyal and courtly and generous and strong—and *very* handsome, sir, I'll tell you that. The only thing standing in the way of our true love is . . ." She looked at him with such a feminine affectation of devotion that he actually blushed—then the expression vanished rapidly, and she shoved him away from her, demanding in a nasty voice, "What's your pedigree, sir? A mere landless knight? Bah! I make it a rule only to fall in love with my peers or betters." She thumbed her nose at him theatrically.

The audience, young ladies and old lords alike, laughed at a sentiment that all recognized, complacently, as true to life.

Willem held up his hand for silence and retorted affectionately, "But my lady, does not pure love raise up the humblest to the highest? Am I not instantly of higher status simply for loving you as purely as I do?"

Jouglet dropped the feminine demeanor and announced with gusto to their audience, "This knight is a student of Andreas Cappellanus, the fashionable French chaplain! That's from his first dialogue on perfect love!"

"It is?" said Willem, startled. "I thought I'd made it up." Their audience responded to this with approving laughter, which further flustered him. "I'm serious," he explained earnestly to the room at large, and that only prompted more amusement.

"A seasoned disciple of *The Art of Courtly Love*!" Jouglet declared, determined to keep Willem from looking like an absolute naïf. "If every man in this hall strove to be so gentle, this would be a much-ennobled aristocracy, with much happier ladies." The minstrel winked at the ladies by the chests. "Any one of you could be deserving of that gallantry, you know." She went on, feigning not to see Willem turn scarlet. "He's a little shy, so you would need to let him know, discreetly, that his efforts would not be in vain. He's staying at Walther's inn by the southern gate of town. You may entrust messages to Erec his squire—the burly blond pimply-faced fellow about my height—and also, of course, to me, my darlings." She gave them the smile that Jouglet the Troubadour gave them before performing any love song, and despite the female costume now, most of them responded, as always, with hopeful blushes. Willem was simultaneously embarrassed, impressed, flattered, and amazed by Jouglet's performance, and for several long moments was too distracted even to register what was going on around him.

By the time he had collected himself, the dresses were all dispersed and couples were beginning to exit the hall.

"Chess!" Konrad was informing him cheerfully, joining them in the center of the room. "And bring your fiddle, Jouglet."

"Yes, I would treasure a game of chess," said Paul, suddenly present, with a convincing display of conviviality, as if he had been invited to join them; almost as if he were doing the inviting.

Konrad gave him a withering look. "I'm sure there are others in the castle who play as well as my friends and I."

"But, brother," Paul said, smilingly, "it is for the character, not the talent, that I seek fellow players. I would spend time with you all. If the young knight here is worthy of your great company, no doubt he is worthy of mine, which is humbler than yours."

Before Konrad could cut him down again, they were approached by yet another figure: the Count of Burgundy, drying his hands on the sides of his tunic, having left off the final hand-washing abruptly to include himself in this clutch. "My nephews both seem in good health today, God be praised," he said, smiling. "I would be honored to join this party of an afternoon."

Konrad closed his eyes a moment. "Utterly absurd," he muttered, then looked directly at his uncle. "We are no party, and it is boorish of both yourself and your kinsman here to invite yourselves into your emperor's private chamber. I am retiring with these two young gallants, and nobody else."

"Actually, sire," Paul said, a smarmy smile frozen on his face, "I received a missive from His Holiness the pope today, regarding his interest in your eventual nuptials, and had been hoping to speak to you of its urgent matter, to which the chess would have been merely a pleasant counterpoint. If you want neither myself nor our uncle Alphonse present, then the necessary discussion I would have had with you, I must have instead with him, as the leader of the Assembly of Lords. A group to which you are after all beholden on the matter in question. My good count," he said, bowing to his uncle with exaggerated circumspection. "Will you walk with me? Our emperor is unmarried yet, and His Holiness has strong feelings on the subject. Perhaps the Assembly of Lords does as well."

Konrad had learned years ago how to mask even the sharpest irritation. "Alphonse of Burgundy is not free to speak with you just now," he said in a tired voice. "He is coming to play chess with me, but you alas cannot, as I have only two chessboards and there are already four of us ascending, like the four cardinal virtues, so there is no room for you."

And thus when they were settled into Konrad's dayroom, with the falcon above and the hounds at their feet, the pages in the corner and the guards outside the door, Alphonse was with them—which pleased him very much, but did not please anyone else at all. The page boys were excused to help haul up casting wax for the new chapel bells, from the bottom of the steep castle mount in the downpour. There was, in fact, only one chessboard; Jouglet played the fiddle as Willem in rapid succession lost two games of chess to Konrad and a third to the count.

Sensing his sovereign's extreme indifference to his presence, Alphonse clumsily steered the conversation in such a direction that he was able to say, as if it were a passing comment, "But of course I do not share the pope's views on my nephew's marriage plans."

All three of his companions paused. "Don't you?" Konrad asked with a hint of sarcasm. "The pope wants me to marry the heiress of Besançon. You want me to marry the heiress of Besançon."

"I did," Alphonse conceded. "But I have become convinced the sister of Willem of Dole is a better choice."

Willem stared at him and then in a blunt, suspicious voice, demanded, "Convinced how?"

The count smiled with those flawless teeth that the family was famed for. It was a singular expression, a look that was both superior and sycophantic at the same moment—a look Konrad and Jouglet, both familiar with it, loathed. "Your sister is much fairer a prize than Besançon's dour girl." He reached out to pet the bloodhound, who growled at him as if he gave it indigestion.

Willem's jaw twitched. "Milord Alphonse, the last time you saw Lienor she was not yet ten years old," he said. "And anyhow, you must take me for a country fool if you think I would be satisfied by such an answer. My sister is, in fact, very beautiful, so charming I know she would melt any husband's heart, but I am not such a romantic innocent to believe marriages are about anything but politics."

Jouglet, head bent over the fiddle on the shuttered window seat, bit her lower lip, and Konrad sat back against the cushions of his bed, as if to remove himself from the scene.

Alphonse reached out appeasingly to pat Willem's arm. "I did not mean to gull or insult you," he said in a paternal tone. "Of course, every union serves a purpose. But I think you discredit the god of love to entirely discount his role in politics. Otherwise, why would His Majesty favor you with access to a lady, today at dinner? You may choose whom to worship according to your fancy."

Konrad and Jouglet exchanged looks. Konrad made a gesture of giving permission to the minstrel, and Jouglet scoffed, "That's not it at all. You are supposed to decide which *lord* you would most like to serve. And then woo that lord's wife discreetly to flatter not only her, but her husband."

"*What?*" Willem demanded.

"Of course. The wife repays the flattery with gifts of coin, and the husband with general patronage. Lords are always on the hunt for dedicated soldiers. You landless knights always need a patron, and when His Majesty decides he's had enough of you, you'll need another host, won't you? I *told* you to pick a rich one."

Willem looked at the minstrel as if they were not speaking the same language. "*Gain* is the purpose of choosing a lady? I thought gain was the purpose of choosing a *wife*. Where does love enter into it?"

The minstrel held out a hand and tapped it. "You put a coin in my hand and I write you a love song for her, then a hundred years from now they'll think you were in love with her. That's what she rewards you for—an eternity of fantasy, of filling her loveless political marriage with the comforting thought that someday, people will believe she was adored."

The knight made a face. "That's the most appalling thing I've ever heard."

Konrad laughed. "Then you are indeed an innocent, my friend." Willem winced when the emperor gave him a comradely slap on his bruised shoulder.

To avoid his sovereign's expressing further affection with another such slap, Willem stretched and rose to his feet. "If you will excuse me briefly, sire, I've had a lot of your excellent wine this afternoon and need relief." He bowed and headed to the door. "Your Grace," he added over his shoulder, "I am of course biased, but the cask of Burgundian wine I saw the butler putting down for storage on my way to dinner—"

"That was a small gift from myself," Alphonse preened.

"That was a small and very late feudal due," Konrad corrected, cleaning his fingernails.

"In any case, it's excellent stuff, sire," Willem said. "Since your boys are occupied, perhaps Jouglet could make himself useful and fetch us some."

"I try very hard to avoid being useful," Jouglet said lazily from the window seat and did not get up. Willem shrugged and left.

For a few moments, the three of them sat in silence. "A match, uncle," Konrad said at last, gesturing to the chess pieces with exaggerated boredom.

"Shall Jouglet play for us?" said Alphonse.

Konrad stretched. "Later," he said with a yawn. "Right now I'd like to indulge Willem and sample your wretched wine. Run fetch us some, Jouglet."

The minstrel feared very little in this life, but the storage cellar had always made her edgy; it was notorious as the place for soldiers to bring their fleeting objects of desire, willing and unwilling, women and youths; Jouglet had kicked and bitten her way free of such an encounter three summers ago down here, with a knight banished from Konrad's sight for it.

The cellar was directly below the great hall. It was carved on its western length right out of the rock, and at over thirty paces it spanned the whole width of the mountain crest. The northern end, with a little side entrance near the kitchen, had a few small windows to let in light; at that end vegetables, herbs, and cheeses were kept. In the center were grains and flours and piles of containers, and at the southern end, in the cool dark, was the wine. There was a great broad door at this end, large enough to pull the tuns in after they had been hauled up the rocky mountainside. Several huge casks filled most of this end of the dank space, each one set neatly into its own large rocky niche. On one long table just inside the door, the butler's deputy spent a good part of his day, filling and refilling flagons and jars that were being endlessly whisked away for use upstairs. There were two cisterns and a well outside, but those were used mainly for washing and cooking; the thirst of the mountain was satiated almost entirely by wine.

Jouglet, lamp in hand, had arrived at a moment of uncommon calm—there was nobody here. The butler and his assistants were probably helping to unload carts in the soggy lower courtyard. The lack of company added to her unease. She closed the door behind her, aware of the berating she would get from the butler if he came back and found it open. Not certain which jars contained the Burgundy, she set the lamp beside the rows of ceramic and glass and stared at them, as if waiting for one of them to reveal itself.

Large, rough hands grabbed her from behind, and she felt herself pulled back toward another human body. Faster than thought, she kicked backward at her attacker's groin as hard as she could, leaping toward the weak light of the lamp when he released her with a squeal of pain.

"Dammit, Jouglet," a familiar voice wheezed, pitifully, from the damp stone floor.

"Oh, crap," Jouglet breathed and stepped back to the hulking form lying curled in the darkness. "Sorry! What are you doing down here?"

"Waiting for you," Willem whispered tersely, sounding horribly pained, and cursed breathlessly between clenched teeth.

On instinct she reached casually toward where she'd hurt him, but he made an unhappy sound and pushed her hand away, complaining, ". . . worse than anything on the field yesterday."

"Sorry," she repeated. *"Why* were you waiting for me?"

Still trying to calm his breathing, Willem gestured her to bring her head close to his, and she did, tilting her ear toward him to hear what he was saying. He raised his own head high enough but, instead of speaking, pressed his lips against hers briefly. Then he relaxed his head against the cold damp floor again and looked up at her, the gentle brown eyes hopeful but unassuming in the dim lamplight.

Jouglet was thrown. She stared down at him a moment, then the corners of her mouth jerked a little, one side, then the other. "If I were a lady I'd slap you," she informed him.

"But, of course, you're *not* a lady," he answered, and despite the pain he managed to smile up at her tentatively.

"This is very dangerous," she said. She could almost hear her own heartbeat.

"You're right, I'm sorry," he said at once. "I'll go out first, just give me a moment to recover."

Jouglet hesitated and then kissed him. Both sets of lips parted, both tongues darted, explored, and then nearly pulled away again. Jouglet hummed a low, thrilled sound, trying not to laugh from anxiety, and Willem reached up to wrap his arms around her and pull her to the floor where he still lay curled—but a sound outside was clearly the latch of the door being worked, and they heard the butler's distinctive, phlegmatic cough.

"Hey now, who's in here?" the rain-pecked old knight demanded, squinting into the darkness. This man was so familiar with the sounds of his cellar—an office he took seriously as a source of great honor—he would have noticed a new beetle's lair. He pocketed a lot of coinage on the side for not reporting identities.

"It's just myself, sir, and Willem of Dole," Jouglet said reassuringly, sitting upright. "He was helping me to find the Burgundy wine, but we bumped into each other in the dark." Quickly, before the cellarer's eyes could adjust, she ran her hand along Willem's cheek. He reached for it, to kiss the wrist he had twisted so harshly the night before. Then she had to scramble to her feet to avoid looking suspicious.

The butler found the wine from Burgundy with ease, and they went out together into the gallery of the courtyard, almost able to feel each other's heartbeats and confusion as they returned to Konrad's chamber. The air between them as they climbed the narrow spiral steps side by side felt so charged Willem was surprised it did not crackle audibly. He'd been pleased with himself for arranging this, but now he was fighting hard against an erection, which would be inconvenient back in Konrad's room.

Fortunately, the monarch immediately demanded that Willem play one more round of chess against Alphonse, so he himself could coach Willem to a winning game; this gave Willem an excuse for sitting down. Each time the knight began to move a piece to an ill-considered square (which was nearly every move), Konrad would warn him what all the consequences could be. Despite this intellectual solicitude, Willem still lost to Alphonse, because he was so distracted he could barely keep his eyes, let alone his mind, on the board. Jouglet, who annoyed Konrad by being very distracted too, stared absently at the window shutters for the rest of the afternoon and played tunes of such agitation that the dogs began to whine.

"You are both overwrought from your various exertions yesterday," Konrad announced, by way of grudging pardon, and then informed them, "happily, you will each be recovered by suppertime."

But after the supper entertainment, Willem approached His Majesty to beg an early leave for the night. He had one eye on Jouglet, who was showing one of Konrad's younger squires how to sound the fiddle with the bow. Jouglet frowned at him warningly when she felt his attention on her, but the second time he made eye contact, she looked away, then risked the slightest nod. An anticipatory thrill ran down his spine, and yet again—it had happened all afternoon—he had to concentrate hard to control tumescence. Luckily he was bent deeply over his own midsection in his bow to Konrad.

"Already, Willem?" Konrad said, sounding surprised.

His ubiquitous unwanted brother, perched to his left, said, "Are you taking our friendly young minstrel back to your inn with you?"

Before Willem could work out a response to this, Konrad turned smoothly to his brother, smiling. "Forgive me, Paul, we neglected to invite you. We're going down to the town in search of common women. Already time to put on our disguises, Willem? Would you like to come, brother?"

"You're what?" Paul said, appalled and instantly suspicious.

Willem tried to think of something to say to hide how startled he was by the announcement. "My . . . cousin knows where to find them," he stammered. "They share a house at the edge of town. We went there the other night. With Jouglet," he added helpfully.

Konrad smiled. With the back of his hand he smacked his brother heartily, much harder than he needed to for a friendly gesture, right in the gut. "Much more convenient than in our day, eh, Paul?" he said laughing, as the cardinal grunted. "Remember? Wandering the streets, finding only one and having to take turns? I always let you dive in first, and you never thanked me, little ingrate. But that's all water under the bridge. You can come with us tonight if you like and have your own this time."

"*Absolutely* not," said Paul, with an edge of amusement to his disgust, as if he could not wait to share this anecdote of shamelessness with someone who would snicker at it with him.

Konrad smiled serenely at his brother. "Recall that your sainted namesake thought the world was ending."

"What?" asked Paul.

"Saint Paul. Thought the world. Was ending." Konrad spoke with cocky precision. "His repressive code of conduct was not intended to guide humanity for the next twelve hundred years, only for two or three. If he knew he'd made an arithmetical miscalculation about the Second Coming, he surely would not have objected to *our* coming, in whatever manner suited us." He grinned and poked his brother's midriff. "Wouldn't you say?"

Paul brushed the royal hand away. "You lack the imagination to dream up such a convenient heresy," he announced, imitating his brother's affectation of affection. "Who provided you with such a rationale? Jouglet, I suppose?"

Konrad laughed triumphantly. "No, you did! Shortly after you took your vows. You almost used to be fun, Paul. Willem, tell Jouglet what we're up to. I must go dress for the occasion." Winking at Paul he added slyly, "Just like in the old days."

The porter at the rough half-timbered relay hut thought at first the muddy man on horseback was drunk, or demented, beating furiously on the gate with the flat of his hand. The porter held up a rush light and the rider blinked, cringed, made horrible faces. "Is that His Majesty's steward?" the porter gasped. Marcus nodded, his throat too dry to speak. He tried to push the light away. The porter sucked air into the gap between his mossy bottom teeth. "You look horrible, sir, have you fallen ill?"

Marcus shook his head and gestured impatiently toward the stable. The porter, understanding, called for a fresh mount, a wineskin, and some food. Eyes wide, impressed with himself for recognizing Marcus despite the lack of imperial livery, he asked excitedly, "What's the news, then?"

Marcus shook his head, too uncomfortable to speak, but then forced himself to mouth, "Messengers?"

The porter nodded at once. "Oh, surely, two royal riders there've been, both for Burgundy. Last one came through at nones to trade horses. What's happening in Burgundy, anyhow? Always seemed like a backward place to me."

"No food," Marcus said voicelessly. "No time for food, just give me a new horse." Nones—at least seven hours ago. But the two

couriers had left Sudaustat about ten hours ahead of him; so he'd
gained three hours today. It was a four- or five-day ride to Burgundy;
perhaps he could still overtake one of them. He doubted he was capable of murder, but he'd been calculating all day how large a bribe
he could afford—or, should he manage to overtake Nicholas, what
array of threats might bend the young man to his will.

To keep the party small and unobtrusive Willem and Erec had
been charged with the duty of His Majesty's bodyguard. So four
figures in simple burghers' cloaks and tunics made their way through
the drowsing streets of Sudaustat, toward the brilliant, just-washed
sunset over the western gate of town, an area Konrad usually avoided.
The streets were bad here, with loose rock and holes from the rain-
water sometimes knee-deep. From the north gate they had to pass
the butchers' stalls, where offal sat stinking in the wet sewers and the
waste from tanners and smithies wafted sharply from two streets
over. Everything was slightly squishy with mire. Konrad held a scented
kerchief to his face and followed after Erec, who was thrilled to be
the navigator for this undertaking.

When they came to the small low building with the red-swathed
door, Erec rapped once and stepped out of the way for the trinity of
his elders.

It was quieter inside tonight, since much of the tournament traffic was dispersed; only a handful of the itinerant women were still in
town for business. There was one trestle table up, and about a dozen
men around it, most of them drunk and a couple of them even flirting feebly with the women. Seeing Jouglet, Jeannette and Marthe
clapped their hands together and rushed around the drunken flirters

toward the quartet—then Jeannette, recognizing Willem, pulled up short. Marthe did not; gleefully she made a beeline for the knight and began to run her hands up and down his chest, bending over to show off her cleavage to the others while looking up at him with fluttering eyes. "Oh, milord, I've *missed* you," she said in a throaty, plaintive voice.

Konrad watched her, tickled. "Pity Paul isn't here to see this," he said to no one in particular.

"I haven't enjoyed anything since our tryst. You were so generous, in every sense." To the other prostitutes, she said slyly, performing, "His nose is large because it's been broken, but the rest of him is large by Nature's own designs." And her hand ran down toward Willem's groin; already blushing to his hairline, he grabbed her wrist to stop her, with a weak, polite smile.

"He's a gentleman," Konrad said to Marthe, explaining Willem's unwillingness to be publicly groped. "He wants to pay you first. So off with you, then." He grinned at Willem. "That's why we're here, after all, and you deserve first pick." He gestured broadly, and for a moment Willem was afraid Konrad was about to wallop his bruised shoulder yet again with one of his enthusiastic displays of regard. "Go find yourself a corner and enjoy a well-earned rut."

"But surely the grand hero deserves special treatment to celebrate his victory," Jouglet declared, and gestured toward the ceiling. "I know there's a private closet in the rafters, the mistress of the house has indulged me in the use of it."

"The charge is tripled for that indulgence," said the mistress of the house, appearing suddenly at the table. She winked at Jouglet.

Jouglet made an expansive, insouciant gesture. "My credit is good here, isn't it? My treat."

Stone-faced, avoiding Jouglet entirely, Willem allowed himself to be taken up the rickety wooden ladder nailed to the wall. He and Marthe disappeared into a cavity in the ceiling.

The three remaining customers looked around. Pointing at Jeannette with a knowing smile, Erec informed His Majesty, "She's good."

Jeannette was staring hard at Jouglet with an occasional glance after Willem and did not react to the commendation. Konrad followed Erec's gesture and his face lit up. "Jeannette!" he boomed without thinking. "Lovely Jeannette!" He grinned at Erec. "You're right, she's very good. Jeannette, tonight you're mine."

Jeannette recovered herself at once and slid up beside the emperor, crooning into his ear, "I recognize you, Your Majesty, so if your pleasure is to remain incognito, perhaps you should take one of the visiting girls."

Konrad had closed a hand over one of her breasts when she had pressed against him, and he squeezed it now, smiling. But with one firm finger she turned his face to meet hers and raised her eyebrows meaningfully, and he released her. "You're right," he said. "No thrill in being secretive when the girl already knows the secret. Find me a snug one."

"The blonde," Jouglet said confidently.

Jeannette nodded and pointed to the smallest of the three young women who had lined up behind them. She was not a blonde; none of them were, really, but she was the palest of the trio. "Jehanne has come all the way from Bremen; she will never recognize you," Jeannette promised in a whisper, and Jehanne, at her gesture, curtsied and took a step forward.

"You're free then, Jeannette," Erec said with a slightly stupid grin. "Come with me—"

"Oh, milord Erec," Jeannette said with an admiring smile. "Don't be stingy with your gifts, give all of us a chance. Susanna!" she called out to the darkest-haired one. "Be worthy of this fine young man." Obediently Susanna plastered a smile to her face and stepped up to him, and he, appraising her cleavage with the finesse of a mason appraising a bridge, was pleased.

"Do you want a drink first, milord?" Jeannette asked. Again she stared hard at Jouglet, who affected not to see her by taking tremendous interest in a bit of dirt stuck in a knothole of the table.

Konrad waved his hand. "We've had our full supper, we just came here for some . . . fulfillment. Where shall we go for fulfillment?"

"There are canvas caves in the yard behind us," Jeannette said. "But I hardly think it suits His Royal—"

"No, no," Konrad said, with an expansive gesture. "Tonight I am simply one of the knights Paul gets in such a state about. I need to know how my men are spending their salt—and their seed." So Jeannette gestured with a meaningful glance at Jehanne and Susanna; both girls curtsied to the men and began to lead them toward the yard.

Konrad paused at the door and glanced over his shoulder at Jouglet. "And you are going with Jeannette?" It was more an order than a question. Jouglet nodded, with an offhand shrug.

Jeannette ran a hand through Jouglet's thick hair. "I'll take good care of him, sir," she promised.

When they were gone, Jeannette, her hand still enmeshed in the fiddler's hair, gently jerked Jouglet's head up, and their eyes met. Jeannette raised her eyebrows questioningly, hopefully, her head cocked a little. "The knight?" she mouthed, releasing her friend.

Jouglet nodded almost imperceptibly, and without realizing chewed her lower lip a moment, nervously.

Jeannette grinned, grabbed Jouglet's hand, and pulled her to standing, dragging her toward the ladder.

Willem was kneeling on a tattered canvas mat looking tense, the unbuckled sword belt with its leather scabbard clutched in his hands.

He scrambled up with obvious relief when Jouglet entered and smacked his head on the low ceiling of the sleeping closet, which sent him back to his knees with a grunt. Marthe, surprised by the new arrivals, looked back and forth between Jouglet and Willem for a moment, her eyes widening with a dawning comprehension.

Jeannette coughed playfully and gestured with her head, and Marthe, nearly chirping with amusement, left, pulling the curtain closed behind her. Jeannette and Jouglet, both stooping beneath the low ceiling, sank to their knees on either side of Willem. The dingy curtain did not cover the entire doorway, and uneven light from a rush lamp gave the little room, barely a crawl space, sharp-angled shadows.

Jeannette finally let herself speak aloud. "I hope milord knight will forgive me my impertinence last night up in the courtyard of Koenigsbourg."

Willem, looking awkward, said, "I deserved it. In fact I'm grateful for it."

She smiled tentatively. "Thank you, milord." Then in a rush of gleeful informality, she leaned into Willem and said confidingly, "You should have seen her the night before the tourney, she was in such a state."

"I was not," Jouglet said.

"Oh, she was, milord," the whore assured him.

"That's enough, Jeannette," Jouglet said pointedly, but Jeannette cheerfully ignored this.

"You're the first man she's ever revealed herself to, milord, did you know that? Usually she just disguises herself as one of us for some thigh-jousting when she requires relief. You must be very special for her to risk revealing herself to someone who knows her as—"

"Our hostess would like some money," Jouglet informed Willem, who was self-consciously trying to look busy in the constricted space without actually undressing in front of the prostitute. He did this mostly by laying down his sword and then picking it up again, as if he'd just noticed it. Jeannette looked pleased that her business had been made clear. "That's what this is about. Although I'm not sure," Jouglet added, glaring at her friend, "if the strategy is to flatter you into a generous mood, or to simply make me desperate to shut her up."

"Why not both?" Jeannette laughed. Jouglet flicked her teeth at her in mock exasperation, then unknotted her overknotted belt-pouch and handed out some silver pennies. Jeannette asked hope-fully, "And will you be using our services often then, milords?"

"No," said Jouglet firmly. "The new darling of the court can't be seen going to the whores regularly, that's as bad as attaching himself to a flagrant sodomite like myself. We are only here now to please Konrad." She met Jeannette's gaze then looked meaningfully at the low, curtained doorway.

"Ah, so she's cultivating you," Jeannette said, ignoring Jouglet's glance. "She's good at that, you know—Marcus the seneschal will be given freeman status, and have a duchy and a royal wife soon thanks to Jouglet."

"That's just a rumor," Jouglet said impatiently. "For God's sake, Willem, give her some money, would you? Or she'll never leave."

When they were alone in the slanted shadows—the whores' giggles clearly audible two paces away beyond the grey curtain—Willem and Jouglet, kneeling side by side on the thin canvas mat, each held out a hand to the other. She reached up to untie his mantle.

He stopped her.

"Please don't tell me you want to recite love songs to me first," Jouglet said.

"This seems a sordid and shameful way to carry on."

"Well it's certainly not as dignified as jumping me in the wine cellar," she conceded. "Do you have a better idea?" She shrugged his hand away and finished untying his mantle, pushing it off his shoulders with one hand as with the other she reached under her chin to untie her own.

Willem reached out quickly and stopped her hand again. "What is this we are doing?" he asked quietly. "Who are you to me? What is Jouglet to Willem?"

She swatted his hand away. "That is a pointless conversation. I'm your friend, of course. And your secret sponsor until you can steer yourself aright through the dangerous straits of court policy. If you like, I'll be your lover. But I cannot be your lady, Willem, and you do require a lady, so I'll find you one."

"I don't need a lady now," he said softly. "There is a minstrel who already has a huge measure of my esteem—"

"A lady is more susceptible to poetry, and better for your future," Jouglet said firmly, untying her mantle.

"This . . . if this . . ." He gestured awkwardly between them. "If this is going to be, I cannot seek someone else to be devoted to."

"That could just be for show, Willem, but it's a show you must perform to protect both our reputations."

He shook his head. "Then we can't do this. I would be making a harlot of you."

"Nobody will *know*." Jouglet laughed impatiently, pulling off the mantle and glancing toward the curtain.

"*I'll* know," Willem said. "God will know."

She smiled with exasperation. "Very well, then. How might we proceed intelligently without offending your chivalrous and pious sensibilities?"

"Your sarcasm is not helpful," Willem said with irritation. "I've been thinking about this all afternoon—"

"I thought as much—that noble brow has those little rows of horizontal furrows in it that it tends toward when you are trying very hard to be a good knight."

Still serious, Willem took her hands. "Be my lady. Secretly," he added quickly, seeing her about to burst into dismissive laughter. "The beloved's name ought to be kept secret anyhow. Nobody will ever know but the two of us. This is . . . let me *earn* this from you. If I don't do that somehow, this will be nothing but my baser nature taking advantage of the situation. I want to prove myself, or it will seem to come too cheaply."

"This does *not* come cheaply," Jouglet countered sharply. "For either of us." She took her hands out of his and looked at him almost as seriously as he was looking at her. "Willem's secret lady is a role that I can't play. It would be even more ludicrous than merely being your secret lover, you know that. And forgive me for distrusting your chivalrous behavior, but you want me to play the role mostly so that *you* can play a role, too—and it's a worthy role, but I'm one of the only people with whom you don't need to play it, and I like that." She began to unlace her left boot. "We really don't have much time, let's not waste it."

Again Willem reached out to stop her from undressing, very firmly placing her hand back upon her own lap. "We are going no further until we have an understanding of what I would be doing to you."

Jouglet looked almost cross. "Konrad will not linger in a muddy canvas tent. We only have a few moments alone in here, Willem, how do you want to spend them?"

He considered her in the dim light, his eyes quickly, involuntarily, flickering over the whole of her body before returning to her face. "I want to undress you, of course," he said, with disarming sheepishness.

She was taken by surprise, and laughed a little. She kissed him, and smiled when he grabbed her by both arms. His hands worked their way across her still-clothed body and began to feel for the breasts his cheek has rested on earlier.

"They're still there," she assured him, and they were.

It felt thrillingly bizarre to each of them for Willem to take the lead. For Jouglet there was also an unfamiliar relief, that for once she allowed herself the forbidden luxury of being acted upon, instead of acting. She helped him only passively, raising an arm or a knee to add grace to his fumbling, hurried disrobing of her, but otherwise she literally put herself entirely into his hands.

When he had peeled everything away he stretched her nude body down across the mat, running his hand up the middle of her torso, trying to spread his fingers to touch both nipples at once. "This is your body," he murmured. He cupped a hand around one small breast in the shadows. "This"—the other hand went to one hip—"and this"—the first hand moved along the delicate curve of her rib cage, and her waist—"and all this, has been here all the time—"

"We don't have time for that," Jouglet whispered, smiling at the warmth of his touch. She reached up to pull at the gold pin of his tunic. "Join me."

He blushed. "I'm shy to undress before you."

She laughed. "But I've already seen you naked."

"I know. It's absurd."

"I'll close my eyes," she offered and did so.

He kissed her eyelids. "No, I'm man enough to handle this."

"Then so am I," she grinned, eyes opening again.

Stooping under the sloped ceiling, he unceremoniously disrobed. Then he knelt on the understuffed mat and shifted one large leg to straddle her.

Jouglet saw the look that flitted across his face, and she raised a hand to touch his bare chest lightly. "Yes, Willem," she said softly, answering the unasked question. "I've done this more than you have, and with more partners. But," she promised, whispering, "you are by far the most cherished man who has ever found himself where you are now."

Willem smiled and kissed her forehead, then carefully lowered his weight onto her. His eyes were close to Jouglet's cool, familiar face as his body felt the outlines of the warm and unknown woman underneath him. When her legs parted as he pressed down between them, when he pushed into her and felt her clench around him in response, Jouglet's face and voice responded too, timed so exactly to his actions there was no way to ignore that he was possessing, entering, taking his best friend. Nothing had ever felt so complicated. It was enthralling.

11

Rhetoric

[the art of ethical persuasion]

15 July

Marcus reached Oricourt Castle in Burgundy in the middle of a morning, at the end of he did not know how many days. Memory, instinct, and his good sense of direction had brought him through unfamiliar Vosges mountain passes. The air was clean and fresh after the rainstorm he had ridden through, but he himself was not.

He'd been received here formally before; they knew him at the outer gate. They also knew why he had come, and the porter's boys avoided making eye contact with him. It was obvious from this that the messenger had been here, that the axe had already fallen.

He hardly noticed what happened next. He was in the outer courtyard, the odor of livestock oddly comforting after days of unfamiliar marsh and mountain scents. He was by the stables. He was breathing even harder than his horse, and the bay, almost white with sweaty foam, was about to collapse. The stableboy, on the alert, had already run inside; by the time Marcus was dismounting, Alphonse's stout wife, Monique, Countess of Burgundy, was standing at the opening to the inner courtyard, under the great arching stone gate-lintel, bracing herself for a confrontation. Even in his anguish and exhaustion, he appreciated the genuine decency of the woman—meeting him alone, not flanked by threatening retainers.

Marcus stumbled when he landed on the ground, because the bad leg was still numb. *That stupid injury.* He walked stiff legged, like an old man with arthritis—for three steps, and then his body crumpled underneath him into the sandy mud and he heard, as if from a great distance, his own voice moan with pain.

The next thing he saw clearly was the enormous, elongated under-jaw of a hunting hound, its damp nose anxiously sniffling at his hair. A female voice called the dog to heel; in its absence, a woman's face bent over him, frowning, but now he was inside. On a cold floor, near a warm hearth. On musty rushes. His sword was gone. He tried to remember where he was, and why the face was so familiar. That was Monique—the daughter of the family in whose home he had been raised. He had been fond of her. Why was she here?

He saw behind her a whitewashed wall with a banner hanging on it, visible from the light of a small, parchment-covered window: gold with angled double bars of red across it. Where did he know that from?

The Burgundian coat of arms.

Oh, God.

"Your sword is with the porter," Monique said reassuringly, in greeting. "It will be returned on your departure."

He sat up, using his elbows to keep his balance on the floor. Monique took a few steps away from the fire to give him space, and with a gesture commanded the dog to do likewise. "Good milady, I have come to seek audience with your daughter," he said, as polite and formal as he could make it sound, willing her not to notice his filthy clothes, dirty face, and wanton-looking hair.

The plump aristocratic woman shook her head. "You cannot see her, Marcus. She is dictating a letter that you had best go back to Koenigsbourg to receive."

He dragged himself to his knees, slid toward her on the rushes and then prostrated himself right at her feet, clinging to her low leather boots. The hound moved closer with a delicate growl. "Please. Please, Monique, for the love of God, please let me see her."

"You are making a spectacle of yourself, Marcus," she said softly. "I do not think you would venture such behavior with anyone else, and you should not venture it with me."

He rolled over on the rushes and stared miserably at the low arched ceiling. "Please let me see her. You can stay in the room. I'm not asking to be let into her chamber, let her come out here."

"She is not in a mood to be seen," Monique informed him, gently.

He indulged in a short, exhausted, bitter laugh. "She will want to see me."

"Marcus, I know you took a genuine affection for each other—I hadn't realized how genuine until her reaction to the message from her father—but it will only exacerbate the pain for both of you."

"Did he say why he's done it? Has he named the new intended husband?" Marcus demanded, resisting the urge to spit. She lowered her eyes and tried to seem nonchalant, which gave Marcus his answer. "What if Imogen refuses? Good God, does Willem even know your husband's intentions? Is Willem the least bit interested in marrying her?"

"The issue is not whom she will marry but whom she won't," Monique said uncomfortably. "She will not marry you."

In that moment, Marcus—who did not like deception and was

almost never good at it—knew exactly what he would have to do. With masonic precision every step of the plan lay open in his mind. A thrill, a surge went through him: it would not be a pleasant process, or an honorable one, but at the end of it, he would have his lover as his wife.

Affecting resignation, he sat up and tried, uselessly, to comb his fingers through matted hair. He rubbed his sleeve against his face, but the sleeve was so filthy that he only put himself into worse appearance.

"I must be a mess," he said in a husky voice, barely above a whisper. "Please forgive me, milady, for appearing in your home so out of sorts." In obvious pain, he pulled himself up to his knees and then with further wincing got to his feet. He bowed politely, then stood at attention near the hearth, with his head slightly lowered, as if awaiting her instructions. This was the public stance he adopted with Konrad—it was a gesture of how entirely he seemed to place himself at her disposal. "How kind of you to receive me on my journey south as the emperor's ambassador," he added, giving both of them an excuse for this encounter.

Monique looked at him, troubled, for a long silent moment, then she sighed and adopted a suddenly formal air. "As loyal subjects my daughter and I would of course be delighted to receive our emperor's ambassador."

His heart leapt. "Do you mean you will—"

"It is not the custom to allow gentlemen into my daughter's room, but perhaps our minstrel can entertain you with a song while I fetch my daughter out." At his look of crazed hope she lowered her voice to add, "You will accomplish nothing by it, Marcus."

He at once bent in half with a second bow, but she gestured him, rather sharply, to rise. "A supplicant for my daughter's hand might bow so. The emperor's proxy does not."

The minstrel played Bertran de Born songs for what seemed

like months while Monique was away. Bertran de Born—the troubadour-knight who'd turned young Henry of England against his king and father. It seemed painfully appropriate. Perhaps it was due to his agitated state, but Marcus found the music graceless and flat, and the singer's voice was entirely dull compared to Jouglet's husky tenor. For a fourth time Marcus pushed away the attentive hound and suddenly wished he'd stayed at court and employed Jouglet to aid in this—Jouglet was a skilled manipulator, and Marcus was not; Jouglet had caused these problems, but without knowing of the dire consequences, and would surely amend the scheme if apprised of the whole situation.

Perhaps. Perhaps not. Jouglet's schemes were often too subtle for Marcus to track; it might be in the minstrel's interest for the heir of Burgundy to be married to the first Imperial Knight—although *why*, Marcus could not guess.

He glanced around the hall, surprised by how repressive and damp it felt, even compared to the harsh environment of Koenigsbourg. The room was hardly large enough for entertaining—not that Alphonse was likely to have many guests on this isolated hilltop, far from even his few devoted vassals. It was a new building, built within Marcus's lifetime, but it was dowdy and dark; no wonder the count was willing to endure the endless small humiliations Konrad foisted on him for the pleasure of staying anywhere but here. He had always pitied Monique for her marriage; now he pitied her entire situation.

The countess finally reappeared from the door to the yard. Behind her was Imogen, dressed in white. Marcus had a brief, glorious, insane fantasy of grabbing her and fleeing with her across the countryside.

Instead he stood at polite attention as the two drew near the fire. Imogen's face was livid from sobbing. He wondered when the message had been delivered, by how many hours he had failed to intercept it. Their eyes met. She looked besotted with affection for him, even now. He was enraged to think of another man ever seeing such regard on her face. Of another man feeling her warm hands undressing him. Of another man feeling the cool smooth skin of her buttocks pressing up against him. A man who did not know her and was worth less than Marcus himself, a man who did not deserve her. And would reject her, perhaps denounce her, once he knew the truth. He saw her entire body start slightly, realized she was barely checking the urge to throw herself into his arms. "Milady," he said hoarsely with a polite bow to Monique. His voice was trembling. He was trembling. He cleared his throat and tried again. "Milady, may I have dispensation to embrace your daughter? It is a gesture of regard from Emperor Konrad."

Monique looked at the ground, hesitated, sighed, then said, "Very well. As long as it does not surpass what the emperor himself would deem seemly."

He did not tell her the emperor's idea of seemliness would practically allow him to mount Imogen naked on the rushes. He held his arms out slightly and took half a step toward her; she ran to him and wrapped her arms around his neck, dissolving at once into such pathetic weeping that he could barely keep his own sobs in check. "Dearest," he whispered. "I can remedy this."

Imogen pulled her head back to peer up at his face. In the exaggerated shadows of the hall, she looked not only miserable, but frightened. Marcus wanted desperately to say more, to tell her what he would do now, but he could think of no words that would not somehow give them away to Monique. He wanted to kiss her; her little body felt so familiar in his arms, it was maddening not to do what was familiar now and caress her. Her frightened expression shifted, softening to the warmth of his body against hers. She closed her eyes, nestled against him, quivering.

Monique, sensing the rising heat, cut it off immediately. "Very well, sir, you have more than expressed His Majesty's chaste affection for my daughter."

They let go of each other, reluctantly. Marcus was too moved to think of anything to say, even any gracious, empty courtier's comments.

So Monique took the matter in hand. With firmness, she excused Imogen from the room, and the girl drifted out like a ghost, walking backward, her eyes on her lover until she had disappeared from view. He felt his throat constrict and a single drop of ice-water move through his heart. "We thank you again, good sir, for condescending to stop for a visit on your journey," Monique said. "Before you continue your trip south and westward, do you wish to bathe?" And lowering her voice, "Marcus, what *is* your journey south and westward? Please reassure me you are not so far gone that you have come all the way here just to sob at my feet."

Marcus hesitated a moment, then explained briskly, "I must congratulate our future empress. I assume your husband has told you of these plans in his . . . missive."

She nodded, avoiding his glance, understanding as clearly as he did why the royal match had inspired Alphonse to break this betrothal.

He knew what to do now, and he could hardly wait to get away . . . but a good night's sleep would make him more presentable. "If I may trouble your servants for a bath, and you for a bed, and your groom to trade a mount for the one I have brought here—he is an excellent racer, I would be happy with a docile gelding if that would make the exchange more attractive to you. And please tell your daughter she should face her future with perfect equanimity."

Monique looked relieved. "Thank you, Marcus. I think of you as a brother from the days you served in my father's home, and I would like to believe it is possible that in the future you might visit with us, even with Imogen's husband beside her."

"It is possible," he said, smiling. "It is almost certain."

Still in a twilight state before he had quite reached consciousness, Willem became aware of a wonderful, unfamiliar feeling: beside him under the sheets was the warm, smooth body of a woman. He wasn't sure who she was at first, but she smelled pleasant and familiar. And her hair was short.

"Oh Lord," he chuckled involuntarily, suddenly wide awake. Despite the minstrel's clever machinations, this was the first night they had managed to spend together—in fact, the first time since the trip to the whores they had managed to steal any time alone at all.

Jouglet had been extremely vigilant about the general public's perception of the knight. So she had seen to it for four days the two of them had had the chance to interact only in public, only as friends; Jouglet's company, in company, was so enjoyable that he could have resigned himself to nothing more than that. But last night she had convinced the emperor he wanted the visiting minnesinger Albert Johansdorf to play him to sleep, and she had come down to the inn to entertain in the yard for three dances, before slipping unnoticed up to Willem's room and waiting for him to join her there himself. She'd negotiated with Jeannette to keep Erec away until dawn; the page boys and servant were happy to obey their master's request that they sleep out in the yard on such a hot, muggy night. So Jouglet and Willem had the room alone.

He had never in his life awoken naked beside a woman; it was ferociously erotic. He slid one hand between her thighs and watched her face for a response.

Jouglet stirred and opened her eyes, staring straight up at him. She was alarmed for half a heartbeat; she had never in her life awoken naked beside a man. She blinked once, twice. Then she relaxed, smiled, and reached up with delicate but calloused fingers to stroke his face. He leaned over her at once to kiss her lips, ready to start the morning with some more earnest fornication.

Erec's voice sounded from the yard, and footsteps began to pound up the stairs outside. With astonishing alacrity, Jouglet fell out of the bed, reaching out for her discarded tunic so that it was halfway over her head before she had even settled on the floor. She curled up like a sleeping child, closed her eyes, and seemed to be slumbering, clothed and contented in the strewing herbs, when Erec threw the door open less than three heartbeats later to let in cool, bright sunshine. He looked cheerier and more relaxed than Willem had ever seen him in his life. "Cousin!" he cried out. "Wake up, champion, the emperor awaits us! It's hawking today, he's even bought you your own falcon! And you've slept through breakfast again."

Jouglet's eyes opened slowly and squinted, as if just now adjusting to the light in the room. "Goodness you're loud," the minstrel said, yawning again. "I'm never that bouncy after a whole night with Jeannette! How's a body to sleep?"

"You're a bad influence on my cousin," Erec rebuked good-naturedly. "This is the third time since we arrived he's slept through breakfast."

With a tired laugh, Jouglet reached for the smaller pair of breeches on the floor, and slowly stood. As she pulled the drawers on, Willem distracted Erec by throwing off his sheets and saying, "Erec, help me find my shirt, I was drunk last night and can't remember where I put anything."

"We had some women in here, maybe they stole the champion's

breeches," Jouglet suggested, and winked at Willem. "That tall thin one, with the low voice—I wouldn't trust her with my own shadow."

Willem started laughing, nervously. He glanced back and forth between Jouglet and Erec, amazed as he was every day that Erec could not see Jouglet for what she was.

And yet, once they were both fully dressed, Willem found it hard to believe—as he did every day—that the minstrel was anything but a young man. There were no affected mannerisms, either way, nothing obvious that changed between Jouglet as woman and Jouglet as man and minstrel. The same vocal inflections, the same gestures, that same infectious laugh, changed without changing. It was seamless. And—when Willem was not near her—vexing.

The day spent hawking was wonderful, especially for Erec. They were attended by tremendous pomp, a pipe-and-tabor player, a herald with the royal flag; the animals were finer and faster than Willem's own beloved falcon, whom he had left behind in Dole. They went up into the hills west and north of the mountain, where the air was dryer and cool. It was a perfect day. Birches and hazelnuts were heavy with green fruit; lindens and blackberry blossoms flooded the air with their pollen.

Paul, on his Castilian dun, in his ceremonial black and scarlet best, was unnervingly attentive to Willem's every move. A flash of near panic on Jouglet's freckled face early in the day explained the danger clearly, and then Willem felt foolish for not understanding earlier: Paul wanted the church's proffered bride in Besançon chosen over Lienor, and was eager for opportunities to discredit her by discrediting any member of her camp. A charge of sodomy might not get her brother burned at the stake, but it was a convenient and increasingly forceful means of political manipulation. That was, Willem argued to himself, an excellent reason for Jouglet to finally end her long-term charade and let the world know she was a woman. He would not force the issue, and he had sworn not to betray her secret, but every passing day made him more determined to convince her to be truthful. Paul's obvious intention to cause trouble for them surely would support his cause.

Alphonse, Count of Burgundy, in contrast to his crony and nephew the cardinal, was becoming increasingly sycophantic. The tall potbellied lord was especially attentive whenever Konrad or Jouglet turned the conversation to the belle Lienor and the presumed approaching nuptials. The emperor, more out of his regard for Willem than from any native interest in proving himself a good husband, played the groom eager to please his bride in all things, and passed the idler moments of the hunt querying Jouglet and Willem about Lienor's preferences—the foods she liked most, the cut of fabrics she favored in her gowns, the style of music ("anything I play," Jouglet said smugly), her preferred sports and pastimes. They crested a hill known for its tricky air currents and watched Konrad's falcon pounce on a small female buzzard high overhead—and Willem adroitly told stories of how well his sister shrugged off metaphorically similar attentions from a variety of lords and knights.

Willem's short-winged hawk, the latest of many gifts from Konrad, got a pheasant—the largest game of the day. This set Jouglet to improvising a ballad, set to an old dance tune, in which the minstrel insinuated Willem's manly prowess accounted for the driving strength of his bird's fierce talons. That evening in the hall, at supper, Konrad declared him Hero of the Hunt and offered him as gift anything his heart wanted in the castle, beside the royal crown or the favorite royal mistress.

Willem, seated beside His Majesty, as was now the given custom, pretended he had to think it over.

"I suppose . . . ," he said at length, chewing on a saffron-gilded chicken leg, "I suppose I'd like a gift that I may in turn share with others."

"A noble impulse," Konrad said. "I would expect nothing less from you."

"Thank you, sire. Music is most easily shared, and my fellow lodgers are given to late-night dancing."

Konrad gave him a scrutinizing look. Paul was glancing back and forth between them with anticipation, so Konrad forced himself to smile. "Done. A costly gift, but given freely." He looked over toward the lower end of the hall, where Jouglet was waiting to be served. "Jouglet, did you hear? After supper you'll spend the evening entertaining at the inn where Willem is staying."

A flicker of a dangerous smile tickled the cardinal's lips, and for a moment Willem feared that he had blundered.

Jouglet made a face. "The floor of an inn is hardly equal to Your Majesty's cushioned window seat," she said. "Nonetheless, if Your Majesty wills it, I am as always your obedient servant."

When she knew Paul was looking away, she frowned at Willem, not sure if she should be delighted or disturbed by his aptness as a pupil.

*L*ienor and her mother had dismissed all the male servants from the house so that the two of them and their women could shriek unselfconsciously with their astonished glee.

The gold-sealed missive had arrived that morning, delivered by charming Nicholas in his spotless livery and ermine cape. He was delighted by the duty. Maria had not wished Lienor to receive even this man in her brother's absence, especially since the men assigned to guard the place were in the village playing chess with the chaplain, or so they claimed. But after it was made quite clear to Nicholas that the family would never normally allow this sort of thing, Lienor, in a conservative green tunic, came into the hall, greeted the imperial messenger demurely, in the presence of her mother and all the male indoor servants, and received the scroll.

"May I tell you what it contains?" Nicholas had asked, trying to mask his eagerness. Five days' anticipation of this moment had given it a wildly romantic sheen for him. This was a moment minstrels would sing about; he could not wait to get home and describe it to Jouglet.

"I hope it is news of my brother's success in the tournament," said Lienor, smiling. "And I think from your expression that must be it. May I save the seal? I kept the one from your first visit, I was going to make a brooch of it for mother. Now we may have matching ones. And I have a lovely pearl pin to give you in exchange." She began to pull off the seal, beaming.

He held up a polite hand. "I left halfway through the tournament, but your brother was already winning the day—"

"I knew it!" she sang, clapping her hands around the scroll in excitement. "Mother, did you hear? Are the details in here?"

"That is not what the message concerns," Nicholas said. Maria joined them from the kitchen screen where she had been hovering, pleased by the news about her son—but like any doting mother with exceptional children, not at all surprised. "The message is a request from the emperor to you directly."

Lienor was astonished. "To me?" she echoed, and turned red. She bit her lower lip, like a bashful child, struggling to find her voice. "What would the emperor want of me?"

Nicholas smiled broadly and announced, "If you are willing, your hand in marriage."

Her eyes got very wide and then—to her mother's consternation—she began to laugh hysterically. "For the love of God!" she cried out.

"I don't believe it!" She sobered a little, then said with affected terseness, "You are mocking me, sir."

"I am not, I swear it. But there is a caveat."

"What is it?" Maria demanded. Her breathing seemed fast and shallow, but she said nothing more.

He bowed politely, hiding how startled he was to hear Maria speak; he had assumed she was a mute. "The Assembly of Lords must approve His Majesty's choice, and they are meeting on the first of August. He will propose the young lady as his choice of bride. If the majority of the Assembly finds it a fit match, and he believes they will, he will send the official proposal to you, with much more celebration and public proclamations along the way. Before making such a gesture, he of course wants your consent. He already has your brother's."

Lienor sat stunned. Maria cleared her voice and politely demanded, "What would keep the lords from approving my daughter? She is certainly fit for the emperor's bed."

"Mother!" Lienor gasped. Then more collected, to Nicholas: "The lords will not want me because we're so poor."

Nicholas nodded. "Yes. But His Majesty believes he has deflected the issue. Your brother has made a tremendous impression on the court. He was already being celebrated before he even arrived—"

"That would be Jouglet again," Lienor murmured, looking pleased.

"Yes, but now his own deeds will mark him out for approbation. A nearly landless orphan girl will never win approval by the Assembly. Willem of Dole's sister may. If nothing else they would do it just to affirm your brother's ties to the emperor."

She smiled, satisfied by the reply.

"So," Nicholas concluded. "You may keep the gold seal, my lady, but only as a reminder of the days when you would feel the need to do so. You will soon be swimming in gold that is much finer than mere foil."

She started laughing again and turned to her mother, who, besides shining eyes, refrained from expressing her excitement in front of a stranger. "Mother, can you believe all that is happening to your two little children?"

"His Majesty suggests you prepare yourself and put your affairs down here in order, so that you may go off instantly upon his formal proposal. I hope to return with that, within a week of the August first Assembly."

"Oh, dear." Lienor sighed happily, with mock exhaustion, clasping her hands together. "I *suppose* we can find the time to do that. Mother, will you see that the good messenger has something to eat. I must begin to . . . *prepare* myself." She stood up, still laughing, and curtsied gracefully to him. "Good sir, I cannot thank you enough for your news. You are welcome to stay as a guest for as long as you like."

"Thank you." Nicholas smiled, bowing back. "But I have a room at the inn, and I am expected there. Besides I think your brother would not like your sharing board with a man you hardly know."

"He would make an exception for this," Lienor assured him.

He bowed again. "Perhaps, milady. But really I have other business to attend to. I am delighted to have been given the honor to share this happy news with you." He put his hand to his heart. "I wish you and your family all the best, my lady Lienor."

And when Nicholas was gone, they sent the male servants from the house.

And when the male servants were gone, Maria led the hubbub of uproarious delight, sobbing with joy, drowning her daughter in maternal kisses, and allowing even the lowest female house servants to come into their private quarters for a shared flagon of Willem's best wine.

*I*t was late afternoon when Marcus spotted Nicholas to the northeast of Dole, with barely a moment to turn off into a small grove of woods to hide. The messenger would not have seen him anyhow; he turned to the west to head into the little burg. But Marcus waited until he was safely gone, and then at a slow walk, he brought his horse back on the road, turning south toward the river Doubs. His palms were sweating and his fingers trembled as he held the reins. It was not fatigue or hunger now. It was his conscience, but over the course of the day's ride from Oricourt, it had already lost the fight.

Soon he came into view of Willem's tiny estate—good fertile soil from the river plain, green and golden as sunset approached, so small the whole of it could be seen in one glance. He was spotted by somebody on the roof of a storage silo, and he heard voices calling out to one another cheerfully to announce that a new rider was approaching. His heart quickened. One of those voices was surely . . . hers.

*B*ut, Mother," Lienor begged in her chamber, as the now-tipsy female population of the manor was finally calming down from their gleeful cheering. The slanting light of late afternoon gave her a golden glow that made her look—and even feel—imperial, although she was in nothing but her shift. "No evil came of my receiving male company an hour ago. In fact, something splendid happened! Perhaps it will again."

Maria shook her head and adjusted her grey wimple. "You were just the sister of a poor knight when I allowed Nicholas in to see you. Now you belong to the emperor, and forgive me, but I must be strict."

Lienor sighed. She tossed down the vermillion gown she'd been about to try. "I do not mean to be ungracious, Mother, but I find this a cruel conundrum, that first I was caged because I was a child, then I was caged for being a woman but unattached, and now I must be caged because I am a woman and attached! When am I allowed out of the cage?"

Her mother gave her a patient, knowing smile. "When you are a widow," she explained.

Marcus was announced and escorted into what struck him as a humble, dark, plain—and yet very homey—hall. Maria (quite tipsy now) received him with a curtsy and expressed surprise and gratitude when he offered up his sword to her steward. "Another messenger from the emperor," she said pleasantly. "Is this to do with the wedding?"

He had known, of course, that Konrad's message was a marriage proposal, but hearing a member of this household refer to it directly gave him a rush of dread. "In a sense, milady," he said, stammering a little. "His Majesty wanted his betrothed to have the honor of being greeted by more than a mere messenger. He wanted me personally to convey his delight at the prospect of matrimony." Inspired, he pulled a gold and onyx ring he'd had from Konrad off his right index finger. "And I would be honored if she accepted this as a token of regard from me."

To Maria the entire world now revolved around this marriage, and his feeble explanation sounded reasonable to her. "Thank you, sir, we are again deeply honored. I shall convey your message to her." She held out her hand for the ring.

This was a wrinkle Marcus had somehow not anticipated. "May . . . may I not see her myself?"

"Oh, no." Maria smiled. "She is naturally sequestered in her brother's absence, she does not receive gentlemen." She took the ring politely from Marcus's distracted grip. "May I offer you refreshment?"

"There is actually a discussion I must have with her," Marcus said, trying to think of what it was and trying also not to sound desperate. "He . . . Konrad . . . His Majesty would, would like to know if there are any questions or concerns she has, or requests of any kind, that I might take back to him regarding what is to follow. Matters of the household, I'm sure you will appreciate—"

Maria mused on this. "No," she announced comfortably.

Marcus considered her a moment, wondering what to try next. Perhaps his plan could still work. It had to. Perhaps the mother herself would afford an opportunity. "Thank you, I would love some refreshment. Something strong, perhaps. Will you drink with me, milady?"

The request flustered Maria out of her quiet composure. "I?" she stammered.

"Pardon me, is that improper?" he asked mildly. He looked around. "We could have a servant present."

"It's not improper," she said hurriedly. "But it has never happened. Men of the world have no interest in an old woman like me."

Marcus looked at her in amazement. "You're not old," he said, meaning it sincerely. "You are hardly older than I am."

"But I offer little conversation," she insisted, blushing. "I have never had my daughter's wit. I can speak only of domestic matters."

Marcus smiled and relaxed a little. This was his entry. "But I am myself deeply versed in domestic matters, milady, did you not hear that I am the emperor's chief steward? I run the court as you run your house. Hence my errand for His Majesty. I am sure the similarities would surprise us both. So again, I ask you, as your humble servant—will you join me for a drink?"

Three bottles later he finally had her drunk enough, and she did not realize it. Her servants would have, but she had banished them from the room so she could gossip about them, with one who understood the burden of inefficient underlings. She and Marcus had just finished an entire jar of something much more sour and potent than wine, and Maria almost never stopped talking, amazed that a handsome man took such a sincere interest in her little life. She offered him as gestures of gratitude nearly all the jewelry she had on her person; Marcus, with many thanks, accepted only the onyx ring he'd given her before.

She took him up to the roof, squinting into the brilliant setting sun, to point out their humble vineyards and orchards ("We have superior cherries and peaches, milord, because of how we prune our trees"), then down into the cellar to parse the wine together, bringing several jars back up with them so that she might satisfy her guest's desire to sample what was local. As they rambled physically they also rambled verbally; they discussed their most- and least-liked kinds of servants, exchanged advice on bookkeeping, and Marcus managed, as her tongue loosened, to affect an interest in learning about the preparation of flax. Finally, well after dark, when Marcus had managed to get her back to the trestle table in the small half-timbered hall, he turned the talk to family matters.

He listened patiently to a dozen unremarkable tales of Lienor and Willem when they were children, examples of how extremely endearing and bright and honorable they were, of how superior they were to their humble mother in all regards, although Lienor had inherited her mother's single attraction of bright green eyes. He tried every subtle angle he could think of to get her to tell an anecdote that was not quite so flattering, that was perhaps even a little damning in a winsome way, but she did not follow hints. Finally, frustrated, with a chummy smile plastered on his face, he said, "But surely your angels have had moments of deviltry, haven't they?"

She thought about it, then gasped with drunken theatricality. "Why, yes, there was one time when they were very willful—or Lienor was, anyhow." Trying not to look eager, he gestured for her to continue. "They were very young, perhaps on either side of ten." That was too young; whatever the sin was it could be dismissed as childhood foolishness, but if it was all the material she had to offer, he would take it. "Yes, it was when His Majesty the Emperor—the old one, not my future son-in-law—was dying. Has Willem told you how we came to be so poor in land?"

"Oh, somewhat," Marcus said vaguely. "But if you would be so kind as to remind me of the details."

The widow's wandering attention was distracted to the corner of the room. "Ach," she muttered. "That dish must be changed, just a moment, milord," and she rose to call an old manservant in, who fetched from the corner a small dish of a foul-looking syrup littered with dead flies. The man removed it wordlessly, giving Marcus a curious glance, and left the room again. "Excuse me, milord, it's milk and hare's gall, absolutely poisonous for the flies, and there are so many of them this time of year. Almost as bad as the mosquitoes."

Marcus managed to mask his disgust. "At the castle we simply use alder leaves," he said. "Which are . . . less odious, I imagine, to prepare."

Maria's face lit up. "What an excellent idea! I shall have to try that. Fresh or dried, I wonder? Alder leaves, I rather like that idea."

"Your Ladyship was telling me about your family estates—"

"Oh, yes," Maria said, wistfully. "The details are complicated and boring. We were robbed, sir, that is the final truth to it. We held a magnificent estate, several of them, directly from the emperor—the town of Dole was ours, *and* the fortress there, in fact I was married before the chapel of that fort! *and* all those salt mines to the south, *and* two silver mines and one for copper—*and* besides all that, half the land from here to Besançon was my husband's by right of birth, not benefice. Well, perhaps a third. My noble husband, who was—if you can imagine it—even more handsome than my son, was cut down in the prime of life defending his emperor's borders, and in the shock of it I trusted somebody I should not have trusted, and suddenly we were bereft of everything. Somehow it ended up belonging directly to the count—not just what he had by benefice, but all of it. There was a lot of that happening at the time."

Good God, thought Marcus—"the count" was Alphonse of Burgundy, of course. No wonder Willem had responded to him as he did, his first night at Koenigsbourg.

"Well, as the children were growing up, sir, of course I did not want them feeling cheated, so I did not speak of what we had lost, I only taught them to appreciate what we had. It was safer that way— have you heard of frontier justice? Things can be a bit rough out here. I wanted them kept safe, and that required their ignorance. But some inferior people cannot keep well enough alone, or do not understand discretion, and one of those people was our former steward Jehan. He had served my husband very faithfully, and he could not reconcile himself to the injustice done us, which was good-hearted but wrongheaded of him. He, or perhaps it was his wife or one of his brats, took it upon himself to approach my children in secret, and tell them the whole truth. The count, Alphonse, had issued deeds to make our land not merely under his regency—as is proper for a liege lord to do of an orphaned heir like Willem—but actually to annex our estates permanently and fully."

She sighed and lapsed into frowning silence. Marcus said nothing, waiting to hear the resolution. He respected Willem, despite the trouble the knight had unwittingly brought him, and for a moment let himself care about the story.

"Well. Something got into Lienor's head, I don't know what, she had been such a docile lass. Do you remember about a decade ago, when the old Emperor Konrad was doing us in Burgundy the great honor of dying here? He took sick and wasted away at Oricourt, the home of his brother the count. Lienor took it into her head to march up to Oricourt and demand to speak to His Majesty about Alphonse taking our lands. I told her no, and she, the silly child, she ran away from home! I'm sure one of Jehan's brats was behind it, Lienor would never've done it on her own. Willem was being raised in my sainted brother's house, and I was quite hysterical, so I sent for his help although he was just a boy himself—Willem I mean, not my brother, who was fully grown with two young sons himself and moreover had granted us this estate to keep ourselves on, God pour blessing down upon his departed soul, his goodness lives on in his son Erec but not quite so brightly, I think." She paused a moment, having lost the thread of her own narrative in her labyrinthine tangential comment. "Anyhow, Willem went after her, but by the time he found her she was already near Oricourt—the count's castle—and the children were caught trespassing and taken to the count. The count thought it was very amusing and put them in prison overnight to teach them a lesson. I suppose he isn't such a bad character, the count, except for being greedy, which is a fault common to all men. Except my son. Anyhow, I tell you, sir, I was beside myself twice over, I thought I had lost everything. It's because of my distress back then that Willem is so protective of his sister now, he blames himself for what happened, but he would never admit that of course, that is a mother speaking, sir, a mother understands her children better than they themselves do sometimes, would you not agree? Do you think the alder leaves work for horses?"

"Pardon?" Marcus asked with a blink.

"We have a devil of a time with flies bothering the horses, I always fret when Lienor goes out with her brother in the summer

months, that some fly will bite the horse and the horse will throw her
and snap that lovely little neck of hers—I make the groom put salted
grease on the horses to ward off flies, but my daughter complains
about the smell something awful, her senses are so keen, you know.
Is there some other strategy you know of at the king's court?"

"I'm afraid not," Marcus said with forced patience and then offered, "I shall ask the chief groom if you like, and convey the information to Willem."

She looked pleased. "He would like that very much, I don't suppose a horse smelling of lard makes such a good impression at the
royal stables."

"I would be happy to inquire for you. But perhaps you will continue with your story? What happened to the children?"

"Oh, yes, the children! My children." She pulled at the stopper
from the first flagon. "I went the next day to beg their release from
the count Alphonse, and of course he was already planning to release them—he was very preoccupied, what with his brother the
emperor *dying* there and all, and we all knew he and young Konrad
his nephew would vie to be voted new emperor, so they were all
concerned with bigger matters, my children were a silly distraction.
But when we went to retrieve them, they had—imagine this, little
children—had *escaped* somehow! Well *that* made it worse, of course,
because now once again the count thought he had to teach them a
lesson, so—"

"—so he caught them again and incarcerated them a second
time?" Marcus ventured, getting bored.

"Oh, no, he did something far more extreme." Her hands paused
their working at the beechwood stopper, and she suddenly looked
grave. "But I don't like to talk about that bit, it isn't very nice,
and anyhow it has nothing to do with Willem and Lienor, only that
little bastard of Jehan's, and I use the term in the worst possible way,
as an expression of character, not legitimacy. All right then, I'll tell

you if you insist"—Marcus had done no such thing—"he killed Jehan's brat—with his own hands!—just to teach Willem and Lienor a
lesson, and he publicized it, and sent the child's guts in a sack to our
gate; Willem and Lienor behaved themselves after that, and it is
them you were interested in, was it not?"

"Mm, yes," Marcus said with a tight, polite smile, appalled. He
hadn't known until that moment that his opinion of Alphonse could
dip any lower. He held out his hand to offer help, annoyed that he
had been gulled into sitting through yet another useless anecdote.
"I'd particularly enjoyed the stories of their being naughty. Those are
entertaining. I would think the older they were, the more entertaining tales of their mischief would sound." He opened the container
and poured her some wine.

Maria sighed happily. "I have such good children, they are never
naughty." She took a sip and made an awful face. "Oh, this is a bad
batch! It's far too sour, I'll have to strain the lot through sand."

"I believe at the castle they use boiled wheat for the same task,"
Marcus said in a companionable voice, his mind racing to return the
conversation to useful material. He set the jar aside and reached for
another one.

"We can't afford to waste our wheat that way." Maria sighed
tragically. Then, brightening with effort, she suggested, "Let's not
despair of that flagon, milord, there is hippocras to sweeten it in the
kitchen, I'll just call the steward." With wobbly steps she rose and
crossed back to the unadorned kitchen screens, and gestured until
the manservant came to her. "We would like some hippocras for this
awful wine," she announced, gesturing to the table where it still sat.
"And bring the gentleman something to eat."

"I'm fine, milady," Marcus demurred.

"Bring us some gingered bread and pears," she insisted. She sat
across from Marcus and grinned mischievously while the old man
fetched the bottle from the table; he was the servant she had most

complained about, although she was actually quite fond of him. She almost began to tell another mocking story about him then remembered that her guest was more interested, as indeed he should be, in her beguiling children.

"Willem once told me a very mischievous story about Lienor from that time, although I will never know if it was true; Lienor swears it isn't."

Something she was ashamed of. That sounded promising. "Tell me?"

"Well. I don't know how they escaped from Oricourt, but they had made it all the way to the outer gate of the count's demesne, and there was a fellow watching the gate who hadn't heard about any of the fuss. Lienor went up to him as if she owned the place, according to her brother, and said, as if she belonged there—to this big strong youth she said, 'You there, boy, open the gates for us.' And he said, 'What'll you give me if I do?'—he didn't realize they were gentle, of course, he thought they were peasants, they were filthy after their ordeal—our servants in these parts are never normally impertinent to us that way ordinarily, sir, it's nothing like it is in Bavaria—and where was I? Oh, yes, and *she* said, 'Why, I'll show you a very pretty flower,' and she started to pull up her tunic to show him her birthmark."

"Her birthmark?" Marcus said with forced attentiveness, wishing he had not encouraged the resumption of this blathering.

"Oh, yes." Marie laughed and lowered her voice "Oh, did I not mention it? She has the most exquisite birthmark, the shape of a perfect little rose and just as red—without the stem of course, without the thorns, just the flower."

"And it is indecorously high up her shin, is that it?" He tried not to sound sarcastic.

She chuckled with amusement. "No, sir, that's not worth an anecdote, we are not such prudes in Burgundy, whatever they say about us. No, it is . . . well, I'll show you." She stood up and gestured him around the trestle to join her. Oh, God, Marcus thought miserably, he had heard about widows. The last thing he wanted to have to do was extract himself from a would-be seduction. "It is this high up," she said, smiling, and pulled up the skirt of her tunic almost to her waist. She pointed to a spot on her upper, inner left thigh that was very close to things he did not want to see. "Right there," she whispered, giggling drunkenly. Marcus glanced obediently, surprised to see her skin was actually smooth and pale, not repulsive as he'd feared. Still, he braced himself for something horribly embarrassing, but Maria, having finished the demonstration, casually tossed down her skirt and gestured him to sit again. Thrown, but relieved, he did so. "Willem stopped her, of course. It's our little family secret, that birthmark, only the three of us know it, since the nurse and midwife died."

He stared at her and almost kissed her. "The four of us, you must say now," he said after a beat, with affected camaraderie.

"Oh, yes." She giggled. "But you won't tell a soul about that, will you?"

"I swear to you, my lady, the secret is as safe with me as it has been with you."

And that was the truth.

She had told only one person.

He would tell only one person.

12

Travesty

[a work deflating something that someone else has highly praised]

19 July

*I*t was hard for Willem to believe it had been little more than a week; his life was permanently altered, and he was already used to it. He had a lover, who was—most confoundingly—his best friend, and a friend who was—almost as confoundingly—his *emperor*. At Konrad's insistence the three of them spent the leisure hours of every afternoon together, once affairs of state and squire training were completed. On the three occasions when affairs of state (often in the form of jealous, intruding courtiers) demanded Konrad's attention through the day, the lovers were adept at spiriting themselves away, twice into the cellar and once down to the densely wooded hillside below the castle. Just by taking off her clothes, Jouglet would make the remarkable transformation into a woman, and for a while he'd forget this was the fellow whose eye he'd blackened back in Dole last month, even forget it was the jongleur who made him and Konrad laugh so hard watching the squires at their practices.

Willem had despaired of convincing her to reveal herself publicly. No woman could retain the status Jouglet now did as favored court performer. And unmasking would be dangerous: the more public the revelation, the more foolish Konrad would appear for having been deceived, and thus the more needful of meting out a public comeuppance. But danger presented itself from another quarter too: Paul pressed his campaign to gather evidence to denounce them as sodomites. So Jouglet insisted the best way to combat both these threats was for Willem to find himself a court lady and become publicly enamored of her. At least once a day the minstrel would playfully encourage various ladies to flirt with him. He hated it. He was bad at flirting; he much preferred to watch Jouglet's bantering with the women. Such occasions, however, sparked in him a mild jealousy, although he was never certain whom he envied—Jouglet for being so delightful to the ladies, or the ladies for being the public object of Jouglet's delight.

Alphonse often managed to insinuate himself into their social gatherings, to Willem's unease; likewise Erec, of whom Willem was becoming rightly proud. Having reassured himself there was a constant supply of female flesh to cool his overabundance of dry, hot humor (although the physician had expressed concern he was depleting his internal heat and moisture), the squire from County Burgundy was maturing into a fine young man. An able fighter, he might be fit for knighthood, as Willem had been, before he had even reached his majority.

The emperor had decided Willem should continue his training program for all the royal squires; before his muscles had stopped aching from his tournament victory, he was spending each morning working a pack of devoted, almost worshipful youths. Konrad came down briefly each day to visit with his full imperial processional, banner lofted high lest any of the squires or watching villagers mistake him for some other emperor.

Today's training, postponed to afternoon, was an exercise Willem had improvised to prepare the boys for jousting. The full royal entourage followed him out to the rocky walled yard on the north flank of the castle, by the hawk house. The footing was sharply sloped and uneven here, so Konrad had had a long stretch of boards laid out, leveled and fastened, forming a deck.

Willem, at one end, ordered each squire in turn to sprint at him from the other end while aiming a blunted, lightweight training lance straight at his chest. He himself also had a lance and leapt at them dramatically as they approached. Almost without exception, the boys would flinch or close their eyes when he sprang. Willem wanted to make them stop that, to make them keep their gaze steady, because a rider had to see not only his target, but at least a third of his own unwieldy lance clearly, to have any chance of striking true. He asked the entourage to stand behind him, studying the squires' faces as they neared. If a boy ever looked down or closed his eyes—in other words, if his aim ever wavered—the entire audience would shout at him from the front, which would lead to his peers jeering at him from behind, and thumbing their noses at his backside while producing sounds akin to flatulence. Peer pressure had remarkable effects on boys this age.

Erec, a seasoned veteran of this humiliation from training back in Dole, was excused from the afternoon's drill and allowed to stand with the adult jeerers on the platform behind Willem. Between the squires' sallies, he made himself useful, assisting Willem and Jouglet in entertaining the emperor by describing the lovely lady His Majesty might end up married to. Her brother emphasized the ways in which she was a good Christian maiden, devoted to her family, adept at all the womanly arts that make a good wife. But Jouglet and Erec, huddled together beside Konrad's left elbow when not ridiculing the squires, knew what His Majesty really wanted to hear about: they had teamed up to paint a merry picture of Lienor's physical charms. Every curve on her body was given poetical (by Jouglet) or porno-graphic (by Erec) elaboration, and both of them groaned with exag-gerated lechery about the effect her face produced in them. The emperor, already in good humor from shouting at the squires, had been grinning without pause for an hour.

"When we first met, we nearly came to blows over her," Jouglet reminded Erec cheerfully, as if perversely delighted by the memory.

Alphonse edged in between Paul and Konrad and turned his back on his younger nephew to face his older one directly. "Such is the desirability of she who will be our future empress," he chimed in, obsequious.

Paul gave the back of Alphonse's head an accusing look, as if he'd been betrayed, and muttered, "Uncle, your fellow lords may have another view. Remember how popular was your earlier proposition of the Besançon girl."

Alphonse, more interested in what was good for him than in what was good for nobility in general, ignored this. "Judging by her brother's merit she is of excellent stock, it isn't as if His Majesty were planning to marry a ministerial's spawn." To Willem, almost confidingly, he said, "Did you know the ministerials are actually serfs? Most peculiar custom, I don't think it ever caught on in Bur-gundy. Marcus, His Majesty's own steward, for all his pomp, is legally really nothing but a bondsman. You and your sister far out-grace—"

"He may be nothing but a bondsman, but he very nearly runs my government," Konrad interrupted, his voice a little tight.

"There is little to run, sire," Alphonse countered. "The princes and dukes are all independent, even the cities self-govern. There re-quires only a ruler, and you alone, in your wisdom and ability, fill that role."

"The princes and dukes are not *that* independent," Konrad said sharply.

Alphonse tried to make up for the gaffe. "No, no, sire, but they are very *loyal*, of course, they don't need whipping-in, especially by upstarts."

Konrad regarded him for a moment and then turned to Willem. "Our uncle is a snob," he explained loftily. "He clings to certain class distinctions in a most old-fashioned way."

"Proudly," the count agreed. "Or I would be a poor father when it comes to my daughter's future."

As Willem, feeling awkward by this discussion, lifted his lance in preparation of the next oncoming squire, Cardinal Paul frowned at Count Alphonse and muttered quietly, "If you were truly interested in your daughter's future, you wouldn't contemplate—"

He was cut off by a call from the curtain wall above them. They all looked up: a garrison knight was calling down to them, and having gotten their attention, gestured broadly down behind the squires, toward a slow-moving, dark-haired figure descending to the yard.

"That's Marcus," Konrad said at once, and held up his hand for a pause. Willem and the squire lowered their lances. "What's wrong with him? He looks dreadful."

Soon the steward had arrived in the rocky yard, all the young squires clustered in curiosity behind him. The rest of the group, around Konrad, waited at the other end of the run, intrigued and concerned.

Marcus cringed inwardly at the timing of his arrival. There were nearly fifty people here; he had not anticipated a crowd. He had not even anticipated Willem and Alphonse, although obviously it made sense that the Count of Burgundy would attach himself to Willem like a tick. The thought of Imogen's name passing between those two brought the taste of bile to his mouth and cemented his determination to go through with his plan.

"God's balls, man, are you all right?" Konrad demanded. "Where the devil have you been? You look half dead!"

"Your Majesty," Marcus said in a lifeless voice, bowing. Enervated, he crossed the length of the decking. "Your Majesty, forgive me, but I must speak to you in private. It's very urgent."

"Personal or political?" Konrad asked.

"Both, Your Grace," Marcus said, dropping his gaze.

"Excellent," Konrad said playfully. "I assume that means it will embarrass some immediate member of my family, so please share it with us all."

"Alone, I beg you, sire." Stiffly, slowly, Marcus lowered himself to his knees before Konrad.

Konrad grimaced. "Wouldn't you like to collect yourself first? We're having a marvelous time terrorizing our little greenlings here."

"I think, sire, you will want to hear what I have to tell you straightaway."

"Is it a border issue?" Alphonse demanded worriedly.

"Oh, Lord, something has happened to His Majesty's niece!" one of the women said to another fretfully at the back of the crowd—"niece" being the polite way to refer to Konrad's bastard daughter.

"Has the pope excommunicated His Majesty again?" asked an older lord near the back of the group.

"Reginaud," Paul said sharply.

"Your Majesty, please," Marcus repeated. *"Alone."*

Konrad pointed up to the curtain wall. "We'll watch from there as we speak."

Marcus grimaced. He wanted to be out of Willem's reach for this. "Even the clouds have ears, my lord. This would be better done within a closed room."

"Such mystery." Konrad sighed. Marcus again looked down, silent. "Oh, very *well*," the king said at last. "To my suite. The rest of you stay here, Willem may continue with the humiliation. With Marcus's permission?" he added archly. Marcus nodded, not looking up. His hands were trembling, and his own skin looked grey to him. Would he really do it? When the moment came—would he even be able to speak? "Good!" Konrad said. "We'll be back shortly, and then I want all of you lads ready to show me how well you keep your eyes open."

Even more stiffly, Marcus rose to his feet. The two old friends climbed the steep slope toward the palace wall.

"Well then," Konrad said soon after, gesturing around the dayroom. "You asked for privacy. Here it is. What is the mystery?" He crossed his arms and remained standing, determined not to be kept long from the yard.

"No, absolute privacy," Marcus said, nodding toward the page boys at the doors. Konrad dismissed them with a wave, and they stepped into the two outlying rooms of the imperial suite. "No," Marcus said firmly. "Go outside, all of you. Even the guards." Bemused, they retreated farther yet, two out of the bedroom to the west, two out of the receiving room to the east, each shadowed by a frowning guard. Marcus waited until the doors were closed.

Konrad made a gesture of expectancy. "What is this dread news? Where have you been for the past ten days? I sent for you in Aachen, and they said you had no ailing uncle. I never really thought you had an uncle in Aachen; I'm relieved to know that he is well."

"I did not go to Aachen," Marcus said, in a hangdog voice. "Sire, I did something very foolish, and I have been debating all these days on the road if I should tell you this or not, but I think I must. I would not rest easy in my conscience if I didn't."

"Then do it quickly. There is a future generation of my soldiers waiting on us."

Marcus took a deep sigh and began. He crossed near to Konrad, lowering his head respectfully, and leaned in to speak softly, although there was nobody else around. "I learned that Alphonse was calling off my engagement to Imogen—"

"He was what?" Konrad snapped. "He can't do that without my consent!"

Marcus hesitated. Perhaps he had been alarmist; perhaps his fears could all be handled very simply and honestly, with Konrad's support.

But on second thought, that was most unlikely. "Would you deny your consent if his intention was to marry her to Willem instead?"

Konrad calmed immediately. "Oh, that's different, that would be a very good match. And then you might marry my daughter, like Jouglet's always said you should. I'd been toying with that idea, anyhow. That all works out excellently, in fact."

"It does not work out well for me. I was distraught about it. I went a little out of my head."

"I am sorry for you, Marcus, but I think this was not a total surprise."

"I rode down there, I can't even tell you why, because I wanted . . . I don't know, I suppose I thought that if I got there before the messenger I could keep it from happening. Of course I couldn't."

Konrad took a step away and considered Marcus shrewdly, knowingly. "You've taken her, haven't you?"

The king's tone seemed to encourage confession, and Marcus opened his mouth to comply, about to sob with shame and relief at what he would now not have to do. *Yes,* he would say, *Yes, forgive me and forgive her,* and then he would be chastised, perhaps publicly humiliated, but then the wedding would take place because it would be the best way to salvage everybody's honor—

But then Konrad continued speaking. "You've taken her *after swearing to me you wouldn't.* Is that it? Is that what you've become,

Marcus? I won't give away a wanton as a bride, especially if she's my cousin—how does that reflect on me, that I can't even control a kinswoman? If you've ruined her, she's to an abbey for life, which I don't mind frankly, since then Burgundy would revert to me when Alphonse dies—but you will be at Alphonse's mercy, and you know as well as I do that he'll kill you." He grimaced and looked directly at Marcus, who somehow managed to return the look steadily. "Please tell me that the man whose judgment I rely on to run my court has not committed such a monumental act of betrayal and *idiocy*."

So the last honest door slammed closed.

"I swore I had not had her," Marcus said unsteadily. "I did not lie."

"Good!" Konrad boomed, visibly relaxing, and headed toward the door.

"But, sire, that is only the beginning."

With theatrical exasperation, Konrad returned, perched on the bed and gestured. "So. To your business."

"I . . . I gave my horse his head and let him wander for a day or so, and eventually I found myself in a field, I did not even know where I was. There was a beautiful blond woman in the field, well dressed and very debonair. Lovely, and playful, and I would have taken her for a novice nun until she began to flirt with me."

"Yes, yes, women always flirt with you, Marcus," Konrad said with impatient affection. "Are you feeling guilty for enjoying the attention of another woman so soon after losing Imogen? Is this one of those *romantic* dilemmas? And if so, do you need me to pardon you? I do, Marcus, I do, and now I really must—"

"We made love, sire. She was . . ." He hesitated. "She seemed experienced and sure, until it came to the very act, and then she proved to be a virgin, but she begged me to, so I . . . did."

"Marvelous! A woman's virginity is the cure for so many things these days." Konrad rose to leave. "Please, Marcus, I have more enter-taining things to—"

"Bear with me a moment, Your Grace, and you'll see why I am telling you this." He could hardly believe it was his own voice com-ing out of his mouth. "Afterward, we were lying in the grass, and she pointed out we did not even know each other's names. I told her mine. And she told me hers."

Konrad sighed with growing impatience. "This is the sort of story you ought to be sharing with Jouglet, he can make a song of it. What is it that you want from me? Do you want to invite her back to court? Do you want to marry her?"

"I want to tell you who she is, sire," Marcus said, sounding strained, and stood up. He took a long moment to steady his breath-ing. Konrad crossed his arms impatiently. "She said her name . . ." He could barely make himself say it. "Her name was Lienor of Dole, sister to Willem the knight."

"What?" Konrad spat. He leapt back across the room at him, startling the sleeping dogs, who yelped with frightened indigna-tion; he grabbed Marcus by the shoulders and raised him off his feet, shaking him roughly. "What are you telling me? Are you *mad?"*

"I didn't know who she was!" Marcus insisted. "Good God, sire, do you think I would—"

"How do you know she was telling the truth?" Konrad de-manded, but he released him. He crossed himself on reflex with one jeweled hand. "There must be many around those parts who would be jealous of Lienor and try to ruin her name. I won't believe it's her without proof. I cannot think that of Willem's sister."

"I have proof," Marcus said miserably, rubbing his arm where Konrad had gripped him. "If I had the slightest doubt, I would never trouble you with it. I can describe her body. There is a little birth-mark on her upper left thigh, in the shape of a rose. She told me only her family knows about it—and frankly, if he is a decent man, Willem himself will hardly remember it since infancy."

Konrad glared at him. He strode across the room, through the receiving room, and hurled opened the door. "Bring me Willem of Dole," he ordered one of the pages outside. *"Immediately."*

Marcus cringed. "Sire, Konrad, please, I beg you as a friend, don't make me be here with you when he arrives. That will only make us both wretched. I've told you what I have to tell; please, ask him about the birthmark alone, and act accordingly."

"If you took her virginity, you are accountable to the head of her family," Konrad said furiously. "This is almost as bad as if you'd taken Imogen."

"I did not take it, she gave it to me," Marcus insisted. "And as I said, for all the rest—*all* the rest—she was clearly seasoned. She's a beautiful woman, sire, she is enchantingly beautiful. She is also a harlot." The back of his mouth tasted like tin; he felt as if a solid, heavy bar of it stretched from his gut up his throat.

"For the love of Christ," Konrad said hoarsely, then sat down in his leather chair and did not move.

"May I be excused?" Marcus asked.

"No, you may not," he snapped. "I did not make this mess, I am only the victim of it—you will have to do the dirty work." He groaned a little. "And then I will end up with that Besançon bitch."

They sat in tense silence, punctuated occasionally by Konrad's indignant cursing and the hounds' soft whining as they pressed their worried canine noses against his fingertips. He ignored them, which only increased their solicitude.

Finally Willem and Jouglet appeared together in the doorway.

"Not Jouglet," Marcus and Konrad said in the same voice, with the same gesture pointing at the minstrel to leave. The two in the doorway exchanged glances.

"Very well, sire. Willem my friend, shall I see you at supper?"

"Yes," said Willem and, without thinking, almost kissed the minstrel. He chucked her on the shoulder in a chummy sort of way instead, and she slipped away down into the red stone courtyard.

"Willem, step inside and shut the door," the emperor said gruffly. "Keep the boys outside. And the dogs." The pages, after summoning the hounds, retreated again, but they were starting to look extremely curious.

The three men stared at one another: Willem with confusion; Konrad with muted fury; Marcus with a very real combination of fear and guilt. "Yes, sire?" Willem asked, bowing. "What do you need of me?"

"Marcus has a little question to ask you about your sister," Konrad said in a tight voice. "You must answer honestly. Our futures both rest on it."

Jouglet had decided to wait in sight of the king's receiving-room door for the trio to emerge. Two pages and a guard waited outside the door, looking like banished pets. Jouglet played half-penny prick with the cook's children, who were alarmingly talented at knife throwing. Upstairs, the three men were secluded for as long as it might take to walk a mile. She had a bad feeling about this—which accelerated to alarm when she saw Willem emerge. His face was colorless beneath his light brown beard. He looked shaky as he passed the guard and pages, and began to descend the steps to the courtyard. She shooed the children off and ran up the steps to meet him halfway. "What is it?" she asked.

He did not look at her; he seemed incapable of turning his head. "I need to be alone," he said tonelessly and kept walking past her down the stairs. She started descending with him, but he brushed her away, as if she were a small dog he did not want to pay attention to. Confused, she looked back up toward the king's door; Marcus had come out onto the landing. He looked as distraught as Willem, but his face was red, and he seemed frightened, or cowed. "Willem," he called down miserably, but the knight, without looking back at him, shook his head with the same stunned slowness and continued walking down the steps; at the bottom he turned left and then left again, to begin the descent down to the stable. Workers and a knight or two, crossing the small courtyard on their own business, looked up at Marcus with curiosity, and then down at Willem as he descended.

"What's happened?" the minstrel demanded, running back up the steps to meet Marcus. "Marcus, tell me what's wrong. I've never seen him like that."

"Jouglet," Marcus said with frustration, glancing at the guard and boys, who were openly eavesdropping. "It is not a topic for public discussion."

"I won't tell anyone." She looked down at the half-dozen people who were taking an interest in what was happening. "Go away," she ordered.

"You're the worst gossip in the Empire," Marcus said irritably. "There are some things, Jouglet, that must be respected, there are some secrets that should not see the light of day." His throat constricted; he was still shaken by what he had just done. Not ecstatic; not relieved. He hoped those feelings would come later; for now he was just shaken. He had achieved his goal: Lienor would never be the empress. He had expected Willem to attack him, and now almost wished for that. No doubt it was yet to come.

"What has happened?" Jouglet demanded again as they stepped off the stairs into the courtyard.

"There really are some things that are beyond your understanding," Marcus said gently. "You are too young, and you do not understand the pressures on the aristocracy regarding private matters.

Leave it alone." A few steps away was the opening to the covered spiral stair that led up to his room, and he stepped toward it.

"I'll talk to Konrad," Jouglet announced defiantly. "He tells me everything." The cook and butler, walking together into the courtyard, glanced at them with curiosity.

"He may not tell you this." Marcus nodded his head to end the conversation, and disappeared into the stairwell.

She heard a sound above and looked up to see Konrad standing in the doorway, looking dismayed. "Sire!" Jouglet cried out, and again ran up the steps.

He smiled a tired, fatherly smile. "Jouglet, I should have known you'd stick your nose in it at once."

"Stick my nose in *what*?" Jouglet begged.

Konrad sighed sadly and then—aware of the attention they were getting—dismissed the ejected attendants down the stairs. He said in a gentle whisper intended only for the minstrel's hearing, "I will not marry Willem's sister."

Jouglet gaped, then rudely and furiously demanded, "Why not?!"

This caught the attention of everyone who was in any room that opened onto the tight and echoing courtyard; in other words, approximately the entire upper palace.

Konrad pursed his lips a moment. Still in a whisper, he answered, "I think Willem is the one who should share that with you, if it is to be shared. It is not my story to tell." He started to retreat into the room, then looked back and said to Jouglet, "It's good he has you as a friend. He will need encouragement these next few days."

"Has something happened to her, sire?" Jouglet demanded frantically. "Is she dead?"

Konrad grimaced. "Almost worse than that."

Jouglet gasped. "Has she been violated?"

This cemented the attention of all those who had been only half paying attention.

Konrad grimaced harder and shook his head. "It would almost have been better for her if she had been. Then she could at least claim to have an unsullied reputation." Seeing the minstrel's consternation, Konrad sighed and gestured Jouglet to come up into his suite. "Willem wouldn't keep this from you, but he's too upset to speak right now. Come inside, then, but you must swear to me this will not end up in one of your little songs."

The instant the door closed behind them, the eavesdroppers in the courtyard and open windows turned to their neighbors with eager speculation.

There was one hard, angry knock on the door. Marcus took a deep breath and prepared himself to face Willem.

But when he unbolted the door and stepped aside, what flew into his anteroom was half Willem's size and almost unrecognizable with rage. Jouglet slammed the door closed, hard, then turned on Marcus, who jumped back in surprise and almost tripped. Jouglet leapt at him and had him by the collar, practically spitting on him. "How did you really learn about that rose?" the minstrel hissed.

Marcus was prepared to be confronted, but not this way, and certainly not by this adversary. "I saw it when we lay together," he said stiffly and wrestled Jouglet off his collar. "Calm yourself, lad. The windows are open, they'll hear you in the courtyard."

"You are lying," Jouglet snarled, shaking a curled fist under his nose. "It never happened. I know that girl, and anyhow, her brother locks her up like a king's coffer when he's away, you would never have had the chance."

"I explained to His Majesty the details of the story because it concerns him," Marcus said and coughed, straightening his neat clothes.

Wincing, he rubbed his upper arm where Konrad had grabbed him. "It does not concern you. I'm remorseful enough about it, please go away."

Jouglet ran to the window and heaved the heavy wooden shutters closed. The room darkened and instantly felt smaller. "This is a lady's honor you are playing with! Her entire life!" she snapped furiously.

"I know that," Marcus said, barely above a whisper. "I am more concerned with a lady's honor than anyone at court. Leave me, Jouglet—"

Jouglet stamped one booted foot hard and grunted with frustration. "It is not too late to unsay it, Marcus. You didn't do it, she didn't do it. Do not impinge her honor!" *And ruin all my plans,* she added to herself, almost sick with rage.

"What do you know about a lady's honor, you hypocrite," Marcus scoffed. "You've never known anything but whores. Get out of my room."

"Tell me why you did this," Jouglet demanded through clenched teeth. "Willem's no threat to you, Konrad will give you a duchy someday! What do you gain by such convoluted treachery? I'm not leaving here until I understand the fullness of your mischief. After all I've done in your interest!"

"There was no *mischief,*" Marcus protested, marveling at his new ability to lie so fluidly. Already the bar of cold tin at the back of his throat was disappearing. "I was approached by a beautiful young woman who literally threw herself at me—she did not tell me who she was until afterward. I would still protect her reputation, Jouglet, I would only the emperor had known—if it becomes common knowledge it's because *you* are running around shrieking about it, not I. She lost her honor on her own—she'll lose her reputation thanks to *you.*"

"Every word out of your mouth is a lie," Jouglet said at once. "Tell me why you did it."

"I've told you the truth, there's nothing more to say." Marcus sighed what he hoped was a condescending sigh and settled before his writing chest as if he were in the middle of something else. He fiddled with his folding scales and tried to think of something he could pretend to have to weigh.

Jouglet clapped. "I have it! You don't want to lose the betrothal to Alphonse's pale little spawn." And with suspicious curiosity, "Why not?"

"You are inventing labyrinthine plots when the truth is far simpler, and more tragic."

"You don't want to lose that fat dowry," Jouglet said triumphantly, then pressed on eagerly, "but Marcus, you idiot, now you can marry Konrad's bastard—I've been cultivating that for *years*! Konrad will offer her within a day or two, and if he doesn't, I'll navigate his thinking in that direction, I promise. What she'll bring you will dwarf what Alphonse's daughter could have brought you. This is good! This is to your advantage! Your ambition benefits from my ambition, why the *devil* are you thwarting it?"

Marcus looked up and shook his head slowly, exhausted by the stress of the day. "I will swear on all that I hold holy, Jouglet, this is not about ambition or dowry lands. And that is the end of the matter. Good day." He gestured toward the door.

"Whoreson," Jouglet spat and added warningly, "I'll disprove it."

"Go ahead and try," Marcus said in a disinterested voice. *Just let me marry Imogen first.*

"Even if it were true, why did you tell Konrad?" Jouglet pressed. "What is served in that?"

"Jouglet," Marcus said, trying to sound very patient and patronizing. He stood and moved closer to the shuttered window. "If he had married her and then found on their wedding night what she really was, it would have been disastrous. She would be shamed, and he would look like a fool in the eyes of the world. I was trying to avert that greater evil with the pain of my confession. That is the end of this discussion." He reached out to open the shutter.

"Tell me the *truth!*" Jouglet shouted and hurled herself on him again.

Marcus wrestled the attack off, surprised by its ferocity. He shoved Jouglet hard to the floor, then pinned the minstrel's neck under his foot, the freckled face pressed hard against the rushes covering the planks. He shook his head as Jouglet growled in protest. "The proof that I am not lying is that I have nothing left to lose. Nor to gain. I have nothing to fight for. All I ever desired has been taken from me."

Jouglet made a sneering face from the uncomfortable prone position. "What are you talking about? Do you mean your engagement to Alphonse's daughter? Are you deaf? I just promised you *Konrad's* daughter—"

"It is not a matter of the purse but of the heart," Marcus said and lifted his foot. He moved away from the window, without opening the shutter.

Jouglet scrambled up, arms raised defensively, with an incredulous look on her face. "You are upset that you will not have Alphonse of Burgundy to call father? Marcus, he's one of the most repulsive men alive, why would you value him—"

"I value *her*," Marcus said sharply. Jouglet looked even more surprised. Very little escaped her attention; this somehow had. It was probably not requited; this had to be some very personal confession that nobody else knew about. Or else, more likely, it was not even true, but a lie intended to confuse the issue. To the best of her knowledge Marcus and Imogen had only even met twice or thrice, and then briefly and in public. Seeing the look on Jouglet's face, Marcus nodded. "I do not deserve her, but I am in love with her, Jouglet."

Jouglet, still brandishing her fists, took a step backward and shrugged impatiently. "So be in love with her. What does that have to do with marriage? People don't marry the one they're in love with. I will never marry the one I cherish most."

Marcus made a disgusted expression. "That's probably because she's a prostitute."

"Willem can never marry the woman he's in love with either."

"Who would that be, his sister?" Marcus said in a nasty voice, crossing his arms.

Jouglet relaxed the martial stance, considering him with narrowed eyes. "I think *you're* the one in love with his sister. You must have met her somehow. This is some twisted way to assure that you can claim her."

Marcus smiled, pained. "Yes, my tale would serve that end very well, but it is not an end I have the slightest interest in."

"Oh?" Jouglet challenged, smug and angry, thinking she had solved it. "Do you claim you would not be pleased if the emperor ordered you to marry Lienor now, to protect her brother's honor?"

This alarming possibility had never crossed his mind. "No, I would not be pleased," he said firmly. "In fact I would refuse. I know her too well already; she will never make a constant wife. As I told Konrad, I took her maidenhead but I didn't take her innocence. The flower had been fondled many times before I actually plucked it."

Jouglet crossed her arms, mimicking him. "That is a neat trick, considering her brother keeps her under guard within the house."

"No," Marcus said promptly. "The neat trick is that she knows how to get out in secret. You yourself have gone on ad nauseam about her cleverness. She complained bitterly to me that he is overprotective, because of some childhood mishap. I didn't press for details; something about being taken prisoner by Alphonse overnight, something about an estate." He thanked the saints that he had endured the mother's blathering on about that. Jouglet's face revealed surprise, and for the first time a hint of uncertainty, and Marcus risked more. "Yes, she told me that she slipped out of the house and found men to . . . lend herself to, simply to rebel against his strictness. This time she was particularly upset because he was sequestering her for his entire absence, so she decided to undermine him by giving away that which he was most obsessed with protecting." He felt in control of the situation now and was able to assume a gentle, compassionate tone as he explained in a lower voice, "That is what hurt Willem the most I think, realizing his own behavior contributed to this regrettable coincidence. He swore her innocence, even when I described the birthmark. It took what I just said for him to yield to the news." With genuine remorse he finished quietly, "You do not know how dreadful it is to see a great man slain by your very words."

Jouglet was staring at him, mouth hanging slightly open. Every instinct inside her still shrieked that he was lying . . . but now he had given an account that was entirely in keeping with Lienor's character. She would never do it for lust; lust had no hold on her. But to rebel, to make a point? Yes. Lienor just might do that. *Might.* Might not, but . . . might. It was no longer in the realm of the unthinkable.

Or perhaps Marcus was more subtle and sophisticated at deceit than she'd realized. In which case keeping an eye on him was more important than ever. So she swallowed the fury, the self-righteousness, the panic, and managed to look extremely sheepish.

"I apologize," she said in a hoarse whisper, looking down at her fidgeting hands. "Please forgive me. I was so upset on Willem's account that I lost my head." And looking up: "It is still very hard for me to believe what you have said, but I no longer feel certain you are lying, especially since I do not know you as a liar." That was better, more nuanced, than an outright shift in sympathy.

Marcus shrugged. "If that is the most you can bring yourself to say, I feel moderately vindicated. Thank you." He tried not to listen to his own words.

Jouglet affected a poignant grimace. "I imagine it will be a bit awkward for you around Konrad and Willem for a while. If I can sweeten any bitterness there, please let me know. If you were serious about being in love with Imogen, perhaps I can—"

"That? No," Marcus said casually, sounding so convincing he spooked himself. "That *was* a lie, and I apologize for it—you frightened me so with your intensity that I was trying to think of whatever I could to shut you up."

"Oh, I see," Jouglet said, risking a small ironic laugh. "So it is my fault that you felt forced to be deceitful."

Marcus looked at the minstrel thoughtfully a moment and nodded. "Yes," he said. "Yes, it is."

Worried, Jouglet left Koenigsbourg and hurried down into town. As she neared Willem's inn from the green market, a baritone roar of fury, humiliation, and hurt resounded from the building. She had never heard Willem raise his voice before, except briefly on the tourney field. She had certainly never heard him—or could ever have imagined him—sounding like this, and for a moment she was actually frightened of approaching.

Inside the courtyard, the inn workers and Willem's retinue were running around anxiously, moving to and from the stable under the hall.

Willem and Erec, both with very black looks, were standing on the shadowed side of the small yard, near the stables, brusquely ordering their mounts prepared for travel. They were arguing loudly about how much to bring with them, each freely taking out their distress on the other. As a groom lead Atlas out of the shadows and began to check his girth, Jouglet, arms waving to get the men's attention, demanded, "What are you doing?"

"Can't you tell?" Erec snorted. Willem turned away and busied himself with an imaginary task involving the water trough. "We're going back to Dole."

"No, you're not," Jouglet announced, eyes widening in alarm. "Send Nicholas. Send somebody else. You can't leave—"

"This is a family matter and none of your concern," Erec said sharply, looking around for his riding gloves. A groom held them out, and Erec snatched them out of his hand as if they had been stolen; the groom rushed back under the eaves to fetch Erec's Arabian. "You have already meddled far too much. I am the head of our family, and I say we're going home."

"You can't," Jouglet insisted. "That would look like an admission of defeat."

"Idiot!" Erec shouted, finally turning his full attention on the minstrel. "We're already defeated! My spurs!" he shouted furiously around the courtyard, although the man who had them was already kneeling by him to attach them to his boots.

"Willem," Jouglet said desperately. "You must not leave here. It's the worst thing you can possibly do. Stay here, near Konrad. Send for Lienor and allow her to defend herself—"

"You accursed meddling whoreson! Your reign of managing my family's fortune is *over*, do you hear?" Erec shrieked in a constricted voice. His eyes were tearing up. "Leave my cousin in *peace*!"

"Willem," Jouglet said again, more quietly this time. The knight had kept his eyes focused on his imaginary task at the water trough, but now he turned and faced her. His eyes were red and swollen. He shook his head, determined.

"Damn it, Willem, how can you *possibly* believe this story?" Jouglet demanded. "It is your sister we are speaking of! Lienor! How can you doubt her?"

"How can I not?" Willem said brusquely, his voice catching. "Marcus knows what he could not possibly know if she were innocent. Not just the birthmark, although that's damning enough. He described my sister's character with the intimate exactness of someone who knows her directly."

"*Many* people know her directly!" Jouglet shot back. "She has a world of friends and admirers! Some rejected suitor might have spun a tale that told him enough—"

"None of her rejected suitors know about the birthmark," Willem argued.

"*I* didn't even know about the birthmark!" Erec interjected, stamping the foot that had just had its spur attached. He sounded almost indignant about it.

"We're going home to confront her," Willem explained, as if that ended the discussion, and took Atlas's head from the groom.

"We're going home to *punish* her," Erec corrected furiously. His face was almost liver-colored with rage, and Jouglet felt a horrible foreboding: Erec both venerated and lusted after his pretty cousin. The cousin who had just shamed the family beyond all imagining with her own lust.

Erec's horse had been brought into the sunlit yard now, and a stableboy checked the girth and bridle. Willem mounted Atlas. The page boys and the manservant, Jouglet realized now, were moving with antlike determination between the rented room and the yard, where traveling chests were yawning open to receive whatever the men could not ride out with right away—the accumulated miscellany purchased with Konrad's hundred pounds. The rented room would be abandoned by tomorrow morning.

Jouglet fought off a wave of panic. "I promise you—" She stepped up to Atlas and took hold of the reins. "If you send somebody for her and remain here, dignified, at court, there may be some remedy. If you flee in shame at a rumor, there can be none."

"I cannot stay here and face this shame," Willem hissed in a troubled voice, pulling the reins tight against Jouglet's grip.

"Facing the unpleasant is a knight's duty," Jouglet upbraided him. She laid a soothing hand on Atlas's nose as the horse fidgeted under its master's tension. "Willem, I've *proven* to you that I know how to play these games better than you do—and I *certainly* know them better than this hotheaded *child*," she added, too angry to be prudent.

"I am not a *child*," Erec shouted. "I am his lord, and on this matter Willem *must* do what I tell him. He's my *vassal*!"

"He *shouldn't* be your vassal and he won't be for much longer, *if* he stays here," Jouglet countered, her voice rising. This accomplished what it was meant to: Erec was confused by the assertion and, for a moment, distracted trying to decipher it.

Jouglet tightened her grip on the reins; Willem looked down at her, frowning. "You are caught up in Erec's rage," she insisted quietly. "This is appallingly shortsighted of you. You *cannot* leave. If you don't have your sister's marriage to buoy your fortune, you still have your own merit, but you can only make that evident by staying right here under Konrad's nose. You know I'm right. Besides, this is a twisted scheme of Marcus's that I know I can unravel. It has no staying power."

Willem's face buckled with confusion.

"Come, Willem, we're off," Erec said with a grunt, waving the groom aside impatiently and hoisting himself onto his horse. As he settled into the saddle, he noticed the hesitation on his cousin's face. "Dammit, don't let that . . . *fiddle player* . . . stand in the way of family honor! He's probably only protecting her so he can rut with her later himself."

"That much is inaccurate," said Willem, shaking his head.

"It's *all* inaccurate," said Jouglet, nodding hers.

There was a tense pause. Erec's mare, reacting to his agitation, became likewise agitated. He turned her in quick, tight circles, each one spiraling a little closer to the open gate.

Willem sighed. Then: "We're staying, Erec. Jouglet is right." The authority of a knight speaking to his squire hardened his voice, and Jouglet was relieved to see Erec's comportment shift ever so slightly; he was Willem's lord by law, but in real life, the elder cousin, though milder, was the natural leader. "We'll send a messenger," Willem decided heavily.

"I don't *believe* this!" Erec screamed, his horse beginning to dance sideways with excitement. "*Blackguard*! Opportunistic *beggar*!"

Willem looked burdened, but he would not change his mind now, and Erec knew him well enough to realize that. Jouglet quickly signaled the grooms to come and take the horses' heads.

Then Erec suddenly threw his shoulders back, shedding any hint of a squire's humility. "Well, *whoreson,* if I am the only one in the family who cares about honor and justice, so be it! I'll travel even faster on my own!"

Jouglet, anticipating Erec, leapt at his horse, grabbed his booted leg, and tried to pull him off. He kicked at her shoulder, hard, and she landed with a pained grunt on the courtyard cobblestones. With a click of the tongue and a shift of his weight in the saddle, Erec had his horse turned around and racing out the gate and to the right, toward the southern road out of town.

Jouglet accepted a hand up from one of the grooms, then scrambled toward the gate, clutching her shoulder. Squawking poultry and startled children in the street were the only immediate evidence of Erec's flight in the slumbering merchants' market. Hearing the clack of hooves behind her, she shied toward the gate post, and then she shouted with frustration: Willem was cantering out after his cousin.

"No!" she screamed. "Willem, no!" She forced herself to leap forward and grab at his bridle as he too turned right, and Atlas shied and stumbled. Cursing, Willem pulled the charger up.

"He'll hurt her!" Willem said in a panicked voice.

"He can't get to her, she's *sequestered,* remember?" Jouglet insisted. "And it's many days ride to Dole, that adolescent rage will have exhausted itself. Your best hope of defending your family's honor is to stay here and act honorable." Willem, unconvinced, glanced up at the settling dust that Erec had left behind.

Jouglet could not make herself say any more than that; she was as uncertain as Willem was of what Erec was actually capable. Part of her was afraid that it really was dangerous for Lienor, letting Erec go there without Willem as a moderating influence.

She released the bridle, hoping her uncertainty was not readable.

"Do what you will," she said curtly. "I'm just a *fiddle player.*"

Willem hesitated another moment, until he turned Atlas sharply around and trotted back into the courtyard with a groan of frustrated capitulation.

Jouglet allowed as much time as she thought it would take for him to dismount and collect himself, then went in to comfort him.

But Willem was not in sight. The servants, who were hovering near the traveling chests without unpacking them, glanced meaningfully up at the door to his room. Jouglet nodded thanks and ran up the steps, casually beginning to throw open the door—but Willem was standing against it on the other side to hold it closed. "It's me, let me in," she said.

"Go away," she heard him answer through the thick wood planking. "You got what you wanted. I'm staying. But don't ask any more of me today. This is not a time for me to be receptive to duplicitous women of any sort."

"Don't be ridiculous," Jouglet laughed harshly, and shoved at the door with her shoulder. "Let me in. Or better yet, come out and return to the castle with me to undo this damage immediately. The longer you wallow the less chance we have of rectifying—"

"The last thing I need right now is your trying to *arrange* things to your liking. Whether it's true or not, this only happened in the first place because you lured me away from home with dangerous ambition. *Go away.*"

"Willem, please, let me in," she said more gently.

"I told you to go away," the answer came, slightly choked and nasal.

She stood waiting by the jamb to hear his footsteps move away from the door, but they didn't, and after a while she realized he was waiting to hear her move away as well. Feeling impotent, she made a face at the door and slammed the heel of her hand against it. "All right, I'm going," she muttered loudly.

There was no answer on the other side except a muffled, angry sob. Suddenly she doubted the wisdom of insisting that he stay.

She pulled away and made her way sulkily down to the yard. For a short while she remained on the bottom step to Willem's room, unmoving, occasionally glancing up. But the door did not open, and before very long she made a gesture of resigned disgust toward it, rose from sitting, and walked out of the yard.

That night His Eminence the Cardinal jotted with pleasure in his regular dispatch to Rome that His Majesty Emperor Konrad might be persuaded after all to marry the daughter of Besançon, a lady whose devotion to the advancement of the church was unassailable. His Majesty Emperor Konrad took supper in his room, alone, nothing to distract him but the pointedly lugubrious music of Jouglet the minstrel. Alphonse, Count of Burgundy, sulked by candlelight in his guest chambers and considered what his options were. Marcus the steward, not often a religious man, stayed up all night with a votive in the castle chapel. And Willem Silvan, knight of Dole and new hero of the realm, paced in his rented room at the inn and stared blankly out the window at the fat rising moon, knowing that something inside him was broken.

13

Débat

[a medieval poem in the form of a two-person debate]

20 July

His Majesty awoke under his silks and wools and furs. Boidon stoked the ashes of all three tiled hearths, emptied His Majesty's chamber pot out the window, drew open the bed curtains, swatted the dogs off the coverlet, attended His Majesty's rising, and draped a mantle over him.

The morning fog was as grey as the monarch's mood. Konrad stretched to warm himself before the fire in his dayroom, while in the bedchamber Boidon silently stripped the top sheet and pillows from the bed and put them out to be laundered. Then he combed His Majesty's hair and beard with a sturdy ivory comb and helped him into his hose and boots.

Finally, staring dully at the fire, Konrad said, "Send for Marcus."

When Boidon was gone, Konrad glanced at the form that was curled up on the cushion of the window seat, under a blue woolen mantle. "Give me a tune," he said, and looked back at the fire. "Let's mourn the death of fantasy together."

Jouglet, who had been awake since the bell tolled lauds, brooding on the situation, pretended to stretch, to blink in the foggy light from without, to come gradually to wakefulness. "What does Your Majesty refer to?"

The emperor shook his head, still looking at the fire. "None of that, my friend. You knew the girl yourself and I know how you regarded her. How dreadful this is for Willem."

"May I speak freely, sire?" Jouglet said, pushing away the mantle and adjusting her brown tunic. Not waiting for the answer—knowing he would say yes, but only halfway mean it—the minstrel continued: "I believe the lady has been maligned, or Marcus fooled somehow. Send for her, Your Grace, and question her yourself before you alter plans that meant so much to you."

"If she can deceive her brother so thoroughly, she is a consummate liar and her word cannot be trusted," Konrad said.

Jouglet declined to point out his spectacularly circular reasoning and instead tried this: "Bring her here to be examined by a midwife to see if she's still virgin, sire."

Konrad lifted himself up in the chair to glare over his shoulder directly at Jouglet. "Good God, what are you thinking? I cannot sponsor such a humiliating indignity. Imagine what gossip that would subject her to, especially if Marcus is proved honest."

"But if she's a maiden, then—"

"Then I'm marked as an emperor who would do that to his bride," Konrad huffed, slouching back into his seat. "Can you imagine how *that* would get warped and turned against me as it spread across the miles?" He sighed with frustration. "I am the Holy Roman Emperor, there are certain things I do not do."

"It could be done in secret, sire," Jouglet whispered, trying not to sound desperate.

Konrad looked over his shoulder again with an incredulous expression. "This is the royal court! *Nothing* is a secret long here—God's balls, Jouglet, you're the one ferreting out the secrets half the time, how can you make such a ludicrous suggestion? Give me a *song,* I said, not *advice.* Something about dashed hopes."

Jouglet pulled herself off the window seat and squatted by her fiddle case, contemplating how to mitigate the sense of catastrophe around what had happened. "Forgive me for being impertinent, but His Majesty has never even met the lady—it is not as if you suffer any personal loss over this."

Konrad gestured impatiently for her to open the leather case. "True, the dashed hopes are mostly Willem's—but mine as well, for losing the chance to call him brother. Don't play any of those dance tunes you've been working on."

"He is still your brother in arms," Jouglet said, picking up the instrument and tapping each string in turn to check the tuning. "Appoint him a member of your court and he's as good as family."

"I know," Konrad conceded. "But there was a sense of . . . I don't know what to call it, *domesticity* perhaps, at the prospect of our becoming real family. I'm *fond* of the man. Genuinely. He is so blessedly unlike the members of my court. Or my born kin."

"So's his sister, sire," Jouglet commented with apparent dispassion, listening hard to the third string.

"None of that, Jouglet," Konrad warned.

"Whatever she is accused of, he need not suffer her fate." Jouglet lowered the string half a notch and sounded it now against its neighbor.

"Of course not, but I had intended a household that included Marcus and Willem as my companions, and it will be a long while before they'll be easy in each other's presence, no matter how much

I would will it. I do not like circumstances I cannot control through my own will."

"Provençal, French, or German?" Jouglet asked, settling on the stool with the fiddle on her lap, raising the bow. "Blondel de Nesle seems appropriate today, or perhaps Ventadour—"

But a quiet rap on the door preempted the performance, and Marcus entered, slowly, almost sheepishly. He and Jouglet ignored each other; he crossed straight to Konrad's hearthside chair and bowed deeply. "Your Majesty," he said in a quiet voice. "You have done me the honor of sending for—"

"Shut up." Konrad sighed and gestured to a chest, where a flagon of wine had sat forgotten overnight beside a pewter cup. Marcus immediately filled the cup and handed it to him. "I only called you up here because I do not want you walking on eggshells around me."

"Your Majesty has forgiven me?"

"My Majesty doesn't need to forgive you if you've done nothing treacherous. Your friend Konrad is extremely irritated, but even he knows that is not your fault, you were a victim of capricious fate."

"Thank you, sire, indeed I was," Marcus agreed.

"Mind you, if I discover more to the story, Marcus, you are a dead man," Konrad went on. "If you forced yourself on her, or tricked her, or took her knowing who she was—there is no *benefit* in this for you. If this proves to be some scheme to get Lienor for yourself—"

"Of course not, sire," Marcus said, feeling ill. He could feel Jouglet staring at his back and wondered what the minstrel was assessing.

"And," Konrad continued, "it will be painful for Willem to see you just now. Although I've missed you in your absence, for the next day or so, do not spend too much time in our presence. Catch up on your duties and then confine yourself to your quarters the rest of the day."

"Yes, of course, sire." Marcus bowed again, then turned around to face the window seat. "Good morning, Jouglet," he said experimentally.

Jouglet was noncommittally polite. "Good morning, sir."

"Are things fair between us?"

"As fair as Lienor's darling sky blue eyes," answered Jouglet blandly.

"Lienor's eyes are green," Marcus corrected.

Jouglet looked down a moment. "It is fair between us," she allowed, almost sullenly. "But I adore the girl, sir, and this is a shock to me."

"I know. I regret being the agent of your disillusion." He turned back around to face Konrad. "Your Majesty, if I may distribute the morning alms?"

"Send for Willem to join us," Konrad said in dismissal.

Marcus suppressed a groan and said he would see to it.

Jouglet had gone down to the hall before Willem arrived, anticipating the worst. The knight looked miserable when he entered, even more haggard than at his exhausting triumph at the tournament, just ten days earlier. He was dressed entirely in dark brown; with his grimness, his broken nose made him less like a warrior than a hardened thug. He kept his left hand clutched on his sword belt, as if he expected to be called upon to defend his honor at any moment.

It had become clear at castle mass that the revelation was generally known. The source of the leak was probably a page boy, no doubt bribed or threatened by Paul, but Jouglet had to admit to herself, feeling sick, that her own relentlessness in the courtyard yesterday had helped to bring attention to it. Every pair of eyes, aristocratic and servile alike, rested on Willem for a moment as he walked to the high table, and he seemed to feel each glance as if it were a branding iron. Finally he turned toward Boidon and caught the chamberlain in the act of staring; Boidon looked abashed and greeted him with sympathetic courtesy. The sympathy felt insulting to Willem.

He took a few steps farther, then paused and turned his gaze on another set of prying eyes, surprising Richard of Mainz, the first knight he had defeated in armed combat here. Willem's grip reflexively tightened on his sword. Richard, equally embarrassed for having been caught staring, bowed respectfully—and sympathetically.

The next pair of eyes Willem intuited, and turned to face, belonged to someone who had been trying very hard to earn his friendship: Alphonse, Count of Burgundy. The knight bowed politely, with the diffidence of a younger man to an older one. "Good morning, milord count," he said with a feeble attempt at a smile.

Alphonse nodded brusquely and hurriedly busied himself with something that required him to turn his back on Willem.

Dammit, thought Jouglet, who saw the moment from behind Konrad's table, and saw Willem's face turn pink. She hurried around the dais to distract him, plucked him by the arm, and dragged him toward the row of boys holding the silver washbasins along the western bank of windows.

"My sister's sin is costing me my friends," he whispered bitterly as they walked.

"Alphonse never was your friend," Jouglet assured him. "And I know you never liked him." She held her fingers over the bowl and let the boy pour the floral-scented water over them.

"He's treated me with respect this past fortnight," Willem argued quietly, hands clasped together on his sword belt. "Do you know how satisfying that felt? Like a man of his own standing—"

"Or potentially better than his standing, which is the only reason he was ever kind to you. That wounds you?" she whispered impatiently, seeing the look on his face. "Then you lack both the head and the hide for this world I've brought you to." She knew it sounded unsympathetic, but she was desperate to keep him away from the maudlin depths she suspected he was capable of. For the first time, she wondered if her affection for him had led to severe misjudgment. Perhaps he really was too pure, too good, to survive a royal elevation. Frustrated by his distractedness, she tugged at his sleeve to bring his attention to the washbasin. "Konrad values you no less, he expressly asked me to take you to the high table to show the others there is no disgrace to you. Wash your hands."

After they'd dried their hands, she hesitated a moment before leading him to the upper end of the hall, because she wanted to read the room. Her eyes as usual were on everyone at once. She saw the cardinal, in an unseemly cheerful mood, enter and approach Alphonse at the lower end of the hall, speaking in quiet, earnest tones. So Paul was already capitalizing on Lienor's fall to champion the Besançon woman as future empress. As she watched, there was a brief fanfare and two pages entered, followed by Konrad and a bodyguard.

The emperor paused, meaningfully. Paul, feeling his brother's glare, broke off the conversation and followed Konrad dutifully past the bowed heads of Jouglet, Willem, and dozens more to the high table. Alphonse stayed a moment by the door, looking contemplative.

"Whoreson," Jouglet muttered, which conveniently referred to both of Konrad's kinsmen.

At the lower end of the hall, at the small south-facing window, Marcus was testing the consequences of his venture. He had to win back that whoreson count's regard, or this would all have been for nothing. "Will your lordship be seated?" he asked Alphonse, gesturing toward the high table.

The count had been in another world, preoccupied by Paul's coaxing machinations about the future of the empire. He started at the familiar voice. "What? Oh—am I welcome there today?"

"Indeed your lordship is always very welcome at the table of your royal nephew, as your lordship intends to marry your daughter to an intimate of His Majesty," Marcus said with marvelous vagueness.

Alphonse looked like a rat caught pulling cheese from a trap. "Did I say I was marrying her to that landless brawler? I never said that—"

"Of course you didn't, milord," Marcus agreed, trying to keep his voice smooth. With a smile, he excused himself to see to the servers.

But he could not see to the servers, because Willem, oblivious to his presence, was in his way, agile Jouglet at his elbow as they dawdled toward the dais. A wave of dread washed over the steward, but he made himself keep walking.

Jouglet sensed him approach and stepped aside to observe. Willem, at her withdrawing, turned to follow her gaze—and seeing Marcus, froze and looked down at once. They were almost dead center in the room and eyes were turning toward them.

"My lord," Marcus said in a soft, earnest voice. "Again I beg your forgiveness."

Willem shook his head and pushed aside some strewing herbs with his foot. "I cannot give it yet." He looked Marcus briefly in the face; those eyes were so startlingly hurt and honest that the steward very nearly confessed to everything. "Perhaps there'll be a day when I can look back at this without grief, but for the moment, do not be insulted if I remove myself from you to protect my own heart." He returned his attention to the floor.

Marcus sighed. With relief, but he managed to make it sound passably like regret. Only Willem—only good, upright, honest, chivalrous Willem, who did not understand how absolutely powerless Marcus was, despite his rank—would offer to remove *himself*, instead of demanding Marcus's own removal. "Your lordship—"

"I am not a lord," Willem corrected, still to the floor.

"A lord among men," said Marcus quietly, without a trace of

irony or bathos. His regard for Willem's character was real—which was what most confounded Jouglet. Jouglet was trying to decipher everything that passed between them in some way that would trip the steward up, betray the aim of his scheming. But Marcus's face gave nothing away.

Once on the dais, Willem bowed and accepted his now-customary seat to Konrad's right. Without appetite he waited for the morning meal to be served. Jouglet withdrew to the lower end of the hall, near the drafty door, almost near the serfs—the proper place for minstrels and other vagabonds, no matter how beloved.

Seeing Willem was in no mood for conversation, Konrad turned to his brother. "I see you wasted no time luring Alphonse back to Rome's matrimonial campaign."

"It is not a matter of luring, brother," Paul said with his smarmy smile. "I think in his heart our uncle has always held your best interests supreme, and he is entirely aware that a lord's daughter is more fit for you than is some pretty orphan girl, even if she *had* been pure."

Willem involuntarily made an angry sound and slammed the side of his fist on the table boards, making the saltcellar jump. The royal brothers looked at him, and he turned his head away, ashamed by his lapse of control.

Konrad's attention snapped back around toward Paul. "That was a gratuitously uncouth comment to make in present company," he barked. "If you cannot be decent, leave my table at once and take your meal in the scullery like the sullen, nasty little cat you really are."

Paul flushed as Willem looked back toward them. "Sire," the knight said in a quiet voice, "my presence here this morning is not evoking the best in anybody."

"What, that? I bark at Paul all the time." Konrad laughed, a little forced. "He likes it. It makes him purr."

"I believe my appearing this morning does not contribute to the good spirit of the court in general," Willem insisted in the same quiet voice. "To avoid an even greater rudeness, before the meal begins, I would ask Your Majesty's permission to withdraw back to my lodgings."

"It would be much more interesting were you to challenge Marcus to single combat," Konrad said, awkwardly attempting levity.

Willem shook his head. "I considered that, but it would be wrong of me to set on someone who is not my equal, and although his martial exploits are renowned, his leg wound makes it impossible for him to have a fair chance."

Konrad stared at him. "Willem, my brother, you are too good for your own good. I'd be displeased at your withdrawal, but I would understand it. If I had a sibling whose virtue I believed in the least bit, I'd no doubt be destroyed to learn otherwise. Luckily, there were never any illusions in my case."

"Nor mine," Paul retorted quickly, aping his brother's tone.

Konrad ignored him. "Under the circumstances do what best suits your own humor—but do not let your humor be permanently altered."

"Of course not, sire," Willem said with resignation. He stood, bowed, and drew away from the table.

Jouglet, from her perch near the door, watched him cross by her and leave the room. She looked at once toward the emperor. Konrad met the gaze; he gestured for the minstrel to follow after Willem. Jouglet picked up the fiddle case from the corner and darted out of the hall.

"And what sort of fiddling do you think that presages?" Paul whispered with amusement in Konrad's ear. "The brother is worse than the sister, sire, admit it. But don't fret, Konrad, remember it is only a landless knight. If his character, when tested, disappoints you, it's not as if you've lost an important member of your court."

Konrad made an impatient face. "For a shepherd of human souls, you have remarkably little understanding of your flock."

Back at the inn, Willem threw himself onto the broad bed with a groan. "I never want to set foot in the castle again," he announced.

"You're being ridiculous," Jouglet scoffed.

He rolled over lugubriously to look up at her. "You were not sent to chastise me, you were sent to comfort and distract me."

They looked at each other for a moment without speaking. Then:

"You cannot possibly mean that as a proposition," Jouglet informed him, with a short, harsh laugh. She set down the fiddle case by the open door.

"What else is there to do?" Willem demanded gruffly. "I can't show my face in public thanks to her."

"Oh for God's sake!" Jouglet closed the door firmly behind her, shutting out some of the hum of the courtyard and street. "There is one agreement we *must* come to, which is that your sister is innocent. Your hiding your face will be taken as confirmation of her guilt."

"Listen to me, Jouglet." Willem sat up and rested his hands on his thighs, agitated but controlled. "She has spent the last five years practically locked up in that house. Since we left our wardship with our uncle and I took up the fief myself, I have been . . ." He took an agitated breath. "I've been her jailor," he said, and his voice broke. "And this is the result."

Jouglet watched him struggle to stay controlled. "Is that belief what kept you awake all night?" she asked gently, taking a step closer to the bed.

He buried his face in one hand. "There were signs of the rogue in her from very early. Others suffered for it—someone dear to me was *killed* for it." He crossed himself reflexively. "I hoped if I kept a tight enough rein on her perhaps I could keep her from further mischief. I should have let one of those rich lords take her as a mistress—at least then when this side of her revealed itself it would reflect on him and not on me."

"Willem!" Jouglet scolded. "That sentiment is"—she struggled to find words—"lamentably expectable, from any man's mouth but yours. This is a scheme of Marcus's, I swear."

"You think just because you live for scheming others do as well," Willem countered, taking his head out of his hand. "I have no energy for such games, myself. And from what I know of Marcus, he doesn't either—he has always been the soul of integrity."

She could not argue this point, except to say, "He isn't *now*. But you're right, he's not accustomed to deceit, so if we find the right obstacle for him, he'll trip over it. But I need you at the castle to help me find it."

"Scheming again," Willem said heavily, with distaste.

After a pause, she sat beside him on the bed and tried another tack. "*You* were to have prospered by this wedding—you would have been the emperor's brother. Do you so lack ambition that you will fall over at this vicious rumor and give that up?"

"Is the issue my sister's prospects, or my own?" Willem asked in a tired voice. "I'm not dependent on Lienor's fate for my own fortune."

"You must be the emperor's brother to get the right bride."

"Konrad is fond of me. He's going to make me the first Imperial Knight, and if I asked it he would find me a proper wife."

"Proper for a *landless knight*," Jouglet corrected, slapping her knee with frustration. "You deserve a better wife than that. You deserve a marriage worthy of the emperor's own kinsman."

Willem looked at her. "There is an obvious option you're ignoring. The emperor is very generous to his cronies—look what he's done for Marcus. If his court musician were to unmask herself, and then retire to marry me, I think she would earn quite a fat—"

Jouglet's face pursed up with irritation. "I knew you were thinking that!" she snapped, and stood up, taking an aggravated step away from the bed. "Put it out of your mind, this moment and forever."

"Why?" Willem demanded.

"We've been over this." She pulled a window shutter closed and lowered her voice. "Konrad would not *reward* me for duping him for years, he would kill me—I mean that literally, Willem, he would have me executed."

"No he wouldn't," Willem assured her.

"Don't you know Paul had three men who lived as women whipped last week—one of them was *hanged*."

"Yes, I saw the body in the square," Willem said gruffly. "Konrad rebuked Paul for inciting it; nothing like that will happen again soon. But you are something else altogether. And even if you weren't, surely *you* would be exempt from such punishment."

"Oh yes? What would save me, Konrad's profound regard for women? At best he would have me banished to someplace far enough away that nobody would know he had been gulled." She moved to stand before him, almost scolding. "I will not be a woman in this court, Willem. Women in this court are chattel. We are not the happy couple of *Erec and Enite*. This is not a romance where love and marriage have the chance to commingle and take precedence. I am not your lady, and I'm not your wife, nor am I fit material for either."

Willem made an angry noise and stood up, fists clenched. Then, just as abruptly, he deflated and sank back onto the bed. "That is not proper, Jouglet. And I cannot expect Lienor to be superior to me. I was thinking about this last night, it is part of what kept me awake. If she must be proper, then so must I."

"What does that mean?" Jouglet asked, certain she did not really want to know. She took a step away from where he sat.

"Reveal yourself."

"No," she said with absolute finality.

"I want to make what is between us *right*. No more shameful secrets."

"Stealing my breeches, and all the freedom that comes with them—that would make it *right*?" she demanded, leaning against the wall. "I fail to see how."

He sighed and threw himself back on the bed, trying to think of how to say what was disturbing him. "I don't want to steal anything from you. But I want things irreproachable, and *proper*. I want a proper *woman*."

"There is one under my clothes," Jouglet offered drolly and reached for her belt.

"I don't mean *hidden*!" Willem said with exasperation. "I need there to be nothing suspect in my reputation. We are in real danger with Paul."

"I know that!" Jouglet said impatiently, letting go of her belt. "Why do you think I've been so careful about our assignations all week?"

"I mean I need to be generally known as having a woman."

"I know that too! I offered to help you snare a lady, and you declined the offer," Jouglet said, in a tone not of complaint but observation. "Now you want a lady after all?"

"Not like that. You were offering to find me someone to woo for appearances and gain," Willem countered. "I don't want a lady in that sense. I want someone whose regard for me is a reward both in itself, and in the eyes of the world. A wife, even a concubine. A *mate*."

Jouglet settled onto the chest beneath the window and looked down at her calloused hands, the long-fingered hands roughened by a youth's exposure to the elements. "That's expecting rather a lot from the average lady," she said. "You may find some sweet simperer who'll fondle your cock dutifully but have no idea what to do with your mind—but won't that bore you?"

"I'm not talking about fornication!" he said, and sat up. "I'm talking about companionship."

"I am your companion!"

"The *companionship* of a known *female*. Who *behaves* like a female." He was reaching exasperation.

She slouched back down onto the chest, lying faceup. "So you want your companion as yielding and passive—all the time—as she would be in copulating with you."

"That is *not* what I want, and you know it," said Willem angrily. "I've never said a female must be yielding and passive. Consider the behavior I've allowed my sister." His voice rising, as if she had challenged him, he added, "But then, consider what that allowance has led to! It shows me the value of the natural, the . . . the *normal* way of things! This . . ." He waved one arm. "This . . . between us, this is not normal."

"It is not *ordinary*," Jouglet corrected softly, her fingers reaching up to wipe dust from the windowsill. "But it is glorious. At least, I thought so."

Willem grunted, distressed, and threw himself back onto the bed faceup. "This would almost be easier if you really were a man," he said, accusatory.

She laughed. "Do you think I've never had that thought myself?" she asked.

"I meant it would be easier for *me*," he growled. "If you were either a man or a lady. Then I would know what to *do* with you!"

"I can be a lady," Jouglet offered, and giggled in shrill falsetto. She leapt up from her slouch on the chest and scurried across the room to him and perched beside him on the bed. "Oh, my lord Willem, I've been sitting here sewing all day just thinking about you and how lucky I am to be among your chattel." She made delicate hand

gestures, exaggerated imitations of Lienor, and as she spoke she
wobbled her head a little, girlishly. "I had such an interesting day,
first I carded some wool, and then I spun some wool, and then I
wove some wool into a tapestry that shows you winning a big-big
tournament, and then my brain turned into wool, and I have a little
wool between my legs, would you like to see it?" She leapt up and
lifted her tunic, pulling down her breeches, giggling shrilly. It was
her manic playfulness, as much as her pudenda, that affected him.

"You're a shameless harlot," he announced, and pulled her down
on top of him.

22 July

*T*he air was so clear and bright after the rain that Erec was recognized when he was still a mile away. Lienor, excited by the mystery and urgency of his galloping approach, hurriedly began to dress
to receive him. She was in such a giddy mood she thought she'd even
humor him by wearing something low cut, and so, clad in only her
shift, she was debating between a dark violet from Flanders or a
green from Douai.

Downstairs, Maria was ordering the steward and the cook to
fetch wine and prepare a plate of fruit and cheeses for her nephew
when he burst in unannounced through the front door of the hall,
filthy, breathless, and red-faced.

He had, during his journey, calmed a little. At one point he almost resolved to turn back toward court but decided that he needed
at least an explanation from her. For perhaps ten miles, he doubted
the story entirely and was eager to hear her defense, had decided he

would believe it no matter what it was—but when he tried to imagine that face, those smiling lips and teasing eyes, protesting her sexless innocence, he could not reconcile that with what his body insisted she really was. By the time he approached Dole he was angry again, and at the sight of Willem's manor he was overwhelmed with rage and spurred his exhausted horse into a final sprint. The closer he came to her the more he was newly convinced she was fallen. The knowledge made him feel unaccountably victorious.

"Where is she?" he shouted from the doorway, without otherwise acknowledging Maria's presence.

"Nephew," Maria said, shocked at his wild appearance.

He brushed past her. "Is she in her chambers?" he demanded, looking around.

"Of course," Maria said politely. "Dressing to greet you."

"I'm sure she is!" Erec laughed harshly, and turned back out of the hall to run to the far side of the small sunny courtyard. Maria went after him, more slowly. The servants in the courtyard followed his path with incurious looks, and went about their business. Cousin Erec was a known quantity around the household.

He threw himself up the stairs, stairs he had not climbed since he was at his nursemaid's knee, and hurled open the large oaken door that for years he had gazed at with burning curiosity from below.

Lienor yelped when she saw him, startled to be accosted half-dressed in her own room. He drew his sword, and in almost the same moment pulled a knife from his belt with his left hand to face her doubly-armed, as if she were a Saracen, his eyes huge and angry and his temples sweating. "Whore," he spat.

"Erec, what are you doing in here?" she demanded, rushing to grab her bed-robe.

He anticipated her and reached the bed a step before her, dropped his knife, threw the robe out of reach on the rushes and grabbed her wrist. She cried out wordlessly in shock and pain; he shoved her hard onto the floor at the foot of the bed and she gawked up at him, silent with amazement.

He stepped, deliberately, onto the skirt of her linen shift with his dusty boot, pinning her there, and pressed the tip of his sword against her stomach. She shrieked briefly but did not dare try to move.

"Show me, you whore!" he ordered, his face violet beneath the coat of road dust. "You've disgraced us all now, forever! Show me the damned rose!"

"The what?" she mumbled feebly, too shocked to understand the demand. The summer shift barely covered her nipples, and she automatically folded her arms across her chest protectively.

"You will not play coy with me anymore!" he shouted. Tossing the sword aside, he knelt down, grabbed the skirt of her shift, and ripped it from the hem up to well above her knee, exposing her lower legs.

Lienor screamed so shrilly that dogs in the yard below began barking. Maria's voice suddenly sounded, drawing nearer, crying out for her daughter.

With shaking hands Lienor desperately tried to pull the two sides of the torn skirt back together, but Erec struck her hard across the cheek and ripped them further. She flinched and brought her hands to her face, trying to talk to him with her head turned away, cajoling, pleading: *"Erec, what are you doing?!"* But her protestation only inflamed him and made him more determined. She tried to squeeze away from him, but he straddled her right leg and pushed her left leg away so that she lay, limbs splayed, on the floor; with rough and calloused hands he grabbed her bared thigh and twisted the soft pale flesh in his grip.

"Erec!" she shouted in pain and fear.

"Where is the rose? Show me the *evidence!*" he demanded furiously.

Finally she understood. "My birthmark?" she gasped, breathless. "All this fury for a birthmark?"

Still clutching her thigh between his fingers he hissed, "Show me. Sit up and show me or I'll break your neck now instead of later."

Fighting off sobs, Lienor pulled her upper body from the floor and nervously lifted the skirt higher than his rip had revealed. The sight made his heart thud, and he looked up. Even traumatized, she was still maddeningly beautiful, but he couldn't keep his eyes on her face because the sight below was so much more transfixing.

"Damn you!" he shrieked abruptly, *"Whore-bitch-harlot-cunt!"* Furiously, he tore the shift open all the way up her body to the hem at her neck and pushed her back so that she lay entirely exposed beneath him. She whimpered with fear. "You're dying today for the shame you've brought the family—"

"What shame?" she begged hysterically.

"Lienor!" her mother gasped from the door, afraid to come in. "Nephew! Get off of her!"

Erec glanced up at his aunt with an ugly expression. Servants cowered behind her on the stairway. "You don't tell me what to do, Aunt. I'm your liege lord, and you've raised a whore, a harlot who will open her legs to any cock that asks—"

"What are you *talking* about?" Lienor begged, sobbing with confusion, trying again to pull the shift closed over herself. Angrily, Erec slapped her hands away, grabbed the knife, and pressed it against her naked breastbone.

"Don't try to hide your shame!" he roared. "You gave yourself to Konrad's man!"

"I don't even know Konrad's man!" she protested in teary bewilderment as her mother said, "Who is . . . oh! Marcus! The steward—"

At the name, Erec looked up again. "There! You admit it!"

"I never met him!" Lienor cried. "I was *sequestered.*"

"She didn't meet him, Erec, I'm the only one who spoke with him," Maria insisted tremulously from the door.

Erec gave Maria a contemptuous snort. "You stupid old woman, she had him right under your nose and you didn't know it!"

"What is your proof?" Lienor demanded desperately.

"The rose! The rose is the proof! He described your perfect little rose!" Shifting the knife to his left hand, he used his right to maul her thigh again, but this time, overwhelmed by the warmth of her flesh, his hand moved up to the birthmark and then even higher. She stared at his hand, sobbing loudly, afraid to move. "This was not yours to give away," he hissed. "You've made it common property now."

"The rose!" Maria suddenly shouted, realizing. "Oh my God the rose—put up, Erec, put up, let her go, *I* told him about the rose! It's my sin, Erec, not hers!"

He looked at his aunt through narrowed eyes. "A feeble pretext to defend a harlot," he announced harshly and turned his full attention back to the space between his cousin's thighs. Pulse throbbing in his ears, he moved his hand even higher and was dizzy by the snarled fight between desire and disgust. Lienor was sobbing uncontrollably, trying to scream but unable to find her voice.

Maria, in a terror of self-recrimination, ran to them. Taking advantage of Erec's unseemly distraction, she snatched the knife out of his grip. She stood over him and pressed the blade hard against his throat; he was incredulous to find himself disarmed by an old woman.

"Get away from my daughter," she ordered in a choked voice. "Lecherous cur."

"Don't speak to me like that!" he said contemptuously. She shoved the point harder against his flesh and with a shock of pain he pulled away a little, glaring at her.

"It was I," Maria explained hoarsely. "He spent ages downstairs talking with me, and I forgot myself. I told him about the birthmark, in a story from her *childhood*, Erec—even the way he heard it had nothing indiscreet about it. I don't know what he's done with what I told him, but it's my fault, not my daughter's. Kill me if your overblown sense of honor requires that you kill someone."

Erec stared at her in amazement, mostly because he'd never heard her speak so many words at once, and never any words so adamantly. She used the threat of the knife to move him away from Lienor, then stepped between them and with her free hand, pulled the robe close enough for Lienor to grab it. Shaking violently, Lienor managed to stand and pull it on, turning away from them, sobbing still, but now from relief.

"Take the sword, Lienor," Maria said in an unsteady voice, eyes on Erec. Lienor could barely lift it, but she stood it upright with the tip on the ground and the hilt grasped hard in both her shaking hands.

"As God is my witness, nephew, she never even saw him from an upstairs window. They would not know each other if they met in the street." She turned the blade of the knife toward herself and offered the handle to Erec. "Kill me if you must punish the wrongdoer."

"Mother," Lienor said in a raspy voice, horrified.

Erec looked back and forth between them, unnerved by each one's attitude. "M-Marcus said you seduced him. Marcus is an honest man," he insisted, trying not to sound uncertain.

"I am an honest mother, and this is your honest cousin," Maria said firmly and offered him the knife once again.

Finally composed enough to wipe her face dry, Lienor demanded miserably, "Does my brother believe this of me?"

"*Yes*," Erec said defiantly, regaining a bit of his righteousness. "As does His Majesty, of course."

In an even more defeated, vulnerable voice, she asked softly, "Does Jouglet the minstrel?"

"No," he said after a pause, the righteousness immediately deflated.

"Do you?" she whispered.

He stared up at her, and she met his gaze, sniffling, her eyes red from the sobbing, her whole body trembling within the robe. After an agonized moment he grabbed the knife from Maria and hurled it across the room.

"Oh my God, what have I done," he murmured in a nauseated voice, and dissolving into tears he threw himself at his cousin's feet.

14

Complaint

[a work lamenting or satirizing the ills of society]

22 July

Erec moved the pieces of fruit, breadstuffs, and tableware back to their starting places, and gave his cousin a solicitous look. "Does it make more sense now?" he asked.

Maria, hovering over her daughter, pointed to a saltcellar. "Why is that one Marcus?" she demanded. "Make Marcus a rotten bit of turnip."

Lienor smiled despite her exhaustion. "You're missing the point, Mama." She patted Erec's hand. "Let me see if I can follow." She pointed to each item on the table. "The gold brooch is the emperor, who has promised to marry; his brother the cardinal—who would manipulate the marriage for the pope's benefit—is the bunch of grapes, and the pope is the wine; Alphonse of Burgundy, from whose county the royal bride must come, is the heel of bread, in a bowl of bread crumbs, which represent all the other nobility." She held up a flower with a tired smile. "I am the rose. The jasmine is the daughter of Besançon, who is devoted to the pope and vassal to the Count of Burgundy. Marcus the emperor's steward, who slandered me, is the salt, and Willem is the knife." She sighed. "Quite a board you've set here."

"Can you track it so far?" Erec asked gently. He was trying desperately to make amends and, having no experience at it, imagined how Jouglet might act. He thought the minstrel would arm Lienor with knowledge, but he was not sure he had it straight himself.

Lienor delicately picked up both the rose and the sprig of jasmine and placed them by the gold-foil brooch with Konrad's eagle on it. "On August first, in Mainz, His Majesty will announce which one of us he'll marry. Jouglet and Willem want him to marry me—and so does Alphonse of Burgundy, which is completely unexpected. Everybody else wants him to marry the Besançon heiress. And now His Majesty and all the others believe me to be a harlot." A pause. "Still why would the steward do this?"

Erec shook his head. "I cannot begin to guess."

"And are there any other rude developments I should know about?"

Erec thought a moment. "Not that I'm aware of."

Lienor frowned at the props and pointed as she spoke, her hand darting haltingly over the collection as if she were slowly tracing the flight of a distracted bee. "Either the steward *wants* Konrad to marry Besançon, or he wants to *prevent* Konrad's marrying me. If, as you say, Konrad trusts the steward and distrusts Cardinal Paul, then the steward is unlikely to be helping Paul, so I doubt the steward is for Besançon." She considered briefly. "On the other hand, if I became the empress, Willem would outrank the steward in court, and the steward wants to prevent that for some reason. What might the steward lose if Willem suddenly outranked him? Does he have expectations that haven't been secured yet?"

"He's engaged to Alphonse of Burgundy's daughter," Erec said, with a shrug. "Has been for years, as I hear it."

She blinked in surprise. "A *ministerial* is engaged to a *future countess*?" Then she smiled, plucked a cherry from the bowl of fruit farther down the table, and lay it between the saltcellar and the knife, continuing her graceful semaphoric exercise with more confidence. "That's the daughter, and that explains it all." Speaking rapidly, and emphasizing each player as she pointed to their symbol: "The *steward* doesn't want to be passed over in favor of *Willem,* and *Alphonse* would break the betrothal in a heartbeat if he could instead marry his *daughter* to the *empress's brother.* That's what's going on here. *That's* why *Alphonse* wants *me* to marry *Konrad* despite . . ." She glanced up to see her cousin and her mother both staring at her, dumbfounded.

"What?" she said reasonably. "Surely you aren't so simple to think the Count of Burgundy wanted to see me empress because he considers me a nice young lady?"

Maria was speechless, and Erec scrambled for words. "How . . . how could you sort all that out so quickly? How did your mind come to *work* that way?"

She smiled her shy-coquettish smile. "From listening to Jouglet speak of courtly scandal, I suppose. I was always a more studious audience than my brother was."

Erec shook his head, astonished. "And what does your scandalous education tell you we should do now?"

Lienor mused on the concert of props before her. "Is it possible to set out tomorrow morning and reach Koenigsbourg before Konrad leaves for the Mainz Assembly?"

Erec calculated. "Yes. It would be close, but he planned to leave the morning after the feast of St. Anne. That gives me four days."

Lienor stood up, her fingertips pressed against the trestle table for balance. "No," she corrected, trying to sound confident. "It gives *us* four days."

*W*hen Jouglet had returned alone from town, after following Willem there from his aborted castle breakfast, Konrad realized the young knight would need time. His Majesty was moved by the depths of Willem's feeling, and privately willing to be lenient—but not willing to appear so to the general view. So for the remainder of that day he never mentioned Willem's name and lost all apparent interest in the knight's existence. He gave Jouglet orders to check on Willem in the evening—but he gave these orders in private, and so obliquely that when Jouglet returned with no news of improvement, they could each pretend Konrad had never wanted any, anyhow.

The next morning, and the next again, Jouglet's attempts to conjure Willem to the castle were thwarted by the knight's disappearing into the hills on Atlas. He left word with his servant that he was flushing out bandits, valiantly protecting His Majesty's highway. Since this was—unbeknownst to him—a duty Konrad meted out to the lower-ranking knights of his donjon, neither minstrel nor emperor found the proclamation very helpful.

The third morning, Konrad said simply, without preamble, "That's enough. Get him here or send him home. Today."

She had ignored Erec's warnings of highwaymen and wolves, turned a deaf ear on her mother's cries that she would die of sun exposure or be dishonored by some local lord through whose lands they might pass. "I am going to clear my name," she kept saying, as if it were a prayer or chant, and began with her own hands to pack necessities. Chief among these, for her plan, was a virginal white gown, almost prudish, and all the jewelry she could carry. The night before she'd wrapped it all in two layers of linen within a leather pouch, and then put the whole thing into a saddlebag. Erec, despairing of talking her out of this, and knowing better than she did what she was in for, took the extra step of wrapping both his cousin and her baggage in the foulest things he could bear to offer her, so she would look like a poor nun with a ragged linen veil across her face.

Appearing decidedly eccentric and not the least attractive, Lienor collected what she naively thought would be enough biscuits and dried meat to hold them for the trip. Then she kissed her mother, anointed herself with holy water from the container by the door, said a prayer to St. Appolinarus, whose feast day it was, and stepped out into the dawn fog to call for her horse.

Jouglet rapped sharply on the door and was let in by a worried-looking page boy. Willem sat staring bleakly out the window, a drab, thick wool blanket wrapped around him, looking like an invalid. Jouglet, as infuriated as she was, did feel for him, but she chastised him in front of the page boys; he responded with grumbles and coded requests for fornication. He was not nearly as upset by Lienor's supposed behavior as he was by her supposed deception, and almost above all he was upset by his own contribution toward it. "I turned her into someone who would do this to me," he said with pained, fatalistic resignation.

"Heavens," Jouglet retorted. "So you are both the offender *and* the victim. That takes dexterity, Willem. I'm so impressed."

He smiled at her weakly, sheepishly, and sent the page boys from the room. "Come here?" he said with a gesture, so tentative it sounded like a question. "I know you think I deserve a chiding—"

"You deserve a lot worse than that," Jouglet corrected sharply, staying by the door. "You're lucky Konrad has been indulgent—but he's through with indulgence now. You are to return to the castle today, or you'll be sent back to Dole. His orders."

"He'd do better to give me some errand far away," Willem answered, making a face. "Tell him to send me on assignment somewhere distant. Then nobody at court can see me grieving, yet I'll be known to be in His Majesty's service."

Jouglet was so surprised by this reasoning, it took her a moment to think of a retort. "The court travels to Mainz in less than a week, and you must stay near Konrad."

He sighed tiredly and gestured again; she crossed to his stool near the window. "I've lived, and tried to raise her, by a courtly code of ethics, and it's all been a sham." He folded his arms around her waist and buried his face against her abdomen, like a little boy wanting to be cradled.

Jouglet bit her lip and looked away from him. "I'm not your mother," she said stiffly, and pushed him away. "I'm your escort to the king."

"I just can't face going back there. I'm trying," he said, almost voiceless. "I know I'm disappointing you, but I am *trying* to live up to your ridiculously impossible vision of me."

"It's not impossible," she said sharply. "I know what you're capable of. I've seen it. You are a magnificent soul, Willem. You're being *incredibly* stupid and pigheaded at the moment, but generally you're a magnificent soul, and Konrad knows that." She softened, tipped his chin up to look at him directly. "You're even magnificent in ways he has no knowledge of."

As if he'd been waiting for a cue, Willem pulled her down onto his lap, locked his arms around her shoulders, and kissed her hard on the lips. Taken by surprise, she let him for a moment. But then she pushed away against his chest, although she remained seated on his lap. "That's a bad idea."

"Paul can't see us here," he said. He rubbed his warm lips across her throat, and her body automatically pushed up closer against his. "I know he's always seeking moral cracks," he murmured into her ear, "but he can't see any cracks in this room at all." With a suggestive, hopeful little smile he moved his hand between her thighs.

"I was not referring to Paul," Jouglet said, rolling her eyes a little. She pushed away again, now just perching on his knees. "You must redirect your amorous intentions in a more public and courtly direction."

"You used to say that like you meant it," Willem observed, his attention turning to her belt-tie, which he began to undo. "Now it just sounds like something you say out of habit or desperation, the way Paul utters blessings."

He was right. For the first time in her memory, it bothered her to think some artificial creature's rouged lips and oiled, flowing tresses might, even accidentally, become valued over her own unanointed body. It felt good—too good—to see the look on Willem's face as he steadily untied her belt. This was getting messy. This was not how she had planned it. She pushed him back by the shoulder. "You *must* return to the castle *today*, it's an *order*."

Willem gestured to his unkempt self. "Showing up in this state would be as bad as not showing up at all. But I'm in need of exercise, and there don't seem to be any bandits in the local hills. So either help me to a distant assignment or indulge me in some other exercise." He tugged on her belt again.

She knew she would never get him back to Konrad's court by rewarding his absence from it with off-site fornication. If reason and self-interest could not lure him up the mountainside, she decided, then she would use whatever other bait was handy, however inglorious. So she put her hands over his and removed them from her belt, then removed herself from his lap, and left the room without a word, ignoring his surprised, imploring protest. A few hours later, back at the castle, she sent a message written in Burgundian and delivered by a boy she trusted and paid well, vowing that their next tumble would be in the cellar of Koenigsbourg, or nowhere.

Almost immediately following, despite a sudden thunderstorm, Willem was at the castle.

When his approach was announced, in the middle of the afternoon while many members of the court were at leisure, there was an awkward, collective pause in the hall. Konrad was in his chambers, having issued instructions not to be disturbed. Marcus asked Boidon to see to the visitor, and then he himself disappeared into his rooms.

By the time Willem was escorted in, everyone had busied themselves deeply in some small-group activity: several dice games, an embroidery project, music lessons, a round of backgammon that appeared to require dedicated onlookers. As Willem walked, dripping, silent, and self-conscious, the length of the hall toward the fire, each group welcomed him with varying degrees of ease or lack thereof, and invited him to join them, but nobody seemed put out when he declined.

Boidon sat him near the fire, took his drenched mantle, and offered him some wine, which he accepted. Nobody was rude enough to stare, but he could feel them wanting to. He was the only solitary figure in a room not meant for solitude. He was certain they were laughing at him silently.

He shifted his weight, about to stand again and leave, walk out the castle gates and straight back home to Dole, when he was stopped by a whisper.

"Your friends at the dice game truly meant their welcome." It was Jouglet, suddenly at his side. She nodded at a group of five young men, all of whom had fought under him in the tourney and come out well for it.

"Gaming is not proper for a knight," he said stiffly.

"Neither is *moping*," she hissed, her mouth clenched into a pleasant expression. She was just as aware as he was that the entire room, pretending to be otherwise engaged, had its collective attention fixed on Willem.

"I haven't been moping, I've been scouring the foothills for bandits," Willem said stubbornly.

"Konrad won't acknowledge that, for *your own* sake—it would appear to the court like a relegation. You don't know the rules, Willem. I do. Do what I say."

He arched one eyebrow, and whispered, "Do you really want to hold this conversation in public?" She began to answer and then stopped herself. He nodded, and almost smiled. "Yes, that's a good idea. Why don't you go down there first and I'll join you when my cloak is dry."

She blinked, and looked impressed despite herself. "Have I just been outmaneuvered?"

In the cellar it was virtually black, and he promised they would have the necessary conversation—afterward. They made love with her warm body pressed up against his, along the side of a huge wine cask. There was nothing poetic or romantic about Jouglet, little conventionally

feminine beyond the fact of her sex. She lacked the easy female softness that had made the Widow Sunia's body like a cushion to settle
upon, but there was an athleticism that Willem found surprisingly
appealing. Jouglet let him take the lead in lovemaking, so different
from the other aspects of their friendship. But she had, from the
start, been full of ideas that were distressingly erotic, and the habit of
frank conversation between them made her very casual about describing them. Everything about this shattered his conception of
how lovers were meant to be together, but unlike the shattering of
his sister's reputation, he enjoyed this, reveled in it. In fact, he was all
too aware that he was now in danger of wallowing in it.

Afterward, he spread his cloak for her amidst the baskets and
wineskins so they could rest for a moment, listening to the muted
symphony of thunder outside. He loved how their bodies nested together: her cheek fit comfortably in the hollow of his shoulder as she
lay beside him, with his big arm curled around her; her arm draped
with perfect ease across his chest, her leg folded over his thighs as if
one soft, curving piece of wood had been their mutual source.

"Now," Jouglet announced, as the afterglow was fading. She dis-
engaged and sat up, hovering over him. With sleepy contentment, he
reached up to stroke her hair. "Now that you are content, go back
upstairs and *radiate* contentment to the court. Remind them what a
glorious knight they have in you."

Willem sighed with sudden aggravation, pushed her away gently
and sat up to dress. "I can't abide their . . . *sympathy,*" he said, pulling
on his tunic.

"Then let them know there is no need of it," she countered instantly.

"How? By telling them I'm not bothered that my own tyranny
turned my sister to a harlot?" He groped around in the darkness for
his breeches.

"Do you *honestly* believe Lienor did this?" she demanded and reached for her own tunic. She always dressed much faster in the dark than he could.

"I have learned from *you* what ardor a young woman is capable of—and capable of hiding," Willem grumbled. He found his breeches and began to pull them up.

"Don't be ludicrous, Lienor is nothing like me!" Her breeches were already halfway on.

"My sister has always been more susceptible to the sensory than I have. She is transported by smells and tastes and sounds, so it stands to reason she would be transported by . . ." It troubled him to speak of little Lienor that way, and he hesitated. "There is a saying in Dole, one who cannot master himself has no right to master others."

"It's a saying you should take to heart yourself," she huffed, fastening her belt. "And it proves nothing. Let her defend herself, if you won't do it. Send for her."

Willem sighed heavily and reached for his own belt. "If her rebuttal is the least convincing, Erec will return with her testimony. I do not expect that. We've been over this too many times in the past two days, Jouglet, there is no profit in continuing the argument."

"There's no profit in continuing to *mope*," she said. "If you must think her guilty, at least affect *indifference* about it. Remind the world of what you are besides Lienor's brother."

Willem looked disgusted. "It would take a callous and ignoble soul not to be affected by what's happened. I would not degrade myself with such an affectation."

Jouglet threw her arms up. "This will drive me to madness. It's all a wasted effort, I should have seen that. You're the purest man I've ever known, Willem—it *destroys* me to see that even purity can fester into something twisted. I wash my hands of you. Go with God— apparently He's the only one who's worthy of you."

Stung, he sat there mutely in the darkness to hear whether she would really leave.

She did.

She was enraged and badly in need of air so she could think. She'd snatched up her belt and now headed by habit toward the kitchen opening, which was less noticeable from the courtyard than the large door for the wine casks. The smaller entrance had a short, S-shaped passage to it, and the door was often left ajar, since there was such frequent traffic through it from the kitchen. As she approached the inner end of the passage, tying up her belt, she heard familiar voices outside, and she pulled up short, glad she was still hidden. She pressed herself against the wall to listen, but in the clattering of rain onto the stony courtyard floor, she could not make out what the men were saying for a moment. They seemed to be standing in the indeterminate space between the corner of the courtyard, hidden behind a cistern, and the passage itself.

When she could make out sounds, she heard Paul's voice. "The Lord works in mysterious ways, Uncle. But he never refuses a little help. Does the prospect appeal to you?"

A pause. "Let me consider it," said Alphonse. A pause, and his voice grew tighter. "What about—"

"No news," Paul said tersely.

"Paul, he's still at *court*—"

"I'll handle it," Paul snapped, cutting his uncle off. "Marrying them—what were you thinking, you stupid hypocrite? I'll handle it, I still have my scouts on it." Jouglet heard the sticky slither of wet silk, and then Paul's voice again. "We must part or we'll be seen, and he will get suspicious. Think on what I said and speak to me tomorrow after mass. You leave first, I have another errand down here that may obviate all we've discussed."

Jouglet panicked when she realized Paul was actually about to walk into the cellar. His intention was no doubt finally to catch the emperor's favorite knight and favorite minstrel alone together; she prayed that Willem had taken the far exit by the wine casks.

Scurrying about had never had a place in her bag of tricks; she was far more accustomed to hiding in plain sight, but that would not help now. She had to move fast and that was hard to do barefoot in a dark storeroom full of irregular shapes, even with her eyes adjusted. There was planking down the center of the cellar that would take her to the far door, but it would mean running, and that could not be done in silence. She wondered if she should try to hide behind or under something until he left. But there were too many possible hiding places, none of them very good, and she hesitated trying to make her choice. It cost her.

Paul had entered, dripping wet—with a lamp, which she was not expecting. He saw at once that somebody was moving in the darkness of the cellar, and near him; surprised and alarmed, he pivoted quickly toward the form he'd seen, lamp thrust ahead of him.

The look on his face warned Jouglet she was in much greater danger now than if he'd caught her with Willem. Panicked instinct took over, and instead of fleeing to the far end of the room, she ran to the nearest cask of wine and tried to hide on the other side of it, against the damp stone of the alcove wall.

The cardinal didn't know whom he pursued, but after he'd grabbed one strong, thin arm and pulled the fleeing youth around to face him, he took in a quick breath, cursing quietly. For a moment the two of them stared at each other, Jouglet blinking from the light, her free hand hovering protectively over her purse. The smell of wet wool, must, and her own fear almost stupefied her.

"Oh, my dear boy," Paul said in a low voice. "I would that it were anyone but you. If you were some ignorant peasant it would perhaps have sufficed to cut your tongue out to keep you quiet. But you, dammit, will have to be entirely disposed of."

Jouglet made a move to break past him, but Paul had already set the lamp down on the rock floor and pulled out a bared knife from his boot. Before she could take a breath, he had wrapped one arm around her waist and had the cold blade against her throat.

His entire body, clothed in sopping wool and silk, was pressing into hers; she tried to edge away, but he pulled her back against him. "I smell sex on you," he whispered, his mouth contorting into strange expressions. "You have been sinning. But I, I am a man of God." He pinned her lower body against the barrel with the pressure of one leg. His breath was shaky for a moment. "I will grant you extreme unction, I will say the last rites over you before you have quite left us. You could not ask for a more thoughtful executioner."

"I heard nothing," Jouglet whispered back quickly, trying not to sound terrified. "But I am a creature of opportunity, milord, and if you are on the cusp of some great thing, pay me and I'll deliver Alphonse to you, I know how to talk to him—"

"Shut up," Paul muttered, pressing the knife harder against her skin. Under his breath he muttered, "Lord forgive me," and she felt him tense in preparation to run the blade across her throat.

Before he could do it, his body was wrenched away from hers. They both shouted aloud in surprise as he fell against a pile of baskets and then crashed to the stone floor with such force that he lay stunned; Willem easily snatched the knife out of his hand. Shaking with rage the knight knelt over the cardinal, and pressed the tip of the blade inside Paul's left nostril. "I will cut your nose from your face if you try to move or call out," Willem whispered. "How dare you wear those robes when you would murder a defenseless innocent in cold blood?"

He tossed the knife toward Jouglet. The cardinal was nearly as big as he was, but he hoisted him roughly to his feet, with one fist grasping either side of Paul's ermine collar. Jouglet picked up both the knife and the lamp.

"Young man, please," Paul said soothingly, managing to reclaim a superior, priestly tone. "You clearly misunderstood the chat you interrupted."

"You were threatening the life of somebody close to me, and you should die for it," Willem seethed. "Given an opportunity where it would insult neither Konrad nor the pope, I will kill you. I swear it on all that I hold holy—I swear it on Jouglet's very life." Glowing with his self-righteousness, he released one side of Paul's collar to reach out for the knife. Reluctantly, Jouglet handed it over. He shoved it point-up under the cardinal's chin. "Now *you* will swear on all that *you* hold holy that you will never again, by direct or indirect means, attempt to harm my friend Jouglet. Swear!"

"I swear, I swear," Paul gasped, when Willem poked the underside of his chin with the knife. "I swear on my own faith."

"That's false," Willem spat, and in a flash had the knife down at Paul's groin. "Swear on your own testicles, or I'll cut them off."

Paul laughed nervously, but Willem was humorless.

"Jouglet, move his robe aside, lift up his shirt for me," he ordered, eyes still boring into Paul's.

"I swear! I swear on my life!" Paul insisted.

Willem relaxed the knife a little, and his breathing calmed. "Very well," he said gravely. "Then I require only one more thing from you." The hand still on Paul's collar hauled him over closer to Jouglet and effortlessly tossed him to his knees. "Beg the minstrel's pardon."

"What?" Paul and Jouglet said in exactly the same voice, as if he had suddenly spoken a different language.

"Beg his pardon for having wronged him," Willem said in a tighter voice. "Now."

Paul looked up at Jouglet. "I beg your pardon," he said flatly.

"Now kiss his feet," Willem ordered, standing over him.

"Willem don't do this," Jouglet warned, as Paul gawked.

"Kiss his feet!" Willem hissed, enraged, and brandished the knife.

Looking sickened, Paul lowered his head to the ground before Jouglet's bare feet and pressed his lips briefly on the dirty stone.

"There, I have kissed the ground he walks on," he said in a voice of dry sarcasm. "Will that suffice?"

"Yes," Willem said shortly, still humorless. Paul muttered something under his breath that sounded like a threat of vengeance; Willem seemed profoundly unimpressed by it. Sticking the knife in his belt he again grabbed Paul by the collar and hoisted him to standing. Then he dragged him past the bags of grain and flour, toward the kitchen entrance, and pushed him hard. Paul stumbled around the corner, through the passage, and out into the thunderstorm.

Willem spun around to finally look directly at Jouglet. His face glowed with relief in the dim lamplight. "The prospect of losing you made my heart stop."

"You stupid idiot!" she snapped, stamping her foot in frustration.

Willem was flummoxed. "I just saved your life."

"I thank you, yes, but you should have stopped there," she said angrily.

"What did I do wrong?" he demanded.

"If there were any doubts before, he knows we're lovers now. You made that absurdly clear, playing my avenging angel. Kiss my *feet*? What were you *thinking*?"

"He already knew we were lovers," Willem protested.

"If he thought he had evidence of that, he would keep me alive to be burned at the stake while he intoned prayers for the populace. No, Willem, he thinks I overheard something I shouldn't have."

"What?"

"I didn't actually hear enough to find out! But he *thinks* I did, that's what he was upset about. He didn't know you were in here with me until you made your grand appearance trying to be my white knight."

"Oh," said Willem, not knowing what else to say.

"Now he thinks I know something I don't—something apparently worth killing me over—*and* he has the fodder to accuse us of miscreant behavior."

"Oh," said Willem again.

There was a pause and the rain sounded very loud outside, through the small and high-up window. Willem's stomach sank as he anticipated—correctly—what Jouglet would say next: "It is not in your interest or my own—or Konrad's—for you to try turning me into your lady. I know it's only your need to do what seems right, moving you to say and do things that are exasperating. It is dangerous to us both. I do not *fault* you, but neither can I allow it to continue."

"I apologize," Willem said quickly. "I won't do it again."

Jouglet shook her head. "It is not your behavior, it's your *nature*." She frowned at him thoughtfully. "I should have realized this sooner. What we're doing together requires a greater level of duplicity than your blood can stand. That makes you a good man, Willem. Too good, in fact, for me. Very well, then." She grabbed his hands in both of hers—her palms were clammy, Willem noticed, and she sounded like she needed to cough. "Go and find a real lady whose white knight you can be. Let *me* be the white knight for your sister. I'll interrogate Marcus, find out why he's doing this and what could make him recant. You just worry about reclaiming your place as Konrad's martial pet. Under the circumstance, staying away from each other may be the best way to work together. We may salvage your sister yet." Dropping his hands, she pressed past him and exited the cellar through the kitchen end, into the downpour.

Jouglet went straight from the wine cellar to Konrad's chambers, arriving damp from sprinting through the courtyard. Two pages stood outside the bedroom with the usual guard, which suggested His Majesty had a woman with him, but she did not pause. The guard made a feint to stop her, but Jouglet eyed him warningly and he pulled back; it was remarkable how forceful a presence the slender unarmed figure could be when necessary. She swung open the door and took a broad step inside, proclaiming loudly, "Your Majesty!"

There was a woman there, but she was already dressing to leave; Jouglet waited at the door to usher her out. The windows were shuttered and the little light came from the hearth; the room had a wintry, claustrophobic smell and feel. Konrad, sprawled drowsy and naked on his unmade bed, scowled. "Do not walk in on me in my leisure."

"I come on urgent business—there's a conspiracy you must attend to immediately," Jouglet insisted. "I just overheard Alphonse and Paul talking in the cellar—"

"No you didn't," Konrad interrupted with finality. "Fetch me my robe there on the floor."

Biting her lip, she retrieved the golden robe and offered it to him. Konrad sat up sluggishly and shrugged his upper body into it. His was the heavy mass of a fighter slouching slowly toward plumpness. "I must be getting old," he said with a rueful grin. "What once relaxed me now exhausts me. And I start to creak when it rains like this."

"Sire, please, this is important—"

"Jouglet, listen to me," Konrad said calmly, reclining back onto the quilted bedcover. He seemed to address his own jeweled hands. "You heard nothing in the cellar. Because—you see—you never go to the cellar unless I send you there to get some wine."

Jouglet pursed her lips, understanding, but pressed on. "Then I heard it somewhere else. You need to know what I heard, not where I heard it. They're scheming."

"That would not be news," Konrad harrumphed. "Paul has—"

Again the door burst open. Willem flew in, brown hair darkened from the rain, shrugging off the gloved paw of the guard. Konrad called the man off with a gesture, but the guard stayed in the room, his eyes glued angrily to Willem's scabbard. Willem threw himself to his knees by Konrad's bed without looking at Jouglet. "Your Majesty," he said in an agitated voice. "Forgive my presumption, but I must tell you that your brother is armed—was armed—beneath his priest's robes—"

"That is no surprise to me, either," Konrad said with a yawn. He gestured to Willem's own sword, wryly.

"He tried to kill Jouglet, Your Majesty," Willem said, immediately unbuckling his sword-belt. He handed it to the guard, who left the room, glowering. "I had to disarm him by force, Your Majesty. I did not hurt him, but I think he is a danger to your court."

Konrad took a deep breath, slow and pensive, slouched against the pillows of his bed. "Where did this happen, Willem?" he asked at last, a patient father querying a cowed but wayward child.

"In the cell—" Willem began, then cut himself off when Konrad slowly shook his head. "But it did, sire," he said quietly. "I know what you think that implies, but you need to know your brother is a danger."

"A danger to those who visit the cellar," Jouglet contributed. "Nobody in this room ever goes to the cellar."

Konrad nodded once. "Quite right, Jouglet."

A third time the door flew open, and this time it was Paul who entered, looking stricken and much wetter than the other two. Konrad snickered sarcastically. "This is becoming a charming farce," he said. "What complaint have you to add to the argument?"

Paul glanced between the other suppliants, trying to assess what damage had been done and how best to salvage it. He waited until the guard had patted him down for weapons and left the room again before he spoke. "Sire, I am here to defend myself. I know the minstrel overheard a conversation and I am confident he will misrepresent me to Your Majesty. I want to be accused to my face so that I may defend myself fairly."

Jouglet frowned, looking confused. "I overheard nothing. Where was this?"

"In the cellar," Paul snapped. "Do not play games with me, Jouglet. I demand to be accused to my face."

"The only thing these two accused you of is trying to slice Jouglet's throat," Konrad assured him. "It would be in their interest to see you compromised—just as it would be in your interest to see them compromised—but staggering as the thought is, Paul, they have no means to do it. Your coming in here to defend yourself is more damning than their coming in here to complain about you. They didn't know, for example, that you've told our uncle the Besançon girl is believed by her physicians to be barren, which means I'd leave no son, and therefore Cousin Imogen's child would be my most direct heir, making Alphonse grandfather of the next probable emperor. They, distracted as they've been lately, hadn't heard that rumor yet." He smiled, his lips pressed together. "But I did. And as much as I enjoy seeing him taken advantage of in general, I'm seeing to it that Alphonse is disabused at once of the notion that some whelp of Imogen will ever ascend my father's throne."

Paul became unattractively pale. Then an unpleasant little smile tightened his lips. "I had been about to disabuse Alphonse myself," he said. "But I was distracted by sounds of a . . . most specific nature from within the cellar. I pursued those sounds."

"I am not interested in what they were," Konrad said, tension in his voice.

Paul nodded, as if with understanding. "Then I shan't burden you with it, sire, I'll burden His Holiness in my next dispatch to Rome instead."

Konrad sighed with aggravation. "You are a small, round,

extremely compacted turd, Paul. Tell me what I must do to keep such a dispatch out of Rome. Agree to marry Besançon, I assume?"

The cardinal was pleasantly surprised at having won so easily. "Oh, nothing so significant, sire. Merely reassure me that if your nonpareil of Christian knighthood here cannot control his impulses, he'll go the way of Nicholas. I don't expect much from your little minstrel—moral uprightness is not expected of his class—but how do I justify my emperor and brother, ruler of an empire deemed by its very nature to be sacred, endorsing such behavior in a courtier? It's one thing when a pack of knights are traveling together and have no other outlet but their squires, but he's indulging right here in the castle where there are women in every corner."

Konrad grimaced meaningfully at Jouglet, who avoided the look. "What exactly did you hear, Paul? How do you know they weren't sharing a woman? They are both partial to the whores, I've gone there with them myself."

"He may have ridden a whore, but it was Jouglet's feet he ordered me to *kiss*," Paul retorted with quiet triumph, and glanced at the knight. "A mistake he'll pay for in time, believe me."

Konrad made an exasperated, disgusted sound. "There is not one man in this entire accursed moldy sandbag of a fortress I can trust to behave reasonably," he growled, glaring at all three of them. Pointing at Paul, but speaking to Willem, he continued, "I cannot remove *him* from my court for failing to be what he should be, although he's failed many times over. You are a different matter. And so are you," he added, turning his glare on Jouglet. "I've more use for a fighter than for a fiddler, or for a spy so distracted that he knows less than *I* do about court intrigues. If I must, I'll say you led Willem astray and then I'll throw *you* out. Or worse. Do you understand?"

"Yes, sire," said Jouglet quickly.

"What was it you once said?" Konrad pressed irritably. "As close to Galahad as any man could hope to be?" The imperial gaze snapped back to Willem. "That is your new assignment, Willem. You are hereby Galahad."

Willem nodded, crimson, eyes averted. "Yes, sire. May I point out that Galahad spent much of his time traveling his master's realm in service to him, which in this case would provide a chance for me to—"

Konrad cut him off with a sharp wave of his hand. "Do you think I hadn't considered that? Sending you away on some knightly errand would give the appearance that I was ashamed of something about you—whether your sister's propensity for lovers or your own. The bosom of my court is the place you need to shine right now. I know that is the hardest place for you to be, but it's where you are most useful to me, so you will be here anyhow. Consider it a public test of character—public tests being the only ones that matter in politics."

"I shall endeavor, Your Majesty, although I'm only human—"

"Not anymore you're not," Konrad corrected angrily. "If you're content with being only human, go back to Dole, you don't belong in my service. Here you must be superhuman—or occasionally, as in my brother's case, subhuman. You are all dismissed. Willem, return to your inn without Jouglet and contemplate your circumstances. Unless you have an exceptional excuse, I expect you back in my court by tomorrow supper."

The moment he was alone, the fuming monarch sent for Marcus and Nicholas. To the messenger he gave an easy assignment, merely to summon his favorite mistress to fulfill a simple but important task in town.

Alone with Marcus, the ubiquitous pages in the next room, he gestured the steward to sit on a stool facing him as he remained lounging on his bed in the golden robe, looking now far more wearied than relaxed. He voiced with quiet bitterness his fear that Willem might disappoint him, after all, and so . . . "And so you, Marcus, are the safest man to put in charge of my daughter's dower lands. I'd been thinking of Willem, but as things are developing, you are a better investment." Marcus's eyes widened but he said nothing, which Konrad interpreted as happy amazement: it was gratifying that *somebody* was behaving appropriately today. "Yes. With all that it involves—I will give you the lands in Aachen as a genuine fief, and make a dukedom of them. You will be the Duke of Aachen, and married to your emperor's closest living relative. That's quite a rise from 'son of a serf' as our boorish Alphonse likes to call you, eh?"

Marcus took a deep breath and let it out very fast. "Yes, sire. Although Alphonse is, I believe, reconsidering the alliance with Imo—"

"Well, he's too late, you're mine, I need you for my daughter," Konrad said comfortably. There was another pause, during which Marcus looked straight down at the rush-covered floor and the emperor's satisfaction with his steward's behavior dwindled to a mote; he eventually amended, sarcastically, "Your gratitude overwhelms me, Marcus."

Marcus shook his head and looked up, trying to organize his thoughts. "Sire, good lord, of course I would be grateful beyond words for the duchy and my freedom—"

"And for my daughter!" Konrad added. "She may be illegitimate, but she's still sprung from these loins."

"Yes, sire, I . . ." He lowered his voice nearly to a whisper, and glanced over his shoulder at the opening to the dayroom, where the pages were. "May I be blunt, Konrad?"

Konrad gave him a curious look, then started laughing as it dawned on him. "Oh, of course—Imogen makes you randy. I must tell you that confounds me, but we can arrange something, that has nothing to do with whom you marry. You're marrying my daughter.

We'll make it public at the Assembly. I'll give you the duchy the day of the betrothal."

The steward felt a wave of panic wash over him, and he tried to look appropriately grateful. But he failed, and Konrad saw this.

"Marcus, I am altering your destiny."

"Yes, sire," Marcus said, and forced a smile. Throughout his youth he would have sold his soul for what was being offered; but now all he could think was that he had once again lost Imogen—and far worse, that whoever *gained* Imogen could denounce her on her wedding night. Some bridegrooms might wink at her soiled state, for the sake of her ample dowry; righteous Willem, if he got her, would never wink at anything. Marcus did a passable job of looking grateful, but Konrad knew him too well.

"Do not annoy me, Marcus," Konrad said through clenched teeth, sitting up a little. "Retire to your room to muse upon your extraordinary fortune—and don't come out until you can demonstrate that you realize how indebted you are."

Marcus stepped out of the emperor's bedroom into the galley to the hall stairs, radiating unhappiness. He paused a moment by the guard's station, torn between the urge to run back inside and fall pleading at Konrad's feet, and rushing away somewhere, anywhere, to try to do something useful—but he could not imagine what.

He stepped into the enclosed spiral stairs and came up short with an abbreviated gasp: Standing on the top step, with an air of having been waiting for him, was Cardinal Paul.

"There is no love lost between us, steward," Paul said softly. "But the ground we both tend knows a western weed in need of plucking. Shall we speak later?"

So it's come to this, Marcus thought, meeting the light eyes that were unnervingly similar to his lord and master's. *Would I join forces with one of the most loathsome men I know?* And something inside him died as he realized that yes, he would.

By sunset, to Erec's astonishment, they were in Montbéliard. "And we've been going up into the hills!" he exclaimed as they reined in near the manor house that overlooked the town. Their horses were exhausted. "This is farther than we got the first day when I came through with Willem!"

Lienor was tired but pleased, almost preening, on her dun. She lowered her linen veil; there was the thinnest mask of tiredness around her eyes, creased in the corners, but otherwise she looked her usual pretty self. "God is smiling on our endeavor," she announced. "We did not meet with bear or boar or wolf or wildcat or highwaymen of any sort. It was really rather dull, in fact. I'm starting to be suspicious of the tales of errant knights."

Erec, as a landed lord, had the right to demand shelter at other lords' homes when evening fell. Lienor was nervous about taking this prerogative, but the only other option was to get rooms in the roadside inns, and he did not want to expose her to the gawking eyes of beggars, monks, and merchants—and far worse, men of his own breeding, young knights wandering the countryside looking for tournaments to win or heiresses to kidnap. They decided she would be disguised, to avoid being recognized by courtiers along the way and having word reach Konrad's court ahead of time about her coming. Now she replaced the linen veil, bowed her head, and let him lead her up to the gate of the manor house.

That evening a mist blinded castle and township from each other. Willem picked at his supper in his room, and sent away his pages, who had offered to keep him company. When he had finished eating, he went to the door to call Musette to take his platter away. There was an unfamiliar figure climbing the steps to the outdoor landing toward him.

"Who are you?" he asked, startled.

Instead of answering right away, she smiled, and her smile made it clear to Willem exactly what her intentions were and her absolute certainty that she would achieve them. "His Majesty the Emperor asked me to pay you a visit."

Willem stared at her dumbfounded. She took another step toward him. His guilty conscience compared her immediately to Jouglet. She was just as cheerfully confident toward him, but the similarities ended there: she was smaller, prettier, infinitely more feminine in her demeanor and speech, and most impressive of all, she was rounder, softer, everywhere. She wore only a reddish cloak over her sleeveless shift, and when she stepped past him into his room she dropped the cloak to the floor.

Still speechless—in part because he was a little drunk—he followed her back into his lamplit room. She glanced around, as if she had bought it and was trying to decide what changes to make. "You were the hero of the tournament, weren't you?" she said, with a lazing, appraising voice that somehow still implied admiration. She was well schooled in this delivery, but Willem, not knowing that, was simply floored by her attention to him. "While I was watching you I hoped we'd have a chance to do this."

She strolled across the chamber and pushed open a shutter, which let in a little light, then considered the ambiance of the room, and pulled it closed again. Willem could only stare at her, and she enjoyed the staring, occasionally meeting his eye with a knowing look, which made him blush and look away. She crossed to the table, lifted up an unlit beeswax candle stub Konrad had given him, lit it by the fire in the lantern, then set the candle stub down again and blew out the brighter lamp. "There," she said with calm satisfaction. "That's what we want to start with, I think. Unless of course you'd like to see me more clearly while you are undressing me?" And she laughed softly because he seemed unable to speak. But when she said, teasing, "Shall I undress myself, then?" he made it clear at once that however mute he was, he was entirely ready to welcome her. She was soft in his arms; she smelled of rose water and cinnamon. She was entirely foreign in a way that Jouglet never could be, and he was fascinated by that, by her unknown-ness; she offered him no hint of her character, of her interests or passions or wit; she offered simply a female body and its willingness to please him. He did not even know her name. Possessing her was nothing whatsoever beyond the immediate moment of conquest and satisfaction.

Nothing had ever felt so uncomplicated. It was enthralling.

15

Saga

[the story of a great family told through several generations]

23 July, night

Marcus had a prie-dieu in his bedroom, and he knelt at it that evening with a dull sense of dread. He already knew there would be a rap from the passage that led to the hall, and knew who it would be, and why. So when it sounded, he sent the pages from their beds into the antechamber, and remained unmoving at the prie-dieu as the cardinal entered, striding into the small chamber and taking stock of it.

Paul in a hungry mood was kinetic. He hardly stopped moving from the moment he entered—not as though he were nervous or angry, just so full of determined energy that he could not contain himself in one spot.

"I will not ask your reasons, and you will not ask mine," he said quietly without greeting or preamble. "But we both would benefit from Willem of Dole's removal."

Marcus, still kneeling, kept his head bowed. "I admire the man and I would not have material harm befall him," he replied, hardly above a whisper. "I don't care if he remains at court as long as he doesn't rob me of what's mine."

"Nothing's *yours*, Marcus, you're a serf," Paul said with a casual laugh, experimentally opening and closing the shutters of the windows looking onto the courtyard. There was an edge to the laugh, an edge Marcus remembered from their youth in the old emperor's court. "Even if you were made a duke for marrying his bastard, it would profit you nothing. Your child would never gain. Who would marry the offspring of a serf and a bastard, even a royal serf and a royal bastard? Konrad is blinded by affection for you. It is an idiotic promotion, there's no future advancement in it. Her inheritance accomplishes much greater good if it is given to the church."

"You're right, Your Eminence, it is a foolish match and I want no part of it. Can you help me?"

"Only if you help me," said Paul. The wainscoted room was apparently far more engaging than its occupant, whom he had not yet bothered looking at. Now he turned his attention to the stand holding the washbasin and the pitcher. He poured fresh water into the basin, then delicately swished his hands around in it, delighting in keeping Marcus on edge. "She's my goddaughter and we're both of the cloth. I know she doesn't want to wed, and I can invoke God's will to allow her to remain cloistered."

That was a wonderfully simple solution. "Will you do as much?" Marcus asked. "For your niece as well as for me?"

"Certainly," Paul said comfortably and reached for the hand towel. "If you help me remove Willem of Dole from the court."

Marcus did not move from the prayerful position. In a constricted voice, he whispered, "There are servants in the next room."

Paul strode instantly to the door and opened it. "Leave," he ordered the page boys. "Go and wait down in the courtyard until we tell you that you may return." He stood there, his head in the door until he had been obeyed, then returned to pacing the bedroom. "There are so many options available. The easiest, frankly, is to catch him in sodomy—"

"That's not necessarily a banishable offense," Marcus said sardonically. "As you yourself know personally."

Paul reddened and turned on him in irritation. He tossed the hand cloth to the floor with a dramatic flourish. Marcus remained unmoving at the prie-dieu. After a moment, Paul said, in a meaningful tone, "As steward you have direct access to his food."

Marcus finally looked up, sharply. "I will not do that!" In a slightly softer voice, returning his head to a position of prayer, he muttered, as if astonished by the revelation, "In the name of Christ, you're fouler than Alphonse."

"Speak to me with respect, you clod of dirt," Paul snapped. He careened through the room again, now toward Marcus's bed. "I am your better."

"No, Your Eminence," Marcus said with a weary laugh. "You most certainly are not that. And it is enough, surely, that he leave the court." He threw a suspicious glance up at Paul. "His sister is out of favor for empress. Thanks to the clod of dirt. Why are you still leery of him?"

Paul hesitated. "None of your concern. Anyhow, until Konrad is actually married to Besançon, Lienor and therefore her brother are still thorns to me."

"But I have absolutely ruined Lienor's chances for any future at all," Marcus said in a tight voice. He felt a new wash of guilt: until this moment, only the inherent sin of lying had pained him, and the abstract fact of treachery; he had not thought much about the concrete, long-term consequences.

"Your story could be called into question," Paul said, throwing himself supine onto the angled bed. "Your word counts less than a free man's in court, if it came to that. Jouglet is determined to warm Konrad to Lienor again. Jouglet is far more conniving and manipulative than you are. He'll get his way."

"Then *Jouglet* is the one to get rid of!" Marcus said, agitated. His interlacing fingers jerked tightly, whitening his knuckles.

Paul considered this. "True. Willem without Jouglet is nothing but a docile pup. Jouglet's food can be . . . seasoned as easily as Willem's, surely." Seeing the look on Marcus's face, Paul smiled paternally. "There is no risk to you, Marcus. I will supply the potion, I will assist you to expiate your sins, and I will cover for you should the law suspect you."

Marcus laughed sarcastically. "No. You'll see the serf is hanged for it, and then you'll be entirely free of suspicion."

Paul scowled and sat up a little. "I respect your intelligence, Marcus, please respect mine. You've been on warm terms with Jouglet for years, while both of you have no love for me. If you're caught and you tell Konrad I'm behind it, he will believe you. So it is not in my interest for you to be caught." He relaxed again against the striped head cushion and went on, comfortably. "There are poisons that kill painlessly. It's not as if Jouglet were leaving behind mouths to feed. He's just a vagabond."

"I will not kill an innocent man," Marcus said weakly from the prie-dieu.

"Oh?" Paul scoffed. He sat up, set his feet on the floor, his hands on his knees, and looked levelly at Marcus for the first time. "Then under the circumstances, how do you intend to get what you want?"

Marcus considered for a moment. His heartbeat suddenly sounded louder to him. "I shall tell the truth," he said at last.

"You'll tell Konrad that you lied about Lienor?"

Marcus went white and scrambled to his feet. "What are you—"

"An educated guess." Paul smiled. "Calm yourself. It is the obvious answer, but Konrad cannot see it because he's so accustomed to your integrity. We can use that, you know. We probably have three months left to exploit his blind trust before he grows suspicious, so we'll have to work quickly to get everything we want."

Marcus fought back a wave of nausea. "We'll do no such thing," he said in a disgusted whisper. "I'll go to him at once and explain everything."

With calm conviction, Paul announced, "If you confess to him now, you are a dead man. Do you understand that? He'll have to kill you. Slander about his intended bride is a mild form of treason, plus you made him look like a fool—plus Willem will simply take your head off. I don't know why you did it, but that will come to light as well, and I doubt to your benefit. Honesty is not an option open to you any longer, Marcus." The smug grin on Paul's face was welcoming, an invitation to embrace the fallen state and gain from it.

"I shall at least make amends by being honest—from this moment forward," the steward insisted.

Paul laughed. "You can try that, but I doubt it will get you very far." He rose and headed for the door with a lazy assurance that reminded Marcus of the emperor. "We'll speak again when circumstances have made your choices a little clearer."

"Jouglet," said Marcus gravely in the shadows outside Konrad's receiving chamber very soon after. "I want to show you something.

Come with me to my chamber." He followed the minstrel down the stairs.

"He expects me back in a moment with a fresh flagon," Jouglet protested.

"That's a lie. If you were going down to get wine you'd have taken the other stairway."

"He wants it mulled from the kitchen," Jouglet insisted as they arrived on the pavement.

"This will only take a moment."

Jouglet warily followed up the internal spiral stairs to Marcus's rooms. A fire was already burning in the large anteroom, tended by a page boy, and a torch was lit; without pausing in his stride Marcus went straight to one of the ornate wooden chests lining his walls, and pulled open the top. He gestured for Jouglet to close the door, as he himself took out a battered-looking piece of parchment, an inkwell, and a reed pen.

"What's that for?" Jouglet asked, taken with his mysteriousness despite herself. He was a bastard, but at least he was more intriguing in despondency than Willem was.

"Jouglet, I know you may be suspicious of me still, but you must believe one thing. I am in love with Alphonse's daughter."

"Of course you are," Jouglet said, hoping very much he wasn't, and then realizing by the look on his face that in fact he was.

Which was calamitous, because there wasn't a thing Jouglet could do to change it.

"I am. If you are serious in your desire to look out for my best interests, I beg you, work on Konrad and the count to go ahead with my marriage to Imogen."

So that was what he wanted after all. She blinked a few times quickly, trying to decide if Marcus, of all people, would let his personal desires ruin his emperor's future.

Marcus had misread her blank expression. "You don't believe me that my only desire is Imogen. Witness me write to her so you can see firsthand how I feel about her."

"That really isn't necessary," Jouglet said, pretending to stifle a yawn. "I would like nothing more, Marcus, than to curl up before the fire now, and get some sleep. It has been a trying day." She needed time alone, immediately, to sort this out.

"I am going to write anyhow," Marcus insisted. "Can you read? I want you to witness it. If you are sincere in your friendship to me, be my witness in case someday I'm called to account for what's happened."

"Very well," the minstrel said at last, resigned. The pseudo-stifled yawn had made her realize how tired she actually was, and sore from resisting Paul's attack in the cellar. And sore at Willem too. In fact, the whole day had been a quiet series of disasters. She bowed with a weary sort of archness. "Your witness."

He dipped the reed pen into the inkwell, and in his quick, efficient hand he wrote: "Imogen, my dear, my heart is full of you tonight. I see you in the face of every lady at court, and your image over theirs makes their faces seem that much lovelier, although none—"

"Yes, all right, we do not need the poetry this evening," Jouglet interrupted, reading along over his shoulder. "Just get to the point, I beg you, Marcus."

She tapped her foot while he continued his flowery language, and finally he wrote: "I am so distraught at this separation, my beloved, I do not know how to turn your father's heart, or Konrad's either anymore, to be kind to us. Please, if your able mind can think of anything, write to me at once. I will do your bidding without hesitation. My friend Jouglet, His Majesty's musician, has promised to help us in any way he can, and is a witness to this letter. I send you as always my unending love, to be yours until death and beyond." He signed it "M" with a very dramatic-looking flourish beneath it. "A love knot," he explained, sounding so sheepishly sincere that Jouglet almost felt a twinge of pity for him. He sealed the note with wax and string, and then offered it to Jouglet. "You may see it messengered yourself," he announced. Jouglet was impressed.

"I will," she warned, intrigued.

Marcus gestured, pushed it more in Jouglet's direction. "Please," he offered.

Jouglet opted merely to witness a page's taking the note for dispatch, mostly because she did not want to be bothered with the task. The intent was what mattered, and what puzzled her. Even if Marcus loved the girl, he hardly knew her, and so Imogen, upon reading the note, would surely think the sender was insane. This was a risk Marcus was apparently prepared take. Why?

So he did love her. Perhaps she loved him too. But Marcus was not self-serving enough to sacrifice his master's marriage for his own. So he did love her. That alone could not justify this scheme. So he did love her. Well, too bad. It would not change anything now.

Unless Jouglet could turn that knowledge to her own advantage. But she could not think how.

She returned to Konrad's room, finally, with the hot mulled wine for His Majesty and a pilfered sausage for the door guard. Konrad had summoned a woman in the minstrel's absence and was unceremoniously disrobing her on his bed as Jouglet entered. The woman was blond, unfamiliar, and because her tunic was already tossed out of sight behind the bed, Jouglet could not readily tell what her status might have been. She seemed dully content to being here, and smiled, somewhat tiredly, when Konrad told her to.

"Oh, Jouglet, you returned after all," Konrad said companionably, as if he were peeling an apple, not a human being. "Put the wine by my bed. All this talk of women made me want to remind myself that they're actually good for something. But please make yourself at home, you can sleep in the dayroom with the dogs, they're very warm."

"I am not in need of warmth, but thank you, sire."

As Jouglet spoke, Konrad pressed the blonde onto the bed and pushed her knees apart, running an appraising hand over her crotch and smiling with satisfaction at the warmth.

Jouglet slipped into the dayroom and curled up near the dozing page boys, trying to ignore the emperor's grunting pleasure as he mounted the woman, pleasure audible even through the closed door. She thought of going back down to the hall to sleep, but there it was even worse—there she might encounter actual lovers who engaged each other with genuine affection, making the quiet, happy noises she and Willem had become used to making. Despite her frantic need to solve the mystery of dealing with Marcus, despite her irritable intention to dismiss plans and people that were obviously doomed to fail, her body ached for Willem with an acuteness she was unused to. She was painfully aware of her own femaleness, of wanting to be filled with him, of wanting to feel his bearded chin against her cheek, her neck, her breasts, her thighs. It was very hard to sleep that night.

24 July

This, their second day on the road, had not been as easy as their first, but they did reach Mulhausen, so they were on schedule: they would arrive at Koenigsbourg before the royal retinue left for Mainz, and that made all the suffering worth it.

The mosquitoes were getting worse as they approached the entrance to the Rhine valley, and although the roads remained shaded, they were in bad condition here and getting crowded. The weather was still lovely, but as they descended to the flood plain, the crisp mountain breezes tapered off to be replaced by slower, denser, wetter crawls of air.

Lienor had awoken hardly able to stand up but insisted they get an early start right after mass. They'd brought salted meat with them, but her calculations reckoned this a fast day: the feast of St. Christopher would be tomorrow, and this was hardly the time to disrespect the saint of travelers. So when the sun was high overhead, they'd bought some fresh trout in a tiny fishing hamlet, fish being allowed on fast days. They cooked it at a riverside campfire made of alder branches and then (at Lienor's insistence) eaten it as they rode, which gave her indigestion.

Her worst silent complaint, however, was boredom. Any excitement she'd had about what might be out here in the world had proven far too optimistic. She was leery of speaking to any of the people they shared the broken road with, irrationally certain they would know her story and recognize her. Occasionally there was a musician or a storyteller to eavesdrop on; the pilgrims, perhaps in the interest of baring their souls before God, had by far the most engrossing tales.

But in between the groups of travelers, there was no distraction; few villages lay along their path. It was nothing but birch trees, oak trees, beech trees, chestnut trees, some maples, apples, pears, blackberry bushes, yew trees, bush-roses with dying flowers, elderberry bushes, walnut trees, and lindens. Even the lovely floral smells became monotonous after a day. The birdsong was riotous; swallows were the main sound of the sun-baked hours, and they were piercing, relentless, hardly melodious; in the evening they would be replaced by the cuckoos and mourning doves she loved so well, but by then she would be too sound asleep to hear. At least, she *hoped* St. Christopher would let her fall asleep.

24 July

*W*hen it was warm and sunny again, Konrad sent his minstrel into Sudaustat to check in on Willem. He gave Jouglet the assignment with a look that informed her this was a test of some sort, so she headed out of the castle gate with an uncomfortable mix of feelings. But as she moved through the bustling town streets, the sensory heat of the day, the quick glimpse of a couple enjoying each other behind the baking ovens, another pair groping near the silversmiths' alley . . . she knew what would happen if they had a sanctioned excuse to be closed in together for a while. With growing good humor and even quiet glee, the fiddler arrived at the inn, exchanged boyish flirtations with the mistress and her younger daughter, hearty greetings with Willem's servant and pages, then ran up the stairs to the room. She wondered briefly why there was nobody seated before his door, then opened the door and skipped into the room.

"Lazy man!" she called out before her eyes had quite adjusted to the darkened space—the shutters were all closed against the sun, and yet strangely the room itself was warm. "What could possibly compel you to stay in on such a beautiful day?" And then she realized there was a naked woman in his bed.

Jouglet's eyes and Willem's met briefly and he almost cringed. She glanced aside to examine his companion. Jouglet knew this woman—it was Konrad's most regular bedmate, someone who would have sold her own mother to earn points with the men of the court.

She was not among the few who knew a thing about Jouglet, and Jouglet wanted to keep it that way. Like Jouglet, she had little use for the femininity of the weak ladies of the aristocratic circles; unlike Jouglet, she relied entirely on her own kind of femininity to get what she wanted. Konrad, who saw women merely as bodies to possess or virgins to arrange political alliances around, thought she was marvelous and kept her well fed and well supplied with jewelry.

Something on the minstrel's face had given Willem the message. The knight managed to push aside his own mortification and say, with forced heartiness, "Jouglet, can't a fellow enjoy a little privacy?"

"The emperor sent me," Jouglet said evenly, recovering. "My apologies, Lady Ever-open, but I'm afraid that trumps mere—"

"The emperor sent me too," she retorted lazily.

Jouglet was—almost imperceptibly—soothed by the revelation, although obviously Konrad had sent his minstrel here to encounter them together. Affecting offhandedness, Jouglet opened a shutter to let in the bright late-afternoon sun. "Ah. How attentive our Konrad is to keep the distractions rolling into your room in such rapid succession."

There was a pause, then: "Actually, the emperor sent me yesterday, and I've been here ever since." The brunette giggled throatily, pleased with herself, and gave Willem a darting, intimate grin, which instantly made the moment more unpleasant for Jouglet. Especially when Willem returned a smile, on reflex, before reddening and looking away from both of them, deliberately causing the sheet to drape over his face.

"Ah," Jouglet said again after a beat. Then, heartily, "You greedy girl, sucking up everything he has to offer and leaving nothing for anyone else who might want a bite of him. All the others will resent you."

"I can live with that," she purred. "I'm already resented for being Konrad's favorite."

Seeing Willem briefly freeze under the sheet at that was more satisfying than Jouglet wanted to admit to herself.

"Yes, we're aware of your status as His Majesty's favorite concubine," she told the girl brightly, to make sure Willem was in fact aware of it. "But he seemed *very* taken with a pretty blonde last night in your absence, so if you want to keep your position, so to speak, you might pull your legs together enough to hie yourself back to His Majesty's bedchamber. Speaking on behalf of His Majesty, I thank you heartily for distracting Willem from the wretched fact of his sister's lechery and whoring."

The irony was lost on the woman, but Jouglet could see Willem grimace, even under the sheet, and took satisfaction in seeing it.

When she was gone, there was a loud silence. Finally, with an impatience that implied he had been goaded into it, Willem snatched the sheet from off his face and sat up a little into a defiant slouch. He took one look at Jouglet—who was expressionless—and then was instantly contrite.

"I can't express how—"

"Then don't bother trying," Jouglet interrupted, apparently fascinated with the design of Willem's beaded belt, lying discarded on a stool. "Thank the saints Konrad did that—and especially with such a gossip as she is. I hope you gave her plenty to gossip about. Paul is champing at the bit to call you a . . . Bulgarian, I hear is the newest term for it. For what they think we are."

"But for you to have to walk in on—"

"The benefits outweigh that," Jouglet decided briskly, moving to the window to better examine the belt in the sunlight. Willem frowned.

"You are not so unfeeling. In fact you were obviously jealous," he insisted.

"Obvious to your ruffled sense of honor perhaps, but I assure you it was lost on her. Is this local workmanship?"

"You can feign indifference but you do want an apology. Or at least an explanation."

"I had the explanation from her—the emperor sent her. Refusing her would have been brainless of you, after what happened yesterday." She paused, staying artificially focused on the belt, and when she spoke again her voice was a little quieter. "Had she really been here since last night?"

"You see, you do want an apology," he said, almost eager. It felt good to him that it would matter to her. "Let me make it up to you."

Jouglet laughed a little. "You just spent an entire night and most of a day riding some tart, how could you possibly have the strength left to give me what I've come to expect from you?" She tossed the belt down with apparent indifference, and crossed back to the door. "Get a little rest. Clearly you need replenishing."

"Where are you going?" he asked as she reached for the bolt.

"To see Jeannette," Jouglet said offhandedly. "She has a blond fall that is quite fetching on me and entirely alters my features."

Willem sat bolt upright. "And why would you need that?"

"Dear heart," Jouglet said smoothly, "I came here with the hope of being ravished, but it appears I must go elsewhere for satisfaction. Obviously I don't want to be recogni—"

"Jouglet!" he said, horrified. "You will do no such thing—"

"Oh, don't worry," she reassured him. "I know how to avoid detection. She used to help me with this sort of thing all the time, we're a very competent team. Will you *please* come to the court for supper tonight?"

Willem leapt naked out of the bed, and despite herself Jouglet enjoyed looking at his body, blithely ignoring how enraged he had become. "You are not to give yourself to another man!"

She sobered. "You are not to tell me what to do."

"I won't have you whoring yourself as my sister does—"

"That is the most ludicrous sentence ever to come out of your mouth," Jouglet snapped, suddenly fierce. She stepped away from the door farther into the room. "First because Lienor never whored herself, and if you'd give me a chance I would prove it. Second because you can't *begin* to compare her state and mine, when the whole point of hers is to remain chaste and the whole point of mine is to have liberty."

"Liberty to do what?" Willem demanded angrily. "Go whoring? Forgive me for stating the obvious, Jouglet, but no matter how successfully you pass as a man with your clothes on, you cannot actually *go whoring*. You can only whore yourself."

"Hypocrite! I'm simply doing what you've been doing—and rather less objectionably, I would say, as *I* am only looking for another partner because my preferred one has *depleted* himself into someone else—"

"You said that was the right thing to have done!" Willem nearly shouted, exasperated and bordering on bewilderment.

"Yes, beloved, it was, but looking at your naked body is driving me desperate with desire and since you—"

"Get on the bed," Willem ordered in a pitched voice, pointing to it with gratuitous drama. "I'll show you how depleted I am."

She threw her head back and laughed bitterly. "Oh, Willem, you are being *comically* masculine."

"I won't have my woman giving herself to—"

"I am not your woman," Jouglet said, with such gravity that he closed his mouth. "I am Jouglet the minstrel." There was an awkward silence. Jouglet nodded once, wishing the gesture could good-naturedly end the tension. She did not, in fact, have much of an impulse to go strolling the streets of the neighboring villages in disguise, but she would sooner be strangled than let him know that now.

Willem grabbed his robe and put it on, looking self-conscious.

Jouglet reached again for the bolt and had nearly pushed the door open when he growled, almost tonelessly, "If you open that door I will tell everyone you are a woman."

Angrily she slapped it closed and spun around to face him down. "Damn you if you forswear your oath to keep a secret," she spat. But the rest of the angry admonition surprised him: "Besides, haven't you learned *anything*? That sort of blackmail should be saved for circumstances in which you would actually *benefit* from carrying out the threat. You'd gain nothing by revealing me, you'd only lose a lover."

"I don't want a lover who will blithely go about giving herself to others!" Willem protested.

She pursed her lips together and nodded understandingly. "Neither do I," she said quietly. "But I would never dream of forbidding it."

He sighed with exasperation. "I'm a *man*."

She looked deeply unimpressed by this revelation. "And?" she finally prompted.

He sat on the bed. "I realize you cannot understand this, but part of the benefit of being a man is *being known* as a man."

She laughed briefly and leaned back against the door, arms crossed. "Nobody appreciates the benefit of being *known* as a man better than I do, duck!"

"But *I lose* by *your* doing that. No one may ever know the truth about us, or you're undone."

Jouglet threw up her arms in mock triumph. "Perfect! The model of courtly love. So I *am* your lady after all."

Willem considered this and abruptly started laughing. "All right then," he said, a challenge. "Give me your silken glove to wear the next time I ride in a tournament. Let me write bad poetry about your milky white brow, and sing it tunelessly in front of other people." He laughed a tired-hysterical giggle, and flopped back against the cushions.

"That's the first time I've heard you laugh in days," Jouglet said quietly, without a hint of remonstrance or annoyance. "I suppose all that fornication agrees with you." A thoughtful pause. "Or rather, all that fornication with someone other than me." A sigh, and she crossed her arms again, trying to sound casual. "Yes, I suppose Konrad knew what he was doing, we'd better give him what he wants—"

Willem stopped laughing and sat up again. "If you want to be estranged from me entirely—"

Jouglet interrupted him by rushing to his side and kneeling beside the bed, staring intently into his face. "We were the best of friends for three entire years without anything resembling fornication. The deepest part of our regard was born within our friendship. I'm not suggesting we be strangers, Willem. I want us to take delight in each other's company the way we used to. Now that all the clever plotting has come undone, and we're left with little resource but each other, and we know we'll never manage to be lovers in the normal sense—let us be true friends at least."

"I . . ." He hesitated, and frowned. "You've changed the subject."

"No, not really. The subject—as usual—is *what are we*? And I'm proposing that we're friends. Friends who are allied to try to salvage a wrecked set of circumstances." She sat back on her heels, waiting for a response.

He looked slightly at a loss, then sheepish. "I don't know how to be . . . allied with a woman," he said at last. "While *knowing* she's a woman." He frowned again. "Except my sister, who has taught me nothing but that women are false allies."

"What, again?" Jouglet said with mild exasperation. "Isn't it enough her future's spoiled? Must she be subjected to her own brother's sullying her name? It's a lie, Willem. You add gratuitous misery to your heart to believe it."

Willem sighed. "I don't know what to believe anymore."

"Then do not believe she's guilty until you must! Why do you dismiss my judgment? When have I ever been wrong?"

He had an immediate response to this: "You thought I would never be intimate with Jouglet the minstrel merely because Jouglet the minstrel was a man." He laughed, a little bitterly. "With political machinations I trust your judgment. In evaluating my family's carnal curiosity, I do not. You tend to underestimate us."

"I can tell you stories about your sister to remind you of her goodness," Jouglet offered, to avoid another argument.

"And *I* can tell *you* a story that trumps all the others, that proves she has always been a willful little wench who enjoys getting herself and other people into trouble."

"Oh, for the love of Christ, not *that* again!" Jouglet said impatiently, starting to get up from her kneel on the floor.

Willem was taken aback. "You know what I'm referring to?"

Jouglet froze, not quite standing upright yet, and for a moment seemed to be calculating something.

"I recognize that look," Willem warned. "Tell me what you know."

Jouglet bit her lower lip, straightened up, and backed away from him. "I know about the night at Alphonse's." He reddened slightly and stared at her. Ignoring his surprise, she planted herself on the chest at the window and went on defiantly, "I fail to see how it suggests your sister is a harlot."

"How do you know about that? I've never spoken of it."

Jouglet hesitated. She was suddenly a little pale.

"Did Lienor tell you?" he demanded. "I suppose she thought it was amusing."

Jouglet, like a trapped rabbit, stared at him but said nothing.

"I want to know what Lienor's told you," he said. It was polite, but it was a command. "I'm sure she's skewed the story somehow in her favor. If we are to be allies, let's set the record straight."

Jouglet kept looking up at him, at his soft brown eyes and sad expressive brows. She felt her heartbeat quicken a little. This moment had taken her by surprise. There was a long silence as she contemplated the entirety of her enterprise, of everything that had gone well, that had gone wrong, that might still come to pass. She took a deep breath. Perhaps this was the moment that would shift the game back to her cause.

"All right," she said at last. "All right then, yes, I will tell you the entire story, as far as I am qualified to tell it." Another pause. She rose from the chest, then after a hesitation, crossed and sat down beside him, facing him, on the bed. "Lienor was eight, you were eleven. Your old steward Jehan, in a fit of misplaced loyalty, sought you out and told both of you the real story, that your father had held land directly from Konrad's father, but Alphonse, Count of Burgundy, had swindled you out of it when your mother became a widow. Lienor promptly walked three days to Oricourt, to complain to the count for his having taken your land, and you went after her. Actually she went to complain to the emperor, who lay dying in Alphonse's bedroom. You overtook her in a small grove of old trees near the top of the hill by Oricourt. She did not want to turn back."

She glanced up at him and saw him staring at her with his mouth slack, hardly breathing. She looked down and made herself continue.

"You argued, you were overheard by one of Alphonse's men guarding the grove against poachers, and you were taken to the castle. Alphonse put you in prison overnight—well, there was no prison really, so he put you in the dovecote, fenced in between the trap that collected all the pigeon shit, and a hole where they had just put poison down for rats. Alphonse told you he would hang you in the morning, although he later insisted to your mother that had been a friendly joke. The penned-in area was so narrow you had to stand upright side by side all night, and it smelled of birdshit, and rotting rat carcasses, and there was a lot of grain dust in the air that made Lienor sneeze incessantly. You passed the time by telling stories—Lienor's favorite was a ghost story you came up with about your avenging ancestors. You discussed ways to escape. And then you realized you could, in fact, escape, that Lienor was just small enough to push her way out through the hole the rats had chewed. She ran around to the side door and let you out, and then under a full moon in a clear sky you somehow sprinted through the outer court and slipped out of the cattle list without being seen."

Willem shook his head, looking weary. "How long did Lienor spend boasting about it, for you to know so many details?" He made a resigned face. "My sister seems to be made of indiscretion."

"This is not a story about your sister's indiscretion."

"Yes it is. Anyhow, she omitted a major part. It wasn't just the two of us." He looked deeply pained. "There was another child, my age, old steward Jehan's girl. She was with Lienor all along—in fact she probably gave Lienor the idea in the first place, she was always getting into trouble." He winced and reflexively crossed himself. "I understand why Lienor would not have mentioned that, because of what happened. After we escaped, she decided to go back and try again—alone, because I would not let Lienor out of my sight again. And . . . Oh, God . . ." He hesitated.

Jouglet, in a gentle tone, picked up the story. "She went back to try again, and was caught. You never saw her again, but a bag containing her alleged innards showed up at your gate a few days later."

Willem nodded grimly. "So you do know that part."

"Oh, I know that and more," said Jouglet. "Shall I tell you what happened when I went back to the castle?"

He gasped in shock and started violently, staring at her, looking terrified. Jouglet gave him an apologetic smile and reached out to take one of his hands in both of hers. It was hard to tell who was shaking more.

"I never claimed I heard the story from Lienor," she pointed out.

"You can't," he gasped, as if he'd been slugged in the stomach. "You can't have been that girl—"

"I certainly did not *want* to be that girl, that's why I became Jouglet the minstrel," she said. "Jouglet the apprentice minstrel, first, of course, who immediately fled Burgundy, and was lucky and gifted enough to be taken in by Konrad's aging court musician. Jouglet the apprentice minstrel was never rounded up by the count, because Jouglet the apprentice minstrel did not go back to the land of Burgundy for more than seven years, until he had earned his name in Konrad's court as a youth of prodigious talents."

Willem shook his head and brought a hand to his temple, overwhelmed. "You must stop *springing* these revelations on me!"

"Perhaps I should have told you when I first revealed myself, but I thought it would be too much at once."

He held out his arms in a helpless gesture, let his hands fall onto his lap. "We mourned for you. We thought you were dead, I thought it was my fault for not stopping you."

"I mourned for both of you. For everything I left behind. But I couldn't risk going back or even sending word. I'd have been hunted down."

"Why? What happened?" His eyes widened. "Alphonse doesn't know it's you, does he?"

"If he knew, I would be longtime and extremely dead," Jouglet assured him. "The day after our night in the dovecote, when he realized his right to your land could be called publicly into question, he forged a document purporting to be the old emperor's revocation of the estate from your father, and immediately granting it to himself."

"How do you know this?"

She held up a hand. "I'm explaining. He had a cohort in his forgery—can you guess who?"

"His nephew Paul," said Willem in a tired voice, suddenly understanding the entirety of the cardinal's behavior toward him.

"Yes, who was angling for the archbishopric of Burgundy and no doubt told himself the bond of church and state needed this sort of nepotistic boost. His assignment was to briefly 'borrow' his father's signet ring to seal the forgery. That was easy to do—Paul and Konrad were standing vigil at the emperor's deathbed right there at Oricourt. Paul and his uncle were in the chapel penning the forgery, and Paul was antsy to get the ring back on his father's finger before Konrad noticed it was gone. I slipped into the courtyard by the chapel gate, and the chapel was half-sunken—I happened to be sneaking by the chapel window as they were arguing about using the ring to seal the forgery. The document was lying on the window oriel. When I realized what it was, I just stuck my hand in and grabbed it without thinking—it was *right there*, those idiots, it was too tempting. They caught me, of course, got it back from me, and Alphonse was about to kill me—but I have very sharp teeth. I wriggled out of their hands and ran away." She smiled almost sheepishly. "As I wriggled, I managed to abscond with the emperor's signet ring. I just grabbed at it, impetuously—I think at the time I only half-knew the magnitude of what it was to have it. They've been looking for me ever since. Looking for *her.* And meanwhile of course Count Alphonse claimed he'd caught me doing something or other of an upstartish nature and executed me—those innards probably came from a pig—to send you the message not to meddle anymore, and so I became officially dead to the world. But they kept looking for her. They're still looking for her, in fact. She's taken on mythic proportions in their guilty souls, I think and hope." She took a long and careful sigh, as if she had been holding her breath for far too long. And shrugged.

Willem reached out a beckoning hand. She moved nearer to him, and he wrapped both arms around her in a long, silent embrace, almost crushing her against him. After a moment of internal hesitation, she put her arms around him too, and rocked him.

When he had regained himself, and spent a while stroking her face and hair, staring at her eyes, trying to recognize the child he had known, he said grimly, "I am going to kill the count."

"No you're not," she informed him firmly. "You're going to marry his daughter and get your land back through her dowry. What do you think I have been working toward all these years?"

16

Imbroglio

[a passage in which diverse elements combine to create dramatic tension]

25 July

They had merged onto the main trade road up the Rhine valley, which was far more crowded than Lienor would have expected. Many of the people they encountered were familiar to her, or at least expected, especially the churchmen: messengers wearing the papal insignia, a bishop circuiting his see, monks and occasionally nuns, floods and floods of summer pilgrims. And of course in the summer heat there were regular messengers as well, and soldiers riding to or from assignments, and then on foot there were tinkers and peddlers and Jewish merchants and poor freemen seeking harvest work, peasants sneaking toward the freedom of town walls, shepherds and cowherds moving their charges. There were cripples and lepers, ringing bells to warn of their approach. There were itinerant musicians and other performers, which gave Lienor a pang: a part of her was disappointed that Jouglet had not come storming down to Dole in her defense.

She was tired, and sore, and in need of sleep. The sun was covered by a white glare of clouds that made her squint; she could hear her mother's quiet admonition not to, and had mostly kept her face behind the veil—but she had to see, or she became nauseated after more than five miles in the saddle. Her initial zeal had worn off; her distant reputation seemed a trifle compared to the immediate well-being of her body. She was aching all over; organs and muscles she had never been aware of before were crying out in constant protest. She couldn't believe a party could ride so far and still not come to its destination. And the valley was settling itself for a storm from the southwest: the air became heavier and wetter, so wet that Erec could not get the torch of hay to light, to chase away mosquitoes with the smoke. There seemed to be no local lord within miles; they would have to stay the night at an inn, if they could find one, something she had never done or ever contemplated doing. She knew only the inn in Dole, the locus of whores and drunks and greasy-faced merchants.

The world was huge, and loud, and dirty, and unsafe. At every moment she fought the urge to beg Erec to take her back to Dole.

*T*he royal court would be moving to Mainz for the August first Assembly, which Konrad had sworn that spring would feature the publishing of the imperial marriage banns. The court was always followed to such Assemblies by its many unofficial sycophants, concubines, and general hangers-on. Konrad had invited Willem although Willem had, after the event in the cellar, once again disappeared from court. The first day, of course, had been largely taken up by his riding Konrad's concubine, and Konrad could excuse that. In fact, he'd publicized it, and made Jouglet do likewise. Willem's failure to appear the second day was rather more irksome, and Konrad contemplated revoking the invitation to Mainz. "We've resurrected the good name of his cock, but not the rest of him," the emperor groused to his musician. "I don't know who's more infuriating, him or Marcus."

Willem's absence was even more irritating to Jouglet. She knew the reason for it. Willem insisted, without irony, that his absence from court was the necessary first step to recovering his place there: she had made him swear not to confront Alphonse and Paul publicly, and he did not trust himself to refrain from attacking either of them until he had his emotions under control. So he'd headed out early in the morning with a bow and several quivers, to take out his rage on the local wildlife. By noon, several boars had gone to their swinish reward, but Atlas was lame from Willem's careless overexertion. The knight sobered himself with effort, dismounted, walked beside his horse back to the inn, and gave Atlas over to the expert care of the groom there. The exertion of a mountain trek did nothing to calm him, but it was by then too late in the day to continue his antiswine crusade even with a hired mount, so he retreated to his room, having decided the safest way to rein in his anger was with drink. An hour later, his rage was thoroughly drowned by good Moselle wine, but so was the rest of his character.

That evening, as the air grew unnaturally still outside in anticipation of a coming storm, Jouglet lambasted him from across the room while he lay, naked and tentatively hopeful, on the wide bed. "You're as bad as Partonopeus," she chided, just arrived to deliver an invitation to the court for supper. "Who'd've sooner been eaten by wild animals than get over his passivity when those in power were manipulating him." She took a step from the door to pick up Willem's sword, which lay discarded where he'd dropped it after badly damaging the low rafters of the room. She found the sword belt and resheathed the weapon. She took in a deep breath. "Ah, the odor of freshly slaughtered oak."

"I've already paid the damages," Willem slurred defensively, when Jouglet made a gesture toward the splintered wood. "I just needed a little exercise."

"We are going to salvage your marriage to Imogen. That means you show up at Koenigsbourg and cozy up to Alphonse. *Now.* I will not have all my years of preparation thrown away in a drunken binge. You'll lose even Konrad's regard soon if you don't pull yourself together, and then what will you be? A landless knight who's fallen out of favor, rumored to be a sexual deviant and brother to a harlot. And a drunkard, if you're seen like this."

Willem looked down at the sculpted expanse of his flesh. "But a *magnificent* drunkard, I've been told," he slurred, with a sad little laugh.

"Stop that! Your future is bleak without Konrad's regard, and Lienor's future is *ruined* if Marcus is not exposed. I have a new idea for tripping Marcus up. Are you sober enough to follow it?"

Willem lay back on his bed, looking weary. "Your belt looks like it wants to be untied, Jouglet, come over here and let me help you with it."

"Enough!" she snapped. "*Your future.* We need to guarantee your future. Without position or property, how shall you provide for Lienor and your mother? Hunting boar and bandits, do you think?"

Willem was not of a mind, at this moment, to try to guarantee anything but a round of fornication safely completed before his servants returned for the evening. He grinned at her with the disarming sheepish smile that so many women liked, the smile that was out of place on the handsome, battered face. "I promised you to be obedient tomorrow and you know I never break my promises. But it's not tomorrow yet. So here's my answer for today: As long as you're in my future, I'm content. Or rather, as long as I'm in you while you're in my future, I'm content." He laughed drunkenly and shifted on the mattress, patting the space beside him near his groin. "Let's start working on that right now, shall we?"

She made a pained face. "Willem, you're wasting time! I don't belong in your future that way, don't you understand that? We need to get you a wife, and she needs to be Imogen. You must start cozying up to Alphonse. Can you *possibly* pull yourself together enough to come up to the castle tonight and charm him? And Konrad? And—"

Consternation flashed across his face. "What do you mean you don't belong in my future?"

"I mean as a lover. I'll become very inconvenient to you, and it will be best to keep me as a memory. That's how it should be, Willem." To appease him she crossed to the bed and perched beside him, and even ran her hands across his chest. That was a mistake because it made her want to run them across the rest of him. She pulled away a little.

He had paled visibly in the light from the window. "This is the first time you've said such a thing. If that was part of the plan you should have told me so."

"Of course it wasn't part of the *plan*," Jouglet argued. "The *plan* never involved us becoming lovers in the first place. The *plan* never involved half of what has come to pass."

He sat up, the fearful, confused look increasing, trying to think clearly through the haze of inebriation. "Everything you do is for a reason, even your beneficence is part of some scheme. Tell me where I fit into that. I have a right to know."

She made an enervated gesture and took one of his hands in both of hers. "Schemer that I am, it was an innocent and schemeless impulse that began all this. I wanted to see justice done. That meant your land restored to you and your sister married well. My life was uprooted and permanently changed—what else to do but try to resurrect your lives as they should have been, which might have let me resurrect my own?"

He looked hopeful and reached out to curve his hand around her waist. "Your resurrected life will be as my steward's heir, Jouglet, we can be together always—"

She stopped him gently with a raised hand. "I don't want to resurrect my old life anymore, Willem. I much prefer what I've grown into over what I was."

"Then why need you bother about the rest of it?" he asked, almost plaintive. "When it would separate us?" He reached up to stroke her face, but she batted his hand away, looking pained and serious.

"I bother about it for the satisfaction of seeing a wrong righted—*two* wrongs now, with Lienor's reputation to restore—and seeing Paul and Alphonse fittingly discomfited, and Marcus brought to task, and really, just for the thrill of seeing what a runaway serving girl can effect in the world—for all of that, I chose to do all this. I thought I could do it alone. I was wrong. I need—and want—your help." She saw a small, hopeful smile warm his face, and she shook her head apologetically. "But not as my white knight, Willem. We have to beat the villains at their own game, which is politics. I know you disdain that game, and that disdain is to your credit—I envy you the luxury of it, and so does Konrad. But you defeat a decade of my life, if you will not help me now by playing the game, and playing to win."

For the first time in her memory she felt her throat constrict with sobs. When Willem, struggling toward sobriety, bundled her gently into his warm naked arms, she wept.

26 July

It was the feast of St. Anne and they should have reached the castle, but there was a downpour so severe that even sections of the raised road were flooded out. The innkeeper in Colmar—who looked to Lienor's veiled eyes like the prostitutes, the drunks, *and* the greasy merchants of the inn in Dole, all rolled up into one— assured them that when the rain stopped the waters would go down again immediately, since they were far from the river and the land here was never oversaturated; however, it was best not to venture forth until the storm had quieted.

So they kept the horses saddled in the stable, but they spent a miserable day inside, Erec pacing the small common room of the inn like a caged wild beast, invoking St. Barbara with every roll of thunder from outside. The rain did not stop, but after dinner the worst of it seemed to have passed, and she begged that they continue on. At least there would be no mosquitoes in the rain, she pointed out.

Marcus was grateful for the responsibility of the packing up. This was hardly the biggest move he had to orchestrate, but still it was a huge undertaking—it would take twenty draft horses for the packing and a dozen more for carts (half of them half-filled with gifts for Konrad to bestow on all and sundry) to descend the steep hillside and move north through the Rhine valley. Aware Konrad was still annoyed at his lackluster reaction to the latest matrimonial plan, Marcus tried to be even more impressively efficient than usual, although he could not stop thinking about Imogen. Twice he thought he saw her among the servants, three times thought he heard her voice, once imagined her hands resting on his shoulders, which made him almost cry out with longing. Mastering himself, he directed various servants to pack clothes, weapons, household goods, and kitchen equipment; he assigned the older squires to be harbingers, riding ahead to announce the arrival of His Majesty and his retinue, so that food, beds, and feminine distractions could be properly arranged. Because they did this regularly, the army of workers was well rehearsed and the imperial household could be readied to decamp in a single day. But it was a long day, and Marcus was exhausted by the end of it. He was almost too exhausted to care that he had lost any chance to canvass Alphonse.

Until he crossed Alphonse's path that night after supper.

Konrad had retired to his chamber with Jouglet, announcing he was sick of hearing love songs. As the court was settling by the smoky fire to listen to a visiting French singer, Marcus was surprised to see Alphonse seated by himself, without oily ubiquitous Cardinal Paul slithering around him. He had to seize the opportunity. He approached the count from the side and stood slightly behind him, in a demure posture, as if he were informing him what wines or other delicacies were available for his enjoyment later on. "Excuse me, milord, may I speak with you?"

Alphonse recognized the voice, shifted uncomfortably and ignored him.

"I make no entreaties," Marcus continued, understanding his reaction. "But I thought it might be in your lordship's interest to be aware that I am to be made a duke on August first, at the close of the Assembly. That is less than a week away. The emperor has proposed to betroth me to his daughter."

Alphonse was gratifyingly taken aback. "But you are . . ." He hesitated. "Has my daughter called off her betrothal to you?"

Accursed whoreson, Marcus thought. Politely he answered in his ear, "I have not received any letter from her yet but I understand there may be one on the way."

"But you have not received it," Alphonse pressed, and Marcus shook his head. "Then your betrothal to her holds, does it not?"

"I really do not know the answer to that, sir," Marcus said evenly. "Apparently I have risen so high in His Majesty's esteem that he would do all this for me, but I am hardly of a station to naysay him. However, if Your Lordship wanted to take the matter up with him, I would be amenable to the original arrangement." How very like a cleric he sounded. How equivocal, how entirely controlled.

Alphonse excused himself, and to Marcus's immense satisfaction, headed toward the far end of the hall, and the steps to Konrad's room.

"I am sick of this round-robin." Konrad yawned irritably at the back of Alphonse's head as the older man knelt before him by the fire. Jouglet had silenced the fiddle. Konrad reached out one ringed hand, and a page boy instantly gave him his evening wine cup. "Nobody is marrying anyone. Ever. The wedding mass is hereby banned."

Marcus had followed Alphonse in, with the conveniently truthful excuse that he had to pack up the royal coffers from the wardrobe; only he and Boiden were allowed to touch the emperor's treasury directly.

"Sire," he heard Alphonse say, "the betrothal between Imogen and Marcus was blessed by both yourself and the archbishop of Mainz—"

"I don't care if Christ popped out of the baptismal font to bless it with his own testicles! I have loftier plans for Marcus, and I want no mention of marriage—or women at all—in my presence for at least a week. None, do you understand? Jouglet, we'll spend the week listening to the *Song of Roland,* so bury your besotted romances the while." He drank off half the cup. "If it were in my power I would order everyone celibate for the next week and boot all the women out of the castle." He drank down the second half and held it out for a refill. "Rise, dammit, Alphonse, and leave the room. Marcus, do not hover over my gold that way, pack what is coming with us and get out. Jouglet, how does it begin, 'Charles the King, our own great Charlemagne has been in Spain for seven years,' isn't that it?"

"Usually, sire, it is phrased so that *Spain* and *Charlemagne* form a rhymed couplet, but otherwise you're spot on," said the minstrel and began to bow the familiar melody.

*M*any miles away that night, in County Burgundy, a very young and deceptively fragile-looking dark-haired lady slipped out of a dowdy castle into the faltering rain. With one guard and one maidservant for company and protection, all of them on borrowed—that is, stolen—horses, Imogen rode north through muddy roads toward Mainz. She was a good rider, hardened by her long clandestine trips to tryst with Marcus. But this would be a ride like no other, and she fought back panic as she rode.

27 July

*W*illem and his pages appeared the next morning before dawn to attend mass and break the fast with Konrad. Konrad was aggravated with Willem, at least as aggravated as he was with Marcus, but was willing to give him the length and exercise of the journey to Mainz to reform himself. Jouglet had promised His Majesty that Willem finally understood what was required of a knight in Konrad's court. And indeed Willem's behavior all morning was admirable; he was suddenly the same earnest and upright youth who'd first appeared a month ago and won the king's affection almost instantly.

The entire royal retinue descended the crooked sandstone steps to the less-protected lower courtyard, where the servants and the livestock lived. Every horse in the stable was either saddled or loaded down with baggage, and several more had been brought up from the village. It was very crowded. Konrad mounted first; then Marcus; then Willem, on his recovered horse; then Alphonse and Paul; and then the hundred-odd remaining members of the court and keep.

Paul was displeased that Willem had been invited to mount ahead of him. He was even more displeased when he saw Alphonse watching Willem, who'd dismounted again to help the pregnant Duchess of Lorraine onto her horse.

Paul knew how his uncle's mind worked. "You cannot really

think to marry Imogen to him," he whispered angrily into Alphonse's ear.

"Marcus is not available. Who else is there?" Alphonse murmured back stubbornly. "If Marcus is Konrad's right arm, Willem is now his left. He will have status."

"He was the victim of our mutual plotting," Paul argued. He pointed out a hawk of some sort high above them as if it were of great interest, as if this were what they were discussing. "You cannot possibly contrive to help him gain in power, Uncle, are you crazy? You're endangering yourself. And me!"

"There is nobody else," Alphonse repeated firmly, apparently studying the hawk's flight pattern with him. "Marcus is being married to Konrad's bastard."

"I shall prevent that," Paul said at once, and almost shook his uncle's shoulder in desperation. "She wants to keep the veil, and I can see she does. Marry Imogen to Marcus. Then he'll be indebted to us, so he can help clinch Konrad's willingness to marry Besançon. And it keeps Willem away from any position where he could harm us."

Across the courtyard Willem remounted, watching them whispering. It took tremendous self-control not to shriek at them and call them to account before the assembled court. Instead he turned his attention to Konrad and began a detailed conversation about training horses to switch leads while cantering.

By the time village church bells rang terce, they were well on their way up the Rhine valley, in the clear, bright air. Pipe-and-tabor players heralded their procession on ponies at either end of the magnificent spectacle, which included over two hundred riders, dogs and packhorses in the train behind them; half a dozen illustrated banners let the countryside know exactly who was passing. Awestruck peasants watched openmouthed from the field, scythes in hand, as Konrad and members of the court rode along the raised Roman roads straight through the flat, marshy river valley.

The four-day ride under white-hot skies would take them through armies of mosquitoes and occasional swamps to cathedral towns—Strasbourg, Speyer, Worms, and finally Mainz—and at each stop, Konrad would spend the night in the archbishop's palace. While in Mainz he would stay with His Eminence Konrad von Wittelsbach—a friend, although Bavarian—and remain only long enough for the Assembly, before returning three days south to his favorite castle, Hagenau. So most of the pack animals would be diverted directly to Hagenau, which meant much of the trip could go quickly and, it was wrongly assumed, without incident.

28 July

*B*y the time the duo from Dole reached Sudaustat, shortly after midday on one of the hottest days in living memory, Lienor had never been half so pained and distressed in her life. Her tunic was soaked through, and despite the rain that had delayed them yesterday, road dust had collected thick enough on the tunic to render it dully dun. Sweat stung her eyes, caked her hair flat against her head under the riding veil, made the leather reins slippery in her chafing fingers. The only thing worse than staying in the saddle was getting down from it—although she'd been sore so long now that she was almost used to it. And yet she felt a small thrill of triumph as they came near the end of their journey: by force of will she had survived this, and soon she would be exonerated. Finally they were in sight of Koenigsbourg, perched magnificently atop its symmetrical cliffed hilltop . . .

. . . without the emperor's flag of residence flying.

She whimpered to herself a little, trying to make light of it. She rested by a linden, and Erec rode ahead to the porter's lodge for news. When he returned, he told her apologetically that the royal court had left at dawn. Willem of Dole and Jouglet the minstrel had both gone. If Erec and Lienor could not overtake them, it would be another four days' ride to Mainz, which in Lienor's current state was flatly impossible. Erec delivered this news in a tone suggesting he thought they should return to Dole.

Lienor's face crumpled, but she battled hard to keep herself in control. She brought a sunburned hand to her mouth to stifle a sob; the dirt on her sleeve stung the cracks in her lower lip. Erec considered her, feeling like a mother hen. He could not take her to the castle, obviously, and she was loath to go to the inn where Willem had been staying, terrified that people would suss out who she was and judge her by the rumors. Anonymity was essential, but she desperately needed rest and a bath and a change of clothes.

There was only one place he could think to take her.

To spare her riding through the worst part of Sudaustat, they skirted left around the town walls and entered at the seldom used western gate. Inside, they turned at once to their right and halted at the first small house, the one with the bright swath of scarlet across the door. Gingerly, Erec helped her to dismount, and Lienor almost collapsed against him, the noisome smells of the town the final insult to her overwhelmed senses.

It was quiet here in the heat of the day, and the women were spinning wool on handheld spindles, their secondary source of revenue. They looked up curiously when Erec flung the door open. "Where are we?" Lienor asked, sounding feverish. She stared at the three women, and they stared back at her, all three getting to their feet; she took in their outfits, the setting, the one midday customer trying to slip out unobtrusively, and her enervated gasp suggested she had answered her question for herself.

"You must be Lienor," Jeannette said, with her usual mix of sympathy and amusement. She nodded approvingly to Erec. "Good of you not to kill her."

Lienor looked alarmed that a whore could be familiar with her name. "How do you know me?" she whispered, barely moving her cracking lips.

Jeannette shrugged agreeably. "If you didn't look half dead, you'd pretty much match Jouglet's descriptions."

"How do you know *Jouglet*?" she demanded, her voice louder. She tensed in Erec's arms and pushed away from him to stand upright on her own. "He would never come to a place like this."

The common women exchanged amused glances. Jeannette grinned hopefully at Erec, seeking permission to respond frankly, but he shook his head.

"She's very weak, we need your help," Erec said, with a hopeless gesture. "We missed the king. Please may she just sleep here until she gets her strength back, before we head back home? I'll pay you—"

Lienor drew herself up. "We are not going home," she announced, as firmly as her exhausted body would allow. "We are going on to Mainz. My name will *not* remain sullied, I will *not* be known as a *whore*."

Erec grimaced. There was a moment of loud, leaden silence, and Marthe, looking nowhere in particular, bit her thumb at something.

"I thought ladies were taught manners," she said tartly and returned her attention to her spinning.

"Or at least common sense." Jeannette snorted. "If you bite the hand before it feeds you, you will not be fed, my girl."

Lienor blushed. She took a moment to collect herself and then explained, a shadow of her coquettish smile on her lips, sweetly placating, "It is not the title itself that wounds me, but what it does to my security. I would not mind being called a whore if I were *profiting* by the description, as you have the benefit of doing."

Jeannette and Marthe exchanged droll looks, and after a moment, laughed.

"It's not actually the *description* that brings the profit, duck. But all right then. The young lady is going to Mainz," Jeannette said. She looked Lienor over and handed her a cup of wine from the table. Lienor glanced in, hesitated, then drank the whole thing down, sighing with relief. "I'm impressed by your pluck, but I hope you're not planning to approach Konrad in that outfit."

Erec, sensing Lienor wobble, took the cup from her with one hand and caught her with the other. He set her down gently on the nearest bench. "I have a change of clothes well protected," she said. "A white silk tunic, high-collared, long sleeves, waistless—I will look like innocence itself."

Jeannette smiled confidingly. "If you really want to get his attention, I have something that might work a little better."

Lienor blinked. "Wearing a whore's dress is no way to convince him I am not a whore," she said, hoping that in her fatigue she did not sound as sarcastic as she felt.

"It's not a whore's dress," Jeannette said with a hint of smugness in her voice. "It's the gown I was to have worn at my wedding."

The silence thudded in Lienor's ears. She felt her cheeks turn pink again. "I suppose there is a story there," she said stiffly, lowering her eyes.

Jeannette shrugged offhandedly. "Only the usual one. Maiden attracts undue attention. The attention lasts as long as it takes to peel an apple, then the peeler forgets about it and the apple's left to rot. In my case the apple was thus peeled the day before what should have been my wedding, and that was the end of it. I've always wanted to see Mainz," she said, and exited into the kitchen, calling over her shoulder, with a laugh, "I would not mind being called a whore if I'd profited by the description, either."

*N*ear the end of the second afternoon, just as a liveried harbinger had been sent ahead to Speyer, Willem found himself riding alone with Cardinal Paul.

It was not intentional. They were alone, on a wide stretch of tree-lined road that was punishingly hot, humid, and lousy with mosquitoes, between several tighter-reined groups that were murmuring together. Jouglet was chatting cheerfully to Alphonse about what a wonderful and gentle man Willem was, how very respectful of the women in his life, how loving and devoted. How very unable to hold a grudge. Willem had in fact been obediently sociable since they left Koenigsbourg, and Konrad was already treating him as if no debacle had ever occurred, as if there was not and had never been a Lienor to consider, only a Willem who might well be worthy, after all, of originating the office of Imperial Knight. Willem was even so pleasant toward Marcus that Marcus himself almost forgot this was the brother of the woman he had slandered—although he never for a moment forgot that Jouglet was her champion and determined to resurrect her reputation.

Konrad was still displeased about Marcus's lack of delight for his impending dukedom, but out of habit and necessity was treating the steward again as his closest confidant. As they rode, they discussed the mundane logistics of Konrad's rule: which lords he should meet with at each town they passed, what size gift he should bestow on each, whom to press for food along the way. Marcus was by now so obsessed with his concern for Imogen that he answered Konrad automatically, by rote, while his inner attention remained completely fixated on thoughts of her. The party was traveling north, away from her; he wanted some plausible excuse to turn back south alone—then he could keep on southward until he returned to her, abduct her, and disappear into the Italian alps . . . "Yes, sire, I believe the Duke of Austria is visiting the archbishop in Speyer, and I know he had wanted to speak with you about the river tolls . . . ," he heard himself say, as if he took an interest in it.

Sensing this dull discussion would absorb them awhile, Willem dropped back, needing a respite of solitude. Paul was also riding alone, and their horses out of boredom moved to walk together.

Alone beside the cardinal, Willem gave in to his impulse to act directly. He was not forswearing his oath to Jouglet, he decided; his oath was not to do this in front of other people. "Your Eminence," he said sternly. "I find myself sickened by the endless politics of the court."

"It can be very tiresome," Paul said, with a sigh. "I often wish that candor could prevail more often."

"Then would you welcome candor from me now?"

After a hesitation, and a little too heartily, Paul said, "Now and always."

"I know about the forged document and the girl who stole the signet ring," Willem said in an even-tempered voice.

Paul blanched. "I don't know what you speak of," he said.

"You know exactly what I speak of," Willem said, his voice tightening a little. "I want you to do the proper thing, and let justice prevail. Help return to me what was taken, and I'll forgive you all the sins committed against me. I will not make problems for you with the emperor, but I require justice. Give it to me. Or I'll summon that girl from hiding, and all the proof she has to damn you. Alphonse merely robbed me of my land, but you, Your Eminence, committed treason when you stole the ring. You have until tomorrow midday to decide your course of action."

He spurred Atlas ahead into the lengthening shadows.

Konrad's mother was buried in the crypt at Speyer Cathedral, and he went with his servants and bodyguard to pay his respect at her tomb while Marcus, across the way in the archbishop's roomy palace, prepared the archbishop's roomiest chamber to receive His Majesty that night.

There was a knock on the door, and he opened it to see Paul, in his familiar frenetic state. Before Marcus could usher the cardinal into the room, Paul jerked his head out toward where he stood. Perplexed, intrigued, and not the least inclined to help the man, Marcus stepped outside onto the small landing that looked over the hall.

Paul held two scrolled papers. In the dim light from a torch by the stairs, he lifted one, and without greeting explained briskly: "This is an edict from the papal nuncio—myself—telling Konrad that his daughter will remain a veiled maiden." Seeing the relieved look on Marcus's face, he lowered that scroll and lifted the other. "This one is from Alphonse, Count of Burgundy, requesting the king's blessing to marry you to Imogen immediately."

Marcus took a breath of amazement. He tentatively reached out for the scrolls, but Paul whisked them away behind his back. "They will be delivered to Konrad as soon as Willem of Dole has been delivered to his reward." And then he smiled like a cat.

Marcus heard himself utter a low, pained sound. "I cannot do that, Paul," he said. "If you rely on me for it to happen you will be disappointed, no matter how I crave the reward you offer."

Paul shrugged, apparently unconcerned. "I knew you would lack the stomach for it. But you should be aware that it is intended, and you will assist when called upon to do so, if you want to see your own expectations fulfilled."

Marcus did not remember Paul's leaving the balcony, so instantly was he reenveloped by his inner morass. Standing alone outside the bedroom, where he had made himself a pallet near the fire, he found he could not enter. He could no longer remember, or imagine, what guiltless slumber felt like.

He went down the stairs to the hall, wondering if he could learn where Willem was staying.

Then he heard something that made him stop, turn at an angle, and walk instead to the dying embers of the great hall hearth: Jouglet was playing the last tune of the evening.

He squatted down behind the minstrel. "Your knight's in danger," he whispered into the back of Jouglet's head. "Keep an eye out." He rose and walked back to the steps to Konrad's room, hoping he might be able to sleep now.

17

Reiselied

[a song of travel]

29 July

Speyer Cathedral was easily the most extraordinary work of man
Willem had ever seen. The vaulted ceilings seemed too high to
have been built by mortal hands, even after the soaring outer walls of
Koenigsbourg. And while Koenigsbourg had merely been intimidat-
ing, here he was overwhelmed with both a sense of peace and a feeling of elation. He wished Jouglet could have been beside him as he
stood in line to take communion during mass the next morning, but
they were obeying Konrad's order and keeping away from each other
throughout the journey. He was so distracted that Paul, who was
celebrating mass, had to physically turn the knight's head around
straight to offer him the eucharist.

They left Speyer heading north to Worms directly after mass. As
they rode along the raised and shaded road, the hills to the west

growing smaller and misty, Willem turned a strange color, became ill, and vomited his breakfast onto the roadside. Feeling Jouglet's furious, suspicious gaze on him, Marcus hurriedly announced that he would personally test the knight's food at every meal for the rest of the trip.

When they stopped for dinner in a small grove in the heat of the day, Willem was growing weaker and convulsed with dry heaves, and Konrad invited him to join him in his resting spot beneath the willow that gave the deepest shade.

Jouglet at once went in search of Marcus and found him by a large spring near the sluggish river, refilling the pot that would replenish Konrad's water skin. The task, normally performed by a servant, was now—with a poisoner in their midst—appropriate for no one but Marcus himself. "Who did it?" Jouglet demanded without preamble. "What do you know?"

Marcus looked innocent. "Don't you think they're wasting their time?" he said with forced offhandedness, gesturing across the river to a group of heavily perspiring peasants, who were pounding great vats of sand dredged up from the water, in search of Rhine-gold.

"You warned me last night that Willem was in danger."

Marcus, his attention now on balancing the pot in his damp grip, avoided Jouglet's glare. Realizing, he winced inwardly at his own carelessness. "Why would I warn *you*? Considering you're under watch and under orders from Konrad to keep your distance, you are now doomed to impotence as Willem's self-appointed guardian angel. Whoever warned you should have thought of that, and gone directly to Konrad." He looked back across the river at the fruitlessly industrious peasants. Their labor struck him as a painful metaphor.

Jouglet huffed with an indignant laugh. "You must be a very tortured soul, Marcus," she whispered. "I would like to think you've conscience enough that you are in an unending state of torment."

"It is my conscience that has brought me where I am," Marcus answered quietly, still staring grimly at the sand miners.

"Then bring your conscience along right now and speak to Konrad," Jouglet urged. "Tell him why you warned me last night."

"I didn't warn you."

"Marcus!" Jouglet snapped.

Marcus's eyes flickered along the resting, sweaty convoy. "I'll tell you what I know, and you tell Konrad. That's better than my telling him directly while the count and the cardinal are watching us."

"You don't want to be held accountable for what you tell me," the minstrel shot back.

"You're probably the only man at court he trusts right now," Marcus said bitterly. "He'll believe you. Tell him Paul offered to secure me my heart's desire if I got rid of Willem, but I would not."

"And that is the balefully beautiful Imogen, I suppose?"

"Yes," Marcus said, so miserable that Jouglet finally understood, too late, what he was truly capable of.

"*There* are certainly some advantages to whoredom," Jeannette said sweetly from behind Erec's saddle, brushing away a cloud of buzzing insects. "For instance, we're so low that we're considered incapable of obeying the law, so it doesn't apply to us. I certainly count that an advantage! It lets me get away with all sorts of awful things!"

Erec elbowed her to stop, but he knew why she was doing this, and he was actually grateful: Lienor was sick with exhaustion, and the heavy humid heat, and her only energy reserve seemed to lie in intense emotion. Jeannette, realizing this, was happy to keep her in high dudgeon as much as possible. It had worked for a day and a half; from what Erec could tell from the detritus before them on the roadside, they had not gained on the imperial retinue, but neither had they fallen behind.

But now even the dudgeon was depleted. "That's interesting," Lienor said in a less-than-interested voice, her entire body swaying, almost to exaggeration, along with her dun.

"And the church doesn't tithe us because it does not want to profit from the wages of sin. Which is particularly ironic if you think about who some of our most frequent customers are." She and Erec, on Erec's horse, glanced over at Lienor, who was squinting into the very far distance.

"That's interesting," she said in the same tone.

Jeannette chewed her lower lip a moment, trying to think of something inflammatory. "But St. Augustine, God bless him, thought prostitution was for the public good, since its eradication would lead to utter chaos."

"That's interesting," Lienor intoned, glassy eyed.

"Jouglet screws me almost every day," Jeannette said experimentally.

"That's interesting," said Lienor. Erec reached out to take her reins.

"Cousin, you're in bad shape," he said with concern.

*W*illem was awakened from his drugged midday slumber in the willow's shade by the emperor, who nudged his shoulder with a jeweled fist. "Willem," Konrad was repeating in a low growl. Somewhere nearby a fly was making a monstrous amount of noise. "Willem, wake up. It was Paul. It was Paul who poisoned you. We must know why he would try to do that. What's happened between you?"

A wave of nausea rolled over him. He saw Jouglet, with an expression of womanly worry, peering over Konrad's shoulder at him. "The truth?" he managed to mutter, as if to Konrad, awaiting Jouglet's answer.

"Of course," Jouglet said impatiently, frowning to hide her anxiety.

He kept his eyes on the emperor. "He knows I know," he said weakly, and rolled onto his side with dry heaves.

The involuntary gasp behind Konrad made Konrad reach back, without looking, to grab Jouglet and yank the minstrel before him on the blanket. "You obviously know what he's talking about. Explain." As Jouglet opened her mouth he added, firmly, "And don't say he's ranting or delirious. No dissembling. You know exactly what he's talking about. Explain."

She took a breath, trying to decide how best to dissemble. "Willem's family land was stolen by the count—"

"You said that was a *rumor*," he interrupted impatiently. "I've invited Willem to speak candidly, and he's never made the accusation. Besides, what does *Paul* have to do with that?"

She hesitated, and hurled a frown at Willem, who was oblivious to everything but his own gastric issues. "Yes, it was a rumor. There was also a rumor going around that Paul covered Count Alphonse's tracks for him. Somehow."

Like anything that might reflect badly on his priestly brother, this news caught Konrad's full attention. "Detestable ass. What evidence do we have of it?"

"We don't have any," she fumbled. "Willem was bluffing. Apparently he's very good at it."

Konrad gave her a knowing look. "Willem would not bluff even if his life depended on it, it's not *knightly*. If poisoning is Paul's response to Willem's threat, then Willem's threat had real weight to it. It was not just the repetition of a *rumor*." Jouglet shrugged and tried to look busy moving a bucket of water slightly closer to Willem's head.

Konrad studied the slender form a moment, then, unhappily but with breathtaking speed, he closed his hand around Jouglet's throat and had the minstrel wriggling faceup nearly on his lap, her fingers clawing desperately at his. "Sire, please," she managed to gasp.

He slacked his grip but didn't release it, and pushed her by the throat farther away from him. "What do you have to tell me?" he demanded.

On hands and knees, she coughed harshly, and brought a protective hand to her own throat. "Nothing sire—agh!" He had retightened his grip, and her hands clutched at his again. Again, he loosed the grip and looked at her expectantly. Again, she coughed to clear her windpipe, and met his gaze. After a moment, she repeated, "*Nothing*, sire."

"Very well, then," he said testily, and finally released her. "I'll interrogate Willem when he's recovered, he's much less work than you are. And then I'll ask him why you wouldn't tell me more yourself."

She cleared her throat a final time, uncomfortably. "You'll be disappointed with the answer, sire, there's really nothing to it." She took a damp rag from an attendant, rinsed it in the bucket, and dedicated her attention to wringing out the excess wet.

Konrad considered her a moment. "Now I see it all," he said. "From the very top. You wanted all along for him to marry Imogen so he could get his land back in her dowry."

Jouglet's cheeks pinked. She stopped pretending to be busy

and gave the rag back to the page boy. "You grasped that very quickly, sire. Willem himself never saw it at all until I told him."

"That's part of why we love him, Jouglet," Konrad said. "We love that there is someone good and useful in the world who does not think like we do." The minstrel nodded in agreement. Konrad slapped Jouglet's knee. "It is a good scheme of yours, and he should not suffer for his sister's fate. I'll tell Alphonse my wish is to see them married, and quickly. Before Willem is poisoned again."

Something in Jouglet relaxed, even rejoiced, but—"Your Majesty does not want to accost Paul?"

"Not without hard proof," Konrad said. "Accost the pope's representative? That will get me excommunicated all over again."

"What if he tries again? What if Alphonse does? If the rumor is true, Alphonse is even more compromised by Willem's claims—"

"That won't happen," the king said with a dismissive gesture. "Paul is trying to hide a crime, but if Willem gets his land back in marriage, the crime is effectively undone." He gave her a meaningful look. "If there were material *proof* of evil by Paul, it would be different. Then we could move against him, denounce him to the pope. Do you see how useful proof would be?"

"There is no proof," she said stiffly, realizing he was waiting on her answer.

"Whoever offered such proof could expect a very satisfying reward," he said in the same weighted tone.

"There is no proof," she repeated, more firmly.

"Then for now Willem marrying Imogen saves everyone—except Marcus of course, but he'll get a dukedom, so he really has nothing to complain about." He bent over the knight, lying curled on his side in the shade, a page boy wiping his mouth from the latest round of dry heaves. "Willem, did you hear that? You're to be married to Imogen my cousin! You're to become my cousin!"

Twenty paces away, Marcus heard this declaration and almost threw himself into the putrid green waters of the Rhine.

30 July

Willem insisted on staying mounted and keeping pace with the rest of the group. At one point he had to strap himself into the saddle with leather thongs, and his pages on their shared hackney kept dousing him with water, but he would not be put aside as an invalid, to take a litter or a river barge behind them. Konrad surreptitiously assigned two knights to watch him, and he told Jouglet to keep an eye on Alphonse and Paul. Between that assignment and concern over Willem, the minstrel had to leave off, temporarily, developing any new machinations toward Marcus. Marcus's expression, mood, and body language were impossible to read throughout the rest of the trip. He may as well have been stone. In fact, he wished he were.

The convoy arrived in Mainz the following evening, finishing their journey by skirting the eastern town walls, along the Rhine shore. The river workers were the first to greet them as they made their way, with reverberating fanfare, through the main gates of the city. Across the Rhine, audible and visible, was an enormous, elaborate campsite, where the lords of the Assembly had collected from throughout the empire. Every possible form of visual proclamation—banners, pennants, flags, livery—announced who was lord of what land, and where they were bivouacked. Two mornings from now, Konrad would be among them, making official the name of his intended bride and publicly offering Marcus precisely what Marcus was desperate to avoid. The steward had spent almost the whole of the journey picking over the situation in his mind, trying to find some way out of this, preferably some way to exonerate himself. He could discover no variant in which he might be spared his entrails.

Willem, still feeble—in fact, looking much worse—insisted on escorting His Majesty's train into the middle of town to the gates of the archbishop's quarters, where Marcus mechanically began to organize the diminished pack train in the stable yard.

The royal party stood on the steps to the small palace, stretched and dusted its collective limbs, and rubbed its collective buttocks after a long day in the saddle. Konrad gestured Jouglet to stand beside him. Willem had not dismounted and did not look well enough to stand on his own if he did. His Majesty cast a worried eye on the knight. "Stay with him," he said quietly to Jouglet. "Do not leave his side."

"What about your Galahad?" Jouglet asked. She had deliberately refrained from going near Willem for this very reason.

"I would rather have Willem alive than Galahad dead," Konrad answered. "And you will be no use to me if you are fretting about him while he's away from you. Where is he staying?"

Jouglet began to answer—and then stopped. And then began again. "Willem of Dole is staying at the inn off the Cherry Garden," she said, with a little more projection than she needed to. A few heads glanced in their direction briefly. Including Paul's.

Konrad gave her a subtle nod of understanding.

She bowed to His Majesty and descended the steps to approach Willem. Without asking permission or offering an explanation, she took Atlas's reins and led him out of the archbishop's gate, down the narrow street between the towering church and stony cemetery, through the broad cobbled market called the Cherry Garden, ringed by trees burdened with the darkening fruit. Between two of the biggest trees stood the door to Mainz's best inn. Openly publicizing her companion's identity, Jouglet was able to requisition a room for them, a small one but one they need not share with others, because the knight was so ill. The innkeeper saw them settled comfortably in and then brought up Flemish broth of egg yolks and white wine in

water for Willem, who was slanting toward delirium. Below, the
lodgers could hear the innkeeper trying to cajole the party that had
lost its room to Willem of Dole.

The humidity had been getting worse all day; Lienor was a pud-
dle trapped in human skin. She had recovered from the sunstroke of the previous day, but now she could hardly breathe. The
butter-based concoction Jeannette had mixed up for her cracked lips
was working, but it smelled rancid and was a great delight to flies.
They had run out of water and did not dare drink from the foul
Rhine—they had heard about the Rhine—and they had long run
out of food. For all the fulsome vegetation around them, it was only
the occasional feral cherry tree or wild strawberry plant that provided
them with edible fruit; the hazelnuts and walnuts were still green, as
were the apples. She was aware, through the general haze of malaise,
that Jeannette was handling all of this much better than she was, and
she envied the common woman for her fortitude. Her shame and
jealousy had roused in her the last reserves of physical and mental
strength, and somehow she'd managed to continue on a pace with
Erec. But now again she was losing her resolve.

They had spent the previous night in another inn, just south of
Worms, because Lienor's appalling state would rouse too much attention in a castle. Here, as at every place they'd stopped for food,
German ale was served in place of wine; it made her shudder. She
could not get over how *foreign* it tasted, how sour and grainy. And as
she looked around the crowded little inn, trapped there by another
passing thunderstorm, the travelers from the north and all the local
denizens looked foreign too, but for the strangest reason: many of

them looked like herself and Erec. The cousins' fair coloring had made them stand out in Dole; certainly Lienor's blond hair had been one of her most touted and striking charms. But half the people here, including women who were really very homely, sported paler skin and hair and eyes than she was used to seeing in the general population, especially among the lower classes. Why was she rushing into a venue where even if she were to triumph—unlikely in itself—she would no longer be special?

Then she remembered, with a jolt, what it was to feel prized, beautiful, unique, and safe—and shut up in her room at home. Suddenly every moment of this nightmare trip felt like a privilege.

30–31 July

There had been a brief, tremendous storm that night, and Jouglet had meant to stay awake throughout it. But when Willem at last fell soundly asleep, she also drifted into slumber.

She was awakened by familiar hands gently touching her face and hair. She opened her eyes and took a breath of relief, seeing that Willem's color was back. He hovered over her with a candle in one hand. "I'm surprised you weren't groping around beneath my tunic," she said.

"That would be ungentlemanly," Willem announced, and kissed her. She returned the kiss, and his hand drifted toward her tunic skirt. He smiled a little. "But of course, you *like* ungentlemanly—"

Sobering, she shook her head, and saw him wilt a little. "Willem, the crisis isn't over. We have to get you out of here." He looked confused. "The whole point of letting people know you're *here* is so they don't know where you *really* are. Now that you're alert enough to move on foot, you're going elsewhere to recover."

"I am recovered," he assured her and took her hand to slide it down his still-clothed body. "Shall I prove it to you?"

"No," she said with some exasperation, and pulled her hand out of his. "You aren't recovered at all, you're at death's gate."

He sat up, his ardor squelched, and sighed with resignation. "What is the game *this* time?" He held out the candle to place it on a clear spot on the floor. His hand shook; he was still weak, she realized. She rested her cheek on his forehead to test how warm it was.

"You're still feverish, so nothing but cooked pears for you until tomorrow's supper."

"You sound so very womanish," Willem said, with a weak smile. "I like it."

She made an aggravated sound and began to fidget with her purse ties. "There are all sorts of things happening at the archbishop's palace and I am missing all of it," she informed him. "I'm certain Alphonse and Paul are plotting again—to force the match with Besançon, to finish you off somehow at last, to lure Marcus further into their camp. And if Marcus knows that you're to have Imogen, Lord knows what he's planning right now to prevent it." Willem groaned a little, and she gave him a sour look. "Well, speak then," she said, in an irritable tone. "Say something infuriating, like, *Go on, I'd hate to keep you from your favorite pastime while I'm busy being sullen.*"

"I'm not sullen," he protested, and kissed her forehead. "I wasn't sullen the entire journey, except when I was practically unconscious. I'll be at death's door, now, if you require it. But why do you require it?"

Jouglet propped herself up on her elbows so they were face-to-face. "As long as you're at the gates of Paradise but not yet crossed over, Paul's in check. So you're at the gates of Paradise until I set things to my liking here on earth. Then you'll recover—and Paul will make another move, and I'll be ready for him. But first I'm taking you somewhere safely secret, so he can't send someone in to knife you while you're low."

Willem lay back on the bed and looked up at her with a wan smile. "Honestly, Jouglet, must you persist in playing my white knight? When will you accept that I simply cannot be your lady?"

Cloaked, on foot, Willem's sword wrapped and hidden, and without a lamp in the grey dawn air, she led him slowly through several twisting lanes with half-timbered houses packed together, to the street where the town's draft animals were lodged, and finally to the handsome building on the corner, at the edge of the small, sequestered Jewish quarter of the city. He was exhausted by the time they got there. The innkeepers were just rising. They did not know Jouglet and had never heard of Willem, but they were used to comforting travelers whose roads had been sometimes hostile. Without questions, they provided a clean, dry, warm room alone for the two strangers.

Jouglet crawled naked into the bed beside him, knowing this might be the last time she would be allowed such a luxury. Despite his earlier claims, he was not yet recovered enough for lovemaking, but they caressed and held each other gently until he sank into slumber, as the sounds of the city came to life outside. He looked restful and comfortable for the first time in days.

Jouglet left money and instructions for Willem's convalescence, then hurried back to the inn at the Cherry Garden. Here she made a show of asking for more Flemish broth for the invalid upstairs, whose fever had risen with the sun. She was dearly tempted to go to the archbishop's. But her greatest hope of profit lay elsewhere, in a void she could neither see into nor control. So—with a knife in her grip, for security—she sat on the small landing in front of the empty sickroom, tending to the imaginary patient, whose fictional and slowly worsening state was whispered about across the Cherry Garden and northward to the archbishop's. She sat and waited, and prayed she had not misjudged the only person who had never disappointed her.

The day yawned onward, the sun arched slowly overhead, the sounds and smells of the town outside the walls of the inn changed with the shadows. Town life went on, and peaked, and slowed, and stopped, and it was night. And she was still sitting there. And still she sat, until, depleted by anxiety, she fell asleep.

1 August

The predawn meeting was in the archbishop's main chamber, where Konrad had slept. He had his brother sent for, trundled Marcus and the sleepy-headed pages from the room, and blew out all but one of the beeswax candles that he traveled with to keep each unfamiliar room smelling like his own.

"This is a family meeting, not a political one," he began gravely. "Let there be an absolute understanding between the two of us on this much: nothing bad is to happen to Willem of Dole again. I know you were behind the poisoning, and I will not look the other way if this happens again, even if I have no proof. Even if it is not your fault, you will be blamed and I will hang both you and Alphonse. I'll hang you both if he does not recover now. If he does recover, keep an eye out for his well-being, do you understand that?"

Paul looked affronted. "Brother, I do not know what—"

"I invite you to shove the entirety of your sacred frock down your gullet, but you will not lie to me on this," Konrad said. "I know you tried to poison him, and I know why." He was very satisfied to see Paul's coloring turn a pale bluish green. So Paul did have something to hide. He would have to ask Willem what it actually was, since Jouglet refused to do so. "Yes. I do. So you see this marriage between Imogen and Willem of Dole is in *your interest*. You are restoring what you helped take from him. If you don't, your clerical privilege aside, I'll see you hanged in my own court for what you did to him, and I'll declare the day of your death an annual holiday."

"Does Your Majesty have other news to . . . discuss with me?" Paul asked, trying not to faint.

"This is not news," Konrad informed him with a nasty smile. "It is a direct threat. Pass it on to our crony uncle, I don't want to waste my breath on him. I expect the Assembly to go as we all assume it will. We will do the business of the empire, and then announce my own betrothal to the Besançon girl, and Willem's to Imogen, and Marcus's to my daughter. Thank God we sorted that all out!" he said with an exaggerated sigh. "And Marcus will be made a duke at last."

Finally approaching Mainz, the trio had not dared the castles and manors of the local lords, who might recognize Erec and whose guests might recognize Lienor. So it had been a common inn for them again, in a village south of Mainz, just off the track of the enormous traffic the Assembly was bringing into the city. The Assembly was the next day, but with luck, it would begin late, as huge ceremonial events usually do, giving them time to hunt down

Willem—and more important, Jouglet, whom all of them agreed
would be the one to fix things.

"But then, really, what is there to fix?" Lienor sighed in the room
the three of them were sharing. She sat slumped on the floor, with all
the effervescence and aroma of an old wet rag. "I'm a disgusting
mess. To present me to the emperor now would be begging him to
mock us. Even if I could reclaim my reputation, I could never possibly be made presentable to him." She smiled apologetically to Erec,
who stood by the door. "I'm afraid this was a waste of time and
effort."

Jeannette, comfortably sprawled on the bed, clicked her tongue.
"Tch. If you are willing to resort to some sluttish tricks, I can make
you look remarkable," she said. She patted the bag she had brought
with her from Sudaustat, which lay on the floor by the bed. "This
isn't just the wedding tunic in here, you know. I have a few miracle
concoctions, too. But let's start with giving you a tub and hairwash."

Lienor, thoroughly cleansed, slept soundly in the bed beside Jeannette; Erec slept on the floor. The next morning Jeannette expertly
mixed up her sluttish concoction in the room while Erec waited outside. Using white lead mixed with rose water and a pinch of a mysterious red powder, she experimented until she had a whitening
paste that nearly matched Lienor's skin tone. She applied it first
around the eyes where a week of squinting in the sun had left its
mark, and then a finer layer all over her entire face and the backs of
her hands. Then she opened the door and presented her to Erec.

"Good God," Erec said, "you gave her back her face! Cousin, you
are . . ." He shook his head with wordless admiration, and knelt
grandly at her feet.

Lienor turned to Jeannette, unsure what to say for gratitude, and
finally just threw her arms around her.

"Don't cry, or it will run," Jeannette said brusquely, but she was pleased by the embrace.

They set out on the brief final leg of the voyage into Mainz. Erec had never been here, but it was easy to find directions to the best inn of the town. As they approached, both horses lifted their heads, sniffed the air, and then began to whinny loudly and repeatedly. In a pause between the neighing, another horse from within the inn's walls answered them. "I trust horse sense," Erec said, alighting. "I'm positive that's Atlas."

And it was. The inn was large and handsome, facing the Cherry Garden, and they were directed up the steps that were directly beside the hall door.

Erec looked at Lienor solicitously. "Are you sure you're ready for this?" he asked softly. "Would you like me to go up first to prepare him for you?"

She shook her head. "I'll do it," she said.

They climbed the stairs, Jeannette a few steps behind them.

At the top, on the small, railed landing, a young guard had fallen asleep before the door, chin dropping over chest, unmoving. Lienor tried to walk around the sleeping figure, but the sleeping figure suddenly sprang up and grabbed her, furiously, and pushed her back against the railing, whipping out a knife and holding it against her pale throat.

Jouglet's face was barely a lash's length away from hers and they locked eyes, the knife wavering in the musician's hand. Erec was afraid to raise a cry, afraid that any sudden movement would make Jouglet strike on reflex. "It's me," Lienor whispered, frightened, trying to stay calm. "Jouglet, friend, it's me, I'm innocent, I know you know I'm innocent, *please*—"

Jouglet, spooked, dropped the knife from a trembling hand. "Milady," the minstrel said hoarsely, and bowed. "For the Love of God, milady, I almost slit your throat." She sank back onto the balcony floor, hands clasped, nearly hyperventilating. Then, recovering a little: "I knew you'd come, milady. I've been waiting for you. *You* are the white knight—white bosom and all." And then, sobering: "Where's that *accursed* Erec?"

"I'm here," he said, without defensiveness, from the top step.

Jouglet looked warily, almost accusingly, between them. "Did he hurt you?" she demanded of Lienor.

"No," Lienor said reassuringly as Erec reddened. "My mother realized what had happened and prevented him." At a frown from the minstrel, she explained, "The steward heard about the birthmark from my mother. He got her drinking, and she spoke too much."

Jouglet looked incredulous. "Your mother? Spoke too *much*?" Then Jouglet, glancing between them, noticed Jeannette on a lower stair, and her eyes widened. "Good heavens," the minstrel said at last, looking now between the three of them. "Must have been an interesting journey."

Lienor knelt down beside Jouglet on the balcony. "I've come to clear my name with Willem—"

"Not with Willem," Jouglet corrected. "No, milady, you must clear it with the emperor."

"If I explain the situation to Willem, he will understand and surely be able to explain it to the emp—"

"No, no, no," Jouglet said firmly, and got back to her feet, wincing with a sudden awareness of how stiff she was. "That's not enough. This has gotten out of hand, there have been rumors feeding rumors, you need a very public exoneration." She frowned into the bright early morning sunshine, thinking, and stretched each limb gingerly.

"Do you have a better idea than going to my brother?"

"Of course I do." A pause. "Give me a moment to figure out what it is."

"Can't I see him while you're thinking about it?" Lienor begged. "I cannot bear the thought of his believing ill of me, I want to—"

But Jouglet already had a plan. "He's not really here, milady, and there is no time now to go to him, the Assembly is . . . assembling. Luckily Konrad decided to pull rank yesterday—he sent out heralds ordering them to assemble here, outside the church, and not across the river as they usually do. That buys us several hours while the lords all ferry over. Quickly, do you have any of your jewelry with you?"

"I have all of it," Lienor answered.

"And a wedding dress," Jeannette answered, one corner of her mouth grinning.

Marcus, in his official livery of black and gold, was in the otherwise abandoned bedchamber of the archbishop's palace, trimming his beard and thinking how easy it would be to slit his own throat. He had been plunged back into grief and panic from the moment Konrad announced that Willem would marry Imogen. It would take a miracle—or someone else's extremely clever, unexpected scheme, since he had no more stomach for such measures—for him to protect his beloved now.

There was a rap on his door, and he opened it to find the messenger Nicholas, his black hair combed back smoothly, his face as usual pleasant but with little expression. He bowed to Marcus. "Sir, I'm glad I found you in and not yet gone to the Assembly. I've brought you a parcel and a message that was delivered with some urgency to the archbishop's gate."

"You've just caught me in time," Marcus said, forcing himself not to sound morose. "Thank you." He gave the young man a few coins and excused himself to see what he had received.

It was a dictated note, a brief one: "My beloved. Forgive the strange hand, this is dictated for reasons you will soon understand. There are complications you do not know about and which it is not safe for me to commit to paper. If you read this in time, and if you love me, I beg you to bring what is enclosed, hidden, to the Assembly. Please trust me, love. This is a necessary scheme to restore our expectations. All will be well, all will be made clear before midday today. My unending love, to be yours until death and beyond, Imogen." There was the flourish of the love knot.

Midday today? Was she here in Mainz? He drew a short, sharp breath and felt his pulse quicken. His hands began to tremble as he tore the parcel open. Inside was an enormous emerald ring set in gold with rubies all around it, and a beaded belt that a woman might wear over a surcoat for decoration.

This was strangely melodramatic for Imogen, but she would not make such an odd request unless there was good reason for it. And like many things odd in appearance, there was no doubt an explanation that, once heard, would make this seem quite reasonable. At least she had a plan of some sort; that was more than he had managed.

The ring fit on his little finger, but there was only one way he could think of to keep the belt with him. He could not bring a hand parcel with him to the Assembly, where he would be on his feet and moving almost constantly all day seeing things were smoothly run. He pulled off his black and gold ceremonial tunic and loosened the belt stays as far as they would go. The fit was very tight, but bearable. He put the tunic back on, smoothed his hair and beard, and hurried out to the Assembly.

18

Palinode

[a poem retracting what was said before; a recantation]

1 August

There were ten thousand noblemen in Konrad's empire. The highest among these were eight dukes, six dozen minor princes, and several hundred counts, landgraves, margraves, and burgraves. None alone within this upper echelon had great power; collectively they had a right to dictate much of Konrad's political life.

But Konrad had the right to dictate where they did the dictating, and so when he announced that he felt like staying on the west bank of the Rhine, the Assembly was severely delayed as they were all ferried across. It was, of course, a power play. The huge market square between the cathedral and the archbishop's modest palace was not only large enough to hold them all, but they also would be open to the scrutiny of the citizens of Mainz, who were among Konrad's most affectionately loyal subjects, since he had been knighted here by his father nearly twenty years ago. If he argued with his Assembly today, he would be cheered for it by the masses, and report of that would make its way handily up and down the Rhine. Not that he had much to do with the masses, but anytime he could publicly show up his lords, he was a happy man.

So he'd had his dais set up in the shadow of the church, facing north over the square, and ascended as the bells rang terce. The lords had been told to bring the camp stools they would have used across the river anyhow, and commoners were officially told to leave the square, but unofficially welcomed to return to it once the nobility was seated.

And now the nobility was nearly seated. Nicholas's streamlined form slipped nimbly through the rounded throng that was trying to settle in. He met Jouglet at the corner of the church and described how the seneschal was dressed this morning. Jouglet gave him a gold mark and dispatched him on an errand that would last the day.

"I want to hear what this is all about when I'm back," objected Nicholas.

"Oh, you will," Jouglet promised. "From everybody."

Lienor stood in a bustle of merchants who were craning their necks for a better view of His Imperial Majesty. Her head was wrapped in a dark blue wimple and her body covered entirely by a shapeless but expensive blue mantle. She did not stand out as the poor country girl she suddenly felt she was. Jeannette's cosmetic ministrations had been recently reapplied. She took a deep breath to calm her trembling; there were possibly more people here in this wide, open square than she had ever seen, cumulatively, in the whole of her life. Her heart was pounding, and her throat was dry. She crossed herself repeatedly.

"Marcus is wearing black and gold, with chevrons," Erec whispered from behind her. "And Jouglet will be standing beside him in a moment. You must make your move as soon as you see them. I will never be more than a few paces away from you if something goes wrong, but people know me here, you must not look at me."

She nodded once, feeling faint, and crossed herself again with a shaking hand.

"Cousin, you can do this," he said softly, then moved out of her hearing.

Her eyes searched the crowd for Jouglet. The merchants and artisans and farmers whose stalls had been removed for the occasion were milling about and muttering in clusters along the edges of the square, as the aristocrats settled onto their unaristocratic seating. There were some preposterously overwrought outfits in the crowd; Lienor could not focus on them but saw a surfeit of red, gold, silver, and violet. Heralds holding up the various coats of arms only added to the visual cacophony. Almost everyone but Konrad and his guards, in the sliver of the cathedral's midday shadow, had to squint; there was no other shade. The light wind carried with it the smell of cooling bread from the bakers' street. It was a comforting smell, but she was not comforted by it.

As the lurking groups of commoners moved in to stand around behind the seated lords, creating a multitextured sea of heads and head coverings, she heard her name once, whispered to her left with sheepish relish. It almost made her start sobbing; then again it was sounded ahead of her, and then here and there throughout the crowd. The whispered word *rose* percolated around the marketplace, and *thigh*. And other things somewhat less circumspect. Everyone knew that His Imperial Majesty had meant to marry the sister of the great Willem of Dole, and would have announced the betrothal here today. Marcus's name was mentioned rarely, and then usually in a nervous giggle by young ladies; twice or thrice a man's voice said it with a kind of guilty envy. His reputation was inflated by the now-legendary event that had demolished hers.

Erec, behind her somewhere, heard it as well, and said through clenched teeth, "They'll all be eating their words soon."

At last she saw the minstrel in the sliver of shade by the dais, in a bright golden tunic with black dagging all along the skirt—looking like a garish courtier who hated looking like a garish courtier. Jouglet was speaking to a tallish, slender man with dark hair who was dressed in a black tunic with a gold belt and gold decorations. She shuddered. He was not bad-looking, in fact was attractive, which disturbed her; here was a man a girl might very well fall for, to her ruin. With his narrow well-formed face and sad dark eyes, the steward looked not only too benign but too conventional to have schemed her undoing—he looked to be an honest man. A tense man, at least today, but an honest one.

"Quite a morning," Jouglet said, looking around.

Marcus nodded, scouring the throng for hints of Imogen's proximity. The hissed words *Lienor* and *sister* and *Dole* and *birthmark* rose up from the crowd like darts. It horrified him that the slander had leaked out and spread, that he had so misjudged Willem's popularity not to realize how hungry every servant girl and village tailor would be to learn and share whatever sundry detail could be known about the knight. He tried to tell himself he would not have done this if he'd realized the public damage it would cause, relieved that he could never know if he were lying to himself. What was done, was done, and had been necessary.

And in vain.

"Do you think he's going to do it?" Jouglet asked. "Tell them he'll marry the Besançon girl?"

Marcus nodded. "Yes. It is very sad that his preferred plan did not work out, but I think he's reconciled to it. Between us, I think politically this is a more sensible match." A pause, and then he said heavily and sincerely, "But I am sorry for the grief that I contributed to. I wish that I could somehow take it back."

Jouglet shrugged. "You did what you felt was right. That makes you an honorable man."

"Thank you," Marcus said, feeling ill. He turned to look around for Imogen again, when his gaze was struck by a pretty but traumatized-looking young woman dressed in dark robes and wimple. At the moment he saw her she was stepping out of the crowd directly into the open circle before the throne. This alone might not have called much attention to her, but she, after a hesitation, ran through the glaring sunlight, across the circle toward the dais into the shade, and fell on her knees before Konrad's feet, her face bent over his boots, wailing, "Please, Your Majesty, you must hear me!"

Everyone else in the square gasped and stopped speaking, to gape at her.

"Please, Your Majesty!" she begged with the hint of a familiar accent. "I beg justice, I beg your justice, before your assembled knights and lords!"

Immediately the two royal guards rushed toward her to remove her, but Konrad held up his hand, staring at the back of her head, as if she were insane. "Whoever you are, get up. This is no place for a lady to prostrate herself at my feet. Rise and tell us your complaint."

"I will not rise until you've heard me out!" she cried and grabbed the edge of the gilded wooden dais as if she could hold herself there should the men try to wrestle her away.

Konrad looked over at Marcus impatiently.

"Make her rise," Marcus ordered the larger guard, who could have easily lifted her over his head. When she felt his hand on her wrist, she pulled away from him, grabbed at her mantle strings, and then looked up, terrified, straight into Konrad's face.

Her mantle fell from her shoulders and with it, the wimple was pulled free as well, dramatically revealing the thick, curling mane of shining blond hair. Freed from the mantle she stood up taller, and Jouglet almost hooted with admiration: Jeannette had given her a green, fitted, low-cut tunic over a low-cut shift, and a bright gold clasp placed deliberately too low on her shift drew instant attention to her breasts, of which more flesh could be seen than had been exposed publicly since infancy. Her face was pale in just the right way, and then a little pink in just the right places. She was laden with the jewelry she'd gathered from three years of adoring wooers. She looked magnificent.

"Wait," Konrad said, stopping the guards. He smiled a little despite himself—she was pretty, and he found it entertaining that she was so shamelessly relying on that fact. "Young woman, you have one sentence to tell me what your complaint is, and then you will be thrown from the city walls."

"I was raped and robbed by a member of your court while I was sitting sewing in my room at home," she said promptly.

"A member of my court?" Konrad echoed incredulously. "Are you saying somebody present now?"

"Yes, Your Majesty, I can point him out and prove to you at once that he wronged me. I was a virgin until he took me! Unless you would be known as a ruler who allows his men to run roughshod over a lady's only treasure, I beg you grant me justice."

Konrad looked up around the collected faces. He hardly knew a nobleman who hadn't helped himself to some pretty virgin beneath him on the social ladder. In fact, there was something charmingly quaint that the young woman thought her case merited attention. He wondered vaguely if her father might not be important—virgins of certain lineage *did* warrant royal protection. And if he did not take her seriously no doubt Paul would commandeer the moment in her defense as an example of the evils of unbridled secular power. So he would have to at least appear to take her seriously.

Happily, this was precisely the chain of thought Jouglet had anticipated from Konrad.

His Imperial Majesty looked astonished and shook his head. "This is a serious charge, and a most dramatic way of bringing it to my attention. If this turns out to be nonsense, we will have your head on a platter before the Assembly is called to order. Stand and step forward."

Unsteadily, she did so, her hesitation caused as much by travel weariness as fear. Then for a moment she did nothing, looking too cowed to speak. Murmurs began to grow.

"Hurry up then!" Jouglet snapped. "There are more important—"

"Jouglet, that is no way to speak to—" Marcus began sternly but was interrupted by her shrill cry. He looked over at her and saw to his astonishment that she was pointing directly at him.

"That is him, my lord! That is the very criminal! Give me justice, sire!"

All eyes swept toward Marcus, who blinked, surprised but unruffled. "Sire," he said firmly, "I have never seen this lady in my life, I swear."

"Don't lie about me!" she shouted with sudden ferociousness, almost sobbing with fury. Her face went red with rage. "You raped me and took my virginity and you even bragged about it!"

"I did no such thing," Marcus said disdainfully.

"And you robbed me, not only of my virginity, but of my jewelry, too."

"You're gaudy with jewelry," he scoffed, taking a single step toward her into the circular space. "Crazy woman, what are you talking about? Remove her," he instructed the guard, but the guard looked to His Majesty for guidance. His Majesty, riveted by the bizarre scenario—and intuiting some current running under it—held up his hand: not yet.

"Sire, if you will excuse my speaking before the Assembly,"

Jouglet said loudly, also taking a step to stay beside Marcus, "take this poor disturbed creature out of here and have the physician attend to her, so you may get on with the tasks before you."

Lienor raised a violently shaking arm and pointed again at Marcus. "Just moments ago this man stole my best gold emerald ring set with rubies and a beaded belt I was saving for my wedding day!"

Marcus went white and for a moment was too flummoxed to think. In that moment, Jouglet leapt forward another step and sneered at her. "Stupid woman, he's been standing here with me all morning. Where would he hide such a belt? Under his clothes, I suppose?" And radiating self-righteousness, the minstrel reached out for the steward's tunic and flipped up the skirt.

Revealing the beaded belt.

"What?" Konrad said in astonishment.

Jouglet cried out and dropped the tunic skirt, leaping away from Marcus and insisting, "There's some mistake here, sire!"

Konrad gaped. "Marcus, lift your tunic," he ordered. In the background the crowd murmured and then shushed itself.

Marcus, almost hyperventilating, put a hand defensively on the skirt of the tunic. "Sire, I must tell you in private how I came to—"

"Lift. Your. Tunic."

The steward looked like he might faint, and Jouglet took a step closer, solicitously holding out an arm to steady him. Marcus took it, and then very slowly, choking back the coppery taste of fear in the back of his throat, he lifted up his tunic skirt, and there, as before, was a woman's beaded belt.

"My God, Marcus," Konrad said, flinty. "Hold out your hand."

Marcus sighed shakily with resignation and held out his left hand. On the smallest finger, turned in toward his palm, was the emerald ring. It glinted mockingly up at him in the sunlight. Again the crowd murmured and again shushed itself sharply.

"This is witchcraft," Jouglet said with a venomous hiss toward the woman in green. "Sire! He is your closest friend, that is a stranger. How can you believe her? This is obviously witchcraft! Or a trick!"

"A trick," Marcus echoed weakly.

"A trick, did you say a trick?" Jouglet demanded, shouting and yet barely noticeable to Marcus through his daze. "Sire, did you hear that, it's a trick! That is not proof of anything!" The minstrel turned to Marcus and shook his shoulders vigorously. "Where did you get the belt from? Let's prove you didn't steal it! Speak!"

Marcus tried to remember. "Nicholas," he gasped and collected himself a little bit. This was some horrible prank that was being played on him—by whom? Perhaps by Alphonse? He did not dare to look around the square in search of that fat wart. Or was this the cardinal punishing his refusal to poison Willem of Dole? "Nicholas brought it to me this morning in a package," he said hoarsely.

"You lie!" she shouted at him. "You had those things off my own body when you took my innocence!"

"Somebody find Nicholas!" Konrad called out.

"Sire, if you please, he's been called away," Erec said apologetically, pushing forward out of the throng and bowing at the foot of the dais. "He was under my hire to go to my home in county Burgundy to check on my ailing mother. He will not be back for ten days or more."

"Somebody chase after him and call him back!" Marcus demanded.

"He's very fast," Jouglet said sadly. Then, anger seeping back onto the freckled brow, the minstrel pointed to the plaintiff woman again and hollered, "Anyhow, she did this, obviously! She's a witch I'm telling you! Burn her!"

"Jouglet!" Marcus said, horrified. "There are better ways to deal with this, the woman is obviously hysterical."

"I'm not a witch! I am not hysterical! I am an innocent victim!" she sobbed. "If you have no reasonable explanation for how he comes to wear my property, sire, you must know him to be guilty. Will you excuse him because he is a friend of yours? Is that what justice has come to in the court of the empire? No wonder in Burgundy they prefer the justice of the papal courts."

"Hear hear!" said Paul from somewhere in the sunbaked, squinting crowd. The Count of Burgundy himself was unreadable, as he was busied with something that appeared to be stuck to the sole of his boot.

"My court is fair in all concerns," Konrad said hotly.

"Then find him guilty, sire!" Lienor demanded.

"Sire!" Marcus said, again stepping forward—again shadowed by Jouglet. They were now standing apart from the crowd, in the open circle, barely five paces from her. "I swear by my decades of friendship and fidelity to you, this must be some trickery or witchcraft, I have never seen this lady ever in my life, nor have I taken her virginity."

"A trial!" Jouglet called out, smirking triumphantly at the distraught young woman. "He deserves a trial! And when he's proven innocent we'll throw her to the wolves."

"It is only his word against hers, Jouglet," Konrad said impatiently.

"A trial by ordeal, sire!"

For a moment, utter silence.

And then a chorus of voices from all around the square, from nobles and commoners alike, in cautious support of this suggestion, as Marcus himself went white again.

"The cathedral is right here!" somebody cried out—somebody who sounded a bit like Erec.

"Yes! And there is a holy well just on the other side!" Jouglet nodded, then turned eagerly to Marcus. "Won't you agree to that, sir? With God as your judge you know you will be exonerated."

Marcus hesitated. "What if God is cross with me for other sins?" he asked quietly. "The calling down of divine—"

"That's not the way it works," Jouglet insisted briskly. "I beg you, prove your innocence, agree to this—the woman is a witch, or working with some scheming charlatan. Don't let her get away with this outrageous accusation."

"Sire," Marcus said, coughing, and Jouglet stepped out of the way so he could face the king directly. "I swear on the honor of every prince and duke here today, I am innocent of this crime, so innocent I'd stake my life on it. May the emperor allow me to prove myself by ordeal as reward for my years of service. Throw me in the holy well and see what God declares." He held up his hands. "The emperor may order my hands bound to take me there, but I will go without a fuss. Because I know that I am innocent!" he shouted suddenly, his attention back on her.

Konrad frowned and considered the request, as a rising chorus of voices excitedly begged him to let this happen. Marcus had many friends at court—and many sycophants, who would try to get the king's attention through him. There was a certain equilibrium that served everyone with Marcus at the king's ear, and everybody wanted to maintain it.

But to call upon God to step into the affairs of humans so directly—that was not an easy call to make, especially for an emperor determined to curtail the church's power. Konrad rather preferred that God remain comfortably in heaven and leave the emperor himself to mete out earthly judgments.

"Brother," called out Paul, who did not care one way or the other what happened to Marcus now, but who was very prompt about public displays of orthodox piety. "Brother you *must* not do this! I forbid it on the pope's authority!"

That settled the matter for Konrad.

"We will do it!" he declared.

There was a roar of approval. Marcus offered himself up to the enormous guard for custody, so that he could not be accused of trying

to escape in the hubbub as the crowd, bubbling with perverse anticipation, crossed past the cemetery below the cathedral. Boidon threw
the trembling accuser's mantle back around her shoulders and led her
by the arm down the brief, narrow lane, muttering to her on the way
that if she were found false for accusing his friend, she might just accidentally find herself falling headfirst into a tanner's vat. Everybody
else in the crowd stared at her, pointed, called her names. She kept
her head high and ignored them.

They reassembled at the pool with their backs to the sun, facing
the church. The crowd had been large before, but politics are not
nearly as riveting as a public trial by ordeal, and now more townspeople joined the throng, coming from the Cherry Garden, from
the Street of the Emperor, pouring out of Cemetery Lane into the
lozenge-shaped square.

The rosy-brown cathedral towered magnificently before them in
the sun. The double-arched windows high up on the dome, through
which only God could look directly, were shadowed slightly at the
top by their own exterior casement, but the sun was beating down on
nearly everyone without relief.

To the other side of the well, across from the cathedral, was a
dignified linden, and Konrad stood in its shade. He refused the heavy
wooden chair that was trundled hastily from the sacristy. The plaintiff was placed to the king's right and the defendant to his left, with
Marcus's righteously concerned friend Jouglet standing beside him as
he was shackled to a narrow log.

"I think there are stones in the hollows of the logs, to make sure
you go down," Jouglet whispered comfortingly.

"I can't swim," Marcus whispered back, not comforted, as two
men attached his wrists and heels. At this point, he would have welcomed death, except he could not abandon Imogen that way.

The archbishop was called out of his private devotions with a
wealthy spinster, and ordered to oversee the process. At first he did

not want to, and Paul heartily endorsed his obstinacy. The church was coming to discourage trials by ordeal; there was talk of banning the practice altogether for being hubristic and immoral. (This of course made it much more exciting to the crowd.) The archbishop himself did not care for it. But neither did he care for an angry mob overrunning his cathedral, so despite Paul's protests, he stood over the pool and blessed it, then addressed the crowd with the formal terms of the ordeal. "Marcus of Aachen, a royal ministerial, is shackled to this wood," he said. "He shall be thrown into the holy pool, which does not accept the flesh of sinners. If he floats, if he is rejected by the sacred water, it is proof by God that he is guilty. If he sinks to the bottom, that is evidence that God has found him pure, and he is innocent."

"And he is drowned," Konrad amended, suddenly looking dubious about the idea.

"He is attached to a rope," the priest corrected reassuringly. "He is drawn up again at once. Steward Marcus of Aachen, will you abide by the judgment of the Lord?"

Marcus nodded shakily. He was lifted by Konrad's two burly guards up and over the sacred pool, a large stone well of greyish water that was four strides across and three times the depth of a tall man. It was in the middle of the green market, and there were doubts about its purity (it smelled slightly of cabbage), but nobody felt compelled to bring that up now—except Paul, who was ignored. The archbishop called for silence, and then the men released Marcus.

Marcus hit the greasy water with a loud splash, and people hovering too near pulled away.

He sank to the bottom, straight as an arrow, and stayed there.

There was a cheer from around the pool, as cornets brought over by Konrad's heralds sounded brightly. Konrad sighed loudly with relief. The pretty young accuser's face was unreadable. Jouglet laughed at her derisively; she ignored it.

"Pull him up, for the love of God!" Konrad shouted out over the noise, and the two who had dunked Marcus pulled up on the ropes, hauling him back to the world of air. They trundled him out, and he lay beside the pool, bound to the log and retching water.

There was more and louder cheering, as he recovered his breath and was unshackled. Then he stood, slowly, gasping for breath, black tunic sodden, black hair disheveled, fury blazing in his dark eyes. The crowd silenced itself with delighted, nasty expectation. "You!" he coughed, pointing to the young woman in the cleavage-exposing green tunic. "You, *ha*! I am innocent! Will you admit it now? I have never laid a hand on you. In the name of God, I have never even laid my eyes on you before this morning!"

All eyes turned to her. Looking still pale, but composed, she said simply, "You will swear that before all these people?"

"Yes!" he snapped back. "I just did! I just *proved* it!" Realizing he was safe now, he let himself feel the fear as outrage. "The Lord Himself has just proved it! Lady, I do not even know who you are!" he said with a triumphant laugh.

She drew herself up very straight. "I am Lienor, sister to Willem of Dole," she said.

19

Irony

[a discrepancy between the expected and the actual]

1 August, night

Before sunset she was an empress.

It happened with such chaotic swiftness that nobody could prove who was responsible for what parts of the breathtaking turn of events, although really everybody guessed it was all due to Jouglet.

Konrad had looked like he'd been speared through several vital organs, staring in horror at his oldest friend. There was no need to ask Marcus's response; his bloodless face revealed his guilt, and he sank to his wet knees on the cobblestones, his hands held up as much in prayer as surrender.

He was condemned to hang the next morning.

Konrad issued the sentence, but he would not watch the jeering mile-long procession through the huddle of town squares, in which Marcus, stripped to his shirt, was forced to carry a heavy saddle to let onlookers know he was a criminal. People spat at him, threw rotten fruit, waggled their fingers in their ears, and bit their thumbs at him, many without knowing what his crime was. The humiliating ordeal ended at the western gate, where he was locked into a corner of the city prison. The emperor avoided witnessing any of this by shutting himself into his private chapel in the cathedral, sobbing with rage and loss.

By the time he emerged, pale from exhaustion, a chant had broken out among the milling outdoor crowd that he should marry this clever and beautiful young lady after all. In fact, the conventional wisdom held quite loudly, it should happen at once. "Why not now?" cried somebody, who again sounded suspiciously like Erec. "We are at the church, we have a priest! An archbishop! We even have a cardinal!"

Konrad, seeing how apoplectic this made his brother, revived enough to announce he would like to do nothing better. He and Lienor, each in their own state of minor shock, hardly aware of the other's presence, managed to exchange vows before the cathedral door. The wedding was blessed by the archbishop of Mainz as well as a scowling Cardinal Paul. To processional marching from tabors and pipes, they were furnished with horses for the brief, ceremonial cross back behind the cathedral and the market square into the high-walled palace of the archbishop.

The dais in the palace hall had been supplemented with a second chair. It took a good part of the afternoon to receive all the lords, during which time Konrad and Lienor hardly had a moment to glance directly at each other, much less speak. When the last and least of the lords, perhaps half a dozen, were still at the base of the dais, the entire hall was distracted by footsteps running, pounding, from the outside main gate that kept the rabble out, through the courtyard and toward the hall. The guards sprang at once to block the door against whoever was intruding, but the large young man in his best red and yellow dress tunic and hurriedly polished boots knocked both of the men to the floor with his bare hands.

Willem stood panting in the doorway, pale in the dusky light. He saw Lienor, with a gold crown flashing gemstones, seated beside the emperor, and voiced a strange sound of disbelief, relief, and confusion all at once. "It's true," he breathed. The room quieted, and all attention turned toward him. Unaware of that, he ran across the hall and threw himself skidding to his knees at the base of the dais. "My lord and master," he said to Konrad's cordovan boots. "You must forgive me for ever doubting the lady's goodness."

"Oh, Willem, for heaven's sake," Lienor said sweetly, and slipped out of her chair to throw her arms around her brother. The crowd cheered.

And then trestle tables were erected in rows within the hall, and the wedding feast began, the entire week's rations for the Assembly of Lords served at once: bear, boar, cranes, geese, venison, fatted calves and suckling pigs, wines both dark and light, peacocks that appeared to have been cooked in their own feathers; one course was literally mythological, a cook's surgical invention of an animal that appeared to be swan above and swine below. There were elaborate dishes of the finest aphrodisiacs: sparrows, sparrow eggs, and pears. For most of a lifetime, Konrad had assumed Marcus would carve and test the meat for him at his wedding feast. Instead this station was divided between the three who'd made the evening possible: Willem, Jouglet, and Erec. No mere minstrel had ever received such an honor; even Jouglet was briefly flabbergasted.

Tables had been cleared away, hands had been washed in rose water, and now the count and cardinal stood on the edge of the mass of dancing, happy, tipsy, overdressed aristocrats. The two watched the hubbub with indifference. "It smells of sulfur in here," Paul said in lieu of conversation.

"It is done," Alphonse said. "Salvage what you can, as I am doing."

"You are the most opportunistic man alive," Paul answered in disgust. "I at least adjust to loyally serve the mother church. You look to nothing but your own coffers."

"I am more honest about my ambition, if that is what you mean," Alphonse said comfortably. "I see what good I can. It has become necessary for both our sakes to marry Willem to Imogen; at least now he has some semblance of being worthy of it. Let it go at that, nephew. You did not serve your church, but you'll save your own skin."

"It's not consummated," Paul argued. "There is time yet for Fate to be kind and bar Lienor from her husband's bed before she even gets there."

The prison was inside the town's westernmost gatehouse, watched tonight by a sullen sentry who felt his knightly background warranted a more dignified post. It was cold, dank, and dark in here, and it smelled horrible.

"I did not want to come," Willem said bluntly, trying to make out the huddled figure of the half-naked, condemned man chained in the corner. "I am only here because my sister begged me to answer your plea. It distresses her greatly that you're to die for this, even though you tried to ruin her life. That is what a sweet, kind, loving lady it is that you misused." His voice was harsh with anger.

"You believed me, Willem. So readily and with such little proof. You are horrified at your own behavior as much as you are at mine." Marcus's voice was so tired it was calm.

Willem glanced at his sword by the threshold, two paces away but morally beyond reach. Much as Konrad might like to be spared Marcus's execution, Willem was not the man to do it for him. "Why did you beg a private audience with me?"

Marcus sighed and began to move, then realized he couldn't, and settled onto the clammy straw-strewn floor again. "Alphonse of Burgundy would marry you to Imogen," he began. Willem said nothing. "I know Konrad approves such a match." Willem still said nothing. "I must know if you will have her."

"Not if she participated in this plot against my sister's—"

"She knows nothing of it," Marcus said quickly. "I am the sole villain. Given that, milord, will you have her?"

Willem's eyes were finally beginning to adjust to the dark. Marcus in his posture of defeated exhaustion looked more at ease than Willem himself was feeling. "There is much sentiment in support of it," he said at last.

Marcus took a slow, pained breath. There was no escaping destiny; he'd been a fool even to try. "Then I must tell you something. She loves me very deeply, more deeply than I have a right to be loved. Please forgive her for that. Please forgive her the trespass of having loved me. Please do not be harsh with her, if she is not what you believe the wife of Willem of Dole should be."

Willem said nothing.

"What I am saying—"

"I understand what you're saying," Willem said brusquely. "I will value her according to her qualities and character, Marcus, nothing more and nothing less. If she is of good character—"

"A woman in love—"

"Being in love is no excuse for weakness. A woman in love is

perfectly capable of choosing to act as though she weren't," Willem
announced, walking out. "I have seen that firsthand."

Standing on the floor between the row of guards and the empress's dais, the jongleur had played three Gace Brulée songs in
a row in celebration of the beautiful and chaste young bride. Lienor
beamed down at Jouglet as if they were back home in Dole. She was
careful not to give the minstrel outright preference, and the minstrel
kept a seemly distance from her at all times. But the spontaneous
gleam in Lienor's eye made her winsomeness toward the rest of the
court seem almost forced. The two of them risked banter so playful
and informal that Konrad finally intervened with warning looks, although he was enjoying the spectacle. "They won't think me a sodomite after my behavior tonight," Jouglet retorted quietly, with a
wink.

"Yes," Konrad agreed. "They'll think you an adulterer and a trai-
tor. Moderation, my friend. Parcel out your affection. Go flirt with
someone else—or join the dance." There was a new circle dance beginning.

Willem reentered the hall, yielding his sword to one of the archbishop's guards. He smiled at Lienor across the room on the raised
dais, and after a moment of searching, saw Jouglet in the swirl of
dancers. He was about to step into the circle to join in beside her
when he saw Alphonse signal to him from the side of the hall.
With resignation he allowed the count to approach, knowing the
intention was to sing his daughter Imogen's praises. For a moment
he hoped Jouglet would break out of the dance to intervene, but

then he realized the minstrel would only add her voice to Alphonse's reedy salesmanship.

Jouglet did meet his gaze a moment as she stomped cheerily by, and winked at him, which only soured his stomach. Of course he wanted his land back, and he understood why this marriage was the way to attain it—indeed, to attain far more than that. But as the moment of truth drew near something in him mourned and wanted to rebel against it. He felt like a pawn—a ridiculous feeling, for he alone benefited from the union, but still he felt like a pawn, and Jouglet was the chess master.

Said chess master was eyeing the room even as she danced, to see where all the pieces were at play. She allowed herself a moment to bask in one facet of her victory: Lienor could do this. She could be the consort to the most powerful man on earth, and enjoy it as if it were just another game that she might play to amuse herself. That, at least, was a simple and uncomplicated success.

Paul had attached himself to the edge of the royal dais and was spending the evening with his eyes glued on Lienor, as if he could will her to make a false move and forfeit her position before it was sanctified by physical surrender. As the dance brought Jouglet close, he felt Jouglet's eyes on him and turned to look. Jouglet indulged in a brief triumphant smirk, and saw Paul's grudging scowl of concession before the circle whirled her away again.

She looked over her shoulder to see how Alphonse was doing with Willem—and almost stopped dancing from astonishment.

Imogen was standing in the hall doorway, between the two men.

She could have been an apparition she was so pale, and as grey as her riding dress. The count put a hand on her shoulder and guided her to a chest along the wall, looking more like a groom leading an injured horse than a father tending to his daughter. She was travel worn, almost sickly, and for a moment Jouglet was irritated; it was already hard to warm Willem to this arrangement, it would be even harder if she was so pathetically wan and distressed.

The moment looked extremely awkward for all of them. Alphonse seemed to be pretending it was an innocent introduction when all of them knew otherwise. Jouglet craned her neck to watch as she danced, fascinated by the count's utter gracelessness at playing matchmaker. Imogen was ashen, and Jouglet thought she might faint even resting on the chest. And Willem, bending awkwardly over her, was distinctly pink. How very annoying. *Must I do it all myself,* Jouglet thought. She had hoped at least to be spared from actually introducing her lover to his future wife. But she dropped her neighbors' hands and slipped through the brocaded silks, spun wools, new cottons, the smells of rose water, wine, cinnamon, and unwashed men, and finally approached the trio.

Alphonse, it turned out, was even more uncouth than she'd assumed: what had looked like an awkward introduction was in fact the establishment of a betrothal. They had both agreed, hesitantly and unhappily, before Jouglet even arrived. She felt a pang of relief, grateful to have been spared that task after all.

"Let me be the first to congratulate you!" the minstrel said heartily, and a little breathless, avoiding Willem. She knelt down ostentatiously and kissed Imogen's limp, clammy hand. She could feel Willem staring hard at the back of her head.

"I am not well," Imogen said, so softly that Jouglet wondered if it were meant to be whispered to her ears alone. "I hope I may be excused. My father and my . . . betrothed will take the happy news to the emperor. And empress," she added hurriedly, apologetically.

"Milady is overwhelmed," Jouglet said in an understanding voice, loudly. "If the gentlemen will permit me to escort her to some fresh air and gentle conversation, surely I can put her mind at ease."

Imogen looked up with eagerness, as if she read some secret promise in this proposal. Jouglet could not imagine what it was—

which made her instantly curious to find out what it was supposed to be.

There was a small private chapel, the door of which was tucked into a hall corner by the stairs to the upper apartments. With Alphonse's permission she steered the girl in this direction, skirting the dancing and the laughing. It was darker here in the thick arched doorway, and marginally quieter. "Willem is an exceptional fellow," the minstrel promised Imogen. "And I've heard the women say he's tender as a lamb." This was not quite accurate, but she trusted he would make an exception for this pale terrified child. "If you are frightened of what it means to become a wife, I promise you, you could never choose a gentler partner than Willem of Dole to escort you to womanhood."

"Yes I could," Imogen said in her murmuring voice, almost under her breath. "And I did." She bit her lip and looked down abruptly. Her hands, briefly, almost imperceptibly, moved to her abdomen before she forced them back to her sides.

It hit Jouglet so hard she almost lost her balance. She grabbed Imogen by the shoulders. "You stupid girl!" she hissed. "You stupid, *stupid* girl!"

Imogen finally broke down sobbing, relieved to have been confronted. "Please," she managed to say coherently, through her tears. She grabbed the hands that were still grabbing her shoulders. "Please, Jouglet, if you have an ounce of sympathy in you, help me away to a nunnery. For the love of the saints, spare all of us the humiliation this would bring." Jouglet did not speak, and so Imogen added, with defiance and a sniffle, "And I am not stupid, I knew what I was doing. When somebody genuinely deserves the one thing you have to give, the one thing everybody else is trying to control—you give it gladly." She turned away, trying to compose herself.

Jouglet studied her, attempting to scowl but already feeling herself capitulating to the fates. "I understand that more than you know. But still—foolish child!"

"Will you help me?" Imogen studied the minstrel's face, hopeful and afraid.

Finally Jouglet nodded grimly. "What choice do I have?" she said, irritably. "Wretch. Do you have any money with you?"

"I have nothing," Imogen said, with an uncomplaining sob. "I rode out from Oricourt in a panic when I realized. I used post horses, but the last one is exhausted. I have two servants with me—they'll say nothing."

"They can't come with us," Jouglet said. "And I'll have to get you money somehow. And apparently a horse." She made a sound of profound aggravation. "Listen then. When the bells ring compline, go to the southern gate of town. Do not be seen by anyone. I'll borrow a hackney from the archbishop's stable, somehow. Be ready to jump up behind me. There is a cloister half a day's ride south of here—you should have just gone there and not come here making things more complicated than they already are."

"I did not know the father of my child was condemned to hang at dawn," Imogen said in a soft, choked voice. "I thought I would arrive here and you, his friend Jouglet, would mend this. He wrote to me saying that you would be our witness and our help."

"By the time the bells ring compline," Jouglet said irritably.

Compline. Hardly enough time. She hurried at once out through the palace gates, through the dancing peasants and merchants in the torchlit market square, through narrow streets bustling with unprecedented nightlife and celebratory gossiping, to the southern gate. She had with her the largest flagon of wine that she could spirit away under the garish violet-opalescent-and-metallic robe Konrad had given his minstrel to celebrate the day. She cursed quietly almost the entire way because she knew that despite herself she was doing the right thing.

Her errand at the southern gate was accomplished in no time at all. The next step briefly stymied her, until she remembered that Marcus, like his master, brought his coffers with him when he traveled. She informed the knight guarding the royal train that His Majesty was donating Marcus's treasury to a nunnery some ten miles south, and even coaxed the man's assistance to carry two bulging saddlebags full of coins down to the archbishop's stable. The archbishop's night groom was easily convinced that she was the ecstatic new owner of the doomed steward's prized Arabian mare and was taking immediate possession of it. Trying to keep her breathing calm, she led the horse out the gates, through the drunken revelers, and down the street to the alley behind the western gatehouse in which the prisoner sat.

This part would be so much harder than any scheming.

She entered the porthouse with a nod to the guard, and then signaled toward the door to the cell, officiously proclaiming, "Here on king's business." In the darkness, Marcus recognized the voice and groaned.

"How's the festivities?" The guard resented being on the outside of court activity, and Jouglet could read it in his voice. She brightened— this might be easier than she'd anticipated.

"Quite lively. Would you like to go over for a few moments, have a dance or two? I can stand deputy for you awhile, if you'll just leave me a dagger in case I need to defend myself."

He was tempted. "I'm not supposed to do that," he began, sounding unconvinced.

"See who's making the offer? I'm the one that helped to get him in here. You can be sure there is no love lost between us. I'm only here on king's business."

Dagger in hand, with nobody else to witness, Jouglet thrust a torch toward the cell, where Marcus sat chained and hunched on a pile of moldy straw, as if he were in mourning.

"Tell me why you did it," Jouglet challenged.

Marcus pursed his lips shut.

"I know it was to keep Willem's star from ascending. Admit to me why you feared such a thing."

Marcus stared in defiant silence, but Jouglet sensed him wavering. Then he scowled. "Because I am a selfish, jealous, ambitious wretch who wanted to marry a rich girl for her land and position," Marcus said in a monotone. "That is the entire truth."

Jouglet considered him a moment. "I like a man who can keep a woman's secrets," the minstrel said decisively. Marcus looked up, alarmed. "But unfortunately, Marcus, certain things will not stay secret by your discretion or even your death."

"I know that," he snapped, miserable.

"Do you know about the child?"

Marcus scrambled to his feet, gaping. Having stood, he panicked and sat down again.

"Apparently not," Jouglet observed.

Marcus began to breathe hard, which in the fetid air of the room instantly nauseated him. "Oh God. What have I done to her?" He leapt up again, pounded his head against the stone wall so hard he stunned himself, and crumpled to his knees. He stood up as if he were going to do it again.

"Stop!" Jouglet interjected sharply, and rattled the door to the cell. Marcus began to pull at his own hair, then fell to the ground, sobbing with deeper grief than Jouglet had ever seen in a man. Even Willem had had rage to animate his distress; this was pure self-recrimination.

Then he looked up at her, his reddened eyes almost frightening in their intense anger. His strong, narrow features were grotesquely exaggerated in the lamplight. "If she comes to harm because of this I will haunt you from beyond the grave until you repent ever bringing Willem of Dole to this court. She is an *innocent*, Jouglet, she was misled by her own heart, not by ambition—"

"Shut up and come outside," Jouglet said brusquely. She took the key from the porter's stand and unlocked the door with one hand, holding out the dagger warningly with the other. Marcus stared at her. She gestured to his arm-chain, and after a confused moment, he held out his wrist; she unlocked the chain. "Remember, you're my prisoner." He stumbled half-crawling out of the cell, then stood up passively, still gasping for breath. She reached up to wrap an arm around his bare shoulders and pressed the knife against his throat. "I am about to do something very, very foolish, and if you annoy me one jot further I will change my mind about it," she explained, hissing, into his ear.

And then they were behind the gatehouse, in the darkness, by the mare, and Jouglet was untying the garish cloak. "Here," she said. "Put this on, draw the hood."

"What are you—"

"Shut up," Jouglet said evenly. "Take the dagger. Get on the horse. Most of your coin worth is in the saddlebags. She's waiting for you near the southern gate of town, and they will let you go through without a question as long as you do not reveal yourself."

Marcus was speechless.

"Hurry up," she ordered. "I've a wedding feast to get back to."

"Jouglet—"

"Go on now."

"Where do we go?"

"I don't know," Jouglet said. "I would head for France or even Flanders if I were you. Get out of the empire, at least. Now *go*," she insisted abruptly, and ran back into the porthouse.

The guard returned eventually, a little drunk, and glancing into the cell saw the figure he expected to see, curled up on the pile of musty straw.

Then the figure uncurled, stood up, and turned out to be not whom he expected.

"Hell!" the guard shouted in alarm. "What's going on?"

"Forgive my impersonation," Jouglet said, "But we are now both in a lot of trouble unless you do exactly as I tell you."

Jouglet passed through the thinned-out crowds in the square and reentered the archbishop's palace. She crossed the twenty paces of the hall to join Willem at the foot of the dais, and bowed deeply to the new empress.

"Your Majesty will forgive me a moment to converse with your esteemed brother?" Jouglet said.

Lienor was obviously delighted that it was in her power to dictate her brother's freedom of movement. "I'm afraid he must remain sequestered," she informed Jouglet, eyelashes fluttering precociously. "Until we can marry him off. For his own safety." Then she laughed and let them go. Konrad watched the three of them, liking their easy intimacy and affection, something generally so absent from his court. It mitigated his still-stunned grief about Marcus, at least a little.

The Count of Burgundy was moving toward the dais, so Jouglet led Willem to the far corner near the chapel door. "There has been a change of plan," she said quietly. "You will not marry Imogen."

Willem shrugged, looking tired. "Very well, what is your new game?"

"It is not my game, friend. Marcus has trumped us."

He frowned. "Marcus? But he—"

"Ah!" She held up a hand warningly to quiet him, then lowering her voice to a whisper explained, "He's gone. They're both gone."

Willem looked relieved, which annoyed Jouglet but did not at all surprise her.

"No, this is *bad* news," she explained. "You have lost the dowry land."

"I have gained an empress for a sister," he said. "I will not be left to starve. All you strove for will be accomplished. Your work is completed, Jouglet."

"No!" Jouglet said stiffly. "*Your* land. What Alphonse took from you. I want him to have to give it back to you. That was the *point*. That was why all of this was started!"

Willem looked at her strangely for a moment. "Poetic justice is not necessary when normal justice will suffice," he informed her. Suddenly he grinned. "I'm *not* the romantic one, Jouglet. *You* are." He was delighted with this insight.

Jouglet scowled. "For such a base insult I may have to challenge you to mortal combat."

"I accept," he said. "We still have a private room at the inn. Let's wrestle there tonight. The scent of your inner arm, just above the elbow, has been on my nostrils all day."

To her surprise, this made her blush. "Thank God *you're* not romantic!" she muttered with forced exasperation to the air.

There was a murmur from the thinning crowd, and they turned to see the source of it: the guard from the western gate, tutored by Jouglet to look distraught, ran into the hall and sprinted toward the dais. "That's the news of Marcus, and I must address it," she said, turning to Willem. His brown eyes were gentle and affectionate, and she let herself admit she wanted more of him. Between his illness, her irritation at his sullenness, and Konrad's Galahad admonishments, they had not made love in nearly a week. "But when I'm done—" She nodded toward the chapel door. "Just for a few moments," she added warningly when she saw the smile creep into the corner of Willem's eyes.

There was a growing hubbub by the dais, and Jouglet hurried toward it.

"Do not pursue the scoundrel, sire," she heard Lienor saying. The bride looked relieved by the news. It was a touching look, genuine humanity—a break in the silly masquerade she was so brilliantly carrying off. "Surely it is enough that he is gone from court."

Konrad's face was a neutral mask barely hiding painfully conflicting emotion. Then Jouglet caught his eye and nodded very slightly, with a subtle hand movement: *let it be.* The emperor made a brief, involuntary gesture, a shudder of relief, and then was in control again. "Very well," he announced grimly, taking Lienor's hand as if he were already familiar with it. "In honor of my bride, and her clemency, we grant amnesty to Marcus of Aachen, our former steward, so long as he never resurfaces within the borders of our Empire."

"Do not ever again try to give me away in marriage," Willem whispered as they untied each other's breeches in the dubious privacy of the small chapel. Steadying himself against the doorjamb, he pushed himself up into her. She gasped a little and fell back against the chapel wall. He pulled her closer, gently, so that she leant her weight against him, against his great broad chest. She could feel and hear his heart thumping, and realized with childlike pleasure that his pulse matched hers exactly. Despite the differences in their temperament she realized there was no one else she felt so near to, no one else she knew so well, or with whom she enjoyed such genuine companionship.

There was no one else. But there was one who came very close, to whom she owed a final revelation.

The royal newlyweds had just allowed themselves to get dragged into a conversation with Paul about church dogma. The festivities were waning, and emperor and empress, still surrounded on three sides of the dais by guards, were trying their hand at small talk. Konrad, having never bothered to converse much at all with a lady, ever, was pleasantly surprised by what he'd married.

The cardinal had been presumptuous enough to climb to the top step of the dais, and his head was now slightly higher than either of theirs. "I understand the area around Dole has been troubled by heretics of late," Paul was saying to Her Majesty in studied terms. "Particularly among the minor aristocracy. A young lady near the border was burned at the stake by a mob, wasn't she? The church does not sanction such a thing, but we cannot, alas, prevent it."

Konrad almost laughed, and was going to make fun of his brother's obvious and leaden desperation, but changed his mind. He wanted to see how his bride would respond.

Lienor lowered her eyes and smiled demurely, letting them know she realized she was being baited. "I do not concern myself much with serious matters, Your Eminence, or with matters much beyond my own doorway. As for heresy, we have been poor, but my brother keeps a chaplain and our uncle kindly built a wooden chapel in our courtyard. If there are dangerous currents about, I assure you they're in waters I do not swim." The slightest pause. And then with the demure cheekiness that was her hallmark, she concluded, "So if you are seeking discreet entrée into such a world, you will have to ask someone else. Perhaps your uncle? He knows Burgundy's naughty secrets better than *any*one."

Konrad laughed aloud as Paul reddened. Lienor's charming expression and bearing had not changed in the least. Now she raised her head a little and smiled warmly at someone across the room. Paul no longer impinged on her serene consciousness.

Willem had reentered the hall, and a moment later Jouglet backed out of the chapel, crossing herself ostentatiously. At Lienor's happy gesturing, they both returned to the foot of the dais, where Willem declined the emperor's invitation to watch his sister laid down in her marriage bed. Jouglet cried with poetic license that seeing Her Majesty in another lover's arms would be too hard to bear, and likewise begged off from the revelry. Lienor was finally escorted away by one

of the old archbishop's serving girls, but she was not a dozen paces
across the hall when she exercised her new-won power and announced, delighting in the liberty to do it, that she wished to be entirely unescorted. This was very irregular, but she did not care. From
a tour of the palace just after the wedding vows, she knew where the
bedchamber was and how to get there—and anyhow it was just up
the steps by the chapel, where she wanted one final moment of maid-
enly solitude to offer thanks to her Savior. The maid left her with a
candle and she sauntered with slow, superior giddiness across the rest
of the hall before disappearing into the deep shadows of the chapel
door.

As the last revelers staggered in search of whatever paths would
take them to their beds, Jouglet directed a clandestine wink at Willem and seemed to disappear.

She went to keep a solemn date she had made more than three
years earlier.

20

Madrigal

[a short poem suitable for singing by three or more voices]

1 August, late night

Entering the chapel, silent as a cat, she pulled the door closed. The dark room now had one beeswax candle lit, wavering on the altar in a bronze enameled holder. There was a high window behind the altar, made of little soldered squares of bluish-greyish-green. The two young figures looked across the empty space at each other without speaking, without moving.

After a moment, Jouglet slipped over toward Lienor and performed a deep and elaborate bow. "My lady," the minstrel intoned with exaggerated lofty diction. "Behold, for I have made you queen of all you survey, and yet this is hardly a trifle of what I would give you to express the profundity of my regard."

Lienor tugged Jouglet's hand to make the minstrel rise. "You are the most remarkable woman in the world," she whispered, and kissed

Jouglet softly on the cheek. They embraced, arms clenched around each other, and stood there in silence. Then at the same moment they began to laugh.

Lienor drew Jouglet to an elaborately carved chest against the far wall, holding one of Jouglet's hands in hers and with her other, gently stroking the minstrel's sun-freckled face. "This is the first moment I feel I can relax since you left us in Dole back in June," she whispered. "You astonish me. You really did it! You have been truly brilliant."

"I've also been extremely foolish, and there is nothing I can do about it. I must tell you something, Lienor." Jouglet hesitated and took a deep breath, afraid to look Lienor in the face. She let the breath out, then after an awkward pause took another breath. Finally she blurted out, with almost motherly compassion, "Willem and I are lovers."

For a moment Lienor looked breathlessly startled, and Jouglet tensed. Then very slowly a shadow of a smile crossed Lienor's face, and a moment later she was laughing, almost giggling. She threw her arms around Jouglet and pulled her close to her on the chest. "Both economical and tasteful of you!"

Jouglet peeled Lienor's arms from around her disbelievingly. "You're not jealous? Milady, with all respect, you are the most jealous woman I have ever known."

Lienor released Jouglet to look at her with almost condescending amusement. "I know you take male lovers. I refuse to consider that mechanical exercise called copulation any threat to what is between us."

Jouglet's laugh was quiet and slightly pained. "And what do you consider is between us?"

"The thing you've spent years making fun of to hide the fact that you're a slave to it," Lienor answered with satisfaction. "The purest, truest love two people can know. You worship me and I inspire you." She was so earnestly effervescent when she spoke that the words did not sound at all inflated or ridiculous.

"Lienor sweet, listen to me," Jouglet said. "I do worship you, or at least revere you—you're the most beautiful and least annoying well-bred woman I have ever known. And you inspire me, that's true or I'd never have begun this mad project. But, Lienor—I must tell you that I love your brother."

The bride smiled her beautiful smile and said reassuringly, "No, darling, you're copulating with him, that's a different thing entirely. We settled this last summer when you were so taken with that Jewish storyteller who came through Dole—"

"I know copulation and love are not the same thing," Jouglet said, speaking in a blunt, rapid voice. "But they *may* coexist and in this case they do."

"You're overreacting," Lienor said with adorable stubbornness.

"I don't think so," Jouglet said. "I fought against it and I only say 'love' because I don't know what else to call it, it's so . . . peculiar."

Lienor mused playfully, as if this were a game and it were her turn. "All right. You are in love with him. Do I lose the affection that you have for me? Am I less lovely to you? Are you less inclined to write poetry about me? Or banter with me?"

"Of course not," Jouglet said quietly.

"Are you going to write poems about how pretty Willem is now too?" She laughed. Jouglet shook her head.

Lienor grinned and shrugged. "So I win!" she declared playfully. "I come first in all the most important things."

Jouglet took Lienor's hands and held them between her own, kissed the fingertips. "Those things are lovely but they aren't the most important," she said gently.

Lienor rolled her eyes. "Oh, very *well*, Jouglet, if you want to *wound* me go ahead and *wound* me, tell me how your love for Willem is *better* than your love for me. Give me your argument for valuing *rutting* above true romance."

"It's not rutting, Lienor, and you're better bred than to use such a—"

"Jouglet," Lienor said impishly, and pointed to the corner of the floor, where a small leather sack lay. "That is my brother's purse, I gave it to him at Christmas. Its presence there, and the earlier choreography of your entrances and exits, suggests a very hurried encounter between you and him of a purely physical nature. In Dole we call that rutting." She seemed to find the subject very droll.

Jouglet considered her a moment and then smiled a smile that was both pensive and affectionate. She shook her head. "There's a lot more to it than that, Lienor, but I don't know if I can make you understand."

"Then I am not threatened by it, so sit by me and regale me with stories of how you've been my white knight, of how selflessly and heroically you labored to bring all this perfection to my life and my family."

"It wasn't perfect, I made mistakes," Jouglet said dismissively. She brought Lienor's hand to her lips to kiss it, a gesture both intimate and respectful. "Your brother's land restored. I botched that entirely and—no disrespect to your imperial potential—that was supposed to be the easy part of the plan."

Lienor smiled comfortably. "But you're the living witness to the original crime, all you need do is testify to Konrad, and Willem will have back what he deserves."

Jouglet dropped Lienor's hand and stared at her, alarmed. "No," she said firmly.

"Why not?" Lienor asked, still smiling, and caught up Jouglet's hand again, rubbing the calloused fingertips. "I realize it's not a convoluted strategy like you're so fond of, it's so obvious and forthright as to be boring, I know, but—"

Jouglet grabbed her hand away roughly, frowning. "Lienor, use your head. That witness is a *woman*, a girl who disappeared ten years ago—"

"And who is about to make a brilliant reappearance!" Lienor said with enthusiastic serenity. "It is the final perfect piece to your exquisitely intricate puzzle. Just think—if you come forward as that girl, as witness to the crimes against my family, Willem will not only suddenly be landed again, but I shall make you my attendant, and we will be allowed in each other's presence constantly." She beamed beneficently.

"You've no idea what you're asking!" Jouglet snapped, standing up and pacing a step or two in claustrophobic agitation. Lienor was taken aback. "I've made you the most privileged woman in the world. You will have treasures beyond imagining. I have one treasure only, and that is my freedom to be Jouglet the minstrel."

"For the love of the saints," Lienor said impatiently. "For doing all this, Konrad will surely give you land, Jouglet—land and safety and security and status—"

"A woman's status," Jouglet interrupted. "No." Seeing the look on Lienor's face, she added coaxingly, "Think honestly, Lienor—you would not love me half so much if I were all day in skirts working at a box loom dutifully beside you."

Lienor beamed at her. "I would love your presence near me in any form at all—"

"You love it most when I am courting you, or performing, or misbehaving somehow. What you love about my attentions to you would be lost if I were found to be a woman. I love you most profoundly, Lienor, but the courtship we enjoy most is an artifice, and we both know that—that's the pleasure of it."

Lienor sighed and looked down at her hands, heavier now by one large gold band. Quickly Jouglet was beside her on the chest again, stroking her arm comfortingly. "We are both at court. We'll be around each other very often. In time it will be with Konrad as it was with Willem—I'll have the honor of being the one man he will trust alone with you."

Suddenly the chapel door swung open and a large figure stood silhouetted in the doorframe. The two women stood up at once and took a step away from each other, but there was no way to disguise that they were in here alone together. The man took a step farther into the room and they could see his face in the candle-light.

It was Willem.

His nostrils flared with a surprised intake of breath. He blinked twice, without comment, trying to understand what he was look-ing at.

"Brother—" Lienor began with a nervous laugh.

Willem turned directly to Jouglet, instantly furious. "*More* duplicity, even *now*? You said my sister did not know what you were!"

"No I didn't," Jouglet said quickly. "I said I did not *tell* her any-thing."

"I recognized her the moment she appeared at our gates three years ago," Lienor explained serenely to her brother. "I never for one moment thought she was a man. She never had to tell me any-thing."

Willem was nearly apoplectic. "A lie by omission *is still a lie*!"

"Be *quiet*," Jouglet said sharply. "God help us, Willem, someone will come running."

Willem slammed the door closed, harder than he meant to; all three of them winced at the sound, and the candle flame jumped as if it would go out in protest.

"Your wallet's just there," Lienor said angelically, and pointed. "I assume that's why you're here."

Willem moved closer to them. "The two of you have been in cahoots against me all along," he said in a low voice, stunned. More hurt than angry, he added, *"Why?"*

They exchanged glances, and Lienor shook her head. "Willem, don't you remember her from childhood? She worshipped you, brother, she wanted your friendship more than anything in the world. You hardly had a second look for her, you disapproved of her tomboyishness."

"What does that have to do with it?" he demanded.

"Would you ever have invited her to ride with you these past three years, spent any time alone with her, told her half the things you did, if you'd known her for a woman?" Lienor asked. "My fondness rested in my knowing, yours rested in your not knowing."

Willem, for the first time in his life, was brought up short by his sister's words. For a long moment he was silent, and perhaps a little red-faced.

"I . . . wish that I could disagree with that." He coughed gruffly, looked uncertain. And finally sighed heavily with resignation. "I interrupted . . . something . . . here."

"Yes you did," Lienor said with a hint of defiance in her tone.

But Willem was not looking at her; he was looking at Jouglet, and the minstrel met his gaze with an unreadable but steady face. For a long moment they stared at each other in the dim light. The knight's expression changed: first disturbed and then simply perplexed. Finally he asked, softly, "Does this—whatever I have interrupted—does it diminish us?"

"No," Jouglet said with absolute sincerity.

He took a moment to let this sink in.

"Konrad will be looking for you soon," he said. "Do not tarry here alone too long." He glanced toward the corner, reached down to retrieve his purse.

Lienor gasped. She leaned toward Jouglet to plant a kiss on her cheek, her hair tumbling forward over her shoulders. "Look at that—he's so hopelessly in love with you, he'd yield you to another lover just to keep you happy! How romantic! You should marry him at once."

Willem huffed uncomfortably as Jouglet snapped, "We are not going to repeat that discussion. I will not be a woman in your court, Lienor, nor out in the world. Even *you* like me most when I'm a minstrel!"

Willem had tied his purse on and taken a step toward the exit. He was reaching for the bolt, when the door swung open abruptly—and this time two large figures stood silhouetted on the threshold. "Is Imogen in here?" one of them demanded of Willem anxiously, as the other held up a lamp.

Jouglet and Lienor tried to leap apart but—"Oh!" Lienor cried out in surprised pain, her long tresses snagged on the sewn-on decorations of Jouglet's tunic. Though they tried to unmesh themselves, they were tethered to each other, the thick spiderweb of Lienor's hair between them.

The two figures entered the room.

The one with the lamp was the emperor. The other one was Paul.

"What is this?" Konrad demanded, shocked.

Paul's face glowed with satisfaction for a moment before he forced a look of disapproval there and cried out loudly, wanting to be heard by Konrad's bodyguards behind them: "This is an outrage! She's a harlot after all! They are all *three* in some sort of illicit . . . arrangement. I'll summon the guards."

Konrad spun on his heel and reached out to grab his brother's arm. "This is staying here," he announced in a low warning voice, and slammed the door closed with his booted foot so hard the candle on the altarpiece went out. Eyes blazing, he turned back to the pair.

Jouglet was still trying to disentangle Lienor's hair from the tunic, her fingers unusually clumsy from nerves. She could for once think of nothing to say.

"It is not what it appears to be, Your Majesty," Willem stammered. "I've been in here with them the whole time—"

Konrad cut him off with a furious look and pointed. "Watching them do *what*, exactly?" he demanded with a snarl. Lienor's hair laced the space between herself and Jouglet, looking more sensual than their actual embrace had been, and was getting further caught up in the protruding gemstones on Jouglet's sleeves and tunic-skirt. Paul made a dash for the door but his brother grabbed him around the waist and virtually tossed him into Willem's arms. "Oh, no, brother, you will not sabotage my marriage." He slammed the lamp down on the altar beside the smoking candlestick, then turning back, glaring, said to Jouglet, "Nor will you, you little whoreson."

Then he started laughing.

Lienor and Jouglet exchanged glances, alarmed by the laughter. "Sire—" Jouglet began carefully.

"God in heaven, Jouglet, but you are a schemer!" the emperor roared. "So *this* is what it's truly all about, eh? So much simpler than I credited you with. Taking such pains to clear your mistress's name so you can have her closer to your own—"

"She isn't my mistress, sire, I beg you," Jouglet insisted. "Take her to your bed this instant, you'll see she is a maiden."

"I'm glad the feast was none too lavish, if it's for a marriage that will not last the night! Tell me the story," Konrad demanded, calming himself to an irritated chuckle. He crossed his arms and adopted a waiting pose, leaning back against the door. "Tell me how you come to be here in the dark in each other's arms, what you planned to do next. All of it. Spare nothing. Entertain me, and if the story is good enough, perhaps I'll let the lady live, if she proves to be a virgin. You, Jouglet, have as long to live as your story takes to tell, so feel free to embellish it."

"My lord husband," Lienor said, "Please, you cannot kill him for a mere—"

"I can and I will. I condemned my best friend merely for claiming to do what Jouglet quite obviously really does regularly. Begin, Jouglet."

"My lord," Lienor tried again, "there is something you must know about Jouglet—"

Jouglet turned on Lienor ferociously, with such an angry, betrayed look that Lienor could not continue the sentence. "His Majesty need hear nothing but the story I choose to tell him," the minstrel hissed. "Sire, there is no treachery here, and no secret, and no shame. In Willem's house I am so entirely considered free of manly tendencies—"

"'Free of manly tendencies,' I like that," Konrad snorted with a sarcastic laugh, and gestured impatiently with one jeweled hand. "Yes, go on. We don't have much time, Paul will explode if we don't let him out to begin his gossip soon, so let's be specific about what that gossip is."

". . . so free of manly tendencies," Jouglet repeated unsurely, "that I am allowed to be alone with the lady. We are friends. I forgot myself. I must learn to correct my behavior now that she is empress."

"That story is not interesting," Konrad said conclusively. "It is hardly worthy of death, Jouglet, but it will have to do. I shall now call the guards, damn you." He uncrossed his arms and reached for the door bolt.

"Willem, *do* something!" said Lienor. He was still holding Paul. The cardinal, knowing he could not muscle his way out of Willem's grip, had stopped struggling, but Willem kept one large arm wrapped around his torso, pinning his arms to his sides.

"Yes, that's an excellent suggestion. Willem, hold forth a moment," Konrad said viciously. He let go of the bolt. "What do you have to say about this? How very ticklish for you."

After a pause Willem said slowly, "I see nothing untoward in what we have encountered here."

Konrad looked irritated. "You Burgundians really are peculiar in your personal relations."

Lienor made a quiet sound of worried protest. "Sire, it is innocent," she insisted. "Jouglet, please—"

"No," Jouglet said mechanically.

"He's going to *kill* you!" Lienor cried. "Willem, for the love of God, help me! Say something useful!"

Willem looked back and forth between them, aware that Konrad was studying his face. "I have sworn not to say anything useful in this matter," he said quietly to his sister, and then gave Jouglet an unhappy look.

"Thank you," said Jouglet quietly. "You are a good man, Willem."

Konrad considered the three of them with disgusted disappointment. "That's it, then? Nothing more?" He reached again for the bolt. "I'll have the guards take you to the prison, Jouglet, and at dawn you will fittingly and economically be placed on the gallows erected for Marcus. If my bride proves to be a virgin after all, *perhaps* I will commute your sentence to banishment."

"I can survive banishment, sire," Jouglet said quietly. "It is preferable to some other fates."

Konrad scowled. "It annoys me to be deprived of my favorite

entertainer just because you do not have a better tale to tell, Jouglet. I am surprised and *extremely* displeased at your not having one."

"Sire," Willem said suddenly, holding up his free hand. "You need not be deprived at all. It is but one aspect of him that troubles you, and I suggest you rid yourself of that and nothing more. Allow me to castrate him."

Lienor visibly relaxed; Jouglet, after a start, gave Willem a look of grudging approval.

Konrad glanced at him sharply, stroking his neat beard with one hand. No, not stroking it exactly—using his hand to hide his mouth. He was actually fighting back a smile. "Don't you think that will be a rather tricky operation?" he asked, barely straight-faced. "Considering Jouglet is a woman?"

The faces of the others went absolutely blank. Willem was so startled he let go of Paul; Paul was so amazed he did not think to escape.

"Yes, I thought I was right about that," Konrad said, in response to the trio's reaction. "And now I'm certain. Which suggests I must reappraise my general view of the female sex. So you see, brother dear, we have interrupted nothing more than a sisterly embrace."

"Sire, you are mistaken—" Jouglet began voicelessly.

"No I'm not, Jouglet, and you will prove it now," the emperor said firmly. "It will save your life."

"Your Majesty is going to extraordinary measures to protect the new empress's reputation," said Jouglet, voice high with tension. "Let us not descend to the level of farce. If you will exonerate Her Ladyship, I will accept the fate of being a fugitive minstrel."

"Accept? I can force you easily, Jouglet," Konrad warned. "I would rather not have it appear to Paul as if you had anything to hide at all."

Jouglet said nothing.

"Brother, this is ludicrous," Paul said, and took a step toward the door. Swiftly Konrad stepped in his way and Paul backed down, knowing here too he would lose the fight.

Konrad turned to Willem in annoyance. "Save your lover, Willem. Tell us what is under the tunic."

Jouglet looked at the floor and cursed under her breath.

Willem made an expression as if he'd eaten something that tickled the inside of his mouth. "A minstrel, sire," he said.

"Do not choose this moment to attempt artfulness, Willem, it is not your forte," Konrad scolded. "This is Jouglet's life at stake."

"Forgive me, sire," Willem said, bowing his head and recovering himself at once. "But if you are after preserving Jouglet's life, I think you should banish the man."

"Willem!" Lienor cried. "How can you say that? Jouglet, are you *mad*?" Jouglet was giving Willem a look of rueful gratitude. Lienor shoved her slightly in frustration.

"I would not have Jouglet caged, Lienor," Willem said quietly. Looking unhappy, he paced to the darkest side of the small stone room, away from the altar and the lamp.

Paul had recovered from his astonishment and was watching these interactions with alacrity. "Even if you banish Jouglet, the empress has been found alone with him in his arms. Your marriage is over, brother."

Jouglet turned on Paul ferociously. Finally freed from Lienor's hair she leapt toward him and with an outstretched hand, a finger pointed, she snarled, "*You!* You are *always* the source of my headaches and misfortunes, you pudgy spiritual midget. After all that's happened to bring about this wedding, I shall *not* let you undo it. Very well then, *yes*, I am a woman. Shall I prove it?" Her hands energized by her fury, she untied her breeches quickly and briefly revealed herself to him. Paul looked dismayed. Konrad, she noticed with appreciation, averted his gaze entirely. "Is that enough for you?" she said, tying the belt up again and straightening her tunic with irritation. "Will you cease this stupid prattle? What objection can there possibly be to a woman's embracing her dearest friend on her wedding day?"

"You were doing more than that I think," Paul said, recovering. "What you were doing may not be treason, but it still falls under the church's censure." With a happy insight, he grinned. "This is even better than your being a man—as a man you merely jeopardized his marriage, as a woman you jeopardize his entire court!"

Lienor made a worried sound and sat down on the chest, but Jouglet laughed scornfully. "Oh bollocks," she said dismissively. She began to untie her purse and reached into it for something.

"If His Majesty surrounds himself with deviant, loose women who go about dressed like men and meddle in state affairs—"

"His Majesty surrounds himself with innocent Burgundians who deserve a little vengeance," Jouglet corrected and pulled out a large gold ring in need of polishing. She shoved it in front of Paul's face; he pulled his chin back a little, making a distasteful expression, but when he realized what he was looking at he gasped. "Where did you get that?" he demanded weakly.

"You know where I got it," Jouglet said with angry satisfaction. "I stole it from you. Shortly after you stole it from your father on his deathbed."

Paul's face went chalk white and he fell to his knees, as Jouglet, despite herself, hooted with laughter.

"What is it?" Konrad snatched it out of her hand, recognized his father's signet ring, and gasped, dumbfounded. "*You?*" he demanded of his brother. He turned back to Jouglet. "How long have you had this? Why have you never brought this to me?" he asked angrily.

"Because it was stolen by a girl, sire," Jouglet said quickly. "And I have not been a girl until just a few moments ago."

Konrad took a moment to collect himself, staring at the ring. Then he glanced up at Jouglet and demanded, unexpectedly, "Imogen has fled with Marcus, hasn't she? She's gone forever?"

Jouglet blinked. "Yes, sire," she said in a voice of surprise. And then added quietly, gaze averted, careful to mask her frustration, "If Your Majesty knew about their mutual regard, I wish you had told me from the start. This past fortnight would have turned out very differently."

Konrad smiled. "I much prefer it this way." He turned to his brother with sudden and absolute serenity. "I think we can now reach an understanding," he said. "I shall keep your head and Alphonse's attached to the rest of your respective wretched bodies. In return, you shall agree to all of the following: I am not a cuckold, my court holds no den of iniquity to write home to the pope about, and it never will. You will bless my marriage bed. You will not harm a hair on Jouglet's head. You will inform Alphonse that all the land he stole, plus an extra thousand acres, will be returned to Willem at once. In addition, inform him that as he no longer has an heir, upon his death the office of Count of Burgundy will be passed to my most deserving vassal, knight, and brother-in-law, Willem of Dole. Let us hope this news hastens his demise." He allowed himself the smallest smile and glanced at the astonished, elated minstrel. "Efficiently done, Jouglet. If somewhat tardy." He saluted with the signet ring. Lienor chirped with excitement as Willem stood staring with his mouth hanging open.

Paul turned a particularly unattractive hue. He tried to rise from his knees from the cool stone floor, could not quite manage it, and didn't try again. "As His Majesty wills it," he said through clenched teeth. "But may I point out, Her Majesty's innocence requires Jouglet to be a woman? And Jouglet's claim against me requires her to be a woman? And the assurance that you will not appear to be a fool by others discovering her secret some day *requires* her to be a woman?"

"I know all that, clearly she will have to be unmasked as such tomorrow—no whining, Jouglet, it's not manly," admonished Konrad, seeing her elation vanish. At this announcement, Willem stirred from his quietude in the corner of the chapel. "And train your nimble wit on finding an excuse to keep me from looking like an idiot for not knowing all along."

"I've unmasked evil and promoted good and my reward is to be punished with a demotion?" Jouglet cried. "I'd sooner take the banishment, Your Majesty, I meant that and I mean it still."

"No, Jouglet—" Lienor began, plaintively.

"Unhappily for you, I don't want to banish you, you're the best musician I have."

"May I also point out," Paul said with quiet viciousness, "that she will now be a detriment to the common opinion of the royal court."

"Nonsense," Konrad said. "Any woman secretly trying to improve herself with manliness should be accounted admirable—I've even heard your brethren say so."

"But now she's *known* to be a woman," Paul said, with airless smugness. "Now you have an entirely untamed female fornicator in the middle of your court. Do you want that? Is it not better to throw her out?"

"Yes!" said Jouglet heartily.

Konrad was taken aback. He frowned. "You may be right." He grimaced. "Yes, an untamed woman is a problem."

"Then throw me out," Jouglet said emphatically. Lienor held out a hand in protest, but Jouglet brushed it away.

Konrad gave Jouglet a knowing smile. "No," he decided. "We'll just have to tame you."

"No," Jouglet said, understanding.

Konrad glanced at Willem, sardonic. "Are you man enough for the challenge?"

"I will not be married off," Jouglet said angrily between clenched teeth. "I have not come so far to reach a . . . such an *ordinary* fate."

"Marriage to you would be anything but ordinary," Willem said wistfully from the shadows, without meaning to say it aloud. Lienor sighed with relief and sat down on the chest.

Jouglet looked toward Willem, and he smiled the sheepish, unassuming smile that revealed so much of what she liked about him.

She looked conflicted, but after a hesitating moment, shook her head once firmly.

"Just a moment ago he suggested banishment over keeping you caged," Lienor reminded her, tugging at Jouglet's sleeve. "He would not see you caged."

"Marriage is a cage," Jouglet said quickly, pulling her arm away. With a bow toward Lienor she amended, "Very pretty if you are an empress, but otherwise a cage. I know how the world works, I've walked among its womenfolk. At court, wives are nothing but pawns, broodmares, and decorations."

Willem took a step toward them, out of the shadows. "The marriage would merely be for show. In private we would just keep having . . . whatever it is we have now."

To this, Jouglet had no retort. She looked at him, mouth hanging slightly open, brows furrowed with confusion. Finally after a long moment she turned to the emperor and asked in a weak but desperate voice, "And if I refuse?"

"Then you leave my court, but as a known woman whom I am banishing for deceit," he answered. "In your disguise, which you confuse for an identity, you are too valuable a commodity. I must expose you for what you are."

Jouglet was affronted. "Sire, I would never betray this court, even as an exile!"

"Technically you've betrayed it several times today alone," Konrad corrected wryly. "But you're missing the point, Jouglet. I don't *want* you as an exile. And yet Paul is right, I cannot have some scheming female of no pedigree in my inner circle. If you were my brother's clever wife, that would be quite another matter. Play the game, Jouglet," he said with a small knowing smile. "You are so fond of games, and this one would last a lifetime. You know what you really are; your soul is not diminished one jot by what others call you."

There was a long silence, all eyes on Jouglet, who looked absolutely flummoxed.

"You may continue your eccentric dress until you are a countess," he offered. "You may continue as my musician whenever you are here with your husband at my court. And you may serenade and banter with my wife without fear of admonition."

She was still flummoxed. She glanced wildly around the room as if somebody—perhaps Christ above the altar—could give her some advice. "Answer this, then," Konrad continued. "What were your ambitions for yourself?"

"To stay your minstrel," she said promptly. "And his lover. And her courtly wooer."

Konrad made a pacifying gesture. "And you may still have all these, in some form or other. You can't *always* refashion life exactly as you want it, Jouglet."

She maintained the broody silence, appearing to absorb this news.

"I will sweeten the pot for you," Konrad said. "Paul will perform the marriage rites."

"I will not!" his brother said hotly.

"Of course you will." Konrad smiled. "The villain's ultimate redemption: to reunite two souls he put asunder many years ago. It pleases the emperor very much."

"Poetic justice is not going to sway me," Jouglet said with a small anxious laugh.

Willem reached out tentatively for Jouglet's hand. She took in a sharp breath at his touch, but she didn't pull away. With absolute sincerity he said, "We will be precisely as married as our priest is holy—entirely in the public eye, and not a whit beyond that."

Jouglet looked up at him with a surprised expression of approval. "That proposal is as honest as you are and as slippery as I am."

He smiled. "So how can you possibly refuse it?"

There was a long silence.

A very long silence.

And then Jouglet said yes.

Author's Three Apologies for Purists

For the historical purist

The Emperor Konrad of this story did not exist. He was inspired by the fictional Emperor Konrad in Jean Renart's thirteenth-century *Roman de la Rose,* who in turn is generally considered a stand-in for the actual Otto IV, of the Welf dynasty (for the information about Otto IV, I am indebted to John Baldwin, *Aristocratic Life in Medieval France*). Because I have not likewise made "my" Konrad a stand-in for Otto, the politics of my story do not correspond to the politics of Otto's reign, although they do reflect the general timbre and mentality of the age. If you try to read this story with the expectation that it is "true-to-life historical fiction," you may get quite exasperated, just as you might if you watched *West Wing* expecting it to feature the true-to-life president of the United States. Please don't do that. Just read it and enjoy it. It's a *story.*

For the geographical purist

The start of the name "Sudaustat" is homonymic to *pseudo,* and that is not a coincidence; those who know the region may recognize it as an unholy union of Sélestat (whose medieval shape it *vaguely* resembles) and St. Hippolyte (whose site it *vaguely* inhabits).

On a broader geographical scale, the history of Burgundy is tragic, vast, and complicated. At the time of this story, there were two (physically abutting but politically distinct) regions both referring to themselves as Burgundy: one an independent duchy to the west of the Saône, the other a more variously defined area to the east, which in the late twelfth century had become part of the Holy (Roman) Empire. The first of these, the former duchy Burgundy, is equivalent to modern-day Burgundy; the former county/kingdom Burgundy, wherein lies Dole and Oricourt, corresponds to the area around modern Franche-Comté. For ease of narrative, I have simplified the history and terminology by referring to the more eastern county/kingdom as Burgundy and the more western duchy (aligned with France) as Bourgogne.

For the linguistic purist

This text is strewn with terms that we associate with the Middle Ages but that were not actually in use in the time and place of the story—for example, "courtly love" (first used in the 1800s), "Holy Roman Empire" (first used in the 1200s), "the Crusades" (largely a post-Renaissance term), or "troubadour" (which should be confined to Provençal language and culture), where *trouvier* or "minnesinger" is correct. It would be confusing to speak to a modern reader of these familiar concepts with the unfamiliar phrases that actually described them in their own age and place. My aim was to create a narrative that flows easily to the modern eye and ear.

Acknowledgments

First, a salute to the thirteenth-century poet Jean Renart for the poem that inspired this project—*The Romance of the Rose.* Also:

I am as ever deeply grateful to Marc H. Glick, Liz Darhansoff, Rich Green, and Jess Taylor, each of whom in their own inimitable way has been my champion.

I am happily indebted to my cousin Stephie Goethals and her family for their boundless hospitality, patience, translations, generosity, and German lessons.

Great thanks to my extraordinary team at HarperCollins. In particular, Jennifer Brehl, Pam Spengler-Jaffee, Lisa Gallagher, Kate Nintzel, and Juliette Shapland.

I am grateful for the thousands of months of research that real historians have labored so painstakingly to attain, so that I may blithely wreak havoc with their wisdom (especially Georges Duby and James Brundage). Also much gratitude to the archivists of the city of Mainz, the librarians of the Bibliothèque Humaniste in Sélestat, the docents of the castles of Haut-Koenigsbourg and Oricourt, and various other sundry professionals I startled with my requests for information. If any of them ever reads this I hope they are not too appalled with the liberties I've taken.

For aiding and abetting, in ways direct and indirect, big and little, I thank: Amy Utstein, Eowyn Mader, Lee Fierro, Jennifer Goethals-Miller, Janice Haynes, Lothlórien Homet, Brian Caspe,

Alan and Maureen Crumpler, Shira Kammen, Laurence Bouvard, Leo Galland, Steve Muhlberger, Christopher Morrison, Jeffrey Korn, Lillian Groag, Elizabeth Lucas, Nicole Steen, Peter Sagal, Beryl Vaughan, Philip Resnik, David and Krista Parr, Bronwyn Eisenberg, Steve Lewis, Tony Taccone and Berkeley Repertory Theatre, and Nick Walker of Aikido Shusekai.

THE HISTORY

BEHIND

THE STORY

Meet Nicole Galland

Nicole Galland hails from Martha's Vineyard, off the coast of Massachusetts. A graduate of Harvard University, she spent most of her time there doing theater, though she was actually getting an honors degree in comparative religion (and with that as an excuse, sojourned in India and Japan, her time abroad including a stint as a Buddhist nun near Kyoto).

Galland repatriated to California and cofounded a theater company for teens that premiered at the Edinburgh Festival Fringe. She was granted a full fellowship to pursue a PhD in drama at the University of California, Berkeley, where she showed great promise at pretentious performance art. Before academia could entirely seduce her, however, she withdrew from the program and split the next several years between the Bay Area and New York City, eking out a living in theater, writing, editing, and, of course, temp work.

After winning an award for her screenplay *The Winter Population*, Galland moved to Los Angeles and spent a few years as a screenwriter. In April 2002 she rediscovered the unfinished outline to *The Fool's Tale*, which she'd begun in college, and was about to delete it from her hard drive when she decided, just for fun, to see what would happen if she finished it instead. Thanks to much serendipity, the book was completed in early 2003. She immediately fled from Los Angeles back to the Bay Area, where she worked for a while as literary manager/dramaturge at Berkeley Repertory Theatre. When *The Fool's Tale* was published to positive reviews in early 2005, she left the Rep to write full-time.

For about a year, she lived out of a backpack, researching and retracing the steps of the ill-fated Fourth Crusade for her upcoming novel, *Crossed*. Finally, after twenty-three years away from her hometown, Galland returned to Martha's Vineyard to live year-round. Here she reconnected with an old high school classmate, Darren Lobdell, whom she hadn't seen in more than twenty years. They became engaged with dazzling speed and will have eloped by the time this book goes to press, though they're not sure it's really eloping when you insist on telling everyone about it.

A Conversation with Nicole Galland

What first inspired you to write this book?

A thirteenth-century poem called "Romance of the Rose, or William of Dole," by Jean Renart. I thought it would make a great novel as soon as I read it, but I ended up writing something only partially inspired by it.

What is the poem about?

The plot's too involved to explain quickly, but it's a sarcastically comic jewel that depicts the medieval lifestyles of the rich and famous—as well as people trying to *become* the rich and famous. (Too bad there's nothing like that in modern American culture. . . .)

And what about it made you want to turn it into a novel?

It has a brilliant plot twist with a strong female character, Lienor, since Jouglet is just a supporting male character who disappears halfway through. Plus it's notable for other things, like it's an early form of musical comedy (the narrative has songs embedded in it, but the story works without the songs and the songs work without the story). And in researching it, I learned how much class-biased propaganda is in it, which piqued my interest.

That's all very interesting but a little academic, don't you think? Anything else?

Yeah, what *really* grabbed me was that the narrator is not playing it straight with his audience, and I began to wonder why. He lies by omission, he hides things from us. At least four times, I found myself wondering, "Hey, what's *really* going on here?" To satisfy my own curiosity, I made up answers, and that became *Revenge of the Rose.*

Can you say a little more about the "class-biased propaganda"? There's a lot of political intrigue in the story, but it doesn't seem to be a "political novel" per se.

No, it's not—and neither is the poem. It was written for a certain class, that being the lower aristocracy, from whence we get the fairy-tale knights in shining armor, damsels in distress, etc. The bad guy in the poem is an unnamed steward—a commoner (in fact, technically a serf) who actually *has a job*; he *works* his way up the socioeconomic ladder. To the aristocracy, that makes him and his class gauche. The two classes were in competition for a certain level of power, and so naturally a story written for one group would make a villain of the other, just like during the Cold War the obvious villain in American action flicks was a Russian spy. Once I realized that the steward was the villain largely *because he worked for a living*, my Yankee sensibility got riled, and I immediately decided to make him more sympathetic.

Your chapter titles are all literary references; did you learn anything unexpected about the literature of the time?

Yes—as I studied the medieval literary approach to "romantic love," the code of chivalry, and all of that, I realized how intensely class-conscious it all was. The stuff that's turned into our democratic, Hollywood-ized "once upon a times" and "happily ever afters" was originally a form of class control.

You've got to be kidding.

Nope. The main point of chivalry was to encourage armed soldiers (knights) to believe that they were bettered through selfless
devotion—in romantic literature it's devotion to a lady, but she's
just an attractive stand-in for either the Church (if she's the Virgin Mary) or the local lord or king (if she's a devout subject,
daughter, or wife).

*But what about all the romances and fairy-tales featuring girls and
young women? Isn't the message there that anybody can be blessed with
love and fortune?*

Ah, but most damsels in distress know and accept their place.
They usually have an aristocratic pedigree, but they don't complain that circumstances have led to their being disempowered
and disenfranchised, and it's their continued undemanding good
nature and selflessness that makes them worthy of being saved
. . . by somebody more powerful than they are. They don't try to
better their own lot; they are encouraged to be beautiful and pas-
sive and well-behaved, which is what Lienor, the damsel-in-
distress in "Roman de la Rose," seems to be until push comes to
shove—and she shoves back!

*How did you balance the need for historical authenticity with the de-
sire to take creative license?*

Although I did a huge amount of research, I don't think of this
story as historical fiction. That it happens to be set eight hundred
years ago is, to me, a technicality; I think of it as literary fiction.
It was inspired by a poem, not by history. The original poem was
full of creative license, and I took creative license even with *that*.
So, to answer the question, there was no *need* for balance. I was
free to go after the creative license every time. This was especially true when it came to women's behavior; just as the heroine's

behavior in the original poem turns out to be exceptional, probably *all* of my female characters are exceptional.

What changed the most as you transformed the story into a novel?

First, I've made Jouglet the central character, which isn't the case in the poem. In the poem he (yes, he) just fades out of view after awhile. And as I said, the poet's villainous steward becomes a sympathetic character in my story; I invented new bad guys: a count and a cardinal. Also, I created two female characters and expanded minor characters from the poem—all to add texture to a theme in my story that is also not in the poem: the attempt to control sexuality in general.

What do you mean by "sexuality in general"?

I have gay characters, prostitutes, a woman who unwisely gives away her politically significant virginity, a Catholic cardinal obsessed with using all such subversions to forward the church's interests. None of that is in the original poem. It's astounding how indifferent to religion the poem is; Renart cheerfully belittles the Church a few times and then his characters *ignore* it for more than five thousand lines. I at least have the Church and its repressive doctrines (made even more repressive by the cardinal) hovering in the background.

What do you think changed least about the story in its new incarnation?

I think the playful, teasing spirit of the thing. My aim is not so much to Depict Real Medieval Life as it is to Tell a Fun Tale. In that way I'm not changing the original at all; I am (I hope) honoring it. And the climactic plot twist I liked from the poem is still there, but it's now just one of several twists in the story.

Your novel has a pretty modern voice. What's the point of setting it in the Middle Ages if you're not going to make it feel medieval?

What does "feel medieval" mean? I suspect a lot of people would read the original thirteenth-century poem and scoff that *it* doesn't feel medieval enough. We think of the Middle Ages as being embarrassingly *earnest*, and we also think of sarcasm as the humor of modern times. But Renart's humor is more sarcastic and cutting than *mine* is; his thirteenth-century poem almost feels *more modern* than my twenty-first-century novel does. I'm not saying the novel doesn't feel modern; I'm just saying that we have a pretty limited and stereotyped sense of what is a "medieval feeling."

So you don't think Jean Renart is turning over in his grave?

No! It's certainly true that the story is embedded with elements that would have been inconceivable in the poem—*not* inconceivable in actual medieval life, mind you, just inconceivable in a medieval poem *depicting* medieval life. There's a perverse irony in there somewhere, of which I think Jean Renart would heartily approve.

An Excerpt from <u>Crossed</u>

Coming from Harper Paperbacks in February 2008, another thrilling novel from Nicole Galland that deftly blends historical fact with imaginative story-telling, wit, and sharp characterization. *Crossed* tells the story of the Fourth Crusade and the dramatic, disastrous sack of Constantinople in 1204.

From San Niccolo, that sweltering sand-bar of an island off the coast of Venice, rose a strange tent-city milling with ten thousand unwashed soldiers and their unwashed squires, whores, cooks, priests, horses, heralds, armorers, and smiths. They called themselves pilgrims, having taken the cross, having sworn to carry out the pope's wishes. This meant they were going to an unknown desert, to wrest an unknown city from its unknown inhabitants.

Their transports and warships, waiting in the lagoon—heavy, strong, capacious, lethal—had been built by the Venetians, would be sailed by the Venetians, and at this moment were being stocked with food and water by the Venetians. In two days, the army and its fleet would finally—*finally*—set sail, after a season of political and financial delays, to do great good for Christendom.

But before they decamped, this would be the site of a gruesome murder-suicide, of such ferocity men would speak of it in fearful whispers, crossing themselves, for years to come.

At least, that was my plan.

As with so many things in this life, I was mistaken.

I leapt from Barzizza's boat when the water was ankle-deep, trudging angrily through the oily green until I had splashed myself to dry land and the edge of the army camp. Venice was mostly paving stone and water; this was the first time in a month I'd been on living soil. Earth felt comforting under my bare wet feet, but I didn't want comfort—I wanted death, and was panicked at the thought of being cheated of it. I'd learned half a dozen languages, taught myself to play music I did not like and eaten food I could barely stomach, grown my beard and my hair and woken up every day forcing myself to go on, for three years, to prepare for my exquisite, redemptive death—a death I now feared I'd been robbed of.

I had no weapon, just a spit of iron small enough to fold my hand around: a spike with a hook on one end, stolen from Barzizza's house, some sort of fishing spear. I don't remember how I learned which pavilion was the high commander's nor what trick I used to distract the guards at the door, but the trick was fast accomplished; I was still seething as I scrambled inside, I could still hear my heartbeat pulsing in my temples as my eyes adjusted to the darkness.

There were only two men in this cool, open space: the army commander himself, and a large young knight kneeling to his right, presumably his bodyguard. Both wore tunics decorated with broad gold braids. They were whispering together. Neither was the man I wanted.

"*Where are the English?*" I shouted.

They started, stared at me; the knight lumbered to his feet grabbing for the dagger in his belt, as the leader responded, in a droll voice, "They are in England, I imagine."

So it was true, what Barzizza had told me; this final trek had been for nothing. A howl of humiliated rage escaped me. Across my mind flashed the journey back to Britain. I would never survive that. My one chance for revenge had been illusory; my intended victim had never even been in reach. With the warped logic of despair and rage, I decided then that I would still forfeit the one life that was yet mine to take: my own.

Both of the men staring at me now were armed. This would be simple, then: I had only to hurl myself upon the leader, and the bodyguard would kill me instantly.

When you know this one is your final heartbeat, time slows for a final savoring of the senses. In less than a blink I noticed more about my surroundings than I had in years: the feel of the woven-grass mats under my feet, the elaborate, bright decorations on the tent walls, the smell of rosewater and woolly must that pervaded the pavilion, the commander's aristocratic handsomeness, the likeable face of the young man who was about to skewer me. He had both sword and dagger in his belt; I wondered which he would use.

I also noticed, in that flicker, that I was interrupting something significant. Although the knight had been kneeling, there was an informality between them, as if they were kin. The lord looked oddly *relieved* by my interruption—until I raised the spike above my head and threw myself at him.

The young man was quick for one so large, but he was nowhere near as quick as I was, and I realized that I could accidentally kill the lord. The lord cringed, but he did not move to protect himself, trusting his knight. I myself did not trust his knight, and as my hands descended, I shirked, pulled back a hair, so that the hooked point of the spike just missed the lord's skull and only my knuckles glanced off his bald brow; by then the knight had me, huge left paw grabbing me around the throat, huge right one shoving the dagger-point against my liver. So this was it: I was over now, finally and despite everything. Suddenly I was flooded with euphoria and involuntarily, I grinned at him—my executioner, my liberator. His hair and beard gave his face a golden glow. I literally loved him more than my own life.

Our eyes locked; all my weight rested in his clenched left fist around my throat, the knife at my gut, as I waited for him to plunge it in.

He didn't.

He yanked the blade away and shoved me hard to the matted ground, where I choked on a mouthful of straw.

Something had gone horribly wrong: I wasn't dead.

The knight said something in a garbled language to the lord, who answered similarly. There was a brief debate, which to this day I cannot remember understanding. Listening in stunned outrage, I gradually recognized it as a Lombard dialect I was familiar with; at that point they could have been speaking in my native tongue and it would have sounded like so much nonsense. I was removed from my own skin, too dazed to understand what was happening.

By the time I registered that I was not only not dead, but—a far worse affair—completely *alive*, the young man had returned his attention to me. "You're not a murderer," he declared. "You're a suicide. Suicide is a sin and by St. John, I will not assist you in it."

I gawked. "I just tried to kill your master!" I protested. "Look, you stupid ass, I'll do it again!" I scrambled to my feet, light-headed, fighting back the urge to scream and laugh hysterically at once, and unsteadily I raised the spike. This time I wouldn't hesitate, I'd show the whoreson I meant business. He'd have no choice but to cut me down.

But everything seemed to slow. He grabbed me again, both of those meaty mitts reaching for my right hand, and again he heaved me down effortlessly. By the time I hit the floor of the tent, *he* held my spike. He tossed it away out of my reach. "You pulled back," he announced. "We both saw it. You made sure not to hurt his lordship the marquis. You are goading me to kill you and I won't do it. Nor will anybody else."

He called out, "Richard," and a sweet-faced boy with a colorless wisp of facial down trotted into the tent. The knight gave him an order and Richard moved toward me, matter-of-factly began to tie my hands in front of me.

"What are you *doing*?" I shouted, horrified.

"You are now my captive," the knight informed me—as if I should consider myself lucky. "No more of this nonsense." Inexplicably, although I no longer liked him, he still seemed to have a warm, earnest *glow* to him, as if this were his normal state.

"I'm a *criminal*," I protested. "*Execute* me, idiot, do the world a favor."

He grimaced disapprovingly and shook his head. And then, as if he were my loving older brother trying to teach me a lesson, he said, "From what I've seen, you are a sinner, not a criminal, and the burden of a sinner is to repent."

This could not really be happening. "You want me to *repent*?" I repeated weakly.

He nodded. The elegant marquis, watching us, looked almost amused now. "You will repent the impulse toward self-murder," announced the knight. "And whatever blackness is in your soul that drove you to such despair in the first place, you must also repent of that."

"And *then* you'll execute me?" I insisted, desperate.

The marquis laughed. The knight did not. The knight seemed to have nothing resembling a sense of humor at all. He was, it now seemed obvious, German.

Ordinarily I would not have sat there passively, letting some boy-child tie me in knots insufficient to keep a tree from running off. But I'd just tossed myself into the arms of Death . . . and Death had tossed me back. I was in a state of shock. So when the boy pulled me to standing, I stood. Then, almost as an afterthought, I struggled against his grip. Only because I dimly remembered that I probably should.

"Bind his wrists, but don't hurt his hands," the knight said to the boy. "Look at those hands. I think he's a musician."

I stopped struggling, startled. I followed the boy out of the tent, blinking stupidly in the brilliant haze of the Venetian afternoon.

The lighter side of HISTORY

REVENGE OF THE ROSE
A Novel
by Nicole Galland

ISBN 978-0-06-084179-9 (paperback)

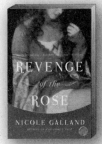

"A tasty fictional stew, mixing elements of twelfth-century
culture together skillfully to produce a veritable reading
feast. . . . The combination of vicious politics, mysterious
doings, betrayals, and double-dealing, added to a leisurely
but engaging plot, will keep those pages turning."
—*Booklist*

PILATE'S WIFE
A Novel of the Roman Empire
by Antoinette May

ISBN 978-0-06-112866-0 (paperback)

"[In *Pilate's Wife*] May creates a portrait of an intriguing
woman. . . . *Pilate's Wife* makes the female experience of past
millennia exotic yet universal. . . . May effectively captures
how the values of the Romans differed from ours."
—*USA Today*

THORNFIELD HALL
Jane Eyre's Hidden Story
by Emma Tennant

ISBN 978-0-06-123988-5 (paperback)

Adèle is a homesick, forlorn eight-year-old when first
brought to Thornfield Hall. She longs to return to the
glitter of Paris—and to the mother who has been lost to
her. But soon a stranger arrives to care for her: a serious yet
intensely loving young governess named Jane Eyre.

REBECCA
The Classic Tale of Romantic Suspense
by Daphne Du Maurier

ISBN 978-0-380-73040-7 (paperback)

"*Last night I dreamt I went to Manderley again. . . .*"
With these words the reader is ushered into an isolated gray
stone manse on the windswept Cornish
coast, as the second Mrs. Maxim de Winter
recalls the chilling events that transpired as
she began her new life as the young bride
of a husband she barely knew.

REBECCA'S TALE
A Novel
by Sally Beauman
ISBN 978-0-06-117467-4 (paperback)

"If you've read *Rebecca* and loved it, Beauman brings it
to more colorful life." —*Chicago Tribune*

"What a savory treat—a mixture of mystery and romance
flavored with intelligence, compassion, and wit."

THE WIDOW'S WAR
A Novel
by Sally Gunning
ISBN 978-0-06-079158-2 (paperback)

"Skillfully employing the language, imagination, and
character that literary fiction demands, [Gunning]
illuminates a fascinating moment in our past."
—Anita Shreve, *Washington Post Book World*

THE FAMILY FORTUNE
A Modern Retelling of Jane Austen's *Persuasion*
by Laurie Horowitz
ISBN 978-0-06-087527-5 (paperback)

"Horowitz has finely captured the bored silliness of
WASP high society, creating a stylish portrait of an
endangered species." —*Kirkus Reviews*

"Rich with divinely dysfunctional contemporary characters
who could have stepped from a Jane Austen novel."
—Mary Kay Andrews, bestselling author of *Savannah Breeze*

AND ONLY TO DECEIVE
A Novel of Suspense
by Tasha Alexander
ISBN 978-0-06-114844-6 (paperback)

"Charming." —*Publishers Weekly*

"This engaging, witty mix of Victorian cozy and
suspense thriller draws its dramatic spark
from the endearingly headstrong
heroine's growth in life and love. A
memorable debut." —*Booklist*

TO THE TOWER BORN
A Novel of the Lost Princes
by Robin Maxwell

ISBN 978-0-06-058052-0 (paperback)

"As she did in *The Wild Irish*, Maxwell once again delivers a fresh take on an old story, giving the world a new theory to debate." —*Library Journal*

DARCY'S STORY
Pride and Prejudice **Told From a Whole New Perspective**
by Janet Aylmer

ISBN 978-0-06-114870-5 (paperback)

Janet Aylmer has cleverly rewritten a beloved classic from a different point of view. Initially seen by Elizabeth as "haughty, reserved, and fastidious," Aylmer's story explains the underlying thoughts, feelings, and motivations behind Mr. Darcy's cold exterior.

THE FOOL'S TALE
A Novel
by Nicole Galland

ISBN 978-0-06-072151-0 (paperback)

"Set in an age when marriage was strategy, love was temptation, and treachery was a tool of survival, Nicole Galland's *The Fool's Tale* creates a vivid 12th-century world and three unforgettable characters."
—William Dietrich, author of *Hadrian's Wall*

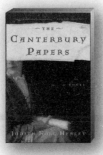

THE CANTERBURY PAPERS
A Novel
by Judith Healey

ISBN 978-0-06-077332-8 (paperback)

"[An] engaging medieval suspense debut . . . Healey's well-researched historical drama . . . delights in poking fun at the stuffiness and misbehavior that characterized the royal families of the time. . . . Fresh and absorbing." —*Publishers Weekly*